the Padre phony

A
JIMMY REDSTONE/ANGELLA MARTINEZ
THRILLER

DAVID HARRY

HOTRAY LLC PUBLISHING

DISCLAIMER: Everything in this book, except for the establishments listed and a few local folks, is fictitious. The words spoken by any of the locals are, of course, also fictional. As I've said to anyone who will listen, South Padre Island is a gem in the sun. Despite its proximity to the drug-related turbulence now occurring in Mexico, SPI remains a safe and extremely friendly place to live, work, or vacation.

Library of Congress Control Number: 2018911136

ISBN: 978-09963650-3-1 Trade paperback
ISBN: 978-09963650-4-8 Ebook

Printed in the United States and published by Hotray, llc.

South Padre Island & Port Isabel Etablishments
Frequented by
JIMMY REDSTONE AND ANGELLA MARTINEZ

* * *

Almost Always Available Locksmith

Bada Bing Bagels

Dirty Al's

F&B

Isla Blanca Park

Isla Grand Hotel

Island Fitness Center

Kay's Beads

Laguna BOB

Lobo Der Mar

Meatball Cafe

Our Lady Star Of The Sea church

Paragraphs On Padre Book Store

Pelican West Band

Pier 19

Rudy's

Schlitterbahn Water Park

Ted's

The Shores

Venus Nails and Spa

Wanna Wanna

*Please don't forget to stop by and tell them
Jimmy and Angella sent you.*

ONE

Being between jobs is stressful no matter who you are. Angella and I are no exception. It was now time to give our past the burial it deserved and to began living our future. In truth, I had been holding out for a night on the town, but that flew in the face of the always practical Angella who didn't want to begin our new careers sporting hangovers. "Let's keep it to sugar highs," she had chided, "nothing good ever comes from the other kind."

Wasn't worth arguing. So here we were having breakfast at Ted's looking forward to a pecan pancake fix in celebration of our newly signed contracts.

September is a typically great weather month on South Padre Island and this year has been no exception. In addition to the wonderful mid-eighty temperatures, the wind has been remarkably steady in the 15-20 mile per hour range. For those people on the island who don't rely on tourist dollars for survival, an added bonus is the limited number of island visitors there are after school goes back into session and before the Winter Texans arrive later in the year.

Ophelia was doing her usual great job of keeping the coffee flowing for the few people who were still lingering over breakfast. My three wonderful looking pecan-filled pancakes and Angella's perfectly prepared huevos rancheros had just been placed on the table when Joy Malcom came bouncing through the door. The word ambush came to mind given the way Joy looked directly at our table even before the door closed behind her. "Cornered," I murmured to Angella, "great way to ruin a celebration."

Karen, Ted's proprietor, moved to intercept Joy, motioning her to an empty corner table. Karen rolled her eyes as Joy brushed past her.

Resigned, I stood in anticipation of the obligatory hug. But this time Joy waved me away and plopped into one of the empty chairs at our table. "Coffee, please," she said in Ophelia's direction.

Ophelia dutifully retreated toward the coffee pots and when she was out of voice range, Joy said, "My lawyer told me to stay away from you both until that messy lawsuit is settled." Blinking and nodding her head in what could only be interpreted as a non-verbal what the hell, she lowered her voice even further and added, "But what does she know. Officially this visit doesn't count."

I suppose in Joy's mind if we hadn't hugged, we hadn't officially met. "So what brings you to Ted's?" I asked, my friendly voice on full display. "I'm told you've been having your morning coffee at Bada Bing Bagels."

"You keeping tabs on me or what, Jimmy?" She batted her eyelids, and when I said nothing, she continued. "Well, actually I'm flattered." To Angella, she said, "Better watch out, your partner's got eyes for me." She laughed her deep-throated smoker-induced laugh. "Just kidding," she added, as if she actually had been just kidding.

On the surface Angella took her comment with a good-natured smile, but I felt a sudden chill. Perhaps reading my thoughts, Angella quipped, "Partners are not forever. One just never knows for certain."

"Technically," I responded, intentionally mis-interpreting Angella's meaning, "we're no longer partners. Co-workers, I believe the proper term is."

"You two quitting Homeland was the topic of conversation all last week over at Venus. You may not know this Jimmy, but you—and Angella I might add—have quite a large following among the, let's say, hair and nail salon crowd."

"I prefer to think of it as retired. We retired from DHS."

"Angella, aren't you a bit young for retire-ment?" Joy asked, her head down, watching An-gella's reaction over the top of her glasses. The way Joy said it made it clear she didn't think I was too young.

"It was time," my lovely partner said, her southern belle smile spread across her face. "It was actually past time."

"Going to work for Great Southern I hear. Insurance investigators. Fits you two perfectly I might add. Heard you're giving up your condo. But I must say, the consensus with the Venus crowd is you'll still be living together. In the fancy Riviera. The penthouse suite no less. You two done yourselves proud, you did."

"Nothing escapes the locals, I see."

"Jimmy, you for one know how important it is to always know what the competition is doing. So, is that a confirmation that the two of you will remain together?"

"It very much is," Angella answered, laying claim to my hand. "Very much so. Great Southern has graciously offered us the use of their suite at the hotel. Combination living quarters and local office."

Mock disappointment flashed across Joy's face. "I know Jimmy here's been named Chief Investigator if I have my facts correct. And what about you, Angella? You working for Jimmy? Or what?"

"For Great Southern. We both are." Angella said, sidestepping the touchy chain of command situation.

Joy leaned forward as if to impart a secret.

"Forty some million in cash gone missing after that bank robbery. Missing with no trace. You two don't need to be working."

"Meaning what?"

"Meaning there are rumors, my friend. Consensus is you two have no need to work."

I suppressed the anger. "So, where's this going?"

"As you well know, my Kings Cup, worth well over a hundred million, is also still missing. And I want it back."

Aside from the hair salon, Joy's source of information was a drug lord now operating from a Mexican jail under protection, I assume, of the Mexican government. And the fact is, the lord's information is usually spot on. "Your point?" I asked.

"I believe you know exactly where my cup is."

"Go on," I said knowing Joy well enough to know this conversation was not about the lawsuit. She had information she wanted to impart. Lawsuit discussion would come through her lawyer, despite her comments to the contrary.

Joy sat back, sipped her coffee for a long minute while making a pretext of thinking about her next words. She leaned in close. "I know I'm not supposed to say this, but we're friends, Jimmy. You and I. We're friends. Right?"

"My pancakes are getting cold, Joy. Just..."

"A little grease will make my suit go away,"

she blurted. "With all that money you won't even notice what I'm asking."

"Joy!" I snapped, wanting no part of this conversation, "That's enough!" Like Joy, I had been instructed on more than one occasion not to discuss the lawsuit with anyone, especially not with Joy Malcom.

"Jimmy, you're wrong about this. You know full well the Kings Cup went missing from my condo during a raid by Homeland Security."

"That's DHS's problem, not mine. Take it up with them."

"You took the picture that allowed those pigs to obtain the search warrant. That was wrong, Jimmy. You violated my trust."

"You know full well I can't discuss any of this. Now please..."

"Five million and the words lawsuit will never be heard again. At least not from me."

"Enough!" I pushed my chair back as if I was about to leave—or toss her out of the restaurant.

"Okay, Jimmy," she said, standing as if to go without assistance from me. "But I know you have the money."

"I'm going to say this once, and once only. I don't have the money. End of conversation."

"Oh, you have the money alright. More accurately, you know where it is. But okay have it your way." Joy took a step toward the door then turned back to face our table. "Just to show I have no hard feelings. Guy was found dead this morning."

"You're telling us this because..."

She returned to the table, tight lips conceal-ing a broken smile. Leaning close, she whispered, "Among other things, he's a horse trainer. Name's Billy Conquesta."

"Why tell us?"

"Great Southern insures horses. Especially valuable horses. Your boss'll be concerned."

For some reason her drug lord husband wanted us to have this information, so I played along. "I can't believe valuable horses are on this island. I thought they were all tourist beach-walking hors-es."

"For one thing, they've been playing polo here for a while now."

"Polo?"

"A polo pony named Lip Sync is rumored to be on island."

"So?"

"Billy is the best there is. So, if Lip Sync is on the island then Billy would be in charge. Simple as that." Joy straightened up as if she had finished what she had come for. "And... Lip Sync is a very valuable horse." Joy blinked a few times as if to emphasis how valuable the horse was.

"You do get around, don't you?" I said, stalling to collect my thoughts. Something she said had triggered a fleeting thought, now gone.

"Jimmy, in your new job with the insurance company you'll be wise to include me in your circle. The whistles and bells you've been accustomed to from the government, the info your handler Tiny gives—gave—you, all that inside government stuff they have no business knowing, well that's all gone now."

Seeing no reaction by Angella or myself, she continued. "Truth be told, I venture to say my information is more accurate—and possibly even more honest—than the 'need to know' crap they've been feeding you."

The fact Joy knew about the insurance company job worried me. No announcement had been made and, in fact, we had only signed the papers late yesterday afternoon. So it wasn't the hair salon crowd, whoever they are. A message was coming from Morris Malcom, Joy's husband, whose real name is Roberto Alterez Santiago, a man I helped put in jail for life. And the message was loud and very clear.

Reading my face, Joy volunteered, "Jimmy, I'm surprised at you. Nothing happens in the Valley, on either side of the river, Morris doesn't know."

"That so?"

"Since you're not police any more I can tell you. The kid Billy was trained by Paco, may his soul rest in peace. Paco was the best mule ever lived. Kid is second. He hauled hay and muck back and forth over the river. Truth is, his muck wagons carried their weight in drugs. Don't say I never gave you nothing." Joy again turned toward the door.

"Hold up a moment," I called, the fleeting thought coming into focus. "You said this Billy character 'among other things' is a horse trainer. What other things?"

"He spent a lot of time digging in the muck so to speak."

"What's that supposed to mean?"

"He's rumored to have dug up a treasure somewhere on this sand bar. Maybe even found your buried treasure my good man. Maybe you done him in. Wouldn't put it past you." This time Joy actually went through the door without so much as a backward glance.

"What was that about?" Angella asked as we turned our attention back to our now cold food.

Before I could spike a mouthful, Karen scooped the plates from the table. "Fresh ones are on the way." Winking, she added, "Give me just a moment and we'll do this the right way."

"Santiago," I began, responding to Angella when Karen was out of hearing range, "just made us an offer he thinks we can't refuse."

"The man's locked away in a Mexican jail, partially your doing. Why on earth would he ever help you do anything? I'm slow this morning. Help me here?"

"We play ball with him and we get access to his information."

"By play ball I assume you mean help him move drugs and contraband across the border."

"Not so overtly. Information is his lifeblood. Without it he can't survive. With it, he controls the lower valley."

"You mean information like positioning of informants, Coast Guard, operations that are pending, that sort of thing?"

"Broadly speaking, that type of thing. But knowing Santiago, right now all he wants from us is the kid's killer. Must have some link to him or his business."

"You're not thinking of going along with him. If you are, count me out."

"Not so fast. You have to give to get. We'll let this play out. See what he really wants."

"You thinking that's why Great Southern hired us in the first place? To play ball with the likes of that rat?"

"Not Santiago specifically. But we were hired because we're connected on both sides of the law — as well as on both sides of the border."

"Talk about frying pans and fires. I think the heat just nipped my ankle. And, Jimmy, I don't like the feel of it. Not one little bit."

TWO

We were walking down the steps on our way out of Teds when our new boss, Jack Silver, CEO of Great Southern Insurance, called.

"Redstone, Silver here," he began, his tone pleasant, but in command, "put Angella on. I mean I want you both on the line together."

I nodded to Angella and hit the speaker button. "You're on speakerphone," I said, "Angella's here. Give us a moment to slip into our car." A moment later I said, "We're alone now."

"Good. Two things. Fun first. I've approved the plans for your apartment. The space is certainly large enough to serve as both an office and a comfortable living area. It's looking good. I'm certain you'll be pleased."

The space Silver was speaking about was the luxurious penthouse apartment in the Riviera Hotel where Philip DePierio had lived. Philip was last seen floating in a raft in the Gulf of Mexico where Mossad General Levi Ben-Yuval was about to descend on him. DePierio was wanted, dead or alive, by the Israeli military. No one was expecting him back on South Padre Island anytime soon. To be more accurate, he wasn't expected to be anywhere at any time in the future.

"We look forward to moving in," I replied. "When should we expect it to be finished?"

"Architect says less than a month. I say two weeks at most. The office may take a bit longer. You two are the face of the company in South Texas, so I want it done up right. Nothing but the best."

We had heard all of this before, but from our observation, Silver liked to repeat himself. Being a billionaire several times over, woe to anyone who failed to indulge him.

"Now down to business. I just learned that Billy Conquesta turned up dead on your lovely island. His throat cut." Angella shot me a glance, but before I could ask the obvious question, Silver continued, "I don't give a shit about who killed him. I mean from a business point of view I don't care. But he's the son of a client, so from a personal aspect I very much care. On the business side, Billy is—was—Lip Sync's trainer and the company has a vested interest in Lip Sync."

"Lip Sync? That's a horse, if I understand correctly. A valuable horse we're told," Angella said.

"Not just any horse. A remarkable polo pony. Perhaps one of the finest polo ponies in the world to be exact. She's out of Jamaica, but sired by Lip Balm, the greatest Argentine polo pony ever. Great Southern has Lip Sync insured for nine million."

"Nine million?" I repeated, "Isn't that on the high side?" I wasn't an expert on horses, let alone those used for polo, but the amount just sounded high.

"It's for both of them. The filly was mated with the Jamaican champion Heymann exactly three hundred thirty-eight days ago."

That meant nothing to me, except that in the normal course of things human babies arrived somewhere around the two hundred seventieth day. "Sorry, but I'm not a horse expert. How..."

"She should be foaling any day now. At birth, that foal could be worth upwards of five million. Some say much more."

"That sounds high," Angella quipped.

"It is. Except, clones are now all the rage. And the foal..."

"I thought you said she was sired by Haymaker. Then the foal will be pure bred and not a clone."

"H-E-Y-M-A-N-N. Heymann, not Haymaker. Exactly. Not being a clone is the key here. If the foal meets expectations, that'll be one hell of a world-class pony. Breeding has been the best of the best for several generations. Bidding on polo ponies right now is at an all-time frenzy. Anyone who ever dreamed of owning a top polo horse will be bidding for Lip Sync's foal. That foal dies, or goes missing, we're out five big ones. The owner will be out even more."

"Do you have reason to believe something's happened to the filly?" Angella asked.

I was about to ask the same question as I tried to understand our role in this.

"I have reason to believe the filly's on the island. A murdered trainer causes me great concern. Can't be that difficult to hide a horse on that sand bar, so find that filly and assure me she's okay. I expect a report sooner rather than later. You hear what I'm saying?"

"We're on it," I said, not knowing how else to answer. Or even what being 'on it' even means in this situation.

"Good. Report directly to me."

"Got it."

"Play it close, you two. I don't want this leaked. As I might have told you, Great Southern is publicity adverse. Our clients prefer to remain out of the news. And heaven forbid the filly or the foal gets caught up in a criminal investigation. That would be disaster."

When the line went dead, Angella said, "I didn't know the island had polo ponies—or even polo for that matter. And now to find out that a priceless pony is among them."

"Actually, in the last few months there have been some exhibition games, usually on Sunday afternoons. I thought they were trucking in the horses, but now I assume some of them are being kept here. Time to drive up to the stables and have a look around."

"Wouldn't Silver know if Lip Sync is actually on the island?" Angella wasn't buying whatever our new boss was selling. Her frown said it all.

"Great Southern is the insurer, not the owner. So maybe that's why Silver wouldn't know exactly where the pony is. But you're right, he wouldn't be calling us if the horse wasn't somewhere near here. But the horse's trainer dying on the island, maybe, just maybe he's simply putting two and two together."

"And possibly getting five. I'm not happy how he dismissed the death of a client's child. Especially when that client is a friend."

"Get the feeling he didn't approve of the kid's occupation? Assuming he knew about moving drugs across the border."

"Drugs may be the best of what he brought across. Silver proves your adage. Follow the money."

"Never known it to fail. Hey, look on the bright side. We could be chasing some terrorist with a bomb. How hard could tracking a horse be?"

It didn't take but six minutes before we pulled off Highway 100 into the hard-packed sand area that had been the parking lot for something called Horse Stables. The commercial riding stables had recently moved five miles further north and the original area was still being used to house a few of the horses. Five horses were visible, all tied along an outside rail of a rickety wooden structure that cast just enough shadows to keep the hot afternoon sun off their backs.

On the short ride up here Angella had managed to download a picture of Lip Sync, a black filly, who, according to her Wikipedia stats, stands 14¾ hands. The picture showed two white circles evenly spaced down the center of her back and a white square on her nose just below her eyes.

No one seemed to be around, so we stepped off the wooden walkway and marched across the sand to where the horses were tethered. Angella tapped my arm and pointed toward a small, mostly decayed structure about thirty yards off to the right. A black horse with white markings was laying in the grass. As we approached, the horse snorted several times and when that didn't stop us, she struggled to her feet and put her head down as if about to charge.

"Watch yourself," I said, "that horse looks..."

"Like she just gave birth. Look over there!"

Sure enough, a small frail-looking foal was sleeping in the spot where the mother had been a moment earlier. "How tall you think she is?"

"Haven't a clue. But she does appear somewhat smaller than the horses back there."

"And more...more sleek. Actually, muscular. More muscular I would say."

"As if she raced."

"Or was used for polo," Angella added as she snapped several pictures of the foal and the filly.

"Stop!" a voice behind us shouted. "Get away from that mare! Hands up over your heads! Both of you!"

The voice sounded young. Perhaps early twenties. Perhaps even younger. I swiveled my head far enough to see a double-barreled shotgun wavering in our general direction.

"Don't turn around!" the voice commanded.

The kid holding the shotgun was slightly built with long straight hair framing a thin face and an almost non-existent chin from whence a few wispy hairs sprouted. Three observations stopped me from going for his legs. First, fear overpowered his voice. Second, his finger was wrapped around both triggers. And third, but critical, that finger was shaking.

Angella, sensing what I was contemplating, said, "Not the time, Jimmy. Not now."

"Yer trespassing! Git away from them horses!"

"Take it easy, son," I said. "We're leaving."

Angella moved ahead of me as we crossed the sand on our way back toward our car. I tried to engage the nervous kid in conversation, but he said nothing until we were back on the gravel walkway at the edge of the parking area.

"Keep go'n," the kid shouted when I turned to

face him. "Keep yer hands where I kin see 'em!"

"Put the shotgun down, son, before someone gets hurt."

"What the hell you think you do'n back there?" he barked, the gun shaking wildly. "This property is private!"

The kid kept moving forward even though I had stopped. His knees were now within diving range. But if his weapon fired before I had him on the ground, Angella would potentially stop a good portion of the shot, most likely with her face.

"Just look'n to hire a couple a horses," I said, "to ride up the beach. Didn't see nobody around is all."

"Nothing's for hire. Git on outta here!"

"If these horses aren't for hire," Angella asked, "what're they doing here?"

"You trespass'n lady! Shoot'n horse thieves in Texas is okay." He took another step forward. "You come back here, I shoot..."

As we had practiced dozens of times, while Angella had been asking questions she had slowly been working herself off to the kid's left, at the same time easing her small purse off her shoulder and into her hand.

Taking my cue from her, I inched off to his right. All we needed now was for him to lower the barrel to a point where a discharge would hit the ground before it hit us.

We both saw the kid's mistake at the same time.

Angella flung her purse directly toward his eyes and I launched my body at the shotgun intending to block it from moving upward while also knocking his legs out from under him.

Angella's aim was right on. The purse slammed into his face. Unfortunately, my timing was off by a hair—hairs being the margin between life and death in our business. I had, however, managed to crash into his legs taking him to the ground. But I missed the barrel of the gun as it fired directly beside my ear. I couldn't be certain if he had discharged both barrels or only one. But out of the corner of my eye I could see Angella down.

I aimed a left hook to his kidney, but again the kid was faster than me, blocking the blow with the shotgun shank and, from where he lay, turning the gun toward Angella at the same time as he busted free of my grasp.

"Putt'n the other barrel direct into her if you don't get your sorry asses outta here!" he shouted, scrambling to his feet. His hands were now rock solid, as if I had scared away the nerves. Blood dripped from beside his right eye where Angella's purse had made contact, but he made no motion to stem the flow.

"Okay," I conceded, mentally preparing to again drive him into the ground with my left shoulder while smashing his head against the wood walkway with my right hand. I braced for the impact telling myself the kid may be skinny, but his

body's rock hard and fast as hell. I wouldn't under
estimate him again.

I took a small step backward, ready to pounce
should I sense he was about to pull the trigger.

Angella stood as well. She was covered in sand.
If she had been hit I couldn't tell. She gave a quick
shake of the head indicating she wasn't hurt.

"Now git outta here," the kid barked. "Won't
say it again." He didn't look old enough to wait
for the school bus without a guardian, but there
was no denying he had given a good accounting
of himself.

"We're going. We're going." I said, turning
away. I was concerned that he—and his shotgun—
were now out of my vision, but without a de-escala-
tion somebody was certain to be injured—or worse.

He stood still while we retreated to the parking area. Other than our car and an old Jeep that
looked as if it had first been used by General Patton
somewhere in Africa, there was no place for us to
seek shelter should he commence firing. So in we
climbed and, crouching low to reduce the target
profile, off we went.

THREE

"What the hell's that kid think he's doing?" Angella asked as we turned south heading back toward town. "He's a nervous wreck. And I don't believe it's about protecting the horses."

"You hit?" I asked, ignoring her question.

"I told you, no."

"You nodded."

"I saw the gun come up and I went down. I actually don't think he meant to shoot. Slamming into him hard as you did jarred his hand."

"Kid's well-coordinated. All muscle. And fast as hell."

"You're not getting any faster, my dear. That's one of the reasons we left the government. Your slamming into people days are behind you. Or should be behind you. Aren't you the one who preaches timing? How many times have you said, 'a hair too slow and the bullet gets you?'"

"Maybe a beat," I admitted. "A beat slower than I'd like."

"A beat's worth a mile. I'm glad we're out. Let's stay out."

I didn't like the way this discussion was going. "So what's your take with him? What's bothering the kid?"

"My take: He's had training. That move wasn't natural. He knew exactly what you were going to do—and exactly when."

"So then why the nerves?"

"Drugs?"

"I don't know what his game is, but I do know what it's not. It's not about horse thievery. Where would a horse thief hide the hapless horse on this island? And if they're that concerned about a horse being stolen then why not just put a gate up? My goodness, there isn't even a sign telling people to keep out."

"Jimmy, actually there's no need to hide the foal. Just drive it off the island. Once across the causeway there's no end to where the horse can be tucked away."

"Not so easy with the camera surveillance at the bridge. But I suppose if there's a will there's a way."

"Now that I think of it, I don't think he's professional," Angella said. "He'd have to be one hell of an actor for his hands to shake that way. I was more concerned about an accidental discharge than

I was about him purposely pulling the trigger. Your chin hit him hard. Sure you're ok?"

"Other than a slight elbow bruise and knuckles that hurt like hell—and... and my bruised ego—I'm fine."

"Something spooked him, Jimmy. Something big—at least big in his mind. Didn't see his car on the way in. Maybe we tripped an alarm or something. So who you calling?"

"Silver. Let him know where Lip Sync and the foal are." The phone vibrated in my hand before I could hit the green dial button. "What the hell! Last person on earth I'd expect."

"Not Tiny?"

"Bingo!"

"You joking? I thought we're beyond the clutches of Homeland Security, or Secret Service, or CIA, or whoever he works for. Don't answer."

"I wouldn't joke about Big Brother following us. But it's him alright. Good plan," I agreed, wanting nothing to do with our former handler.

A moment later, as if to prove nothing is beyond the long arm of our government—especially not beyond Tiny—my cell again came alive. Only this time the sound of a siren replaced the normal ring tone. Tiny had tripped the emergency response code.

"Plan B," Angella said.

"And that is?"

"Answer it! There's no telling what he'll do if you don't. And I don't have a plan C."

Angella was right of course. So I tapped the Accept button. "You're about the last..."

"Say nothing!" Tiny barked. "Listen."

A dozen two-word epitaphs flooded my mind, but I held my tongue. It's never smart to burn bridges. And when the bridge is a high-ranking CIA agent with tentacles reaching deep into government agencies at home and away it's wise to listen when told to listen. It is also wise to listen carefully.

Tiny's message, as usual, was terse. Also, as usual, the line went dead as soon as the one-way communication stopped.

We drove in silence for several minutes before Angella said, "You planning on telling me what Tiny wanted? Or..."

"Or what?"

"I got plenty of or whats. Just tell me what he said."

"I'm digesting his message."

"That's progress. Usually his words choke you."

"I know the words. 'DHS agent in difficulty on SPI, Levi says be careful'. But I don't know what it means."

"Give it a try."

"Is he referring to the dead guy on the beach? If so, he's beyond our help. Or is there another agent he's concerned about? And why would Levi be involved with an DHS agent?"

"I'm assuming the Levi he's talking about is that Israeli Mossad agent we worked with in Mexico, Levi Ben-Yuval."

"Don't know any other Levi. But why send a message through Tiny? Ben-Yuval has my number."

"Maybe he's deep cover or something."

"If his message had been delivered by anyone other than Tiny, I'd blow it off. They're working on something together and it's spilling over to us. I only hope that us not working for DHS doesn't prove to be worse than working for DHS."

Angella fell silent for a moment, her furled brow telling me she was working the mystery. "Perhaps the message is really from Tiny," she finally said, "only he's prohibited from telling us anything. So he couches it as coming from Levi."

"I suppose the possibilities are endless. But when has Tiny ever followed protocol? Just take heed. This may not be a simple homicide—if its homicide at all. So far, all we have is Flaky Joy's word for it. Who knows if there's even a dead guy on the beach. And if there is, guy may have fallen overboard from a shrimper and been washed ashore. Joy, as we know all too well, has an over active imagination."

Angella shot a glance in my direction. "We left DHS to avoid exactly this situation. At least then we were briefed—and armed."

"We might want to consider..."

"Don't even think it! I don't know about you, my friend, but I'm definitely not going back. I don't know what was worse, the criminals or the political double dealings. For God sakes, Jimmy, you ended up with forty some million in the trunk of your car and no one on the right side of the law was willing to claim it. Couldn't even give it to our government!"

"I wasn't thinking of going back, Angella. I was thinking of not allowing our carry permits to expire."

"That I suppose I would welcome. But truthfully how dangerous can it be investigating stolen watches, necklaces and paintings?"

"I hear you, but truth is, desperate people do desperate things. So if we get too close to the truth people can get, well desperate. Maintaining our concealed carry permits would be a good idea — that is if DHS doesn't block it."

"Better check with Silver to see what company policy is before we start packing heat." Angella was using her Bonnie and Clyde voice, so I knew she had put the horse episode behind us. "So, what's our next step?"

"Need to confirm that Conquesta, or whatever's his name, is the only dead body on the island. Let me re-phrase that. First we should confirm there is a dead body on the beach. And, I suppose we should confirm there's only one."

"Jimmy, I have a better idea. How about mind-ing our own business? We found the horse and foal Silver's worried about. That's our charter for now. Our only charter actually. We're not police. Let's stay focused."

I reminded Angella that Tiny's call made the homicide — some homicide — our business.

"Can't we treat the call as just a heads up? Keep our eyes open. That's the extent of it. We have no jurisdiction, no protection. We're naked on this one and that's not a good place to be."

"That kid's behavior bothered both of us. And since when has it ever been to our advantage to ignore Tiny?"

"Peculiar behavior on this island is...well, its SOP. If we investigated everything peculiar we'd never sleep."

"I'm not sure how much sleep we'd get if we ignore Tiny. I'm willing to follow your lead on this one, except...except us looking at a horse shouldn't have caused such obvious panic in that kid. I'd say, something's brewing."

"All I'm saying, Jimmy, is we're civilians, so let's remain focused. What's a horse have to do with DHS?"

"That's exactly what I've been debating. The thought just came to me that you know how art objects have become valuable currency in money laundering and money movement, could horses be used the same way?"

"You thinking buying and selling valuable horses can be used to move terrorist funds around the world?"

"Why not? Big money is involved. No one can pin down the actual value of any horse, so money can move without undue suspicion."

"You thinking Lip Sync falls in that category?"

"The foal is valuable, we know that. That skinny kid's on the rhomb line between an owner with a very valuable object and some wise guy who would like to appropriate the mare — or the foal — for his own account. Not a good place to be and that young man knows it."

"Jimmy, you thinking we have another Kings Cup or Blue Footed Boobie on our hands? Money transfer by way of a valuable object changing hands."

"That's what's making Silver antsy. With governments — especially our government — cracking down on money movement, anything of high value is fair game. Antsy flows downhill."

"And we're downhill is what you're suggesting. I also suppose with Trump's promise to end drug trafficking, the pressure for off the grid financial transactions has skyrocketed."

"How about if we drop in on Lt. Malone. See what's really going on."

"Pretext?" Angella asked, ever the practical one.

"We're overdue for a social visit."

"That's a stretch."

"She came to our retirement party. Least we can do is drop by and say thanks. Bring her up to speed."

"Three people drinking beer and listening to music at the Lobo Del Mar is not exactly a retirement party. Visiting Malone at police headquarters is a leap. And besides I had the feeling she was there to keep an eye on us. See if anything slipped out."

"Such as?"

"Such as a lead to the money that was not found after the bank heist? The forty million Joy was speaking of."

"You're now doing it too!"

"Jimmy, my dear, you have a guilty conscious, if I say so myself. If I were you, I'd keep an eye out for Malone. I hesitate to think of her as a friendly."

"That your version of keep your friends close—and your enemies even closer?"

We were halfway across the parking lot when the police station door flew open and out came Malone, a no-nonsense expression plastered across her face. A young uniformed cop I hadn't seen before trailed two steps behind.

"Sorry, Redstone, Martinez," Malone barked when she saw us, her pace not slowing. "If you two were coming to see me your timing couldn't be worse."

We fell in beside her. "Something breaking?"

"Been advised of a homicide. Reportedly a Homeland Security Agent. On my way up to investigate."

"Location?" I asked.

"About seventeen miles north. On the beach."

"That makes two today," I responded, focusing on the dead guy Joy Malcom had told us about a few hours earlier. I was probing to see if there had been more than one murder.

"What're you talking about?" Turning to the young cop, Malone ordered, "Ortez, load the ATV and bring it around."

The young guy, barely out of his teens, quickly disappeared around the side of the building.

"Alberto Ortez just joined us. What were you saying about two? Two homicides?"

"I'm confused is all. Didn't know your jurisdiction extended that far north? That's Cameron County territory."

"We go where the Texas Rangers want us to go."

"Rangers?" Angella said. "As in Lt. Contentus, Jimmy's former boss?"

"None other."

"How would he..."

"How does he know anything? Got contacts everywhere, including south of the river it seems."

"You suggesting a National told him."

"Not suggesting. Telling. From Joy Malcom's

husband no less."

"Guy's in prison down there," I said, happy to know our small mystery over the dead guy was solved. There was only one — but that one was real, not a washup.

"Once a drug lord, always a drug lord," Malone answered, her eyes moving to the side of the building. "Information keeps the man alive. He pays well."

"So why doesn't Contentus handle it directly?" I asked.

"The nearest Ranger is in McAllen and won't be here for another hour. I'm to secure the scene and do the preliminary work. Babysitting," Malone replied, her pissed eyes not at all matching her smile-curled lips.

"Mind if we join you?" I asked, figuring there's no harm in asking.

"I'd love to have you both. In fact, if I had my way I'd send you there in my place. But considering you're neither a Texas Ranger nor a DHS agent, I can't accept your kind offer."

A police truck with a new-looking red-stripped ATV strapped in the center of its bed, came rattling around the corner. "Ride's here," Malone announced. "Gotta go. Stop back later. Better yet, make it tomorrow. I suppose I'll be busy the rest of this day."

"That woman puzzles me," I said to Angella

when Malone disappeared into the truck. "Don't know why, but she gets to me."

"That's what detectives do, Jimmy. You should know."

"You implying that I..."

"Just letting the facts fall where they will."

"So, tell me this," I said, checking my watch. "Some two and a half hours ago, give or take, our friend Joy Malcom informed us of a dead guy on the beach. She even put a name to him. Why did it take so long for Malone to learn of the death? And even now she doesn't have a name."

"Or Malone is playing you. Just saying."

"Or Malone is playing with us," I agreed.

"Or perhaps there's more than one body and she's holding back."

"Won't be the first time."

"You thinking what I'm thinking?"

"Only if you're thinking of dropping in on Joy Malcom and clearing the confusion. I wouldn't go to the trouble if..."

"...If Tiny hadn't called."

* * *

"Jimmy," Joy gushed, her eyes lighting up, her arms rising as if to hug me. "Oh, and you too, Angella," she said, her arms coming down and her eyes going dead. An act or not I couldn't determine.

Joy had changed from the blouse and slacks she had been wearing a few hours earlier to shorts and what appeared to be a sleeveless sweatshirt. The faded Texas A&M logo across the front of the sweatshirt confused me because Joy was a UT graduate. Or so she had once told me.

"I'm sorry, Jimmy," Joy said, breaking the silence, "but I've been instructed by counsel not to talk to you without her being present." She studied Angella for a long moment, then said, "But my curiosity is getting the better of me. What on earth has brought you both to my condo?"

Now I was really confused. Either this woman was losing her mind or...or perhaps someone was listening to this conversation and she didn't want them to know we had spoken earlier. "Mind if we come in?"

"Can't do that, not a proper thing to do." she winked. "Advice of solicitor and all that poppycock."

"That guy killed on the beach. Just where did it happen?"

Joy's eyes set as hard as I had ever seen them. "I don't know what the hell's got into you two! I've only been out for ten minutes today to walk Slider and I certainly didn't see any dead bodies on the walk. Frankly, Jimmy after what you did to me if I had seen anything, which I didn't, you'd be the last person I'd tell. Now please leave."

"Joy," Angella injected, "this is important. If

you would have seen a dead body where would it have been?"

"You two are nuts! Now get out of here or a I swear I'll call the police."

"What the hell's going on?" Angella exclaimed when we emerged from her building. "That was an Academy Award performance if ever I saw one! Makes no sense. Unless...unless the conversation was being recorded."

"I'll bet my badge she's the one told Morris. Not the other way."

"You ain't got no stink'n badge my friend. And that's a good thing—or so I believe."

"I wouldn't be a bit surprised to learn she also knows who killed him."

"That kid from the stables involved? Could be why he's so...edgy," Angella added.

We were on the same wavelength with regard to the operative facts of the day. "Horse guy murdered on the beach and a few minutes later our phone rings from the insurance company. Go to see the horse and run into a nervous as hell shotgun wielding kid. Not random incidents."

"Don't forget Levi's warning," Angella reminded me. "And the Mexican drug lord's involvement."

"And the fact we found both the mare and the foal. Can you say set up?"

"Those concealed carry permits are looming larger by the moment, I would say."

FOUR

Angella and I, each nursing our second Bud, sat at the Wanna Wanna listening to the band Pelican West finish up their first set of the night. The pressure of a hand on my right shoulder startled me. I looked up into the eyes of a tall, good-looking woman who was sporting a serious expression. "Pardon me," she began when I looked up, her voice soft, but in command, "may I assume you're Jimmy Redstone?"

"That would be a good assumption. And you..."

"And you're Angella Martinez," the woman continued, extending her hand to Angella in greeting.

"And just who's hand do I have the pleasure of...oh, sorry, I recognize you. You're the lawyer, uh, Ayers."

"Merry will do. We need to talk."

I stood. Lawyers get my guard up. At times, I think I'd rather be opposite a thug. "So I must assume this isn't a chance meeting."

"Rather urgent," Ayer's responded. "Can we meet at my office?"

"I don't generally talk with lawyers," I said, sitting back down. "Especially outside business hours. You need to talk, pull over a chair and talk all you want. Just keep the beer coming. Music's too good to pass up."

"This is important." Ayers leaned forward. "My client, Billy Conquesta, was found dead today. I assume you recognize the name."

"I didn't think lawyers assumed anything," I said, not wishing to impart information. "Why would I recognize the name?"

"I prefer my office. Too many eyes and ears here."

"And just why should..."

"Jimmy," Angella injected, "you made your point." Turning to Ayers, Angella said, "Your office is on Padre Boulevard?"

Ayers nodded.

"We'll see you there in ten minutes," Angella said, taking charge of the situation.

Without saying another word, the lawyer walked around the bar and disappeared in the direction of the parking lot.

The front door to the Merry Ayers Law Office was open slightly when we arrived. Entering an unknown structure can be dangerous business.

Those dangers are magnified when one is lured in by a person, or persons, unknown. At least in this situation we knew the lawyer, or thought we did. But we didn't know who else was in the building. As was our custom when we had been weapon-carrying DHS agents, one of us would remain outside to cover the other's back. But now without a weapon our only real option would be to dial 9-1-1. That, by no means, would be fast enough to save us if we were ambushed.

Angella hung back, motioning for me to enter ahead of her. At least we had a chance to fight back if our situation degraded to that point.

"I'm over here," Ayers' voice called from the shadows. "In the conference room to your right."

I entered the room slowly, nodding my intention to Angella before I actually went through the door. She signaled that all seemed in order to her.

The only force of evil in the room as far as I could determine was the kid with the chin whiskers; the one who had escorted us from the horse stable earlier in the day, shotgun in hand. He was now minus the shotgun. Or, more accurately, I didn't see the shotgun.

"Last time I saw you," I said to the kid, "you discharged a load of shot that could have done real damage to my partner. Show me your hands."

When he did so, I said, "Stand slowly."

The kid looked toward Ayers who simply nodded.

Once standing I directed him to a seat at the far corner of the table away from any weapon he could have planted. "Sit down right there and keep your hands above the table."

"He's not armed. I can vouch for that," Ayers said.

The kid shook his head in agreement. The bravado was gone. If anything, this kid was deeply distressed. Or, as Angella had suggested at one point, he could be a great actor.

Suddenly, the kid's eyes went wide and his focus shifted to a location over my shoulder.

Turning slightly, I recognized the problem. Angella was standing in the doorway, but her face was in shadow.

"That's my partner. You met her earlier. Damn near killed her then. Come in Angella and take a seat. Kid doesn't have a weapon."

"Jimmy, Angella," Ayers said while Angella was getting comfortable at the table, "this is Hermes Castro. I take it you've met."

"Under different circumstances to be sure," Angella responded, glaring at the young man. "Darn near took my face off. Didn't much like that."

"Just why are we here?" I asked, playing off Angella's lead, my own discomfort growing. "And why are the lights off?"

"There's enough light coming in from the street to...to be comfortable for what we need here,"

Ayers responded, as if she were chairing a meeting. "Fact is, I'm trying not to call attention to the fact anyone's here at this hour."

"So, why are we here?" I again asked leaning forward against the table.

"Before we get there, in case you're hungry I have bagels and some spreads from Bada Bing Bagels left over from a late afternoon meeting. And there's fresh coffee on the sideboard. Help yourselves."

When no one moved, Ayers continued, her tone turning professional, "As I told you at Wanna Wanna, my client, a guy by the name of Billy Conquesta, was found dead today a few miles..."

"There's been no announcement from what I know," I interrupted, "so just how do you know a homicide has occurred?"

"You're the one calling it a homicide. I didn't. They never announce these things on this island. But more to the point, a woman, Joy Malcom, who I believe you know, came in earlier today. I was in court in Brownsville all morning. In the words of my secretary, she 'camped out' until I got back."

"What time was that?" Angella asked.

"Got back little after one."

"And what time did Joy arrive?"

"I don't know precisely, but my secretary had car problems and arrived late. I'd say Joy was here around ten."

"So how did Joy know? I mean about the death," Angella pressed.

"Apparently someone, I believe she said, called her."

"I told her," the kid interjected.

"Then she hadn't been on the beach and hadn't seen for herself," Angella noted.

"Nope. I told her," Castro repeated.

"How did you know? And why tell her and not the police?" The questions were queuing in my mind faster than I could ask them.

"Doing what he was told," Ayers injected.

Angella turned to Castro. "Do you personally know Conquesta?"

Ayers nodded to Castro as if to tell him it was okay to answer.

"Calls himself William the Conqueror," Castro said. "Conc for short."

"He your boss?" Angella asked.

"Got no boss. Work for myself. Hires me time to time."

"For what?" I asked.

"Stuff needs do'n."

"What kind of stuff?"

"Stuff is all. I do many things."

"Legal or illegal."

Castro waited for the lawyer to nod before answering. "Some of each."

"When you saw us earlier today did you know Conc was dead?"

"Yeah. Dead as can be." The kid pulled on the hairs of his sparse beard. "Just git'n back when I saw you fussing around Lightning...er, Lip Sync."

"Did you actually see this guy Conc up on the beach?"

"We was up there together."

"Doing what?"

The kid continued fussing with his scraggly beard, wrapping strands around his finger, all the time with his eyes focused on the table.

"Look up!" I commanded. "You want our help, you look at us. And answer the questions."

"Am answering the questions." Castro again looked toward Ayers. "If I say, can it be held against me?"

"Assume so," Ayers responded.

"Then I have nothing to say."

"Then we have nothing more to discuss." I pushed my chair back from the table and began to stand.

"Helping bring stuff onto the beach," he said, his eyes darting around the room. "And...and meeting with a man."

I sat back down, but didn't reposition my chair. "What man? On the beach?"

"Stuff we did was on the beach. Man was at the stables."

I pulled my chair back to the table. Angella hadn't moved. "Man have a name?"

"Q."

"Q? That his name?" I asked. "Q?"

"Only name I know."

"What was the meeting about?"

Again, the wild eyes. The hesitation.

I put my hands on the table as if I was about to push away. But waited.

"I found some...some...findings up just...let's say, near...the cut. Very valuable."

This was like pulling teeth. "What was the nature of the...the findings?"

"Tell them all of it," Ayers instructed. "They can't help you unless you do."

Reluctantly, Castro said, "A giant fossil. Woolly Mammoth jaw bone I believe. Never one like it found on the sand bar before. Conc was helping me sell it."

"Was this Q person a buyer?" Angella asked.

"Don't know."

"What did you talk to this...this Q about?"

"Conc talked. I stayed back."

"Why didn't you talk with him? It was your find."

"Didn't want him knowing I had the find. Didn't want it stolen."

"It's that valuable?" Angella asked.

"Changes history. That's what Conc told me. He was my...broker."

"How did he know? Was he an expert?"

"Someone told him."

"Who?"

"Talked to someone. Don't know."

"We'll come back to Mr. Q later. How much stuff you bringing in up there?"

"Two kilos. Pure, uncut."

"So I imagine someone shot Conc, took the drugs."

"Not exactly."

"Explain."

"Throat was cut."

"Are you certain he was dead when you last saw him?"

"Yeah."

"Do you know who did it?"

"No."

It was Angella's turn to lean in. "So someone cut his throat while you watched and you don't know who did it? Is that what we're supposed to believe?"

"I was in the dunes. Looked up. Saw some-one come up and cut his throat. The sun was in my eyes."

"What exactly did you see?" Angella continued. "Tell us exactly what you saw."

"A woman. Think it was a woman. Came out of nowhere. Next thing I saw Conc was down."

"Where did this...woman go?"

"Disappeared. Like into the sun. Disappeared."

"In a boat."

"Didn't see no boat."

"What time was that?" I asked.

"Bout seven. Sun was low over the water. Maybe seven-fifteen. Don't rightly know." He reached into his pocket.

"Get your hands back on the table," I shouted.

Angella stood so quickly that her chair toppled over.

"Just gett'n my phone. See the time."

"It's eight-fifteen," Angella said.

"When he was cut."

"You need your phone for that?"

"A picture came in. Why I was in the dunes. Try'n to see it in the sun. Grass gave shade."

"Tell us again what you were doing up there?" Angella asked. "You weren't visiting the man about a finding, where you?"

"Waiting for the drop," Castro admitted. "Dark when we got there. Might have dozed off, tired from delivering the foal and all. Met with Q and got up there before sunrise."

"You met with Q back at the stable?

"Conc did. Not me."

"Okay, the foal we saw out there with Lip Sync, is that the one you two delivered?"

"Same one. Didn't go easy."

"Let me understand," I said. "You and Conc delivered the foal. Then you met this man by the name of Q and then you went up the beach to help bring in a load of stuff?"

"The load was Conc's deal. I don't get into those things, but he insisted I stay with him."

"You do that before with him?"

"First time."

"Why?" I asked. "Why did you go this time?"

"He was expecting a call. A picture. Wanted me to see it first thing. Timing sucked is all."

"So you had Conc's phone in the dunes when he was killed?"

"Sunlight was too bright by the water. Use'n the dunes so I could see."

"You just stood there watching him get his throat cut? Doing nothing about it?" Angella made it sound as if she was disgusted with him for hanging back.

"I didn't see the woman. I was look'n at the picture. I looked up just as the woman reached out for Conc. By the time I got the camera on she was walking away. Then she disappeared into the sun."

"So, where's the camera now?"

"Left it at Joy's place."

"Why?"

"Conc did work for her husband," Ayers injected.

"That's who set up the drug drop?" I asked.

"Don't rightly know. Could be."

"You do work for Santiago as well?"

The kid looked directly at Ayers.

"Why's all this important," Ayers asked. "I haven't yet told you why you're here."

"Just our nature," I said. "Too many years in law enforcement." My assessment was the kid was through talking about the murder—at least for now. So I asked, "You know Santiago?"

"Father's friend."

"You do work for him?"

"Some stuff. Nothing illegal."

"I find that hard to believe."

"Father says not to."

I turned to the lawyer. "So just why are we here? Conc's dead. Can't help him. This kid says he's done nothing wrong. Can't help him."

"Conc came to me a week ago—actually ten days—and told me he thought his life was in danger. He told me that if he were to be found dead to hire you two to investigate his death. He said to tell you it had to do with Lip Sync, but he didn't know what."

"Why us?"

"Because Santiago, through Joy Malcom, told him you were the best."

"Miss Joy told everyone you two're the best," the kid said. "I need protection."

"Because of Lip Sync? Or the foal?"

"Fossil. It's valuable."

"You held a shotgun on us today," Angella pressed. "Not a good way to get our help."

"Didn't know it's you. You were with the horses. Thought you'd come after me since I saw him get it."

"What makes you think you're in danger?"

"Got Conc didn't they? It's my fossil. Worth a lot of money. I'm next."

I studied the kid for a moment. "I suppose you knew Joy from rehab."

"How'd you know that?"

"Son, your hands are going a mile a minute, your eyes even faster. I'd say the treatment didn't take."

FIVE

Angella sat with young Castro in the conference room while I grabbed a bagel, filled a cup with coffee and followed Merry down a hallway to her office.

Closing the door behind us, she said, "In the interest of full disclosure, I don't usually handle this type of situation."

"What type is that?"

"I consider this criminal. Our practice does handle criminal matters, but I personally handle estates and real property matters. Another disclaimer is..."

"I should make an appointment to see you for my...my situation."

"From what I've been hearing about that missing money, perhaps you should."

I kept silent. This wasn't the time to deny I had the money.

Sensing my displeasure, Ayers said, "The other disclaimer is that I don't really know who's paying Castro's legal fees—or your fees—should you take the assignment."

"That kid must have money somewhere. Rehab doesn't come cheap. But actually, our employment agreement with Great Southern Insurance Company doesn't allow us to freelance."

"If I tell you Jack Silver says it's up to you. Would you accept?"

"You've discussed this with Silver?"

"Great Southern is a client."

"Why on earth would Silver agree to us getting involved with..."

"As you well know, Silver has a lot of money riding, so to speak, on Lip Sync. The horse's trainer is now dead and his assistant believes he's next. The horse is Silver's concern. I suppose he wants your full attention on both the horse and the horse's protectors."

Stalling, I responded, "Need to consult with Angella. Details please."

"Keep him alive. You'll each be paid a flat fee of ten thousand dollars to get him situated and then ten thousand dollars for each month he's in hiding."

"Plus expenses?"

"Plus expenses."

"Expenses include three operatives for twenty-four-seven coverage."

"Reasonable. What else?"

"Back to basics. Best guess as to where the money's coming from?"

"Either Billy Conquesta's family or Castro's family."

"And they are..."

"Conquesta is one of the wealthiest families in Argentina, perhaps in all of South America. Their land holdings make the King Ranch a mere blip. Not only in Argentina, but they have large holdings in Jamaica. Rumor has it also in Texas. The son, Billy grew up with horses and is—was—the best perhaps in the world in training them for polo."

"Then is Lip Sync from Argentina—or Jamaica?"

"Actually, neither. Far as I know, she's owned by the Castro family here in the Valley. The Bar-C Ranch in Jim Hogg County to be exact. The Castro and Conquesta families do very well indeed."

"If Billy's father is paying the bills, then we need to talk with him directly before long. Is he a client as well?"

"Can't discuss our clients, but I can tell you Silver, Conquesta, Castro and of course several others are very tight."

"Who are the others?"

"The only one of importance to you is Santiago."

"Santiago?"

"Relationship goes back at least a generation

if not more. They call themselves brothers and operate in lockstep. I'm telling you this so you know the cartels are with this despite...despite the disappearance of their money."

"You telling me they hold me responsible for the money going missing?"

"It was last known to be in the trunk of your car. You drove the car north into Texas. Let's just say they have strong suspicions you have it."

"Wrong! It was last in the bank here on the island. Not my fault the bank was robbed."

"They're not buying the bank robbery story. Money went missing is what they know. You were in the vicinity. Unlike our American justice system, I really doubt they presume you innocent until proven otherwise."

"And these are the same folks who want Angella and I protecting the kid?"

"I suppose they believe you'll do a good job."

"So who paid for the kid's rehab? His family?"

"The Castro family knows nothing about their son's condition. He'd be disowned if they knew. Conc was taking care of him."

"Not doing a bang-up job from the looks of it."

"Don't judge, my friend. Don't judge."

"Money guaranteed?"

"To the extent you earn it, yes."

The door to Ayers' office flew open.

"He's gone!" Angella announced. "I was interviewing him and suddenly he jumped up mumbling something I didn't fully hear. He ran from the conference room and disappeared. I checked outside and don't see him."

"Is there anywhere in this building he could hide?" I asked Merry.

"One floor," Ayers immediately answered. "No basement. Front and back doors only. If he's not in one of the offices, then he's not in the building."

Within a minute we were satisfied that Hermes Castro wasn't in either head and not under any desks, or behind any file cabinets.

"What's your take on what happened?" I asked Angella.

"I believe someone walked by the window behind me. His eyes went wide — like when I came into the room earlier. I turned around to see what had spooked him but saw nothing. When I turned back, he was already through the door."

"Let's check outside," I said. "It's time we wrap this anyway."

Castro was nowhere to be seen.

"Get anything important from him," I asked Angella as we retreated toward the back lot where our car was parked.

"Not much more than we had. He's sticking to the story that the sun was too bright and in his eyes. He couldn't make out who killed his friend. Got a bit of a description of that guy Q they met with in the middle of the night. He was about to show me a picture of the man when he got spooked."

"Don't believe he doesn't know who the killer is. But go on."

"He claims he ran most of the way back down the beach, a good four, maybe five miles, and went right to Malcom's place."

"Then why didn't she tell us about him?"

"Does Joy do anything straightforward?"

"Good point. What else did you get?"

"Only that he gave Conc's cell to Joy."

"Anything else?"

"That's about it."

"Hey," I exclaimed, taking note of a car parked directly behind ours. "What the hell's this about?"

"It's not that there's a shortage of spaces," Angella noted. "We're the only car in the lot. Someone's purposefully blocking us in. Be careful."

I slowly approached the parked car while Angella hung back a few steps. I couldn't see anybody inside. Angella checked the bushes while I studied buildings across the street. One dumpster was visible, possibly concealing one or more would-be thugs. I pointed toward the dumpster to be certain Angella had situational awareness.

"Jimmy," Angella warned, her voice low, "someone's in that car."

My hand went involuntarily to my non-existent holster. My eyes are not as keen as Angella's, so it took me a while to see what she was seeing. Indeed, a person was in the driver's seat, slumped low, possibly sleeping. Possibly dead.

I took a few tentative steps closer, giving my eyes time to adjust to the low light in the car. Angella moved up beside me, a large rock in each hand.

"Better than nothing," she said sheepishly. "That guy comes for us, he'll at least leave with a headache."

"Is that before or after they haul us away in body bags?"

The body moved, causing Angella to slip a rock into my open palm.

"What the hell you doing with that stone, Redstone?" The voice belonged to Lt. Malone, and it had come from the car. "Been a long day," she said, rolling the window all the way down. "Sun drains you."

"Could have gotten yourself hurt, Lieutenant," I said, "surprising us like that."

"That is your reputation, isn't it? Shoot first and lie about it later."

"That's uncalled for," I said, dropping the rock. "And you know it. Badman Tex died of natural causes."

"Bullet through the brain is not exactly natural causes."

"In a gunslinger's world dying from a bullet is most certainly a natural cause. And for the record, it was self-defense all the way. He shot first."

"My, my, you're sensitive. No need to re-litigate, Jimmy. You were reinstated, so your story's been accepted by the powers that be. Never mind the ballistics doesn't support your timeline."

"Ballistics have been known to be confusing."

"That's your story, I understand that. Hey, sorry we couldn't talk earlier today. I've been replaying our conversation of this morning and you two weren't just stopping by randomly to say hello."

"Now why would you..."

"Too late in the day for your cat and mouse routine, Redstone. You knew about the murder, did you not?"

Lie or tell the truth. As a DHS agent I would have automatically lied. In my new civilian life, I said, "We were told of a dead guy on the beach. Yes."

"Have a name?"

In for a dime, in for a dollar. "Billy Conquesta," I confessed. "Goes by Conc."

"Who told you?"

"Joy Malcom. Tracked us down at Ted's. We were on our way to your office to relay the info. What can you confirm?"

"Shouldn't give you the time of day. Fact is,

you didn't tell me even though you knew I was going up beach to investigate."

"I thought it was a second one. Timing and location seemed off from what I knew."

"Still, you didn't give me what you had. You, of all people, know better. You have something to hide? Something you're not telling me?"

I wasn't ready to give up Castro. Not just yet anyway. "Nothing."

"One theory making the rounds is that Conc was brokering a deal for...shall we say something of high value."

"Any idea what?"

Rumor has it, he, or someone, found buried treasure up island."

"Treasure? Like?"

"Like forty million buried in the dunes," Malone said, a slight smile causing her otherwise blank face to come alive.

"That's not funny."

"Not a joke. Where were you this morning between seven and nine?"

"With Angella. Walking the beach."

"You don't say. Where on the beach?"

"Not where Conc was killed."

"So, tell me Redstone, just how do you know where Conc was killed?"

SIX

Malone was silent, waiting for an answer. "Same way I knew a murder had been committed," I said, forcing my voice to remain calm. Either I was a suspect or I wasn't. I would soon know.

"Joy tell you?"

"She did." I was now in my shade-the-truth mode. Not a smart thing to do, especially if you're the subject of a crime. But until I knew where this was going, old habits die hard. "I take it TOD is between seven and nine."

"I didn't tell you that. I also didn't tell you preliminary tox is negative."

"What else didn't you tell us?" No harm in asking. Malone only imparted information she wanted us to have.

"Several kilos of cocaine were on the beach not far from where he was found."

I could read Malone pretty well. She was holding something back. "I suppose I'm to ask what else you want us to know?"

"You can ask anything you want, Redstone. Conc's throat was cut by someone who most likely has done this before."

"That it?"

"For now. How do you know the Castro kid?"

"What are..."

"I said drop the act. It's late. I'm tired. I was on my way inside when a call came in. Came back to the car for my notes. That's when Castro came bolting out, looking like the devil himself was close behind."

"You go after him?"

"No need. He's known to us. Nothing illegal about running away from a lawyer—and a gumshoe investigator."

The kid was running away from a lot more than the lawyer. "How did you know we'd be here?" I asked, partly to change the subject and partly out of curiosity.

"If the lead criminal investigator in South Texas can't find you two then how could I ever find the bad guys?"

"You insinuating something, Lieutenant?" Being lumped in with drug dealers and other criminals didn't sit well, especially coming after her query about my alibi for this morning.

"You know the saying, if the shoe fits..."

"The shoe most definitely doesn't fit," I shot back, perhaps a bit harsher than I had intended.

"Hit a nerve, did I?"

"If you have nothing further with us, please release our car so we..."

Malone's wheels were spinning even before I finished the sentence. I had to jump back to avoid getting runover. As it was, several pebbles hit my arms and one slammed into my right leg just below the kneecap hard enough to draw blood.

"What's gotten into her?" Angella asked when we were back in the car.

"Frustration, I suppose. We knew about the death hours before she did. Bet she's on her way to Malcom's place."

"At this hour?"

"Eleven's early for a murder investigation," I answered, nostalgically remembering my days with the Texas Rangers and the adrenaline rush of an active case.

"Jimmy, the look on your face tells me you're thinking about going over there now. Tell me I'm wrong."

"Thought did cross my mind," I confessed. "Now that I'm busted, mind if we drive by and see if I'm right about Malone."

Malone's empty car was indeed parked directly in front of the condo building where Joy Malcom lived. "I'm bothered by something," Angella said as we continued down Gulf Boulevard. "Castro and Conc met with a man after spending hours birthing a foal."

"So?"

"But he told me after you left the room, and I quote, when the foal arrives, I had the job to do I was hired for."

"Did he say what kind of job?"

"He had his phone out to show me a picture of the man they met. I think he was also about to show me the message he sent to himself from Conc's phone. But he bolted before he brought up the images. I think he saw a silhouette of Lt. Malone through the window behind me. It spooked him."

"He certainly wasn't on Malone's hot list."

"Not judging from her reaction. But with her you can't always be too certain what she's thinking."

Malone's face popped up on my cell phone. "Speaking of the devil," I said, when I hit the ACCEPT button, "how may I be of service, Lieutenant?"

"You or Angella have Conc's cell phone, or know where it is? Simple yes or no will do. No bull shit!"

"No."

"Joy says a kid she knows as Castro came to her apartment, gave her Conc's phone. Says it was in the apartment when she went out. She spoke to you at Ted's and then came to my office. When I was out she went to see the lawyer Ayers. Spent the rest of the morning over there."

"So just why are you asking..."

"For God's sake, Redstone, you're big as life on the security camera walking up to her door not long after she left the restaurant."

"Didn't go in."

"You're not denying you were at Malcom's at 9:48, now are you?"

This is the point where any decent lawyer would instruct me to say nothing. "If that's what the tape shows, then that's what the tape shows." Admit nothing, confirm only what you know the physical evidence shows.

"Redstone!"

"I'm still here."

"Stop with the games! Have you seen that phone? Do you know what was on that phone?"

"The kid, Castro, took a picture—or a video—of the killer in action. Or so he wants us to believe."

"Find the phone and I find the killer. That your story?"

"Kid says it was right into the sun. He couldn't make out the face. Thinks it was a woman, but not certain."

"I'm positive the lab can extract a face from the sun. That is assuming I can find the phone."

"Assuming you can find the phone."

"Thanks." The sarcastic tone of Malone's voice hung in the air even after the connection dissolved.

SEVEN

It was ten the next morning when we headed out to follow up on a thought Angella had. I was skeptical, but it was worth a chance. The sign in front of our destination read, Kay's Beads. Inside, the place was crammed with bin upon bin of beads of every color, size, shape, and material. Several people were browsing the bins, picking up beads and dropping them in hand-carried trays.

"All the years I've lived on this island," I said to Angella, "I had no idea this is where people come to make their own necklaces and bracelets."

"That only means you don't get out much. You can string them yourself or Maria will do it for you. Best selection of beads anywhere."

"Did I hear my name?" a voice called from behind me. Turning, I found a woman approaching from the back of the store wearing the broadest smile I think I've ever seen.

"That's Maria," Angella informed me, "and if she's not the most pleasant woman you'll ever meet I'll..."

"Hi. I'm Mary," the woman said, extending her hand. "Angella! How are you? Haven't seen you forever. Here, give me a hug."

"Jimmy Redstone," I said, when the women released each other. I reached out to shake her offered hand.

"You here to make her a necklace? If so, it would be better to surprise her. Come in when she's busy some other place and we'll make something nice for her."

"Not this time," Angella answered. "But I'll work on him." Angella studied the faces of the others in the store, lowered her voice and asked, "A guy by the name of Castro, skinny kid, wears a ceramic-glass wrist bracelet. That bracelet come from here by any chance?"

"Over there," Maria said, pointing to the far wall, "is where we have the ceramics. "Pick what you want, I'll string it."

"Did you design the one Castro's wearing?"

"Not exactly."

"You know which one I'm talking about?"

"To my knowledge he only has the one. Texas blue-sky pieces."

"What's 'not exactly' mean?" I sensed a reluctance on Maria's part to talk about it.

"Well...actually, Joy Malcom designed it."

"Joy Malcom," I blurted, momentarily caught off guard. "Are Castro and Joy..."

"An item," Angella finished my thought.

"Oh, heavens no!" Maria quickly added. "Joy had the bracelet made in exchange for...oh I suppose nothing's private on this island anyway. In exchange for a tattoo."

"A tattoo!" Now I was really off balance. "Who got the tattoo?"

"Joy."

"Joy?"

Maria stepped back, the smile mostly gone.

"Don't mind Jimmy," Angella said, "he's old school. Not a tattoo fan. Back when he was a Texas Ranger he worked on several murder cases where the gang members all had tattoos. On their right middle finger if I recall your story correctly, Jimmy."

"Right middle finger," I repeated. "Here." I pointed to the area between the knuckle and the first joint. "Took delight is claiming the last thing a victim would see was the gang logo slamming into his face."

"That's horrible," Maria replied. "I can assure you Joy's was nothing like that. Just her husband's name on her upper arm just below the shoulder blade."

Angella said. "I'm curious. What does Castro have to do with tattoos?"

"Kids a genius. Tattoos, henna, you name it. If it comes to drawing he's the person to see. He's almost as good as a young woman, goes by Kat, who worked for me one summer. Kat defines good, but didn't do tats. Henna was her thing. Castro does it all."

"So, if I'm following correctly," I said, "Joy had you make a bracelet for Castro and you gave that bracelet to him in exchange for Joy getting a tat. Is that right?"

"Right."

"So why didn't Joy just pay Castro for the tat. Why the bracelet?"

"I asked Joy that very question. And what Joy told me, and I quote, 'You have no need to know'. End quote."

"You're saying, it's none of my business."

"That's not what I said. What I said was, I didn't find out because I have no need to know."

"Your best guess, then," I said, not heeding Angella's gesture to drop the subject.

"Joy wanted the work done off the books, so to speak. I think they did it at her apartment and not at the parlor. That's the best I can do. Sorry."

At least the smile was back. On Maria's face, not mine. I was about to ask her what parlor Castro worked at but a woman walked into the store with the cutest little white dog I had ever seen.

"Pardon me, Jimmy, Angella. But I have to say

hello to Franco and Mary." Bending to pet the dog, Maria said, "Hi, Mr. Franco, little dude. You come for a homemade collar?"

"Not today," the woman, a brunette, replied after giving the store proprietor a genuine hug. "We're off tomorrow to New Jersey and I was thinking of necklaces for my granddaughters."

"Megan and Lauren, as I recall."

"What a great memory you have dear lady."

Maria said, "Got work to do. Jimmy, you come back soon and we'll build something nice for your lovely partner." Turning to the brunette, she asked, "So what were you thinking about my dear?" She led the way toward a myriad of bead bins further back in the store.

Our interview was over. Fact is, the interview would have been over anyway because a shadow had passed across the front door. A very recognizable shadow.

"Tiny!" Angella whispered, turning on her heel and heading toward the door. "What the hell's he doing down here?"

"Nothing good," I replied as I followed her out the door.

"Both of us couldn't be mistaken," Angella exclaimed when we couldn't find Tiny after looking up and down Padre Boulevard and searching for him on the street running along the side of the bead shop. "How does a seven-foot-tall man disappear?"

"That's what spooks do. Disappear. It's an art form with him. He's the most invisible big man I've ever known. That shadow was intended to draw our attention. If he didn't want us to see him, we wouldn't have seen him. Let's just start home. He'll find us when he's good and ready."

"Why not call him?"

"If he wanted to talk on the phone he would have called."

I put the car in reverse and started to back out onto Padre Boulevard when the back passenger side door flew open and in slid the big man. Not for the first time I marveled at how a person of his size could maneuver like a cat of prey. He made it seem almost effortless.

Holding his finger across his lips in the universal sign for quiet, he motioned with his free hand to proceed south.

"So Angella," I said, playing along and trying to sound natural, "how about a ride up the Rio Grande River later today? You up for it?"

"Anywhere specific?" Angella asked, going along with the charade.

"Just a ride. Pack a lunch. Better yet, let's have lunch at that great barbecue place."

I glanced in the rear view mirror and got the thumbs up sign from our guest.

"You mean, Rudy's," Angella replied, "Everyone in that place is packing it seems."

Angella was referring to the fact that Rudy's gives a discount to law enforcement folks and the sworn officers from McAllen, Edinburg, Pharr, Mission, Border Patrol, ICE, FBI, Texas Rangers, State Police, you name it, all show up at lunch time. All of them have weapons on their person, but not all of them are in uniform. One day something will startle one of them and half the place will shoot the other half. A real shootout at OK Corral. "Yea, Rudy's. We'll be in the minority without our guns."

"We'll manage just fine, Jimmy. I think before we head out it would be good if we go up to the stable and see how Lip Sync and her foal are doing."

"Good thought."

Tiny refusing to talk in the car was an indication we might again be bugged. My phone began playing the William Tell Overture Finale. I let it ring.

"That's the boss man, Silver," Angella said, "Not a good idea to keep him waiting. No matter what the reason."

I checked the rearview mirror for instructions from Tiny and got a thumbs up.

"Redstone here," I answered, "at your service."

"Something wrong, Redstone?" Silver asked, never one to miss a nuance.

"No, nothing's wrong, sir. What can we do for you?"

"You remember Senator Angel Lopez Garcia? Tells me you saved his life a while back."

"Indeed, I do remember him." How could I forget the man? He talked my ear off half the night, what with his plans for remaking Mexico and eliminating their dependence on drug trafficking.

"He'll be on the island within the hour. Isla Grand. He'll be there until morning. Keep him safe. He'll give you the details. Meet his security guard in the lobby. Angella with you?"

"She is."

"Angella?"

"Listening."

"Garcia's wife, Valencia, goes by Val, has her own security detail. She'll cross the border at McAllen in two hours. As I understand the situation, she plans to do some shopping before proceeding to the island. You're to meet her detail at the hotel as well."

"Will she be leaving with her husband?"

"That's my understanding. Be certain she's not harmed."

Now it was Angella's turn to say, "Yes, sir."

"What about Lip Sync?" I asked. "And the foal?" I hesitated asking about Castro not knowing who else was listening.

"I understand the horses are okay for now. I assume your other charge is as well. Get back to them when the senator is safely off island."

When the phone went dead, Angella said, "Isn't Garcia..."

Angella fell silent when Tiny tapped her on the shoulder, but I knew what she was thinking because the same thought flashed into my mind. If Silver and Castro and Conquesta and Santiago were buddies, and if, as we knew from past history, Santiago and Garcia are bitter enemies, why was Silver assigning us to cover Garcia? Made no sense. And why was Silver covering people anyway? He insured things, valuable things. Not people, no matter how valuable they were—or thought they were.

I checked the mirror for driving instructions. The big guy motioned to keep straight at the base of the causeway. Meaning either we were going all the way south on the island to Dolphin Cove, or...or perhaps we simply were going to Dirty Al's or Pier 19 for lunch.

Schlitterbahn Water Park was also along this stretch of road, but I highly doubted if Tiny had it in mind to don a bathing suit and float along the lazy river, his butt wedged in an inner tube. The thought of it made me laugh. He'd need a tractor tire.

"What's so funny?" Angella asked, as we passed the waterpark. "Clue me in."

"Private thought. For my mind only," I replied, again checking my mirror for directions. Seeing none, I continued south. "No need to know."

Pier 19 was now behind us and Dirty Al's off to the right. We were about to pass through the toll booth into Isla Blanca Park when the direction came, by way of a tap on my right shoulder, to move to the far right onto a dead-end road that runs along the lagoon. Coast Guard Station South Padre Island is located at the end of that road.

Angella and I were now mustered out of Homeland Security so we had no real business out here. Captain Boyle, Head of Station, and I had gotten ourselves crosswise so many times that only by the grace of God had one of us not already committed a capital act with respect to the other. Hopefully, that was now behind us. But this visit, if indeed we were going to the Coast Guard Station, felt strange. Very strange indeed.

EIGHT

"**S**o how's civilian life treating you two?" Tiny asked as we passed the sentry and entered the Coast Guard building.

"Not much going on, not yet anyway," I answered. "Unless you count checking up on a horse as anything. But I suppose you're well aware of that."

"Do I detect a bit of sarcasm, my friend? I hope not. Somebody's gotta have your back. May as well be me."

"May as well," I agreed, knowing I had no choice in the matter regardless of how I felt. And if my back needed watching, Tiny was the best — until he wasn't. "It would be a better world if no one had to have our backs," I needlessly added. "Can't I retire in peace?"

"That world's long behind you my friend. A real long way back. Capisce?"

"You telling me something?"

"Nothing you already don't know." Tiny fell quiet as we walked into the small conference room. Another sentry closed the door behind us. Then Tiny continued. "You're aware, I'm sure, you and Angella made some powerful enemies, enemies with long memories. Their revenge will come whether or not you're a card carrying government employee."

"Are those enemies in or out of our government?"

"Actually, both. One of them is about to join us. I suggest you do nothing to further his...his desire for your skin."

Boyle had started it. But I kept that comment to myself. Sounds like squabbling siblings.

Angella broke the uncomfortable silence, a deep frown on her face. "I've been thinking about Angel Garcia."

"And?"

"As I recall, Jimmy, he was at the Convention Center when the mayor announced a Mexican deal of some sort. He would have been killed had you not tackled the perp." Her frown deepened even further. "Wasn't the would-be killer none other than Shadowy Sal?"

"Disguised as a Muslim," I replied. "Walked calmly through the security check points on her way out. Caught on camera, but to no avail."

"This doesn't feel right. I can't imagine what could be Silver's interest in protecting Angel? Silver reminds us at every opportunity he's a property man, doesn't deal in life insurance. Remember, that's what sealed the deal. We would be investigating property, not people. Property doesn't pack heat, or carry knives."

Tiny, who had been listening from across the room, said, "It hasn't been announced, but Garcia is about to run for President of Mexico. His donors have insured him — actually they have insured a campaign asset known as Senator Lopez Garcia, for well over fifty-million."

"Great Southern the insurer?"

"They have a major piece. Your boss heads up the coalition putting up the collateral."

"I suppose the U. S. has an interest in his well-being as well," I said, still not understanding Tiny's presence this far from Washington and particularly not with respect to an insurance policy. And if Garcia is considered property then we need to rethink our current employment.

"Let's just say my employers have an interest in seeing that the Senator and his wife come and go safely."

"Isn't that the mission of the Secret Service? Or some police organization. How about I call Lt. Malone, let her folks handle this? Or perhaps the Texas Rangers?"

"We have Malone's number on speed dial. If my bosses wanted her, she'd be sitting where you are. You're up at the plate, so concentrate on the pitching mound, not the spectators. Capisce?"

Actually, I didn't capisce and was about to tell Tiny so when he added, "Just so you can't say I keep secrets, Garcia is here for a fund raiser. Big money will be here for a quick lunch. Because he supports the border wall Mogul will introduce him."

That explains Tiny's presence on the island. Advance team for the Secret Service. That also means this little island will be flooded with high-stakes players from both sides of the border. "I didn't think there were that many Mexican nationals in the States to make fund raising up here worthwhile."

"I'm not an expert on foreign election finance laws. But there's a large number of wealthy Mexican business owners who support the wall. Or, more accurately, there are any number of folks who want to see the criminal element in Mexico run out. With Trump being here, the wall will receive major TV coverage. And that plays to Trump's benefit. The announced reason for his visit is the wall, along with immigration issues. Expect protests."

"If Garcia supports the wall," Angella said, "that would put him directly opposite Santiago—and by association Silver. Tell me again why Silver is protecting Garcia?"

"Silver follows the money," Tiny winked. "Isn't that your motto, Redstone? Follow the money. And isn't it true what they say about politics making strange bedfellows?"

"Stranger all the time. Even with a scorecard, I can't keep it all straight."

"Your job isn't to keep the relationships straight. Your job Jimmy is to keep one man alive. And your job Angella is to keep one woman alive. Politics, relationships, money flow, none of that is your concern. As I said, keep your eye on the pitching mound so you don't get thrown a curve you don't see."

"What's that supposed to mean?" Tiny, a man of few words, had said a lot, most of which went over my head.

"The wall stops drug traffic as well as people. Ultimately, that can be good for the Mexican people because it will loosen the drug lords' grip on the country. Silver needs to maintain a balance if he wishes to continue in business."

"Are you saying Silver is involved in illegal activity?"

"You, my friend, are getting ahead of yourself. Just keep them both alive tonight. Wave goodbye in the morning. What can be so difficult?"

What Tiny didn't say, and would never tell us, was why the American government required the help of private citizens in protecting a Mexican husband and wife. Or maybe we weren't as private as we thought.

The door few open and the Captain himself swept in. The sentry saluted and pulled the door closed behind him. Boyle's behavior reminded me of a legend I once heard about the Queen of England. When, as the tale goes, it's time to sit, she sits. It's the unenviable duty of some minion to position a chair such that her butt never touches the ground. If I had been tasked with that job for Boyle his ass would have hit the floor long before now. The corollary: my ass would have long ago been on public display hanging from some gallows.

"Good morning gentlemen — and lady," Boyle began, his voice command perfect. "As you know, yesterday a young man had his throat cut eighteen point three miles north of this room. At the time as it so happened we were tracking a high-speed carbon fiber vessel in that vicinity. Carbon fiber is believed not to be detectable and for that reason vessels made from carbon are used for the delivery of contraband. A well-placed intelligence asset tipped us to the fact that the vessel contained cocaine."

Boyle paused, looked to Tiny, got a nod, then continued. "We have been using highly sophisticated drones along the beach. For all practical purposes they appear from the ground to be pelicans."

"Pelicans equipped with cameras, I suppose."

"Not at liberty to say, Redstone, what the drones contain or don't contain. But I am authorized to show you pictures obtained from a classified source."

One of the many screens came alive and a series of stills appeared. The first one showed Conc and the kid walking at water's edge. There was a shot of Conc bent over his phone. And one of Castro in the dunes, a phone held low as if being shaded by the dune grass. The next one surprised me. A helmeted person head-down on a small Jet Ski driving toward the beach. Then that same helmeted person walking north along the water line, the Jet Ski on the sand in the background.

"Can I assume, the Jet Ski came in off the vessel you were tracking?"

"Assume what you will," Boyle responded.

The next image was of a woman standing behind Conc holding what appeared to be a knife. Then one of Conc on the ground. Then a shot of the woman back on the Jet Ski riding straight out from the beach.

The screen went dark. "So who is the helmeted person?" I asked.

"No need for you to know," Boyle snapped.

Hold your temper, Jimmy. "So then why are we here?"

"Not my idea, hot shot," Boyle sneered. "Not by a long shot. This was at Emerson's request." Boyle nodded toward Tiny. "Care to answer the man's question."

Tiny flashed Boyle his don't-mess-with-me look before saying, "Recognize the figure with the knife?"

"Not immediately," I responded, even though I had.

"Don't play with me, Redstone!" Tiny snapped. "I know you all too well! I'm here to help."

Angella, in an attempt to defuse the situation, said, "The drone didn't capture her face. But I'd say the figure with the knife is supposed to be Lieutenant Malone."

"Give the lady a beer," Tiny said. "But, of course, like you, we ruled Malone out. Anyone else come to mind?"

"Malone have an alibi?" I asked, the Texas Ranger in me surfacing while remembering how she had questioned me last night.

"Not exactly. But...but Malone's right-handed. The knife was in the left hand. Not conclusive. But persuasive—for now."

"So who do you make for it?" I asked. I then recalled the warning from Ben-Yuval that had come through Tiny. I knew the answer even before I finished the question. Shadowy Sal!

"The imposter artist!" Angella blurted. "Sal! That explains something that's been bothering me. When she impersonates someone she takes on their movements as well as their speech patterns. Remember last night at Ayers' office when Castro bolted?"

I nodded.

"He recognized something outside. If Malone— or a Malone imposter—cut Conc's throat, that's what Castro saw! The person who killed Conc moved exactly like the person outside the window. No wonder he bolted."

"Malone walking along the side of the building and then going back to her car to answer a call," I confirmed. "That's what she told us happened."

"Can't blame him for running," Tiny repeated absently, distracted by his communicator.

While the big man studied the tiny screen, I turned to Boyle. "The drone obviously traced the Jet Ski to the beach. Where did it go afterward?"

"No need to know," Boyle answered.

"Answer the question, Captain," Tiny demanded, not looking up.

Not accustomed to being told what to do, Boyle's back stiffened and his eyes set hard. But on reflection, he calmed himself. "The drone continued up the beach and when it circled back the Jet Ski was gone." Boyle's response had been made with scorn in his eyes, as though he was angry with the drone operator as well as being angry at having to confess that his operation was less than perfect.

"Guesses?" I pressed.

"Most likely ran further off-shore than we had expected and met up with a mother ship. Maybe a shrimper. Maybe one of the oil derricks out there waiting for repairs. We really don't know."

"What happened to the cocaine?" I asked, even though I already knew the answer. My way of testing Boyle.

"Malone, the real Malone, recovered it. ATF has it now."

Tiny, finally looking up from the device buried in his large hand, said, "Been a slight change of plans. Mrs. Garcia's female EMP agent has taken sick. Angella, you're needed in McAllen within the hour. EMP protocol will not allow Valencia into a changing room unguarded."

A puzzled look crossed Angella's face. "EMP?"

"Mexican Presidential Guard. Think of it as our Secret Service."

When Tiny didn't comment further, I said, "Just have her skip the shopping. She can buy what she needs here on the island. Or in Houston, or in Dallas for that matter."

"Not an option. The Garcia's have a heavy appearance schedule tomorrow and she insists she requires several outfits. Our hands are tied."

"Who's the money for?" I asked. "Can't raise money in the U. S. for a Mexican political race."

"That's not your concern, Redstone," Tiny replied. "Just focus on keeping Garcia alive while on the island. He's unpopular among the drug trade and I can't imagine them not trying to end his political career before it really begins. South Padre Island would be the perfect location."

"Driving time to McAllen is an hour and a half," Angella said. "Even with a police escort it'll take over an hour."

"Captain," Tiny said, turning toward Boyle. "I assume the station helicopter has a driver in the vicinity."

"Not on your life!" Boyle replied. "That helicopter is scheduled for drug surveillance up island."

"Captain!" Tiny stood. Towering over Boyle, "A drug scan an hour or so late is not a big deal."

"Don't lecture me on how to do my job!"

"I assume," Tiny said, his voice steely hard, "escalation won't be necessary. Capisce?"

Boyle's hesitation caused Tiny's cell to appear. But before the big man could touch a speed-dial button, Boyle leaned forward to the communication panel, pulled a lever and said, "Have the helo ready for takeoff in five minutes."

Tiny continued to glare at the Captain. Boyle again pulled the lever forward. "Make that two minutes. Woman passenger will provide destination info."

"Thank you, Captain," Tiny said. "I'll arrange priority clearance." To Angella he added, "I know you're not armed. That will be arranged as well. You'll have permission to carry—and to shoot if necessary. Same rules and protections apply as before when you were an agent. Just keep the Senator's wife safe."

"Report to?"

"Me. Now get outside. Don't keep the pilot waiting."

Angella disappeared through the door.

Tiny turned his attention to me. "I've had your clearance restored, for now anyway. Here, read this. It will bring you up to speed on what we know about Angel Lopez Garcia and his run for President of Mexico. It includes some of the folks who would be very happy if he doesn't succeed. He's less than an hour out. Get to your place, get your weapon and get your ass back to the hotel. Timing's close. Don't be late. Anything happens, it's on you."

"I assume Angella's cleared as well."

"She is. On a need to know basis."

"And may I assume you'll have our backs? I mean with the carry permits."

"I wouldn't think of doing otherwise? Oh, and Jimmy. If you find it necessary to discharge your weapon be sure it's after you think it through. As a civilian there is really not much I can do for you."

"That's below the belt. Even for you." I paused to listen to the helicopter taking to the air, the whirl of its blades sounding as if the machine was passing through the room we were in. Silently I wished Angella well, but I didn't like the way it was starting out. As always, we only had half the story—and probably not even that much. And the story we had made little sense.

"Just so you know," Tiny said, interrupting the mental wave I was throwing to Angella, "while we were in here your car was swept. Found a few toys. I'd advise you to get it done often. Your apartment as well." He smiled a mischievous smile. "Just remember, you might be finished with the bad

folks, but I can assure you, the bad folks aren't
finished with you."

NINE

I was in the lobby of the Isla Grand Hotel a full five minutes before three burly men burst in from the direction of the front drive. EMP if ever I saw EMP. No different from our Secret Service, except they all sported identical mustaches and not one of them was under two-forty pounds. Or as my Mexican friends would say, a hundred plus kilos. Some flirted with three hundred pounds. Their eyes darted in every direction much as mine had done when I had been assigned to guard the Texas governor many years ago.

Sudden unexpected motion could easily set them off, so I remained seated, weapon out of sight, not knowing what orders they had been given, or even if they would follow those orders.

A moment later the door swung open again and a tall man, flanked by two more EMP agents, swept into the lobby. His eyes quickly took in his surroundings. "Jimmy Redstone!" Angel Lopez

Garcia's familiar voice rang out. "What a pleasure to see you again, my friend. Thank you for doing this for me on such short notice."

"My pleasure, Senator," I replied, grasping his outstretched hand. It was difficult not falling under the influence of this gregarious man, who had sat up half the night on his last visit talking to me about his positive vision for the people of Mexico. He was now putting into action plans he had been dreaming about for years, all geared to his desire to rid his country of the devastation wrought by drug-induced crime.

"Come," he said, signaling to the nearest guard that it was okay for me to join the entourage, "let's go up to the room. We have much to discuss."

In the elevator, Garcia leaned close. "I understand your partner has arrived in McAllen. She should by now be with my wife. That is indeed a relief. But I won't rest comfortably until Valencia is here with me, and under your expert protection."

"She's in good hands," I assured the senator, despite the feeling of dread that had sprung up at the mention of Angella. The whole operation was out of character. Never are these trips allowed without extensive planning by the Secret Service, and, I presume, the EMP. And never would they allow civilians like Angella and I to be center stage. So why now? As always, it was what I didn't know that bothered me more than what I did know.

The elevator door to the fourth floor opened and first off was one of the senator's guards, then

Garcia, then a second guard. I brought up the rear.

No sooner had I stepped into the corridor than one of the burly mustachioed men stationed beside the elevator door grabbed my right arm and pinned it back against the elevator wall. Before Garcia could say anything, a second security man, his hand firmly clamped to my left wrist, located my Berretta and pulled back my jacket to expose it.

"He's okay," the Senator called. "I asked for him to be armed." Turning to me, Garcia explained, "I forgot to warn the floor guards. My sincere apologies my friend. I am not yet accustomed to all this security. Because I am running for President, the EMP insist. Please accept my apologies."

"Accepted." It was the only thing I could say. My trouble meter was above the red zone and still rising.

"Come, we have connecting rooms."

Glancing around I had no idea what I could — or should — add to their security plans. So I followed, saying nothing. A large table had been set in one corner, holding enough food to feed the Mexican army. A uniformed waiter removed covers from a hot tray revealing fajita fixings, beef, chicken, pork and a meat I didn't immediately recognize but guessed to be cabrito. Surrounding the hot tray were plates of cheese, peppers, salsa and at least two types of beans. Hot tortilla's, both corn and flour, sat in serving plates covered with white cloths.

"Help yourself, my friend," Angel said, pointing to the food. "I, for myself, am starved." He walked over to the table and spread a corn tortilla on a plate, selected the mystery meat, added several of the sides and rolled it all up. He then fetched a De Minerva Stout. "My favorite beer, but don't tell anyone. Their competitors donated to my campaign."

I made a fajita taco for myself, also using the unidentified meat. First bite confirmed it was indeed cabrito. "That's good. Surprised they have cabrito here."

"Family recipe, my good friend. Hotel makes it for me when I visit your wonderful island. I'll see that you receive the recipe. Come, let's catch up."

Garcia's idea of catching up was to fill me in on his plans for Mexico as if we had been friends since childhood. It was hard not to get caught up by his enthusiasm. The only time his eyes clouded was when I mentioned Trump's comments on Mexican's being murderers and rapists. But even then the shadow quickly passed. "He was referring only to..." His phone buzzed. "Pardon me. It's my wife. I must take it." Speaking into the phone, he said, "Hi, Val. Get what you want?"

He listened a moment, then asked, "Is everything going well?"

"Okay, then. I will see you here on the island soon."

Putting the phone down, Garcia turned to me. "Vic wanted me to know that she's safe with the

EMPs and all is well, but that your partner re-mained behind in McAllen."

If an imaginary trouble meter could explode, mine had just gone nuclear. Nothing good could have made Angella stay behind. On the off chance she had, she would have called or messaged me. I checked my phone. I had no message. "Did she say why Angella remained behind?"

"Apparently, one of the outfits required a hem. Angella is waiting for it."

There is no possibility Angella would allow a charge out of her sight. I doubted the hem story, but even if it were true, Angella would have ar-ranged for a messenger to deliver the merchandise. Security details don't abandon their posts, period. She was reporting directly to Tiny and EMP's or not, Tiny would never have authorized Angella to stay behind. "Are you certain your wife's okay?"

"Her security detail confirmed everything was going according to plan. They left the store ten minutes ago without incident."

I checked my watch. There hadn't been enough time lapse since the helo took off for Angella to have been in place when Garcia informed me of that fact. It had taken a moment, but I now knew what had been nagging at me. Timing. It was way off.

I called Angella. She answered immediately. "Jimmy. You must be a mind reader. I was just about to call you. Something's wrong. I've been in the store less than five minutes and they're gone!"

"What's the situation there?"

"The store clerk says Valencia arrived with three men who identified themselves as her security team. The clerk had been briefed and was expecting them. Several outfits were waiting in the changing room."

"How long ago?"

"Fifteen minutes before me. Here's the problem. The clerk says I escorted Valencia into the changing room. Valencia was in the room about five minutes and came out."

"And?"

"According to the clerk, I didn't."

"Is the clerk positive it was Valencia?"

"The clerk knew Valencia from previous shopping trips. She also identified her from a picture I showed her on my cell."

"Did the clerk say anything about tailoring?"

"Negative."

"Check the changing room," I said, fearing the worst.

A moment later Angella exclaimed, "Oh, my God! If I didn't know better I'd swear I was lying on the floor!"

"What?"

"In the dressing room. A woman looking exactly like me, and even wearing one of my outfits, is out cold. Breathing is shallow. I'd say drugged.

Gotta get off. Need the phone to arrange things!" The line went dead.

I was confident Angella had the presence of mind to call Tiny and let him arrange the details, so I didn't call him. Things would move faster that way.

At least for the moment I felt we were doing everything possible to recover control of the situation. It was clear we had an imposter on our hands. Odds were good the imposter was Shadowy Sal. Since I was reasonably certain I had been speaking with Angella on the phone, then who was the woman lying drugged on the changing-room floor?

My first thought was the imposter. But that made no sense, unless EMP figured out the hoax and put an end to Ole Sal. But then why not tell the senator what happened?

My phone rang. Angella's picture came up. "The van will be here in less than two minutes," she said when I hit the Accept button, "so I'll talk fast. The woman on the floor is Valencia, or so it appears. Prints have been sent to Tiny. We'll know in a few minutes."

"She okay?"

"If we hadn't found her when we did she wouldn't be. Opioid injection. They got Narcan into her and she's up and moving. Groggy, but I'm told that'll clear in an hour or two. Forehead bruised a bit. Apparently hit a chair on the way down. Gotta go."

Again the line went dead.

It followed that if Garcia hadn't spoken with his wife on the phone a few minutes ago then it had to have been the imposter who called. That meant the EMPs were now guarding Shadowy Sal. Worse, they were bringing her to the hotel to spend the night with her husband. This wasn't going to end well — for anyone.

Time was short and my only real option was to brief Garcia on what I knew. He listened carefully, asked several questions mostly related to why Angella was so late in getting to McAllen. He then demanded to know how she could be so certain it was Valencia she had found. He wasn't buying all that I said, especially the part about Shadowy Sal now being disguised as his wife. In fact, his reaction was especially hostile to the messenger.

Garcia grabbed his phone and hit the speed dial button opposite his wife's name. After several rings Valencia's pre-recorded answering message came on.

"Call me as soon as you get this," Garcia said into the phone the moment the message stopped. "I need to speak with you."

Over my objection, he then immediately typed out a text message and sent that to his wife as well. Assuming Shadowy Sal had the cell phone she would now also know that the senator was aware of the substitution.

"I'm sorry to say this, Jimmy," Garcia said when

he looked up from his phone, "but I now believe it was a mistake asking to include you on my team. I was told...well, anyway, this is not working out. As you know, I personally spoke to Val not more than fifteen minutes ago. I'm positive it was her on the phone. Now you're trying to make me believe it was some...some imposter. Actually, the very same person you blamed for trying to kill me at the Convention Center. I don't know what your game is, but...I want you out of here."

"Senator, I may be wrong about who actually called you, but I can promise you I'm not wrong about where your wife is. Fingerprints will soon confirm I'm right, and I trust Angella."

"I know my own wife's voice! And that was her! You're a fool if you think for one minute I'll instruct the EMP to divert her! You must be loco!"

"I can't allow your wife, the imposter, into this room, Senator. Not until she's properly vetted. I'm sorry, but I can't."

"As your President Trump would say, you're fired! Now get out of my room!"

"Sorry, but I can't."

"You can! And you will!"

"Sorry. But if I'm to leave I'll only do so by orders of—"

"I said, get out! Do I have to call my security team?"

"Call whomever you wish, Senator. I'm here until relieved by our government. On this side of the river Homeland Security is in charge, and I'm here at their request—as well as yours." I had to trust that Tiny had my back on this and that he would have already informed the Mexican authorities that we had a problem. In these matters, coordination—and timing—are everything. If Tiny was good at anything, he was good at coordination at the highest levels. I was about to learn if he really had my back.

A moment later my cell buzzed. Terse message from Tiny: "Hold position. Prints confirmed. A has V."

I relayed the message to Garcia who turned on his heel, went into the bathroom and slammed the door behind him. I had become the enemy.

My cell buzzed again, this time from Angella. "On our way."

The bathroom door flew open. Not knowing if Garcia was armed, my hand went for my weapon.

"So now you're turning on me? You're not to be trusted!"

"Show me both hands. Please."

"My friend. You are the last person I would have thought would turn on me."

"I haven't turned on you, Senator. I'm trying to keep you alive. The woman you spoke with before is an imposter." I went on to explain what I knew about Shadowy Sal and her international reputation, but Garcia wasn't having any of it. I showed him Angella's message, but to no avail.

"So why not kill her?" he asked when I stopped talking.

"Beg your pardon?"

"I said, why didn't this person, this Shadow person, why not kill her?"

"Your wife—or the imposter?"

"My wife. Why didn't this Shadow person just kill Val?"

"Because Angella got there soon enough to keep her from dying. But the plan is to kill you! She, the imposter, substituted herself for Valencia. Your guard team is either in on it, or duped. Either way, they're bringing the imposter directly to you. In due course a killer will come through that door. You'll walk over to greet her and...and she'll cut your throat."

"You actually believe I'm not capable of knowing my own wife! You must be insane! I'll know in an instant if it is not her."

"As I told you a few moments ago, she has impersonated my partner Angella and I can assure you I didn't know."

"You remain alive."

"Because it was information she wanted, not my dead skin. I assure you, had she wanted me dead, I'd be dead."

"You have a plan?" Garcia asked, slumping into a chair. "If not, I'll call the detail and have her arrested when she steps from the elevator. Is that what you want?"

"Please don't do that."

"I thought that's what you wanted me to do."

"I've had time to think. Your team's been in-filtrated. You support the wall. Many in Mexico hate the idea of the wall. Someone on your team's taking directions from an enemy of yours. That's why the original EMP agent didn't show up and why the timing was off in McAllen. Maybe the infiltration was only with your wife's team, but maybe it goes higher. It's possible the instant you speak with them they'll come after you. I'm here because someone...someone doesn't trust your team. So, whatever we do we need to do it on our own. Surprise is the best plan."

"So, what is it you have in mind?"

"When the door opens, walk slowly toward your wife as if you are welcoming her home. Her guards will stop at the door. But don't get close enough for her to reach out and grab you. I'll be behind the door. When she clears the door, I'll disarm her. This won't be our first encounter, but I plan to make it the last."

"Don't kill her in my presence. I can't afford to be involved in an international incident."

"I'll do my best. The important thing, I can't stress this enough, is for you to stay far enough away from her so she can't lunge for you. I know the temptation will be for you to move closer to insure yourself she's a phony. But please don't do that. That woman is fast—and deadly."

TEN

We killed time chatting, but Garcia imparted nothing I already didn't know. Ever the politician, he had written me off, but he did it with a smile, not a kick in the butt.

The conversation was wearing thin when the lobby detail reported Valencia was five minutes out. It seemed an eternity before word came that she was stepping into the elevator.

Lights and camera. Action would come when the imposter made her appearance in our doorway.

We took our respective positions; me behind the door, Garcia remaining in the chair across the room as we had rehearsed.

"You ready?" I asked.

"Not happy, but I heard you."

Steps in the hallway. Two male, one female. The female was wearing heals. The male steps stopped a few feet from the door. The clicking heals continued closer to the door before stopping. No sound for a moment.

Then the card reader on the door buzzed. Slowly the door swung open, but the footsteps remained silent. Shadowy Sal was taking stock of the situation, refusing to blindly walk into a room. The scenario she had orchestrated was playing out exactly as she had visualized it with the target alone in his room, at ease, talking on the phone.

One step forward. Pause. Nothing amiss.

A second step.

She was still being blocked by the door. This woman was even better than I had anticipated, and that's how she had evaded law enforcement on several continents and why she was at the top of Interpol's most wanted fugitives.

Across the room Garcia remained seated. "Hi, Honey," he called, "just finishing up a call. Give me a moment." If Garcia had doubts as to who his visitor was, he gave no indication. I was pleasantly surprised that he was following the script so perfectly.

The imposter's body came even with the open door, but went no further. Something had triggered caution, but she was not yet in a position where I could safely go for her. So I remained frozen in position. The angles were all still wrong.

"I'm tired," she called from the doorway, "and in need of a shower. How about a drink after I'm finished in the loo...toilet."

Was she spooked? Or just being cautious? Criminals at Sal's level have a sixth sense about danger and I was beginning to think she knew about my presence behind the door. Or perhaps it was as simple as her not wanting to make a move while a phone line was open?

But then, why not close the door?

She knows I'm here!

If I push the door into her, she'll end up in the hall. If I pull the door toward me I'll be in an even worse position. But staying still is not an option. She'll make a move toward me any moment now and close quarters favors her knife over my gun. I needed her to move a yard forward, or close the door.

She did neither.

I heard one of the security detail take a step forward. He stopped and I assumed she had signaled for him to wait. If I now appeared in the doorway he wouldn't hesitate to send a bullet in my direction.

Perhaps anticipating my dilemma, Garcia said to his fake phone call, "My wife just arrived. Call you back later." He pushed the end button and put the phone on the table beside him, playing the charade to the last detail. He stood and faced his imposter wife. "How did the shopping trip..."

The door flew closed, leaving me standing in place. I swung my gun around to where Shadowy Sal should have been, but she was already halfway across the room toward Garcia, her left hand down at her side.

"Stop right there, Floratine," I commanded, using the name Interpol knew her as. "One more step and a bullet goes into your brain."

"My God!" exclaimed Garcia taking a step toward the imposter. "Don't shoot! That's Valencia!"

"No!" I barked a moment too late.

Sal grabbed Garcia and spun him around so that he was between us. "We meet yet again, Redstone," she said.

"You're not leaving this room alive," I replied, my confidence level being mostly hat and very little horse.

Calling my bluff, she responded, "Don't be so certain." She moved her left arm just far enough so that I could see the knife at the side of Garcia's throat. "I'm not fool enough to think for a moment you'd hesitate shooting. After all, you'd be sacrificing a Mexican senator—a former senator at that—for someone on the international most wanted list. More than a fair trade, I'd say. But here's the thing. You shoot, all three of us die. Me by your bullet, the senator by my knife, and you, hero you think you are, by bullets from the men just outside that door."

Unfortunately, she was right about that. The men guarding Garcia and Valencia were prime candidates for shooting first and sorting it out later. That's a topic I know all too well.

"So," I conceded, "layout your plan."

"Really simple. The senator and I walk through that door as husband and wife. Guards go with us down to the beach for a stroll. Up the beach a tad and I walk off. As long as the senator here doesn't tip off his guards they'll think I'm going shopping. I'll take my chances getting off the island."

While Sal was talking I was again calculating my shooting options. If I discharged my weapon and the bullet passed through her eye and into her brain she'd be dead before she could nick Garcia. The flaw with that reasoning was obvious—and she had already pointed it out. The security detail in the hall would come through the door loaded for bear. I'd have to drop them both or I'd be dead almost as fast as her. And if my initial shot missed its mark, even by a fraction, Garcia would be dead as well.

"Take the offer, Redstone," Garcia said. "She's right, the EMP will storm the room shooting first. You'll have to kill them and I'll not protect you if you do. Get her on your own time, not mine."

"Deal," I said, still convinced this wasn't going to end well. But I had run out of options and with Shadowy Sal's knife blade pressed against Garcia's throat, even a twitch could end his life. "Take the knife from his neck and I'll lower my weapon."

ELEVEN

"By the time the drone arrived on site," Lieu-tenant Malone was saying, "the senator and his imposter wife, Scumbag Sal, were almost as far north as Joy Malcom's place."

"Who was running the drone?" I asked.

"Detective Cruz. Why is that important?"

"Just filing in the edges. Please go on."

"Actually, since I ordered the drone flight at your suggestion, I was watching over his shoul-der. Anyway, when Scumbag, with the senator in tow, came even with Joy's building, she peeled off toward the building. Garcia abruptly turned and double-timed it back south. That bodyguard team of his better sign up with Teran over at The Island Fitness Center if they have any hope of keeping up with him."

"While on the beach did Garcia call anyone? Use his cell phone?"

"Not that was captured. But keep in mind the drone was following Scumbag. In the short time Garcia was in view he didn't appear to be holding anything. I've put in a request for the phone records. That might be a while. Especially since this is international and according to the report he filed he went along voluntarily. No crime, it seems, has been committed. And since I'm not exactly in the need-to-know community I assume I'll get no help on this one."

Angella's barely perceptive nod indicated she'd check with Tiny to see if NSA could get us access to Garcia's phone records. I wasn't any more optimistic about our chances than Malone was about hers.

"Let's go over again how the drone lost sight of Shadowy Sal."

"When Scumbag left the senator on the beach she walked across the dune line and then went past Malcom's condo on the south side of the building. Cruz had to fly the drone around the north side because of an obstruction located over the walkway on the south side. That was unfortunate because that's how we lost her. Here, I'll show you."

Malone motioned for us to walk around her desk and look over her shoulder at her computer screen. Valencia Garcia's imposter was clearly visible as she made her way up the steps and across the short wooden bridge over the dunes. She then passed along the outside of the fence surrounding the condo's pool area. The drone was still high enough to capture both the pool and the blue Gulf behind Sal.

"Freeze!" Malone said. "See there." Malone pointed to two poles supporting a black net. The poles appeared to be extending from windows on the third or fourth floors.

"Okay, let it run."

When the video restarted, the black net loomed large and nothing below could be seen. The drone turned north, flew over the pool and then turned west over a parking area. A moment later the image showed the front of the parking lot and then a low covered area as the drone passed the front of the building.

Then the figure of a woman walking quickly came into view and it seemed as if the drone had regained its target. However, as the image zoomed in it became clear that the figure that had been 'Valencia Garcia' had now become 'Joy Malcom'. The clothes now on the target were the exact same as when I had seen Joy at her apartment earlier in the day.

"The interesting thing, Jimmy and Angella, is how fast Sal changed. Not time enough to go up to Joy's. She must have anticipated all along that she would have to make a quick change, so she must have stashed her gear in the bushes—or somewhere near the pool."

"Did anybody see her change? We saw people at the pool. Someone must have seen something."

"Checked it out," Malone answered impatiently, showing her displeasure at being second-guessed. "Classic no one saw anything."

"I'm thinking," Angella added, "that she's now using rubber masks. She did a quick change in the dressing room in McAllen and apparently here as well. Just pull a layer overtop, slip on the mask, no need for makeup. Almost don't have to stop moving."

"If she's using masks, they're darn good," I said. "I had an up-close and personal look-see and didn't detect anything that rang phony about her appearance. She even thoroughly fooled her husband."

"Fooling men, I have found," Malone said, a bit of a smile returning to her face, "isn't as hard as you'd expect."

"You forgot to say, 'present company excepted'," I replied, feigning distress. Changing the subject, I said, "I assume you're monitoring all cars leaving the island. You using cameras yet?"

"No cameras, Redstone. And so far, we got zip."

"Know what she's driving?"

"Don't know, Angella. Last seen walking. When I saw Joy on the screen we turned the drone around thinking we were following the wrong person. That's all it took. By the time the drone turned back she was in the wind. My bad."

"I suppose that means Ole Sal knew all along she was being followed by a drone," Angella observed.

"Maybe nothing more than exceptional contingency planning." Malone checked her watch.

"Don't you two need to get back to the Isla Grand and resume your duties?"

"Fired," I confessed. "Mexican government filed a protest with the State Department and they're all over Homeland Security. Even Tiny agrees we need to stay as far from Garcia as possible."

"Actually, what Tiny told Jimmy was that DHS was looking for an excuse to aerate him."

"You run with a fun crowd, my friend."

"Even Silver called," Angella added, "instructed us in no uncertain language to get back on the Lip Sync matter. His parting comment was to the effect he hoped we were better with four-legged clients than with the two-legged kind."

"Really?" Malone said, not breaking even the tiniest of smiles. "I haven't seen any evidence of that. Not a smidgen."

"Horses don't typically run games of their own."

"What's that supposed to mean, Jimmy?" Malone asked, picking up on my gist.

"Just that the whole Garcia incident, from beginning to end, has been wrong. Off key, as it were."

"How?"

"For one thing, timing's all wrong. Garcia's response was wrong. The scumbag having a change of costume just hanging around is...is evidence of preplanning. But yet we're to believe Sal kidnaping the Senator was spontaneous."

"As I said, maybe she's just good at planning for contingencies?"

"Perhaps. We know she's a master. But...but it still feels wrong. Maybe not wrong so much as off. If Sal came to cut his throat so why not cut his throat out on the beach?"

"Bodyguard too close?" Malone answered.

"Feels wrong is all I'm saying. She's so fast with that knife guards a few feet away are essentially useless."

"Point made, Redstone. But maybe Scumbag was delivering a message from the cartels. Cross us and you—or your wife—will become dead real fast. Okay, what else you got?"

"I was thinking of the kid, Castro," Angella said. "What do you have on him?"

"Zippo," Malone answered. "But not surprised. Guys like that go off the radar like smoke. He'll eventually turn up. Most likely on a police blotter, but he's not been seen on the island since he bolted from Lawyer Ayers' office."

"That reminds me," I said, deciding to give Malone something in return for her apparent openness with the drone videos of Angel Garcia. "Earlier today Captain Boyle invited us to view some of his videos. Seems as though the Coast Guard knew about a drug delivery up-island. Caught Conc's murder on camera."

Malone's reaction was immediate. "Son of a bitch didn't bother to share it! So much for our working relationship!" Malone pulled a notepad out of a drawer. "You say he knew about a drug drop. How?"

"Claims he was tracking a carbon fiber boat."

"You don't believe that?"

"In his words, 'a well-placed intelligence asset' informed them of the drop. I'm thinking that was Conc himself. If it was, the kid's far undercover."

"Okay. So who's the perp in the video?"

"You are," I said.

"Stop jerking my chain, Redstone. Enough already!"

"Wouldn't do that, Lieutenant. The video clearly shows you welding the knife. Angella believes that's why Castro took off last night. He saw your silhouette when you walked past the window. To him, you matched the silhouette of Conc's killer."

Malone had stopped listening to me prattle on about the kid being spooked. She had her cell phone to her ear, I assume waiting for Boyle to answer.

"Even if he does share the video with you, you won't learn much."

"Why? Is the quality that poor?"

"Actually, it's rather good. Clearly shows you with the knife in your left hand cutting Conc's throat from behind."

"Thank goodness I'm right handed."

I couldn't resist. Using my best interrogation voice, I asked, "Where were you between the hours of seven and ten on the morning in question?"

"I deserved that. Sorry." Malone slammed the phone down. "He's not answering! And from what you're telling me, Scumbag Sally's impersonating me now as well!"

"You, Angella, Valencia," I said. "I think she's even done me a few times. You're in good company."

"Don't forget Joy Malcom," Angella added. "And those are just the ones we know about."

A thought struck me. "By any chance have you located Conc's cell?"

"Not yet. Malcom confirms it's missing. As I understand it, Castro delivered it to her. So where was Castro when Sal cut Conc's throat?"

"In the dunes trying to get enough shade to see the image on that phone."

"What does the drone video show?"

"Him in the dunes bending over an object."

"Any thought as to why he would hand-deliver a phone to Joy when he could have simply sent the image?"

"Orders. Perhaps they wanted no electronic trace."

"No electronic trace," Angella said, "implies NSA. You think they have Conc's cell on their watch list? Or Castro's?"

"Or the person he would be calling?"

"Malcom?" Angella asked.

"I'm thinking Malcom is the conduit to Morris, her husband." I turned to Malone. "Any update on cars leaving the island."

"Nothing."

"By now she's become someone other than who we think she is," Angella added. "By chance, any cars reported stolen?"

"Good question, Angella. Give me a moment." Malone picked up her radio, mumbled some code numbers into the speaker and clicked off. "Desk Sergeant will be back to me in a moment. The computer shows a stolen-vehicle report entered into the system less than an hour ago. But it was a four-wheel ATV, not a car. But that was found abandoned in the parking lot of Andy Bowie Park."

The radio crackled back on. "Lieutenant," came a female voice. "Stolen vehicle is a kayak trailer. No exact time for the theft. Owner noticed it missing thirty-five minutes ago. Trailer was loaded with four kayaks. Someone hitched it to a truck or something and made off with it."

"Trailer have a plate?" Malone said into the radio, rolling her eyes.

"Affirmative," came the floating voice.

"Get the number in the system. I want to know immediately if that trailer goes onto the causeway."

"Kayak trailer is not your typical get-a-way

ride," Malone said, throwing her pencil onto the desk. "Besides, it still requires a vehicle to pull it. I'd say our perp is still on the island."

"I'm thinking long gone," Angella said. "Why hang around when she knows we're looking for her?"

"That scumbag could be in the next room for all we'd know," Malone snapped, clearly agitated about losing control over her investigation.

What else was bothering the Lieutenant I had no idea. And I had no intention of hanging around long enough to find out.

TWELVE

After taking leave of Lieutenant Malone, Angella suggested we check on Lip Sync and the foal. "Losing two charges in one day is never a good idea, Jimmy. But I don't know what more you could have done about Shadowy Sal."

"Failure is not an option. I failed. Period. There will be consequences."

"You most certainly didn't fail. Garcia's still alive. If we hadn't intercepted the Scumbag, to coin Malone's terminology, he'd most likely be dead. So, I'd say, we passed with flying colors."

"Whatever. Since when do results matter with these folks. It's all commentary. They live by words. Actions are for us worker types."

"How long you gonna beat yourself, Jimmy? Put it behind you and move on."

"Doesn't feel as if we're off to a good start with Silver. We're burning bridges we don't even own."

"Hey, look at the silver-lining. No pun intended. Getting fired by Garcia could keep us from drawing the short straw in future DHS situations. If he's elected and teams up with Trump there'll certainly be plenty of future situations. Best if we stay far away."

"The more I think about it the more I believe I—we—were set up to fail."

"The McAllen operation, as you said, took perfect timing on their part. Had to get Valencia into and out of the dressing room before I arrived. How did Scumbag know the timing? If she had made the swap too soon there was a strong possibility it would have been discovered and the copter would have been diverted back to the island. Or, more likely, tasked to intercept the convoy midway. If I got there too early, then...then there'd be two of me on scene."

It was unlike Angella to be spouting conspiracy theories, so I took notice. "So you think it's no coincidence a chopper just happened to be sitting on the pad idle, or that a pilot was on duty and available."

"Who knows how far up the chain it goes. But if the goal was to kill the senator, they failed. But if they only wanted to scare him into submission, I believe they accomplished their goal. In McAllen I asked the pilot to wait a few minutes so I could verify everyone was in place. 'Orders are orders', he informed me. 'Instructions were to deliver you and that's all I can do.' He was off the pad almost before my feet touched the earth."

We drove in silence a few minutes and just south of the turnoff for the horse stables, Angella exclaimed, "Hey, wasn't that a kayak trailer?" She pointed to a contraption rattling from side to side as it passed us. "It's only got one kayak on it, a pretty large one."

"There must be several of those things on this island. I'm not surprised," I answered, straining to see the opening in the vegetation where the road, if you call hard-packed sand a road, to the stables begins. "Anyway, that's not our concern."

"There it is, Jimmy! Slow down or you'll miss the turn."

Without Angella's sharp lookout I would have flown right past the narrow entrance. A moment later we were parked in the same spot as before. And, as before, there didn't appear to be anyone around. Only this time we could hear Lip Sync snorting around back where we had first seen her. Agitated. And the closer we came, the more agitated she became. Unlike before when she allowed Angella to stroke her nose, she was now hell-bent on nipping.

I looked around for signs of the kid Castro. No such luck. The place was deserted.

"If I didn't know better, Jimmy, I'd tell you this was a different horse."

"She sure doesn't like you today. If she wasn't tied she'd have kicked you by now."

"Don't see the foal. Must be inside."

I pulled out my phone and called Silver. My call went directly to voice mail. I explained to the machine where we were and what we had observed, ending with the suggestion that Silver locate the manager and see to Lip Sync. Without a phone number, I explained, we were unable to follow up.

Not more than five minutes later Tiny's name popped up on the cell screen. Coincidence?

The message read: "Boy Scout campground Dolphin Cove. 15 min. Both of you."

"Just once I'd like to hear him ask. Not demand," Angella said. "This is getting old fast."

"You think'n of blowing him off. Just going home, letting him cool his heels at the campground?"

"All of the above. But, of course, we're going to accommodate his every whim."

"You say that because..."

"Because, Jimmy, that's where our puppet strings lead."

Angella was right of course, but I preferred to believe I was going under free will. I turned my mind to the horse—and to the kid. Nothing was making much sense. "We need to know more about Castro."

"I'll call Ayers and have her set up something with the father for tomorrow. Maybe that'll shed light on it."

We passed through the entrance booth to Isla

Blanca Park without incident and I absent-mindedly drove to the far southwest end of the island and into the parking lot of Dolphin Cove. The new bandstand having been built on the Boy Scout campground, I didn't immediately recognize the once familiar dolphin watching spot. A large chain-link gate blocked the entrance. I parked outside the gate and we sat in the car taking in the surroundings.

Two live-in trailers were parked on the north side of the parking area. Judging from the laundry hanging from every protrusion of the nearest RV and the paraphernalia scattered about the ground, it was easy to conclude they had been there a while and not planning on leaving any time soon. Other than a solitary empty boat trailer parked near the launch ramp, the remainder of the lot was empty.

"I'll check the gate," Angella said. "See if it's unlocked."

"It won't be. But no harm in checking."

A moment later Angella was back. "How'd you know the gate would be locked?" she asked, bending over to talk to me through the open driver side window.

"Typical Tiny BS. The gate only covers the driveway. Keeps cars out." I pointed to a walkway between the east end of the fence and the side of a block building." Anyone can come and go around that way."

"I guess then its show time."

The construction of the stage had required many of the camp buildings to have been torn down. But off to the right there was a green-painted building with the barely visible word 'office' in faded white letters on a door. It appeared from the lack of vegetation around its base that the building had recently been moved from another location.

Nothing appeared to be moving as we passed inside the campgrounds and made our way toward the office. The door was locked. Same with the door to a building marked 'keep out'. "I'm thinking that bunk house looking building over there is where we'll find Tiny. That's the only structure that doesn't appear to have recently been moved."

"You have the Berretta?" Angella asked as we approached the third building.

"No use. This is a perfect set up. If they, whoever they are, wanted us dead, we'd be dead before we could even take aim. Have faith."

"I don't know about you, Jimmy, but Tiny's about worn through any faith I had in him."

"Can't say as I blame you. But he's all we have at the moment. Gotta trust."

"Trust, but verify."

"Can't ever verify a spook." And Tiny, if nothing else, is a master spook.

"Sorry to spook you." We both jumped at the sound of Tiny's voice directly behind us. "But I couldn't resist the opening you just gave me. For the record, you'd be right about being dead if indeed that was the goal. Fortunately for you, it's not."

"So why are we creeping around like...like we're on a scavenger hunt?" I, like Angella was tired of Tiny's games and frankly not knowing how to extract ourselves from more of the same.

"Come, sit on that bench and give me every detail of what you saw or heard from the moment you entered the hotel until Garcia left your sight. And when Jimmy's finished I want the same from you Angella, starting from the instant you stepped off the chopper in McAllen until you met back up with your partner at the police station."

An hour and fifteen minutes later, after both I and Angella had recited everything we could recall, Tiny said, "Now let me hear the details of your visit with Malone. Either one of you can have the honors."

"I'll do it since Jimmy's been doing most of the talking up to now."

When Angella finished, Tiny said, "So what's up with that horse?"

"Why your interest in the horse," I replied. "That's an insurance matter and has nothing to do with DHS—or any other government agency for that matter."

"The person caring for that horse is a DHS agent. Anything he's involved in is very much our business."

Now that was new news. Not a total surprise,

but confirmation. "Was," I replied. "You mean was involved with the horse. Guy's very much dead."

"You heard me right, Jimmy. Is."

I was still processing this information when Angella exclaimed, "So Hermes Castro is the agent! Not Billy Conquesta."

"Bingo! You're slowing down. I would have thought you two would have figured that out by now on your own."

Not put off by Tiny's diversion, Angella said, "So his frightened schoolboy persona is an act? Then I assume the addict act is just that. An act. And we were fooled."

"Former user," Tiny confirmed. "Assuming that's ever possible."

"We were told an agent had been murdered?"

"Unless Conc was also an agent, which is certainly a possibility, the bad guys messed up." Tiny confided in one of his rare moments of candor.

"Is the lawyer Ayers in on it as well?" I asked.

"Conquesta was using her for legal work. And it does provide the agency a way to pass money to you—for Castro's protection, of course. Not that you two need the money."

If it was anyone other than Tiny, my anger would have gotten the best of me. As it was, my only reaction was a narrowing of my eyes.

Tiny, instinctively anticipating my typical reaction, had moved his body away from me ever so slightly. Any hostile movement on my part would have been met in a most unpleasant way. "Couldn't resist. But you're now about to move into perhaps the most posh penthouse on the Island. I understand the place will be furnished to suit...well to suit POTUS should he desire to visit the island sometime in the future."

"You telling us something?" Angella asked.

"Nothing's ever cast in stone. But the scare with Garcia caused Mogul to cancel the lunch with the Senator. I believe it will be rescheduled, probably sooner rather than later, and Silver is hoping he'll take a tour of the building. Remember, he's a real-estate guy at heart. Silver wants to be prepared just in case."

Our apartment was not ready for visitors and Tiny knew that. I couldn't fathom what he was actually telling us, so I changed the subject. "You thinking Conc was killed over the horse?"

"Not saying that at all. In fact, I think not. Again I ask, what's with the horse?"

"Polo pony, actually." Angella studied Tiny a moment before going on. "We saw her yesterday just after foaling. In retrospect, her temperament was okay considering something didn't go right. An hour ago she was as wild and unsettled as I've ever seen a mare."

"Cause?"

"That's what we hoped you'd tell us." Angella said, meeting Tiny's deadpan stare straight on.

Tiny's response was to rise. "That's all I need," he said.

"Mind letting us in on what's going on," Angella called after him.

But Tiny was through the door before her question was complete. She started after him but I put my hand on her arm. "If he wanted us to know, he would have told us. Once a scorpion, always a scorpion. It's their nature, I'm afraid."

THIRTEEN

"**S**o what do you make of what Silver just told us?" I asked Angella as we drove west from the Gulf of Mexico toward the Bar-C ranch.

"For starters, I have doubts about how straight he's being."

"Leave that for later. Second?"

"If he knew all along Lip Sync was not on the island, why didn't he tell us that from the start?"

"I'm assuming he didn't know. Let's for now take him at his word that Lip Sync had been on the island not long ago, but had been replaced by the mare we saw. Go on."

Angella's brow furled as she considered the possibilities. "According to him, the pony we saw, the one with the foal, is named Lightning Strike. I see no reason to doubt that. But I have trouble with who he claims owns Lighting Strike."

"You don't believe Joy Malcom owns that horse?"

"There's no doubt in my mind that if Joy owns the horse then she's being used as a front. It's just that...it's too convenient. Just like with the priceless King's Cup. Remember, it was in Joy's possession before it went missing, but neither of us believes it was Joy's."

"Remember?" I said, anger again rising. "How could I forget? The lawsuit reminds me every day. She claims she had the real cup and someone substituted a phony. She blames me for that. Not my fault at all."

"That's my point, Jimmy, exactly. We have no proof Joy ever had the original of anything. But she seems to believe she owns it. "That's a problem. Maybe the lawyers can get to the bottom of it."

"Not likely to happen. So what's your take about which horse we saw? Lip Sync or an imposter named Lighting Strike?"

Angella remained silent for several miles, then replied, "I'm finding it hard to believe there are two polo ponies with the exact same markings. And that Joy Malcom — or Santiago — owns the look-alike. Cut me a break. They're con artists, Jimmy. Fakes, phonies, sleight of hand, you name the con, they do it. And they're masters."

As was now often the case, Angella was ahead of me. I thought about what she had just said and it finally came to me. "So you're thinking Castro, who we know to be a talented artist, painted..."

"Or tattooed..."

"...or tattooed, white markings onto a black mare. Making Lighting Strike appear to be Lip Sync." I suppose as an insurance company investigator we'd be associating with more than our fair share of forgeries and con artists.

"What I haven't worked out is why?" Angella replied. "Why paint the horse?"

"If Castro is an DHS agent, then DHS knows about the horse imposter. And if DHS knows, then we must assume Tiny knows. Yet he didn't let on."

"No surprise there," Angella said, contorting her jaw into a grimace. "So much for candor. And my back is feeling a bit exposed."

We drove in silence for ten or so miles before it came to me. I turned toward Angella to share my thoughts when she suddenly blurted, "I got it! Jimmy, right in front of us all the time. The pieces fit—well they mostly fit anyway."

"I think they all fit, Angella. You go first."

"Here goes nothing. The kid painted—tattooed, hennaed, I don't know which—a pregnant mare by the name of Lightning Strike having Lip Sync's basic coloring, size, temperament, to impersonate Lip Sync. The purpose obviously being to sell the foal, and possibly Lighting Strike as well, for big bucks. Same scheme as we're seeing with valuable art. Fakes show up all the time. In this case they're selling imitation horses. Fits into a Santiago scheme. But, and here's what's been bothering me. Where's the foal in all this?"

"Go on," I replied. So far Angella was tracking my thinking exactly.

"The foal was stolen! That's why the mother was so...so ill-tempered. The baby was taken from her. We never did see the foal this last time out there."

"So, in your theory, why take the foal of an imposter?" I asked, checking to see if Angella had worked out all the pieces.

I wasn't disappointed with Angella's answer. "Because whomever stole the foal thought the foal was Lip Sync's foal. That would make the little one valuable."

"But," I cautioned, "the imposter foal's colorings wouldn't match Lip Sync's foal's markings."

"Unless the tattoo artist also performed artwork on the foal," Angella replied.

"Bingo! That's what was sent to Conc just before he died—a picture of the real foal. Castro needed that picture so he could perform his artistry."

"So who stole the imposter foal?"

"My guess. And it's only a guess at this point, is Shadowy Sal. She had access to the picture of Lip Sync's foal from the phone—Conc's phone—the one Castro delivered to Joy. As we know, he may have handed the phone to Joy, but the scumbag, impersonating Joy, stole it. That's who we saw when we stopped by Joy's place."

"I assume then Castro's nervousness stems from him being the artist and being a wanted person as soon as the hoax is found out."

"But," I added, "as we now know, it's all an act."

"I don't think that's exactly accurate, Jimmy. I agree the nervousness is an act. But his disappearance from Ayers' place because the police, in the form of Lt. Malone, arrived was real. Being a DHS agent he couldn't be worried about Malone. He simply had to get the artwork on the foal finished. Spending hours with Malone would have messed up his timing." Angella paused, then added, "Also, he might have recognized her shape through the blinds as the person who killed conc."

"And messed up his cover? Malone must not be in on his real identity?" I added. "And for some reason he was instructed to keep it that way."

"If Malone hasn't been read in, that means..."

"The government is playing him closer to the vest than usual."

"Afraid of leaks be my guess." Angella said. "But leaks from where? On the missing foal side of the equation I'm going with Shadowy Sal taking the imposter foal. But if so, how'd she get it off the island?"

"Assuming it's off the island, I'd say inside a hollow kayak on that trailer. Size would be right if the foal were laying on its side and the kayak were large enough."

"So, who's Sal working for?" Angella asked.

"Someone who paid Sal a bunch of money to move that foal. That someone plans to sell the foal for a larger bunch of money. But that only works if the ultimate buyer believes the foal to be Lip Sync's lineage."

"Don't know about you, Jimmy, but I haven't a clue how that works—or who does the due diligence. But what I do know, if the Scumbag is doing all that we think she is, she's one busy person and the timing is almost impossible."

"Since when has timing been a problem for her? Thought strikes me she might be working more than one assignment. For more than one master." I thought about our pending visit to the Bar-C Ranch and said, with more enthusiasm than I felt, "Hopefully, this visit to the family spread will get us back on track."

"Hopefully."

We fell silent for the last several miles, each of us lost in our own thoughts.

"According to Waze, we're about to pull off onto what appears to be a dirt road," Angella suddenly announced. "Keep your eyes peel...oh, there it is," she said, pointing to a long curving oiled-gravel path snaking off to the right.

I slowed, made the turn, and we drove about a 1000 feet before a large white-painted ranch house came into view from behind a stand of live-oak trees.

From the boundaries drawn on the map I had examined earlier, I estimated the Bar-C Ranch as being at least a hundred thousand acres, possibly even larger. From where we were positioned, other than the main house, several close-in buildings, and a single stable about a half-mile away, all that I saw as I scanned the horizon from west to north to east was flat brown land with a bit of scrubby grass thrown in for contrast. Looking south, the landscape appeared to have been ravaged by a winter blizzard, with tufts of snow-white cotton dotting the earth as far as I could see.

"If we weren't already under their observation I'd say turn around and go home. Maybe we should have tied a white flag around the antenna."

Angella was referring to a large-framed, leather-skinned, angry-looking man walking up to our car. If ever a burr was under a man's collar this guy was the poster child.

"Help you?" came the deep resonant voice with an accent that placed his linage in close proximity to the Rio Grande River—one side or the other.

"Looking for José Castro."

"You the folks hired to look after the boy?"

"This the Bar-C?"

"You drove in under the sign. You tell me."

"Now would be a good time to de-escalate," Angella admonished, her hand on my knee. "We're on his land, Jimmy. Curb the hostility. We're working for the family, remember."

Angella was right, of course. The fact that I could visualize a shotgun in his hands was no cause to pick a fight. "I would be he," I answered, my voice smoothing out. "Actually, we both are. Is Mr. Castro here? I believe he's expecting us."

"Yes and no."

"Want to elaborate?"

"Here is a big place."

"Please tell him Jimmy and Angella are here?" I was tempted to add, "his son's babysitters." But Angela's fingers pressing into my leg caught my attention. The fact that the kid was a DHS agent would have made my comment sound stupid — which it actually would have been.

The big man reached behind him. My hand, as did Angella's, instinctively went for our respective holsters. The problem being that neither of us was armed. We continued to tell ourselves, rather naively, that our armed days were behind us.

It wasn't a gun the big guy produced, but rather the current weapon of choice: a cell phone.

He took several steps away from the car and turned his head back toward the house. A moment later he returned to the car, the scowl now gone from his sun-hardened face. "Boss says he'll meet with you when he gets back."

"How long?"

"How long?" The big guy repeated, the scowl again appearing.

"Until he gets here."

"Reckon 'bout two hours. Seems they found an abandoned trailer up on the property. Immigrants locked inside." The scowl deepened. "Says to take you to see Lip Sync. Over there." He pointed to one of the buildings, the only structure with a fence around it. A high fence that appeared to have an electric wire fastened along its top surface.

Images, all horrible, from past investigations I had been involved with flooded to mind. "Any survivors?" I asked, knowing full well the temperature inside a closed vehicle in the hot South Texas sun could easily rise to well over 120 degrees, making survival for any length of time all but impossible.

"Bolt cutters and ambulances are on the way. Boss doesn't think the truck was there long. Just have to see." Without a further word, Tex — or possibly Mex — shuffled across the vegetation passing for a lawn and disappeared around the side of the house. I glanced at Angella who nodded to follow him.

We both opened our doors and swung our legs out of the car onto the gravel. A truck's motor coughed to life and a moment later an ancient half-ton Ford blew by engulfing us in a nasty dirt cloud. We hurried back to our car, slammed the doors closed and threw our own dirt cloud as we raced to catch up.

The building that seemed just across the yard proved to be further away than we had thought. We parked beside the pickup and walked across a gravelly path over to where Tex had stopped to answer his phone. The conversation consisted of several 'yeses', followed quickly by a 'no', and ended with 'got it'.

Coming alongside the big man, I asked, "You got a name?"

"Boss Man works." He pressed his thumb against a pad and the entry gate swung open. We followed him to the stable where he again used his thumb. This time a loud click could be heard before he pushed open the barn door.

I haven't spent much time around stables over my lifetime, but this one was, by far, the cleanest I had ever seen. Boss Man led us down a wide center walkway past five horses on either side. Then we passed two open stalls and in the third stall was a horse, or perhaps, more accurately a pony, that looked almost exactly like the one we had seen on the island, the one we had believed to be Lip Sync, two white ovals on his back and a white square on his nose.

I pulled out my phone and quickly confirmed that the horse in the stall in front of us was a perfect match for the image of Lip Sync now on the screen.

"No Pictures!" Boss Man barked, reaching to confiscate my phone.

"No worries," I snapped back, my hand safely out of his reach. "Just confirming this is Lip Sync."

"It's Lip Sync alright. And her foal, Sync Opate."

Sync Opate was in the stall beside her mother. On closer inspection I could see that the panel between them was constructed to open allowing them to be together.

"I don't know about the mother," Angella said,

"but this foal is certainly not the same one we saw on the island. This one has the hereditary white markings on his back and nose."

"If you say so," I said. "If you say so."

"I said the foal is Sync Opate," Boss Man cut in. "Birthed her myself. You got a problem?"

"No problem, but the insurance company requires us to document Sync Opate." I lifted the camera and took plenty of time to position the camera just perfectly. Boss Man had become nervous and I wanted to flush him out. But he didn't object.

"I don't know what your game is, insurance company or what," he finally snapped, his eyes going dark. "but I've work to do."

"How can you be so certain the horses are who they purport to be?"

Boss Man's stance changed and if he had been armed I would be very much concerned. But his shotgun was in the truck and if he had a concealed weapon it was not in a convenient place for drawing on us.

Angella's head nod indicated that we should leave. Her hands told me she was ready for a physical confrontation.

I held my ground. "I mean, what's to prevent a...a substitution?"

"Markings. No two look perfectly alike."

Before I could suggest alterations—horse cosmetic surgery, or, in our situation, painting—he added, "DNA. You must be aware the insurance company demands that insured animals have DNA on file. First thing that happens when foaling." He turned toward the entrance. "I took the swab myself. It's gone to the lab. Time to go."

Following Angella's lead, I fell in behind the big guy. "Who all has access to this facility?" I casually asked as we exited the barn.

"What's it to you?" came the reply.

"As you said, the insurance company has lots of requirements."

"I do. Two foremen."

"That all? What about the Castros?"

"Of course. All the family does."

"Anyone else?"

"Not that I know." He turned to leave, took a few steps, then turned back. "Listen, I didn't mean to...well, I thought you were the folks coming to examine the ponies for the trip. Sorry."

"What trip? Angella asked.

"Jamaica. Auction."

"Which horses?"

"Lip Sync and her foal, Sync Opate. Too soon. But the boss says do it, so we'll do it. Don't have to like it."

"Isn't it routine? I mean, that's what you do. Buy, sell horses."

"Yea, and we move them back and forth to

Jamaica and Argentina all the time. Those horses travel better than most people do. Boss had a
plane custom fit out. Pampered all the way. But...
but Lip Sync is one special horse, I'm hoping the
boss'll change his mind. I'll miss her if he doesn't."
Boss Man turned back to his truck and this time
kept walking.

FOURTEEN

"Two of those poor souls are in critical condition, but their prognosis looks promising," Castro was saying. "They were all dehydrated, but the medics say they'll all recover. Truck pulled a flat and the driver disappeared. Good thing one of my men spotted the truck when he did. A few more hours and they'd all be dead! I hate this cat and mouse game we play with the lives of people who only want to feed themselves and their families! Government can't get out of its own way!"

I looked away, focusing on the breathtaking panoramic view from Castro's front window. I knew we were seeing only a portion, indeed only a very small portion, of the Castro spread. Driving along the highway Angella had called my attention to the tall green and white flags spaced every mile or so, each with the single word, Agua. I now wondered if Castro was responsible for maintaining the water stations on the roads abutting his land in an effort to keep the illegal immigrants alive.

"Sorry," Castro said, apologizing for the outburst. "I know you're part of Homeland, but it all boils down to economics — on both sides — and these poor souls have drawn the short end."

We, of course, were no longer working for the government, but there was no need to point that out to Castro. "When last did you see your son?" I asked when Castro finally settled into a chair in the living room of his elaborately furnished home.

"Not for several months, Mr. Redstone. We... we had...well, to tell the truth, things were not smooth between us. But I did get a call from him earlier today."

"Did he happen to tell you where he is?"

"Why's that important?"

"Got something for him. About...about the horse he's taking care of."

"Weren't there."

"Pardon me?"

"I mean...weren't nobody on the line when I answered. Happened twice. Just before you walked up, same thing."

Castro reached for his cell and turned it to face Angella and me. I memorized the 956-phone number. "My direct number is on the card I gave you. Please call me when you speak to your son. And please ask him to call me."

"I'll do that Mr. Redstone. But as I say, we've

not spoken in a while and these calls are most unusual."

"Mind telling us what the issue was," Angella asked. "I mean the issue that came between you and your son."

"In a word, drugs. The boy got himself hooked up. Goodness knows, his mother and I gave him everything he ever wanted. Everything." José produced a handkerchief and blew his nose. "I think he's cleaned up now, going straight, but I worry about him."

"What's he do for a living?" I asked, trying to determine how much the father knew about the son.

"He's an artist at heart. Likes to draw. He got himself a job over on the Island doing tattoos and things. Works some with a friend's son."

"The friend's son, his name Billy Conquesta by chance?"

Castro looked hard at me a moment, as if I had stuck him. Then his head bobbed up and down. "They been friends since grade school. Same as I was with Billy's father. That's Billy over there." Castro pointed to a picture on a side table.

"You his Godfather?" I asked out of curiosity.

"Not to Billy. It's a long story. Those are my children, those pictures over there."

Two boys and a girl posed with a slightly built, very attractive woman. Good looking family, their faces revealing heavy traces of a South American country. The older boy had the same eyes as the kid Castro, but nothing else seemed to match. "That your wife in the picture?"

His eyes filled with tears. "Passed three years next week. All this," Castro said, waving his arm in a half circle, "is nothing without her." He blew his nose, nodded in the direction of Conc's picture. "Boy goes by Conc. Hard working young man. Took my son under his wing."

"What work did Conc do with your son?"

"Work with horses. Polo ponies mostly. Same as he does here on the ranch. Like Lip Sync out there. Muck barns. Typical honest ranch work." Castro paused, again pulled out his handkerchief, and this time he coughed into it. "I believe Hermes also now works for our government."

"What makes you say that?" I asked, puzzled as to how the father knew about a supposedly secret undercover operative, especially a father so well connected with the very people the kid would be working to defeat.

"For one thing, Hermes is connected with people well versed in cross-border activities. That, in their minds, makes him perfect for an agent."

"I take it," I responded, taking my lead from the unmasked disdain in our host's eyes, "you don't approve."

"What I approve of is not important. What I care about are the people. This land we are on has been in my family for generations. That national flag you drove under on your way in is the sixth flag to fly in that very same spot. I'm proud to be an American, don't go getting me wrong. But my Granddaddy was just as proud to be Mexican and his Granddaddy swore allegiance to Spain. It's the people who are important. Governments come and go."

"So would it upset you if you learned for certain your son worked for Homeland?"

Castro's brow narrowed and his eyes focused on something in the far distance. Then, as if he had just broken through a barrier that he had been working on for a long while, said, "To stop drugs and weapons from coming north it would be a good thing. To inhibit good people from saving themselves would be...would put us at odds."

"Your son ever tell you he got hired?"

"As I said, we haven't spoken."

"You have occasion to talk with Conc recently?"

"Not directly. He texted me a few weeks back, wanted a picture of the foal when it was born."

"Did you comply?"

Angella leaned forward, started to say something, but remained quiet. A worried look flashed across her face.

"I had the foreman text a picture."

"What time was that? Roughly speaking."

"Right about sunrise. Never got a reply." Castro's eyes clouded. "Not like Billy not to reply."

"You know why Conc wanted the picture?"

Angella was now clearly agitated, but continued to remain silent.

Castro studied me several seconds before responding. "He trained Lip Sync and said he wanted to see the baby, that's all."

Angella made a pretext of studying her watch. "Jimmy, we need to be going if we're to keep our afternoon appointment."

We had no such appointment. But she was right. It wouldn't be long before Castro started asking questions about his son and his buddy Conc, questions we didn't want to—or couldn't—answer.

"Run this cell number," Angella said into the phone to Tiny even before our car turned out of the Bar-C driveway. The proud Texas flag that Castro had referred to was snapping overhead in the stiff afternoon breeze. "Need to know the location of origin if that's possible even if the call was never completed?" Hanging up, she turned to me. "Tiny says they can get a tower ID. Doubts if they can get closer."

"Well, at least that'll tell us if he's north or south of the Rio Grande. That's a start."

"Since when does Homeland hire private citizens to protect one of their own? Doesn't play right?"

"Officially the kid's deep undercover. But someone at DHS thinks the kid's life is in jeopardy, so why not protect him themselves?"

"If it was an external threat, they'd do it themselves."

I thought about what Angella just said. "The logical conclusion then is that Homeland's been infiltrated."

"Kid's gotta be too low on the totem pole for a mole to waste time on."

"Not if the kid's a link to something the mole wants."

"The horse? The foal? What could..." Angella's phone buzzed before she could finish her thought. She listened without saying a word and when she hung up, said, "According to Tiny, several calls originated from Castro's cell, all somewhere on the Island. Only one was answered, but lasted less than thirty seconds."

"Who answered that one?"

"Lawyer Ayers."

"We're almost back. Call her."

"Who do you think I'm dialing?"

"Sorry, Angella. I was concentrating on the rear view mirror. I have the distinct feeling we're being followed."

"You're never wrong when you get that feeling. See anything?"

"Not that I could say definitely. Whoever it is, if they're there, they're good." Too good for my liking.

Angella turned her head and studied the traffic

behind us. "I don't see anything unusual."

Still studying the back window, Angella said into the phone, "Merry Ayers please." Pause. "Okay, tell her Jimmy and Angella will stop by in..."

Angella turned to face me. I mouthed a half-hour.

"Tell her about a half-hour."

The drive time from where we were in Port Isabel to Ayers' office was less than fifteen minutes. But I planned to execute a few evasive moves designed first to establish whether or not we were being followed, and second to lose the tail if, in fact, we had one.

I stopped in the parking lot of Our Lady Star of The Sea church to observe the few cars that came down the street. Three minutes passed, then four. No suspicious vehicle came past. At the five-minute mark my suspicions were confirmed. A white Silverado drove slowly down the street and at the corner of the parking lot turned west. "That's him," I said. "Saw that same truck back in Los Fresnos."

"Jimmy, in the Valley there're more trucks than cars. Perhaps even more trucks than people. White Silverados no less."

"That truck's never been on a farm—or a job site for that matter. Wheels too clean."

"Still not buying it."

"If I told you it was sporting Mexican plates would that persuade you?"

"Now that you point it out, the plates were Mexican. Nuevo León to be exact. What made you spot it?"

"Parked in a corner of the gas station. I noted the plates when we went by. Not many trucks that clean come across the border."

"Monterey's the capital of Nuevo León. Valencia Garcia told me her family's from Monterey. Angel's got a massive spread down in Tamauilpas, but she confided she's not comfortable down there when he's out of the area which he is now that he's campaigning. She's been spending time with her family."

"Angel's bucking the drug lords making it all the worse."

"That's for certain. We saw that yesterday with Shadowy Sal."

"They couldn't kill Valencia in McAllen without messing up the operation to kill Angel or she'd be dead by now. The bad guys own the security detail."

"Since you foiled the plot then you're on their hit list. That the way you got it figured?"

"That's how I got it figured."

I drove slowly down the back streets, doubling back twice. No more sign of the Silverado. Comfortable—for now—I headed out to the highway and across the causeway. We parked behind the law offices a few minutes later than we had promised.

Ayers was waiting for us in the foyer and motioned toward the conference room, the same conference room where we had last seen Hermes Castro.

"I'm happy you two came by. I'm worried for Hermes."

"That's why we're here. Have you heard from him?"

"Actually, yes and no." Ayers got up and closed the door. Resuming her seat, she said, "Got a call on my cell yesterday. I was busy and didn't answer it. Actually, I didn't hear it. But it was there when I went to bed. I listened to what I thought was the message but there wasn't any."

"So, what changed?"

"When you called a while ago I thought of Hermes and the call. Went back and listened to the message again. It was there all along. But very faint." She looked though her purse, produced her phone, and hit several buttons. A moment later she held the phone to my ear. The sound was faint, perhaps a man's voice. Perhaps the wind. "Let Angella listen. Her ears are better than mine."

"Castro's voice," Angella announced almost immediately. "It's muffled, and the only word I heard clearly is 'stable'. I think he said he's something in the stable. Sorry, I can't make out what the something is."

"At least he was alive last night," I said. Let's get on up there and see what we can see."

"Keep me posted," Ayers called to our backs. I

wasn't paying much attention to her. My concentration was on a white Silverado moving out of the parking lot coming from the direction of our car.

I turned back to address the lawyer. "Is that your car, the blue Honda, the one parked behind the building?" I asked Ayers.

"Is there a problem?"

"We need to borrow it for a while."

"I don't understand. Why..."

"My car won't start," I lied. The less she, or anyone, knew the better. "Be back within the hour." I was well on my way to becoming Tiny.

A few minutes later we were heading north, but not on Padre Boulevard. Angella suggested we use Laguna Boulevard as far as it went on the assumption the Silverado was most probably tucked in somewhere along the main drag waiting for us to go by. "Hopefully, they won't spot the blue car, Jimmy. They certainly found yours in the parking lot."

I drove while Angella studied her phone. I was now certain they had a tracking device on my car. The road ended and I turned east for a block and then resumed going north on Padre Boulevard. "Any sign of the truck?"

"Not that I can see. But I did manage a few pictures of the guys in the truck back at Ayers' office. Got a partial face, too blurry to use without enhancement. I sent it on to Tiny and asked for a rush."

"They haven't perfected face recognition on blurry so far's I know." I felt like we were chasing our tails.

"Never know what will turn up. Homeland's got a great library of Monterey faces."

"Might not be Monterey. Nuevo León is a large state."

"Slow down, Jimmy. The stable's not far ahead."

Indeed, Angella was right. We were on top of the turn-off almost immediately after her warning. A moment later we were out of the car. Except for a few restless horses, we saw nothing. The imposter horse was exactly where she had been when we were last here, only now less belligerent.

"My guess, these poor animals haven't been fed in a while. Water trough is almost dry."

There was only one enclosure so that made searching for Castro, at least at this location, easier. I nodded toward the structure, a wooden contraption that appeared to be years beyond the end of its useful life. When I pulled on the door it wouldn't open. Not because it was locked, but because it was jammed. I pulled as hard as I could and still nothing. It was really jammed, or nailed closed.

Angella retrieved a long flat board from the pen area and handed it to me. Raising it to the battering ram position, I said, "Stand back. Watch for flying splinters."

"Wait Jimmy! Door's stuck 'cause the hinge is busted." She pointed to the upper right part of the door where the gap was almost wide enough to see through. "Use the board as a lever over there."

She was right. The door had tipped from the top and the left side of the door was wedged against the frame. The best way to free the door was to wedge something behind the lower right hinge. The board in my hands was too thick for that purpose. Instead, I worked the board under the door and tried to leverage upward, but to no avail. I resorted to the horizontal position and proceeded to ram the door several times, again to no avail.

"You're going to hurt yourself, you keep that up. Here!"

Angella handed me a tire iron that I assumed she had retrieved from Ayers' trunk. I wedged the flat end of the iron between the hinge and the frame, and kicked the metal several times causing the wood to splinter, but the door remained jammed closed. I pushed on the tire iron, but the door wouldn't budge.

"Here, hold this," I instructed Angella.

Sitting on the ground, my back propped against a post, and with Angella holding the tire iron steady, I coiled my knees against my stomach and placed both feet against the metal. It took three bursts of power before I heard the first crack of wood. But I had not yet been able to fully extend my legs.

Two more heaves and my legs shot forward. The door now hung over my head, held up by a single screw. I rolled away just as the door ripped loose and crashed to the ground.

"Jimmy!" Angella shouted, "You...Oh, thank God! Thought it got you!"

"Nicked my head," I replied, touching the hair just above my ear, my fingers coming away sticky. "Nothing serious. Let's see what's in here."

The kid was in the corner, hands behind him, naked from the waist up. Remnants of his shirt hung from his mouth.

Castro was skinny when we last saw him with clothes on. He was a scarecrow as we saw him now, his shirt tied around his head and stuffed in his mouth. "You injured," I asked when I got the shirt untied. His legs were straddling the center post of the shed with his wrists secured behind the post.

"Nothing I can't handle. Get me loose! I couldn't even coax the rats to eat these things."

These things were heavy-duty red tie clasps of the type usually found bundling electrical cables, but more recently a favorite of law enforcement. Castro had struggled to escape, that much was evident by the deep lacerations in his wrists. It was evident, however, that the only way he could have freed himself was to have cut through a wrist.

"There's nothing in the car to cut these with," Angella said. "And I don't see anything here either. Any reason we can't call for help?"

"Please don't. Best they don't know I survived."

"Any idea how we can..."

"Been thinking of nothing since she left but how to get out of here. There's a branding iron over there. Burn them off."

"We'll need a fire to heat the iron," I said.

"That's old school. This one's electric. Plug's on the wall."

While we waited for the iron to heat up, the kid pointed to his cell phone lying several feet away. Before we could ask how he managed to place calls, he nodded toward a riding crop near his feet. "Hit my phone with that and it kinda butt dialed. At first I couldn't talk. Then I worked that stink'n shirt partway out of my mouth. Took a while. I don't know who all I called, but I believe one went to the lawyer."

"It did," Angella confirmed. That's what brought us here. A few went to your father."

"My father? I haven't...How'd you know?"

"Went out to see him. Seems he knows about... about you being Homeland and..."

"How the hell he know that?" The kid hadn't had the shakes one time since we entered the shed. Either the drugs were out of his system—or really weren't there the last time we saw him.

"A friend at the agency tipped him."

"He also know about my rehab?"

"Sorry to say, he did," Angella answered. "You should—"

"All an act. DHS set it up. Wanted me close to

Malcom and that husband of hers. If it's illegal and moving across the border Santiago has a piece of it."

"Get anywhere?"

"Didn't think so, until...until this. Must have hit a nerve somewhere."

"Don't know or not telling?"

"Don't know."

"If we're to protect you, you gotta be straight with us. Capisce?" Now I was sounding like Tiny.

"I been doing a lot of thinking," Castro said, his formerly dancing eyes now deadly quiet, "if DHS thinks I need to be watched by an outsider then they think there's a mole somewhere. I feel like the bait."

"How does that follow?" Angella asked, feigning innocence. I wanted to say, join the crowd, but restrained myself.

"If there was no mole then they'd watch me themselves. But they have you doing it. You report outside the chain of command. But what has me concerned...I suppose I can level with you..."

I nodded.

"...what has me concerned is the mole must be high up. If that's true then...then this business with the foal, the painting, must be high level. But how does it all—"

"Foal's name?" I interrupted.

"I don't know if—"

"If you want our protection...and," I looked at the hot iron in my hand, "if you want released, you'll tell us exactly what's going on here."

"Release first."

"Talk first," I responded.

"No choice, I suppose. He was in the process of stealing the foal when I showed up."

"Back up. Start at the beginning. That horse out there is not Lip Sync. That much we know."

"Lightning Strike."

"She's a dead ringer for Lip Sync," Angella said.

"I touched her up to match Lip Sync."

"Why?"

"That's what I was working on. Don't know." The kid's eyes shot around as if to make certain no one was eavesdropping. "I painted the foal—I'm told his name's Strike One—to look like Lip Sync's foal. That's the image I got from Conc's phone. I transferred the image to my phone, gave Conc's phone to Malcom, then came right over here to get the job done. That's what Conc had told me to do."

"So you say the person who took the painted foal is a man. You certain?"

"How the hell could I confuse a woman for a man?"

"Trust us, it's possible."

"He's a man all right. Took a leak over there." The kid pointed to the wall by the door.

"At least we can get DNA. Probably won't get anywhere, but worth a try."

"Okay, what else do you know about the horse napping?"

"For starters, he loaded the foal into a hollow kayak. Custom made for just that purpose. When he closed the thing up it looked like a real kayak. Only larger."

"Where were you when all this was happening?"

"Out there. I walked up while he was loading the kayak."

"You didn't take action?"

"No weapon. Instructed not to. Observation only. How he knew I was there I don't know."

"What else? Where were they headed?"

"Not exactly certain. He got several calls and from what I could gather, they were holding a plane for the foal. They were running late."

"How do you know it was a plane?"

"At one point he told the caller to 'change the bloody flight plan'. From the timing, I'd say they were flying out of that small airport across the bay."

"Going to?"

"Jamaica, I'd guess."

"Based on?"

"Accent of the guy on the phone. Man was

yelling loud enough for me to hear his cadence. Jamaican all the way."

FIFTEEN

We were back in Ayers' office waiting while the kid polished off an extra-large plate of rigatoni Bolognese freshly made by The Meatball Café. Angella was talking to Merry while I was busy on the phone, first with Silver to update him on our visit to the Bar-C Ranch and to report that we had located Hermes Castro and he was none the worse for wear; and second with Tiny who reported that image matching failed to narrow the identity of the Silverado's driver. Tiny also confirmed that a jet had, indeed, flown out of the Port Isabel airport around the time in question, its flight plan being listed as Houston.

I sat down across from Castro. "Your father told us you were raised with the ponies and are as good as your friend Conc."

"Conc was the best." The kid's eyes went moist. "My best friend. Can't believe he's...dead."

"He was into drugs."

"Importer only. Didn't use or sell them. Anyway, he was getting out. Told me this was his last import."

I wanted to ask him why it is a DHS agent can turn his back on a drug deal in progress, but the question would have shut down communication. Instead, I asked, "You think that's why he was killed?"

"Could be. He always told me not to get involved. Don't know why he did what he did. Not for the money. His family has more than they need."

"As does yours," Angella noted. "Nice spread your folks have out there. By the way, we haven't arranged a place for you yet. So for tonight you're staying in our guest room," Angella announced to my surprise.

"That's more than I can ask for," Hermes replied. The relief on his face spoke volumes.

Ayers nodded her approval and said, "You'll be safe with these two. But frankly, I think the danger's over. Someone seems to have wanted that foal and they got it."

"By the way," I asked, making my question appear to be more casual than it was, "Did Conc know you were DHS?"

His eyes again began their wild motion, but quickly settled down when I glared at him. "I... well, I did tell him."

"I suppose you were under orders not to do that."

"Was. But I wanted him to stop."

"Didn't work, did it?"

Castro's eyes danced for a moment as he seemed to struggle with his answer. "This was to be his last shipment. And he—"

Angella threw me a warning look, but she needn't have bothered. It didn't need saying, but Castro becoming an agent may have doomed his best friend. It was also clear that DHS was leaking like an old wooden boat.

"How much is the foal worth do you think?" the lawyer asked. "I imagine Silver isn't too pleased with you two at this moment."

We hadn't fully briefed Ayers, so she didn't know that the stolen foal was an imposter, just like the woman who impersonated Joy Malcom. And just like the kid across from us. All playing roles. "I think we've worked it all out with Silver," I said. "We'll be fine. Your client will be safe at our place. Angella's arranged with a cop friend of hers to watch the apartment."

Castro looked relieved, but with him I chalked it up to an act. "By the way," he said, "while I was tied up someone came by for several of the horses. That's not unusual, but I don't believe Lighting Strike was moved."

Since Lightning Strike was not insured by Great Southern she wasn't really our concern. "Ayers," I said, "please be sure the horse folks on the island know Lightning Strike needs attention."

"Who is Lightning Strike?"

"Long story. She's tied up at the stables. We'll talk—" I was interrupted by a message from Tiny: Flight plan for foal PIL to IAH changed to MIA. D/N land MIA, believe Jamaica. You and A to Jamaica. Silver will coordinate.

I then called Jack Silver, who promptly instructed us to go down to Jamaica to, in his words, 'grease the skids'. "The foal, Sync Opate, is being auctioned. You'll represent Great Southern, validate the foal. Take some time off, enjoy yourselves down there. Company's picking up the tab."

The fact that this trip came under the auspices of Tiny was cause for big time worry. But it was hard to complain about an all-expense paid trip to one of the world's most beautiful islands.

* * *

We flew out of Brownsville on the Great Southern Insurance Company private jet in the presence of luxury and pampering. The food was great and the massages were even better. Old Jack Silver knew how to live, that much was clear. At least for now, all was well.

Also on a positive note, he had moved up the timetable on finishing out our new penthouse digs and promised all would be ready for our move-in when we finished the pony file. I took that to mean once Sync Opate was sold and off Great Southern's books.

The other horses seemed to be okay. Lip Sync and Sync Opate were on their way to Jamaica for the auction. Even the mare, Lightning Strike, was okay as far as we knew, if you call okay being painted to imitate another horse. But the paint would soon be gone and the horse back to normal. Only the foal Strike One was missing, but as far as we knew the young one had no real value and was not in any danger. My mind drifted to other things and I found it difficult to focus on business issues with a scantily clad, extremely nubile masseuse working on my back and shoulder muscles.

Angella was behind a screen and I could only guess at the clothing level of the person running his fingers up and down her spine. Since our 'retirement' from Homeland Security our relationship in all aspects had improved dramatically. Perhaps it was because of the reduced stress, perhaps because I was no longer her superior officer. Or perhaps it was something different—something called commitment.

I was finally ready to tie the knot and was waiting only for the right moment. My plan was to pop the question while in Jamaica, perhaps over a tall rum drink, the waves lapping at our feet. I had picked out an engagement ring and placed a large deposit on it over in Harlingen, the deposit essentially depleting my entire signing bonus. The deal I had made with the jeweler was that Angella could change the ring when she accepted my proposal. Not wanting an excess of pressure on me, I still had four months before the jeweler was free to sell the ring I tentatively selected to another customer.

Before we left South Padre Island I had retrieved a picture of the ring. My thought being that having the picture would prove my proposal was not simply the result of a rum-induced wonderful moonlit night on a white-sand Caribbean beach with a gorgeous woman.

"We'll be landing in twelve minutes," a far-away voice floating in the ether said. "The island will appear on the port side in eight minutes. Weather is eighty-five degrees Fahrenheit, twenty-nine Celsius, wind from the east-northeast at twenty-five knots, heavy cloud cover. Barometer is beginning to fall. There's a tropical depression forming in the Eastern Caribbean. Expect turbulence as we approach land."

A few minutes later I was heading for my seat looking around for Angella who hadn't yet appeared. The massage had set the mood, now for the rum — and the gorgeous woman.

That's the point where my memory of things becomes hazy. But I do recall looking down at the deep emerald water with just a trace of white flicking across the surface and guessing we were still 15,000 feet up.

I do recall Angella slipping in beside me, kissing me lightly and telling me she loved me. And I recall wrapping my arm around her shoulder and pulling her close and taking in the pleasant aroma of the oils that had been worked into her skin. After that...well after that I remember very little.

SIXTEEN

"This is Angella," I yelled into the phone to Tiny. "Silver's jet is ready for take-off. Jimmy's already been brought aboard," I forced my voice to remain calm despite the turmoil raging beneath the surface. "Just waiting for the doctor who will accompany us to Florida. I'm told Jimmy's stable. They don't anticipate permanent brain damage, but he's better off in Miami."

Tiny thanked me for the update as if I had just reported the weather conditions instead of the fact that my partner had been thrown from a horse—polo pony to be exact—and had landed hard on his head. He had been unresponsive up to this point.

Tiny went on to tell me not to worry, he'll arrange things at the far end. He again expressed his concern that the weather wouldn't ease enough for us to take off.

"What things?" I had the presence of mind to ask.

Transportation for Jimmy, he told me. Adding that since I spent time with the buyer—and with Conquesta–he'd want to debrief me as well, explaining that he needed to know everything that happened and he needed that information in detail.

This trip to Jamaica had been an insurance company matter. Verifying the identity of a horse, coupled with some well deserved R & R. So why the hell was I being debriefed? And what did Tiny know about the weather that I hadn't been told. The wind on the tarmac was gusting to forty-five knots, but I had been assured the winds would cooperate.

Just then Jimmy squeezed my fingers. "Nicki," he said.

All thoughts of Tiny and the game he was playing vanished from my thoughts. Who was 'Nicki'? I thought of the picture of the diamond engagement ring I found in Jimmy's wallet and my stomach knotted with the possibility it was meant not for me but for some Nicki bimbo. I know that wasn't a rational thought, but Jimmy means far too much to me to not be panicky.

"Nicki," Jimmy mumbled again. "I need—"

He fell silent, his eyes again closed. Only the fingers of his right hand and the corner of his mouth had moved, nothing else. His breathing was shallow, but thankfully steady. The monitor showed his pulse rate steady as well. Thank God for the small things.

"Angella," Tiny's voice broke through, "you still there? Doctor's five minutes out. Did I just hear Jimmy's voice?"

"Nicki. That's what he said. Nicki." I responded, wondering just how Tiny knew where the doctor was?

"That all he said? Ask him—"

"He's out," I replied, refraining from telling Tiny I wasn't at all interested in interrogating Jimmy. Truth was, I'm positive Tiny already knew the details of any conversation that had taken place with the broker Serek Powell and the breeder Malik Conquesta. I was also positive, even though he hadn't let on, that he also knew the details of Jimmy's accident. What Tiny really wanted was my assessment of the entire situation, from Conc's death to the theft of the painted pony, to what we learned at the Bar-C spread, and to our interaction with the broker and buyer here at the Jamaican breeding ranch.

Jimmy was in a coma and I was in no mood to share anything with Tiny until he came clean on what all this was about. Remembering what he had said, 'You may be finished with the bad guys, but the bad guys are not finished with you', there was a strong possibility that Jimmy being thrown could have been planned. If so, we were in this a lot deeper than I had realized. So much for retiring from Homeland Security.

"Prepare for takeoff," came the welcome words from the cockpit.

A moment later a man with a military bearing came through the door, walked quickly to where Jimmy was positioned, gently opened first his left eye, then the right, nodded, briefly studied the monitors, then turned to me, and with a trace of mid-east in his voice, said, "I'll examine him more thoroughly when we're in the air. I suggest you belt up." He then stepped to the rear of the plane. A woman, who I took to be the flight attendant, then entered the plane and pulled the door closed behind her. She too had a military presence about her.

The woman came forward, took hold of Jimmy's rolling bed and pulled it toward the rear where she strapped it in place. I started to follow and was motioned back to my seat as the plane began to taxi away from the gate.

In a few minutes we were off the ground and into thick black clouds. The Caribbean may have been below us but visibility was nonexistent. It wouldn't have mattered because I was lost in my own thoughts, angry at this person Nicki who I didn't even know and frightened that the one person in my life who I deeply cared about could now be lost to me.

The single attendant who had replaced the four who had serviced us on the way to the island, had remained at the back of the plane. She came forward to where I was sitting, holding the overhead rack for support against the wildly gyrating plane. "I'm told this will ease up as we gain altitude. Thank goodness we are flying northwest with the wind. The center of the disturbance is stalled south of the island and that works to our advantage. You need anything, just ask." Her tone reinforced my belief that she was more military than commercial. "We've established medical contact with the hospital and your partner will be examined by the world's best brain trauma experts. He's in good hands. We've been cleared to our destination."

My experience with military is they tell you only what they believe you need to know. In that context, this woman was a regular chatterbox. "And what is that destination?" I asked. She could always tell me she didn't know. Or that I had no need to know, which is the government's way of telling you to mind your own business.

She surprised me by responding, "Texas. Houston to be exact."

"What hospital?"

"Above my pay grade."

"But we're going to a hospital. I mean a civilian hospital and...and not a military base."

"That is my understanding. Your friend has traumatic brain injury. Some people come around a hundred percent. Others, well one never knows what head trauma brings with it."

"What are you saying?" The panic in my voice was real. "He was talking to me a moment ago."

"Talking, yes. But not necessarily to you. He's stable, but...but at this point, based on the preliminary results, he's not the Jimmy Redstone you know."

I started to respond but couldn't find the words. He had been holding my hand. Calling me Nicki. It now came to me that his former partner's name was Nicki, and he had sex with her ten years back. Nicki was the woman he had lost his marriage over. "Amnesia?" I finally asked. "Is that what's happened?"

"Labels don't help in these cases. He's got TBI. Traumatic brain injury, and seems to have taken on a...a different...personality."

A sudden thrust of the jet engines pushed me back in my seat and the noise drowned out the attendant's answer. Whoever this woman was, she wasn't a flight attendant. I doubted if the words 'coffee' or 'tea' had ever been spoken by her in this context.

When the noise had subsided, I told her I hadn't heard what she had said a moment ago.

"I said," the woman repeated, "he has TBI. He's providing information inconsistent with his profile."

"He's awake now?"

"Off and on. The awake intervals are increasing. That's good news."

"What's it mean he's giving inconsistent information? What're you saying?"

"Just that his mind thinks he's someone other than Jimmy Redstone."

"How can that be? Who does he think he is?" I was expecting her answer to be something like

Superman. Other than superhero's, all of the hero people I recall Jimmy musing over were dead. But I suppose that wouldn't prevent him from taking on their identities.

"That's just it," the attendant said, "they don't yet know. Perhaps someone from his past." She headed toward the rear of the plane where a curtain had been closed allowing me to see only parts of the table where Jimmy was strapped. I unbuckled my belt to go back to where Jimmy was.

"Keep your seatbelt buckled, Ms. Martinez," the attendant commanded. "I must insist."

"Who are you to insist?" I pivoted my legs sideways in preparation of standing. "That's my... partner back there and I'm..."

The attendant's left hand immediately flew to my left shoulder and forced me back into my seat. "Remain in your seat with your belt on. Do as I say!" There was no humor in her eyes, only steel.

"Just who in the hell do you think you are?" I demanded, remaining seated, but not reaching to buckle my belt.

"Commander Loeb. IDF Medic. General Lazarow and I are attending to your...partner."

IDF! Israel Defense Force. "This is a private plane. You have no authority."

"No law against military catching a ride, now is there? Just helping out friends."

"Tiny set this up?"

"Don't know the name."

"Kelvin Jurald? Or perhaps Emerson Sommers?" All names I know Tiny by. As a spook there's no limit to the number of names he uses—or nationalities for that matter.

"Never heard of any of those people. Now excuse me I'm needed in the back. Please remain seated. And buckle that belt."

"Yes, Commander," I replied mostly swallowing my words. I refrained from throwing a salute as Jimmy would have done. But that didn't stop me from pulling a face. They were keeping my lover alive and for that I was thankful. But the one thing I knew, they weren't doing it out of friendship—and I didn't believe it was a coincidence IDF medics just happened to be in Jamaica when we needed them.

A few minutes later, anger overtaking me, I again unsnapped the belt in preparation of going back and confronting both medics. But to what end? If they were really attending to Jimmy why distract them?

I re-snapped the belt and for the umpteenth time replayed our time in Jamaica. We had spent a delightful two days at a Montego Bay resort called The Half Moon where private cottages are spaced among coconut palms and where gentle waves lap at the white sand of the large half-moon bay.

Jimmy had suggested we go out in the resort's sailboat, but uncharacteristically I took a pass. Swaying in a hammock strung between the trees,

Kindle in my hands, a seemingly bottomless fancy rum something-or-other close by, was all the excitement I craved.

Surprisingly, Jimmy, who doesn't typically read much more than the front page and perhaps the sports section of the newspaper, was content to settle into a hammock of his own, reading what appeared to be a thick novel. All he would say when I quizzed him on it was that he was brushing up on the polo pony business.

Late in the afternoon of our second day, Jimmy met with a man who I had not seen before. They spent about twenty minutes pacing up and down the beach. The man pointed toward the hills several times, his hand waving in the air.

"So," I quizzed Jimmy over dinner, "what was your discussion about? And why wasn't I included?" We were in the outdoor dining area surrounded by fragrant bushes and the gentle sound of waves rolling across the white-sand beach.

"Horse trading was the topic. You weren't there Angella because these Island types are uncomfortable talking business in the presence of a woman. You didn't miss anything."

It wasn't like Jimmy to make me bristle with such blatant sexism. "That you speaking or them?" He had crossed the line and I wanted him to know it.

"You're shooting the messenger here. Didn't think talking horse-trading with an over-indulged minister — or whatever the governing folks are now called—was anything you cared about. Besides, all he wanted, beside possibly something in his pocket to ease his concerns, was to have me cancel the auction."

"And why would he care about a horse auction?"

"The weather has them spooked. That tropical depression seems to be lingering a bit too long. They want the horses off the island, or at least further inland. Says it's going to be bad."

Swallowing my anger, I asked, "So what was so important you had to meet in person? And does Silver know I was excluded?"

"Nothing to do with Silver. The do-it-in-person thing is why I think this was a grease-the-pocket visit. But since there are several foreign folks coming the government is nervous."

"So why don't they just cancel it themselves."

"They tried, but someone in our government refused to consider cancelling. But...and this I found interesting...he asked me to verify that the foal Sync Opate is authentic. They can't seem to get the DNA report."

"You know less than I do about horses. And nothing at all about polo ponies. So why you?"

"Truth is, I don't know. The government just wanted me to assure the buyer that the foal was authentic."

"Isn't that the potential buyer's responsibility? Now I am confused."

"My guess is the buyer didn't want to face anyone who could recognize him in the future. I was the classic cutout."

"Strange," I said to Jimmy. "You'd think with all the money being transferred the buyer would want to be certain of the linage. Certifications from experts, that sort of thing."

"You'd think. My take on this entire transaction is that it's all a sham. Buyer is passing money to the seller and wants the transaction to appear as nothing more than a horse deal when, in fact, it's a payment in support of terrorist activities. Wouldn't be surprised if the foal ends up in a jerky package."

"Jimmy!"

"Just saying. That government guy knew less about horses than I do. And that's saying something."

"So you think there's more going on than meets the eye?"

"Don't know what to think. Tomorrow we go up to Conquesta's ranch where the foal's located. That's when the deal goes down officially."

"Let's skip all that and go home," I told Jimmy. "Tonight wouldn't be too soon! My BS detector is sounding alarm bells and my head is ringing."

"For once, Angella," he answered, "I'm ahead of you. Called Silver and...and...here's where we come in. He wants us both to witness the transaction for insurance purposes. He's concerned about blowback."

"I still say we go home. When I agreed to work for Silver I envisioned solving insurance fraud cases, tracking down thieves and con artists, not babysitting horse traders and money launderers. I say, the hell with them!"

"I'm no happier with this than you are, but we came here on Silver's plane and that's our ride home as well. Now let's enjoy dinner." Jimmy leaned across the table, taking my hands in his. His eyes were sparkling. "Tomorrow night we'll be staying at a special place—a special treat. A little place up island a bit. Private home on a bluff overlooking the water."

"What's that about? I didn't book—" Then, because it was so unlike Jimmy to cut me out of a work related discussion, I asked, "Is that what you were discussing with that man earlier?"

The twinkle deepened. "For me to know and you to—"

"Can't wait."

SEVENTEEN

Conquesta's ranch was snuggled high up in the mountains. Our driver had instructed us that we'd be in the car a good two hours. "So sit back and enjoy the ride. When we turn off this coastal road we'll pass through some of the roughest terrain and at the same time the prettiest terrain anywhere in the world." His accent made me take notice. He certainly wasn't Jamaican. Middle Eastern it sounded like. In fact, at one point I strained to get a better look at his face thinking it was the Israeli Mossad agent, Levi Ben-Yuval. We had worked with Levi in Mexico and he had been the one who had sent a warning through Tiny for us to be careful.

Coincidences always set Jimmy off. A Mossad agent driving us up into the mountains of Jamaica was more than enough to set me off. But to what end I didn't know.

For twenty minutes the road was flat, the turbulent blue-green Caribbean on our left stretched as far as the eye could see, interrupted only by resort villages along the beach. Then the car slowed, turned right onto a well paved and, at places, narrow but very windy roadway cut into what appeared to be solid rock. Soon the rocky walls moved back away from the road and bits of grassy plateau appeared as the road continued to wind its way upward from the beach. Gray stone replaced foliage for long stretches.

Again, the car slowed and went around an almost U-turn switch-back and then we continued our upward climb for another fifteen minutes before turning left onto a rock-strewn path barely wider than the car. We were still going upward, however now the angle had increased so much I had the impression the car would stall at any moment.

At some point I became aware that a second car was now in front and a third had fallen in behind us. "We have an escort," I said to Jimmy.

"I noticed that. Hope they're heavily armed — and on our team."

The further up the mountain we climbed the more desolate the area became and the more I hoped my suspicion of armed security was correct. Also, the further up we went the harder the wind seemed to blow and the car was now being rocked by gusts. One miscue by the driver and we'd disappear into somebody's inferno. My nails dug into Jimmy's hand. His response was to pull me even closer.

"Storm's coming in even faster than they projected," I said. "Sky's all black. Those clouds are fast and thick."

Eventually we turned off the bumpy road onto a hard-packed dirt path, the saving grace being that we were no longer going upward and the path was wide enough for two lanes. Best of all, the bone rattling had ceased. Suddenly, the car made a sharp left turn into what at first appeared to be a cave, but in actuality was a narrow opening in an otherwise steep grey rock-wall face.

A moment later the most gorgeous plateau I had ever seen lay before us. Steep rocky walls towered above us on all sides. A waterfall cascaded into a small lake barely visible in the distance. Horses roamed near the lake and judging from how small they appeared, the plateau must have been much larger than I had at first thought. But the feature that captured my attention was the massive stone chateau that sat off to the left. Fifty rooms at a minimum, all with arched windows, and balconies jutting out from the second and third floors. A castle in heaven if ever there was one.

"Ever see anything like this, Jimmy?"

"I've parachuted into all manner of treacherous and dangerous country, but nothing as protected—or picturesque— as this. Nobody's getting on or off this property without their blessing that's for certain."

"Place is a fortress, you ask me."

"Malik Conquesta," Jimmy said, referencing the research we had done, "is little known outside the breeder world, but as you learned he's one of the world's richest people. Well-connected politically in many countries. Man lives a charmed life."

"I'd say not so charmed with the loss of his son. Maybe that's what all this security's about?"

"I'm thinking there's someone up here, or someone coming up here, who...who's on Interpol's most wanted list. Red tagged."

"Or a group of someones," I added.

"The security is well oiled. This isn't their first rodeo. This place is one of those secrets that everyone knows and no one ever talks about."

"I suppose this is the kind of place where governments meet in secrecy and plan any manner of mischief."

"Think an investigative reporter or photographer could ever infiltrate?"

I told Jimmy I didn't see how anyone could get up here uninvited and asked why Conquesta would allow Mossad to escort us?"

"We're cover for something going down," he answered, then went on to remind me to watch my back.

"From my observation," I told him, "this spread goes far beyond horse breeding. There are cannabis plants as far as the eye can see. What's that about?"

"I've been thinking about that. I figure the plants are a cover for money laundering. And besides, the only way to raid this place with any hope of success would be to use glider parachutes coordinated from highflying aircraft. Without the permission of the Jamaican government, or very sophisticated stealth aircraft, such a mission would be impossible. And, even assuming a raid could be mounted, the operators would be met by deadly cross-fire."

"Welcome, Mr. Jimmy Redstone," perhaps the thinnest man I had ever seen welcomed Jimmy as we emerged from the car, his long slender fingers wrapped themselves around Jimmy's hand. "I'm Malik Conquesta and I trust the ride up here was not too uncomfortable."

"Not so bad," Jimmy responded, his hand still encapsulated by our host. "But this weather, it's deteriorating faster than—"

"Moving the time table up some. Bidding's over and the winner is coming in person. Most unusual, but because of the weather, timing is critical." Conquesta turned toward me. "Oh," he exclaimed, "Angella. I was told you were attractive, but I hadn't anticipated such beauty. Welcome to my humble home. Not large by Texas standards, but it suits our business well." He released Jimmy's hand and immediately took mine and proceeded to move it up to his lips. "Delicious!" he exclaimed, after planting a lingering kiss. "Purely delicious! I understand you two will be remaining overnight. I suspect with the weather, everyone will be remaining. Mr. Serek Powell, our horse broker, will be joining us for dinner. He is anxious to get your take on the horse Lip Sync and her foal. I trust your stay with us will be most pleasant." He bowed deeply, never taking his eyes from me. "I will do everything in my power to make your stay memorable."

Conquesta did not act like a man who had just lost his son. But as Jimmy often pointed out, customs in different countries vary greatly and it is always problematic to extrapolate from one to another. Yet, in my mind some things are universal and grief over a lost child has to be one of those things. I detected no grief in this man and made a mental note to carefully lock the door to my bedroom, assuming there even was a lock—or a door. Grasping Jimmy's hand, I replied, "I'm sure Jimmy and I will find our visit pleasurable, Mr. Conquesta."

"Oh, please, Angella my dear lady, call me Malik. Real friends shorten it to Mal."

Changing the subject, I said, "I understand you raise horses...ah, polo ponies. What makes your ranch special in that regard? I mean, horses...ponies...are born and raised all over the world. So why are—"

"We are high up and the young ones develop strong lungs. And... Well frankly, I pay Mr. Powell handsomely to bring me only the best breeding stock. Lineage is the real key, even more than altitude." Conquesta had moved close to me while he spoke and was now significantly within my private zone. I glanced in Jimmy's direction and he appeared unaware of my discomfort. My anxiety rose.

"And what about lineage?" I forced myself to ask. "What exactly do you look for?"

"Blood line, blood line, blood line. Come," he said, placing his hand on my shoulder, "while the weather holds we'll take a ride over to where the foals and yearlings are. You can see for yourself what we have. I'm certain you'll be well impressed."

I suppose I shouldn't admit it, but...well, his hand on my shoulder had sent a surprisingly pleasant shock through my system. I followed his urging and took a few steps toward an open-top Hummer parked at the edge of the clearing. "Jimmy," I called, pausing to allow my partner time to catch up, "come, we're visiting the foals."

Several men had joined Jimmy and several horses, including one that was either Lip Sync or a dam good imitation of Lip Sync, were being led in their direction. My voice was drowned out by a steadily growing sound of a motor off in the distance. Focusing on the sound I realized the noise had been in the background for several minutes, perhaps a car bringing the buyer up the mountain. I also realized that the sky was now even darker than when we had arrived and the wind gusts were closer together—and getting stronger.

The sound continued to intensify and I turned

my head in time to observe a helicopter break through the clouds overhead. In that instant the machine was tossed from my far right to my left like a toy. The helicopter tipped downward, looking as if it was about to crash into a stand of tress. Then it suddenly rose straight upward, hovered for a moment high overhead, and, fighting the gusty wind, landed shakily between Jimmy's group and where Conquesta and I were standing.

"Come, my dear, time is short. The storm will quickly be upon us. Our guests are arriving earlier than anticipated and I must get back to greet them."

This time I allowed myself to move toward the car. With one foot on the running board I was about to swing up into the back seat. I froze when Conquesta's hand slid down to the small of my back. "Jimmy," I called again, this time as loud as I could and with urgency. "Please come join us."

Jimmy didn't answer. I looked over to where my partner had been. My blood ran cold and my body froze in place. A circle of men had formed around him, the circle moving in the opposite direction.

"Let me assure you, my lady," Conquesta's smooth voice said, "that Mr. Redstone is in good company. He's as safe with them as you are with me. He is taking a quick ride on Lip Sync. The foal Sync Opate has already been verified and we are waiting only for the money to arrive." The warning flags went up and suddenly the welcome sensation on my back became a major threat. Conquesta was far too large for me to take down, but even so, my body pulsed in preparation. But before I could act, the sky lit up with a massive jagged discharge of lightning stretching across the now black horizon and seemingly ending at my feet. Almost immediately the crash of thunder reverberated from the ground around us. As high up as we were, the lightning appeared horizontal in the sky. Something I had never witnessed before. A second burst hit almost immediately, again followed by the loudest crash I've ever heard.

I jumped, partially from the sound and partially to free myself of my host. I landed on the ground off to Conquesta's side. What I hadn't planned on was Conquesta's instant reaction. As I came up, and before I could position my legs for running, his hand clamped on my elbow. "Be careful, Angella," he said, his voice as smooth as always, "the ground is indeed rocky. You went down on that knee hard. Are you hurt? Here, let me take a look."

Before I could resist, he kneeled, forming a platform with his left knee. His large hands clasped my calf and he gently placed my right leg onto the platform. He was gentle, but firm. I wasn't going anywhere and nothing that he had done to this point warranted violence on my part. But even if it did, my assessment was it would be futile. Outwardly, Conquesta had done nothing other than be a gracious host—albeit an over-friendly one.

"Flex your leg, if you can."

I did as he instructed.

"Any pain?"

"Nothing to speak of. I'm okay."

Squeezing the sides of my knee, he said, "Any pain there?"

"Not at all."

"Well then young lady it doesn't appear you've been hurt." His hand closed around my calf and he gently lifted my leg from his thigh and placed my foot on the ground.

While he was still down on one knee was the time to make my get away. But again I asked myself what exactly had he done? Yes, his hands had been all over me. And yes, he had been steering me away from Jimmy to some unknown location. But he did appear genuinely concerned for my wellbeing.

I looked back toward where I had last seen the guards, hoping to catch Jimmy's attention.

But the area was empty.

"They've gone on ahead, Angella," Conquesta said extending his hand. "Let me help you. Don't want you getting hurt. The only doctor we have in the area today is a veterinarian. Wouldn't want him sewing up someone so gorgeous as yourself. Now, would we?"

"I'll be okay. The lightning—"

"Today has indeed been an...an exciting day, my dear. Today the foal Sync Opate was sold. That colt is the product of two of the best, if not the best, polo ponies ever. This will be the largest cash transactions in horse breeding history. A day for celebration."

Conquesta's mind had focused on the financial transaction and in that instant his hand retracted. Before I could take advantage of his distraction another flash of light, followed by ear deafening thunder, blasted across the high plateau effectively stunning me into inaction.

Rain began to fall, a light rain that was wind driven and which promised to grow heavier before it was over. "Come, Angella, time to be inside."

But before we were to the car, a man ran up, his arms waving wildly. He was yelling excitedly in Jamaican English. I couldn't exactly follow what he was saying, but judging from his arm and hand movements it seemed as though he was saying a man was down and badly injured. My immediate assumption was lightning had hit something or someone.

"Come," Conquesta urged, taking my arm, "Redstone has been injured. Hurry."

EIGHTEEN

My eyes cleared and I focused on a man standing above me who was no more than five-five, and only if he had a pocket full of rocks would his weight reach a hundred pounds. Skinniest living person I'd ever seen. Or maybe he was a zombie and I was dreaming.

"My name is Captain Lazarow," the skinny man said. "I'm attending to your partner, Mr. Redstone."

Then I remembered I was on a plane high over the Caribbean and must have dozed off. Jamaica was now far behind us. "How's Jimmy?"

"Resting now. Our assessment at this point is he'll make a full physical recovery. We're ruling out the need for medical intervention, at least for now."

"Physical recovery? I don't understand. What aren't you telling me?"

"TBI takes many forms and, quite frankly, we're

in the early stages with your partner. The lasting results of the TBI will not be known for a while I'm afraid."

"What's that mean? What results?"

"He's had a...a personality change."

"A what? Is it permanent?"

"In situations where the trauma is to the frontal lobe, the patient experiences what we call executive control issues. These issues manifest by lack of emotional control, poor judgment, passivity. But that's not the case with Jimmy. Jimmy seems to have taken on a different personality—actually a different person—than his record indicates."

"I'm still confused."

"Indeed, it is confusing. The short answer is that we see no physical basis for the personality change. But the fact remains he's presenting as if he was a different person."

"Who? I mean who is he? Who does he think he is?"

"Truthfully, I was hoping you could shed light on that. He's referring to himself as something—or someone—that sounds like Tex."

"He lives in Texas. Is that what he's saying?"

"Initially that is what we thought. But his speech has cleared somewhat. He's definitely saying Tex, not Texas. He's also referring to himself in the third person."

"How's that?"

"Ranger Redstone's gonna pay," he said. "Money's mine, earned it fair and square. Redstone got me. I'll get him."

My initial thought turned to the bank robbery on South Padre Island. Could Jimmy be referring to the money everyone believes he hid up north on the island? If so, I better be—

"In my experience, and this is my theory only," the doctor continued, "when TBI patients take on other personalities it usually stems from an emotional—or traumatic—encounter with that other person. And—"

"Badman Tex!" I exclaimed. "Could he be confusing himself with Badman Tex?"

"Yes," Lazarow replied, "the name fits. He's used the phrase bad man several times. I thought he meant there was a bad man, maybe chasing him, as in a dream. Badman Tex makes sense. What is the connection between Jimmy and this Badman person?"

"Jimmy shot and killed him. Tex robbed a bank in Austin. One of many. I didn't know Jimmy then, but at that time he was a Texas Ranger. He and his partner, a man by the name of Lonnie, tracked Tex and while I don't know all the details, I do know Jimmy shot Tex through the head. Single shot. Jimmy and Lonnie's version is that Tex shot at Jimmy and Jimmy fired back."

"Do I detect some...some skepticism on your part?"

"I read the trial transcript. Ballistics supports Jimmy firing first and his partner Lonnie shooting Jimmy in the arm as a cover up. Both were acquitted, so Jimmy's story is what the law says happened. No law officer anywhere believes Jimmy didn't shoot first. He's reminded of that fact routinely."

"It's certainly heavy on his mind. Anyone else?"

"He's killed only one other person that I know about. An international bad character we know as Igletz Touchy. He's the half-brother of another bad actor. Woman named Sally Comings. Known in the trade as Shadowy Sal. Woman's a cold-blooded killer, but what makes her even more dangerous is she's also an extremely talented impersonator. Men as well as women. She can imitate anyone. I promise you if she imitated your wife you'd not know."

Lazarow chuckled. "Not married at the moment. But I'll keep that in mind."

"Ig the Pig."

"Come again?"

"That's what Touchy was known by. Ig the Pig. Jimmy killed him to save his son a few years back."

"Okay. I have what I need for now. Thanks for being candid."

"Anything if it helps Jimmy. Can I see him?"

"Afraid not, Ma'am. While he thinks he's this guy Tex, he could become...well, violent. Particularly violent toward you since you and Redstone are...are involved. Let's give it time. These things tend to work out, especially ...well, especially if this condition is due to drug inducement."

"Drug inducement? What are you—"

"Found traces of lysergic acid diethylamidc and traces of other drugs."

"LSD! What the hell!"

"It's not usual to find LSD injected, mainly because unlike other drugs the time for reaction in the body doesn't change over oral ingestion. So something else knocked him out, but the LSD is what he's reacting to now. But he'll be fine once it's out of his system. It will work out fine."

Of course, they believe it'll work out. Everything tends to work out. But not always in the manner one might desire. "Mind telling me where we are landing?"

"Houston. A private room has been arranged for Jimmy at Hermann. They are nationally ranked, second only to the Rehab Institute of Chicago."

"So, why not Chicago?" I don't believe rankings of this nature have any scientific validity, but I wanted to learn as much as I could before they brought the inevitable iron curtain down between Jimmy and me.

"I trained under Dr. Max Cobalt at Hermann. Believe me, he's the best there is. He wrote the book on TBI. Jimmy will be in good hands."

That sounded ominous. "I thought he was... stable."

"He is. He's actually doing well. Except for the personality shift. But truth is, with TBI we expect the unexpected."

"No offense," I said, "but it sounds like anything can happen at this point."

"Not exactly anything. The personality shift should be temporary, but it's too early to make any definite prognosis."

"So, you're saying he'll return to...to well, being Jimmy. The Jimmy Redstone I know — and love?"

"I would love nothing more than to assure you that will be the case. But truthfully I can't in good faith make such a statement."

I turned away to hide the tears.

"Perhaps Dr. Cobalt will be able to shed more light on this when he examines Jimmy in person."

I didn't dare ask the question that hung in the air. Had Cobalt already examined Jimmy remotely? It sounded as if he had. And if so, Captain Lazarow already knew the answer — and it wasn't good.

NINETEEN

Silver's jet touched down and taxied to a remote hanger at an airport I didn't immediately recognize. From the time we landed until the time the hanger door was closed behind us I saw nothing to give me a clue as to where we were. Captain Lazarow had said Houston, but we weren't at International and neither were we at Hobby. Most likely we had landed at a military airport.

"Miss Martinez," Commander Loeb said, "please remain in your seat a while longer. I'll be accompanying Jimmy over to Memorial Hermann and will remain with him along with Captain Lazarow. I understand you have a visitor coming on board in a few moments."

"Where are we?"

"Houston."

"I mean, what airport?"

"I'm not at liberty to discuss anything further. Please excuse me. I'm needed with Mr. Redstone."

Before I could respond, Loeb disappeared behind the curtain. I immediately went to the front and attempted to twist the handle on the exit door, but it wouldn't move. The exit was locked.

Through the porthole I saw an ambulance maneuver into position just beyond the rear steps. Loeb came into view, walking backward down the steps, her arms outstretched, supporting a wheeled-gurney. Captain Lazarow, holding the head end of the gurney, appeared next. Even though the temperature was in the eighties, a blanket covered Jimmy up to his chin.

My focus shifted to a black limousine that came to a stop directly below where I stood. Dark tinted windows blocked my view to the inside. The right rear door opened and out stepped a man I recognized by the movement of his shoulders even before I could see his face.

"Pardon me, Miss Martinez," a gentle, but firm, female voice said, "I need you to step back so that I can open the hatch." Four bars on her white uniform indicated that the slender black woman standing beside me was the plane's captain.

"And your name is?"

"Captain Freiman. Now if you'll please step back we can allow the boss on board."

So Freiman works for Sliver, or more accurately, Great Southern Insurance—or whoever owns this aircraft. Another mystery I most likely will never solve.

A moment later Jack Silver came through the door, threw a quick salute to the Captain, then turned to me. "Just got an update on Redstone. Don't yet know what to make of his injury, but I'm most hopeful."

"He's not the same," I blurted. "He's...someone else."

"Let's not be too quick to think the worst. He has a great medical team. Doc Cobalt is optimistic he'll come around in due course. I've never known Cobalt to be wrong when it comes to brain trauma. Never."

"I hope you're right. But...but I saw anger in Jimmy's eyes a moment ago when they brought him out of the plane. I never saw that in Jimmy before. It's...it's just not Jimmy. It just isn't."

"Come, let's talk." Silver moved to the middle of the plane, settled into one of the swivel seats and motioned for me to take the seat opposite him.

I felt like a daughter obeying her father, but couldn't help myself. I needed to talk to someone and truth is, I wanted to get to know Silver. Jimmy had done most of the talking during our negotiations, not so much because he wanted it that way, but because I was just happy to be away from the half-truths and outright deceptions that came with being a Homeland Security agent.

When I was seated, Silver said, "For your information, I have arranged an audible and visual link connecting you to Jimmy. Cobalt doesn't yet want you speaking to him, but from time to time they'll turn on the video so you can observe for yourself how he's doing. The link will be available soon."

"And how do I access..."

"Use the Great Southern Employee app, the one I believe you already have on your phone. You'll be notified when the link is live."

"I thought that app was only for giving us assignments and files."

"Generally speaking, that's its use. But we do use it also for special situations such as this."

I hated to think what the term, special situations actually meant. "I appreciate that. Thank you."

"Least I could do. But truth is, the docs said it would be useful to them if you could provide feedback. After all, you know him better than anyone."

"Mind telling me where we are? I mean what field we landed at?"

"Ellington. Handles traffic for the Space Center and at times commercial flights diverted from Hobby. At one point there even was a commercial flight between here and International. Shortest fixed wing scheduled flight in the country. All that's gone now." Silver paused as if contemplating his next statement. "Listen Angella. I know you're worried about Jimmy. Frankly, so am I. But worry doesn't solve a bloody thing. Action is what counts. And we've taken all the action we can up to this point. Jimmy's in the best hands and all we can do is wait."

My anxiety bubbled to the top. "I need to be with him! Not sitting here in a dark hanger."

"The doctors tell me your physical presence while Jimmy believes he's some guy named Bad-man Tex will have a negative effect on him. Whether or not that's true is something neither of us is qualified to say. So for now we wait."

"And do what?" Silver hadn't arranged his schedule to meet me in a Houston hanger simply to tell me to cool my heels. "What is it you want from me?"

"The reason I hired Jimmy—and you—is that you are both exceptionally perceptive. That's what makes you so good at what you do. But you're quite right, Angella, I have a business to run. And frankly, you have a job to do. Let's start with exactly what happened in Jamaica. Who was there? What you saw? What's your take away?"

Silver turned out to be a good listener. He asked questions at the appropriate times, but mostly allowed me to brief him in the free-flow manner that worked so well between Jimmy and I.

"I take it," he said when I fell silent, "you don't believe Jimmy being tossed from the horse was an accident."

"As I said, at first I thought it was the thunder clap that spooked Lip Sync, and that might be what happened. But the fact that Conquesta was intent on separating me from Jimmy—and, in fact, had done so—increases my suspicion that Jimmy being thrown was no accident."

"I've known Malik for more years than I care to remember and while he's definitely a lady's man, he has never to my knowledge taken advantage of any woman who...well suffice it to say no woman has ever filed a complaint about his behavior. There are no rumors of bad behavior—official or unofficial. He's happily married and just...just appreciates beautiful women."

I thought back to my own assessment of Conquesta's actions and recalled that I also had concluded that his behavior might have been over the top, but he certainly hadn't done or said anything warranting a complaint. Yet...yet I had tried to break away from him, hadn't I? I looked at Silver. "I suppose I could be over-reacting to Conquesta. But I do believe Lip Sync throwing Jimmy was set up."

Silver fell silent and appeared to be contemplating his response. Then he said, "Actually, I concur. Polo ponies, by their very training, are not prone to buck the way you say Lip Sync did. Are you certain it was Lip Sync?"

"That's what I was told. Didn't see for myself."

"I know Lip Sync was flown to the island. The initial plan was to auction her off along with the foal, but then I was given some poppycock about getting a higher price for the foal if Lip Sync was not sold. Made me uncomfortable."

"Are you thinking then something's wrong with Lip Sync, they took her off the market?"

"Just asking. Don't know what's going on.

From your perspective, it seemed like it happened when the thunder hit. But from another source I'm told it happened just before that. Did a helo land just before?"

I thought for a moment and remembered the noise—and the near disaster. "As a matter of fact, it did."

"That squares with my source. Speculation is that someone was on that helicopter that Jimmy was not supposed to see."

"They had everything timed so well, I'm surprised Jimmy was anywhere near the helicopter if it carried a...a secret person."

"The storm moved in faster than expected, and was much more intense than predicted. That helicopter came off a private yacht that had to launch early because the sea conditions got ugly. Plan was to circle for a while until Jimmy could be moved safely away. But as you well know, the storm hit too soon. Would have taken that bird right out of the sky had it not been on the ground."

"Who could have been on it?"

"That, my dear, is the twenty-four thousand dollar question—and frankly, not my concern." Changing the subject, Silver said, "Let's talk about Lip Sync's foal if you don't mind, shall we?"

I nodded, not knowing what he actually wanted to discuss.

"Stop me if I'm wrong on this. What we know is that some imposter foal, not the foal of Lip Sync, was tattooed to make it appear that this phony pony if you will is the son of Lip Sync."

"Correct. When you sent us out to find Lip Sync we found a horse that matched. Only it was not Lip Sync. It was that horse whose foal we saw on the island."

"That foal is a phony. And it then disappeared. Correct?"

"Correct," I repeated. The word phony focused my mind on Shadowy Sal and how she also disappeared, both at the same time.

"Well, the scuttlebutt is that the phony was the one brokered to Malik. It's also my understanding that the phony was substituted for Sync Opate, the real foal. Jimmy telling Malik about the phony could be why Jimmy's in the hospital."

"Sounds plausible," I lied. For starters, Jimmy wasn't alone with Malik at any time and not for a moment would that justify Jimmy receiving such high-level military care after his injury. Something much more serious was going on and Silver was sitting here feeding me diversions. I wondered if he was part of an operation or just being duped. Jimmy would have pressed Silver to find out.

"But I don't believe Malik was involved with the accident. Do you?"

Silver thought a moment before saying, "So that you know, Great Southern dropped coverage on the foal. I haven't told Malik why, only that we're over extended. That phony was sold for over fifteen million. Makes no sense to me."

"Isn't he going to be upset with you for not telling him why?"

"He's not an amateur in the horse business. He knows the questions to ask and the tests to demand. The fact he didn't follow his normal protocol is on him—or more accurately, on his staff. And," Silver paused, drew back and debated with himself over his next words. "Listen, let me level with you, Angella. As I'm sure you noted, the folks who brought Jimmy back from Jamaica are military."

"And they just happened to be catching a ride home," I said, not trying to mask the sarcasm. I wasn't about to tell Silver I knew the medical team was Israeli. As Jimmy taught me so well, some hands are best played close.

"Of course it didn't happen that way," Silver confessed. "You're right, the medical team's presence on the island wasn't exactly a coincidence. When Conquesta texted me about the accident I immediately notified both the Jamaican government as well as our own to get expedited service. I didn't want the doctors down there doing something we'd regret. I have a few friends in the Navy. I called in a favor or two."

"Thank you," was all I could think to say. That still didn't account for the IDF. But maybe even he didn't know who exactly had been onboard.

"But there is something troubling me."

"And that is?"

"Patterns. Insurance companies live and die with patterns. A pattern has emerged."

"A death pattern? Who else died?" I certainly didn't know of any other deaths on the island.

"Not deaths. Large money transfers for jewelry, artwork, some of which falls into the antiquities category, and now horses. In the vernacular of the times, illicit cash transfers for forgeries, forgeries of all kinds, have gone viral."

"On Jamaica?"

"Not just in Jamaica, but around the world. Forgeries have become a prime means of moving money in a manner that governments can't trace — or at least can't trace in the short term."

"Isn't that good for business? I mean, if you insure the valuables you can charge good rates."

"It would seem so. But the insurance business runs on statistically determinable risks. These transactions are one of kind and for the most part are transacted by shadowy characters who I dare say have the moral scruples of an alligator. There is no accounting for what they would and wouldn't do. And bear in mind that the reason to make it difficult for governments to easily spot the trans-action is because something untoward, such as a major terrorism action, is being financed. Anyone, and any company, found in the chain of this type of activity will be brought down as sure as you and I are sitting here talking."

"Great Southern has no intention of insuring

what you are calling questionable transactions. Is that what I'm to take away from this conversation?"

"That and the fact that you and your partner will be at the forefront of identifying situations that have the earmarks of a terrorism money transfer."

"I don't know about—"

"That's a discussion for another day. Let's get Jimmy back on board before we go there."

Having recently experienced a forty million dollar bank heist, along with the loss of a hundred-million-dollar art object, I should not have been surprised at what Silver was telling me.

"What falls into your definition of antiquities?"

"Fossils, that sort of thing. Usually smuggled from one country to another. Some of those old bones are worth a great deal. In that regard, rumor has it that an ancient mammoth of some kind has been found on the island."

How this guy gets his information I'll never know. But he's certainly plugged in. "And I suppose that's my assignment?" I said, not wanting to get into the specifics of Castro's interrogation, but trusting the kid was at our condo—and still alive. "Is there something specific you want me to investigate?"

"Just get to the bottom of this mammoth thing quickly."

"Does the company have an interest?" I asked, trying to understand what all was going on. "I mean, is there an insurance policy on a specific antiquity?"

"Not yet, but we could be asked. I need to know what exactly the risks are." Silver stood. "I've asked Captain Freiman to take you home. Good luck with the assignment—and with Jimmy."

As Silver started through the door he turned back to face me. "A friend of yours is about to join you. Enjoy your ride home."

TWENTY

"Tiny!" I exclaimed. "What the hell you doing here?"

"Came to check on Jimmy."

"This look like a hospital to you?"

"Why so hostile?"

"Pardon me for not welcoming you with open arms. But we left Homeland Security because we'd had enough of the double dealing and half-truths. Seems we're back in the thick of it. Just leave us alone already!"

"And allow Jimmy to die in a Jamaican hospital. That what you really want?"

"We shouldn't have been in that situation to begin with. You put us there, then you want praise for getting us out!"

"Just doing Silver's bidding."

"You telling me you're Silver's Navy friend?"

"Let's just say I'm a facilitator."

"With friends like you, we don't—" Going off on the guy who may have saved Jimmy's life made no sense, so I tempered my anger. "Sorry. But it seems to me this whole polo pony thing has more to do with some...some government...operation... than it does with an insurance investigation. Not to mention that little episode with your Mexican Senator friend, Angel Lopez Garcia." I hadn't been paying close attention while concentrating on Tiny, but someone had closed and sealed the plane door and we were now moving across the tarmac. It took me a few more seconds before I realized this meeting had been pre-planned. I hadn't realized how tight Silver was with Tiny.

"I'm told Jimmy shows every sign of a full recovery. I know the docs will never say it that way, but that's what I glean from my briefing."

"As who? Badman Tex?"

"As Jimmy Redstone. He's already begun moving away from that guy Tex."

I took in what Tiny had just said. For the first time in what seemed like forever, I felt a heavy weight begin to lift. "So why am I out over the Gulf of Mexico headed south and not on my way to see him?"

"I can't speak to medical decisions, but what I do know is that you need to get to the bottom of the mammoth situation."

"So now I'm a mammoth investigator? Next it'll be—"

"Get to the bottom of it."

"And just why do you need me for this? Any-one can track down the value of old bones. When you get involved the mammoth must have some-thing to do with smuggling."

"Don't sell yourself short. You've been trained by one of the best."

"That's not an answer."

"You know the answer as well as I do, Angella."

"And that is?"

"Did Conc die because of the mammoth or be-cause Shadowy Sal was busy plying her trade? We need to know which it was and, frankly, we need you on the island—and alert. Tip for you on the mammoth angle. The Harmon Jackson Family land might be at play."

Tiny was right. I don't know how long I had known there was no getting around the fact Sal's behavior with the Senator was bizarre. She's never involved in anything so...so messy. Perhaps it was when Silver was talking about the phony pony, perhaps even before. "Is that why you're really here? To check on Shadowy Sal?"

"One of the reasons. Think of it as a two-bird type of thing."

"If Jimmy's one of your birds, then what—or whom—is the second?"

"You actually. Silver needs you to get to the bottom of the antiquity and I need you to get to the bottom of Shadowy Sal—once and for all we plan to eliminate her."

"Do I take that as it sounds? Once and for all?"

"Would be doing the world's work, you would."

"That's not my—"

"Just the messenger boy. But the powers that be do believe Sal is behind the murder of Conc—and it wasn't just about the pony. That's small potatoes in the new world."

"New world, what's that mean?"

"She was trained by a man known in the trade as The Master. And a master he is. Rumor has it that he had a leg blown off near the end of Shadowy Sal's training. He then dedicated himself to handling her and, as far as we know, has never again impersonated anyone himself. If he has, he's changed his MO significantly."

"You, my friend, are going in circles. If this Master character has been handling Sal all along, what's changed?"

"For years, Sal did jobs that scored money, perhaps for funding terrorist activities, at least according to Interpol. Her typical MO has been impersonating someone to obtain their bank account or safety box info and then heist their money, jewels, artwork, that kind of stuff. Not that she hasn't slit many a throat, but for her that's collateral damage. It's the heist that's been at center stage for her. But now...but now she's being used to change the world order."

"Assassination?"

Tiny nodded, but said nothing.

"I assume you're talking about what went on with the Senator?"

I expected Tiny to remain silent, but he surprised me. "Reasoning goes along these lines. The Senator is mounting a campaign to run for President of Mexico. He must raise large amounts of cash. He's anti-drug, so the money won't come from the cartels. At first he thought he'd raise enough from anti-drug business folks, but...but they're afraid to get involved. So the good Senator has resorted to other means of raising money. With Sal's disguises she gets behind enemy lines before the enemy even knows the war has begun."

The Sal reference threw me. "You're talking in circles again."

"At first we believed Sal's mission was to assassinate the Senator. But now we have good reason to believe her job is to raise funds for his election by—"

"...by stealing art and antiquities. Since when does the U. S. care about Mexican elections? Or who steals what from whom in Mexico?"

"Trump set out to build the wall and the Senator, if elected President, is willing to help pay for it. You know what that will do for Trump's reelection. The bottom line is that the Senator, in addition to his natural Mexican enemies, has now picked up millions of U. S. enemies as well, making it all that much harder to raise money."

Something in the way Tiny said enemies didn't ring right. "These U. S. enemies, I assume, are both in and out of the government."

"I wouldn't be involved if this wasn't government related. You've heard of the Deep State concept. This could be a prime example."

"Explain, please."

"We, and when I say we, I mean the U. S. intelligence community, not me personally, have thought for a long while now that a mole has infiltrated our ranks. Now the mole is believed to have worked his, or I suppose, her, way to the top. We have set various traps along the way and the mole is clever enough, or high enough up, to have sidestepped them all."

"Where's this going?" I asked, trying to fit Jimmy and me into their plan. Then a horrible thought struck. "Oh, my, you don't think it's...us. I mean Jimmy or me? That's not why you're here is it?"

I would have hoped for an immediate and unequivocal no from Tiny. Instead I got, "Should we be thinking along those lines?"

"You can't mean that!" I said jumping out of my seat and walking toward the back of the plane toward where Jimmy had been. "How absurd!"

"Just had to ask. Capisce? Come sit down, briefing's not over."

I hadn't known I was being briefed, but I should have known nothing Tiny says to us is off-the-cuff chit chat. Reluctantly, I went forward and sat.

"The consensus of the community, through extensive surveillance, is that the mole has a deep desire to own, of all things, a world class polo pony. Hence the trap that we set."

"So you now have your mole, I assume."

"Unfortunately, no. The trap was set with Lip Sync being the bait. But...but I hate to admit this, the trap was sprung, only the target got away."

"Got away! How did that happen?"

"That storm messed up our timing. Couldn't get assets up to that ranch no matter how we tried."

"So, where do I come in?"

"When I said the mouse got away, I didn't elaborate. Part of the trap worked, actually the consensus is it all worked. But we're not home yet. We still lack the identity of the mole. Our goal of messing with the timing came off perfectly."

"Details?"

"All I can add is, someone may be about to attempt to assassinate Mogul. That's as much as I can tell you. You'll have to run blind for the rest. Sorry. Part of the mole's plan, we knew, was to funnel a large sum of money to a terrorist operation that was to occur simultaneously in the U. S. and Israel. A money transfer of the magnitude in question was in the twenty million range. The purchase of Lip Sync conceivably could have been the money transfer we've been waiting for."

"So where does this all lead?"

"That's where the phony, Strike One, comes into play. We had to hide that from the mole and that's where Castro came in. The idea being to inject the foal into the mix to mess with the transaction."

"I assume it worked."

"We really don't know for sure. We also don't know for certain if the horse transaction has anything to do with money laundering. That, and with the storm, things went all to hell."

"So, again I ask, what do you want from me?"

"Keep your eyes and ears open. Keep Castro safe, although we believe he's no longer in danger. Keep an eye out for the scumbag, but approach her with caution. Don't alert the locals, this is strictly a federal operation. We need to ferret out the mole."

If I didn't know Tiny as well as I did, I would have concluded he had more to tell me. "Give it to me straight, Big Guy. I know you better than to think I just got all you know about what's about to happen.

Tiny's eyes flickered as if to say I was right on track. But he remained silent for many minutes, with the only noise in the cabin coming from the engine mounted on the fuselage above us. Then he said, "Look, I have my own take on this." Tiny lowered his voice to barely a whisper. "A source tells me Sal received instructions from someone high up in the administration to...to take out Mogul."

"How credible?"

"Secret Service is acting as if it was nothing. But I wouldn't be so certain."

"Did I just receive an assignment?"

"Stay alert."

"What's this have to do with the mole?"

Again, Tiny went silent. But this time he was choosing his words even more carefully than before. When he finally spoke it was to say, "It's my belief, and my belief alone, that the mole is an imposter, trained by the same person who trained Sal. And that it was the imposter who drugged Jimmy."

If I had any doubt before this, it was now abundantly clear. The government was again running my life and it didn't appear as if I had much to say about it.

"You're being unusually quiet," Tiny commented a few minutes later.

"What do you want me to say? I'm thrilled to be under your control again?"

"It's more than that, Angella. You're contemplating going off the reservation. I'd advise against it."

"I didn't know I was on a reservation."

"That, Angella, in a nut shell, is the problem. Listen to me. And listen well. Like it or not, you're in the crosshairs of several active investigations. CIA, FBI, DHS, Secret Service, to name a few. They're all running ops and one misstep could prove...damaging, fatal even. Powerful—hear that as violent—forces are being disrupted, and if the forces of evil don't nail you, the white hats just might."

From past experience with Tiny it was useless to fight him. He had actually just given me much more information that we ever typically receive from him and ignoring what he had said would be at my peril. "Wouldn't it have been prudent for me and Jimmy to have been read-in at the beginning? Why wait until Jimmy's lying brain damaged in a hospital?"

"Just be thankful it occurred on a government sponsored operation. Look, twenty-some million changed hands. And if my source is accurate that's just the first installment. There are several more exchanges planned."

"To what end?"

"Wish I knew. But the horse trade money appears to have gone directly to Hamas."

"So Loeb and Lazarow didn't just happen to be catching a ride home? There's an active IDF op going on as well."

Ignoring my comment, Tiny said, "Just watch yourself. It may all be nothing. I may be on the wrong trail. It happens more often than not. But every thread must be followed, every nuance followed up. Stakes are far too high for anything less."

"What about Silver? What do I tell him?"

"Silver knows you're working for us under his cover. He has no need to know the details. You're on a long tether from him, but he does remain your employer."

"What's that mean?"

"Jewelry, art, antiquities, and any other valuables you find in your possession belong to him. Capisce?"

"I wouldn't dream..."

"Capisce?"

"Capisce!"

TWENTY-ONE

First thing I did when the plane landed was call Lt. Malone. She wasn't available. I left call back instructions and moved down my hastily constructed checklist.

Once I find Castro, I told myself, I had to begin working on mammoth valuations. Steve Hathcock's name immediately came to mind. He being the local historian as well as the best locksmith in the valley. Rumor has it that Steve did a TV episode about hunting for treasure on South Padre Island and actually may have found something while being filmed, but he insisted they turn off the cameras before he dug the treasure out of the sand. But on this island rumors abound, most with little or no merit. So, one never ever knows for certain.

"To what do I owe this pleasure?" Steve said when I entered his place of business. "Is it true what I hear about Jimmy? How's he do'n?"

"Depends upon what you heard."

"Always the government agent. Gather, but don't sow. Or something to that effect."

"Not working with the government anymore. Work for Great Southern Insurance now."

"Now that's news."

"You know everything that happens on this island. But thanks for keeping it to yourself. Jimmy fell off a horse. Has a concussion."

"How bad?"

"Bad enough to keep him in the hospital for a while. Hey," I said, changing the topic, knowing full well Steve would understand, "what do you know about antiquities?"

"I didn't know this was a business call. In that case, why not let's go sit where we can talk in private."

Steve led me through a door that opened into what I'd call an antique store, introduced me to a woman named Kay who he said was the owner, and proceeded through the store to a small patio in the back. I knew Kay to be his wife, but if he wanted to play it close, I was game.

He offered water or anything else I desired to wet my whistle. When I refused, he pointed to two 1950s looking chairs which turned out to be much more comfortable than they appeared. Once seated, he said, "We can talk in private back here. That tree will keep us in shade for another hour or so, but you'll have to be more specific. Antiquities cut a wide swath."

"In confidence. Okay?"

Steve nodded. "Nothing else. I deal in confidences."

"Have you heard about a wooly mammoth found up island? Maybe a mastodon?"

"Go on," Steve's noncommittal voice said.

"Go on with what? It's a simple question. Yes or no."

"Much more complex than that, I assure you. Your interest?"

"Partially my employer. Partially another matter I'm working on."

"Without committing to anything, let me give you a brief history lesson."

"I'm all ears."

"Let us suppose a mammoth has been found. Now this is supposition, not confirmation."

"I understand."

"Okay. First, while mastodons and mammoths are part of the Proboscidea order, they are separate families, both now extinct. Elephants are the only still existing Proboscidea family members."

"Go on," I told Steve. I had the impression that while I had simply asked for the time, I was receiving a history lesson on the origin of clocks. Well, so be it. Steve was always interesting.

"It certainly wouldn't have been a mastodon, the climate this far south was never right for them.

I doubt also it was a wooly mammoth, but...but, and this is hypothetical, I'll accept a Columbian mammoth."

"So it is possible?"

"Possible covers a wide swath. Let's just say if there had been such a finding it would have taken place north of the Mansfield cut and not south."

"How would you know that?"

"Just assume that as a fact. Anyway, the site of the find, if indeed there has been a find, has an interesting history. At one point in time it was privately owned. But, and here is where things get a bit tricky. The land was deeded to the federal government. LBJ was instrumental in the transfer, claiming it was for protection of the shoreline."

"Does it follow, then, that if the mammoth, or whatever it is, was found on federal lands, the government owns the right to the find. Is that what you're saying?"

"Well, not exactly. LBJ insisted that the original landowners be allowed to keep the mineral rights. Which is another way of saying that if—actually not if, but when—oil or natural gas is discovered on that land, the original owners receive the proceeds."

"What's that have to do with fossils?"

"I'm not a legal expert, but I believe there are two problems. Depending upon how the language of the deed is crafted, the government may have rights to any fossil dug up on the land. From the documents I've seen, I'd say the original landowners retain rights to anything found on or under the surface."

"Talk to me about the value of a mammoth find on the land. Ownership rights seem secondary."

"Values come in many forms, depends upon whose ox is being gored." Steve laughed. When I didn't join him, he said, "Hey, pardon the attempt at a pun here. Bad joke. Back to the subject. A mammoth find on the sand bar would indeed be something. I'd say in the right hands, and if the carbon dating confirmed the find back to mammoth times, the value could easily be upwards of twenty million."

"A fossil valuation of that much? Aren't you going overboard a bit?"

"Not if the fossil dates back beyond where civilization is thought to begin."

"What do mammoths have to do with civilization, human civilization?"

"Large topic. Short answer. Speculation is that it wasn't climate change that killed off the mammoths, but rather human civilization. If a mammoth fossil were to be found down here the next step then would be to see if civilization coexisted. That would be in keeping with the theory that civilization may actually date back earlier than originally thought."

Hathcock's statement caught me by surprise. I'd heard recently of some finds that challenged anthropologists understanding of when human existence, as we know it, began. But I hadn't heard anything like that in Texas—and on a shifting sand bar no less. "Are you telling me something I should know?"

"All idle assumption."

But it wasn't idle assumption and we both knew it. "Okay, go on."

"I was discussing the value of the find itself. But...let's just assume, again for the sake of this discussion, a fossil of this nature and scope was indeed found on federal lands. Then there could never be oil drilling at that location. Well, maybe never is too harsh a word. But oil drilling would be postponed until the full extent of the bone pit is determined. There may be a whole civilization, a civilization we know nothing about, under that sand. Can you imagine how long that will take before drilling for fossil fuel will be allowed?"

Hathcock had a point—a very valid point. "So oil interests will pay large amounts of money to bury, so to speak, this find. Is that a fair take-away from what you're saying?"

"Fair enough. But there's more to be lost than just money. Stopping the drilling can easily run into the billons. And when that much money is in the balance, lives are at stake."

"But," I said, "there is, to my knowledge, no drilling taking place on this island or on the land north of this island."

"Drilling, and plans for drilling, are different."

"Are you saying..."

"Speculation."

"Speculation based on what exactly?"

"First hand observation."

Before I could ask, Hathcock pulled out a pencil and a notepad, scribbled something on a page, ripped the page from the pad and handed it to me.

"Coordinates," I said, "of what?"

"Drive up island to the cut. Fly a drone north. I think you can actually program the drone to these. See for yourself."

"Does the name Harmon Jackson mean anything to you?" I asked Steve, remembering the tip Tiny had given me.

"That's the entity owns the land of the coordinates on that paper I gave you."

"Know them?"

"Nobody knows them. That's a made up name of a group of people who own the rights under that land. They may be getting ready to drill up there."

"How'd you know? You up there?"

"Not me. But a lawyer who represents landowners' interests up there has been seen at the records office in Brownsville and here on the island. His law firm, actually his old man's law firm, worked with LBJ on the negotiations with the Feds. The son's now the front man for anyone talking mineral rights on Padre Island, north or south."

"Son have a name?" I asked.

"Quinton King."

"Related to the King Ranch?"

"Distant cousin."

"Where can I find this distant cousin? He have an address? Law firm name?"

"Seven blocks south. Riviera Hotel."

"That's where we'll be living soon. Great Southern's giving us the penthouse."

"Nice place."

"Thanks."

"I'm installing the locks for Silver." Steve's eyes twinkled. "You shouldn't have trouble finding Quinton. Six four. Slender build. Narrow face. Clark Gable mustache. Wears a white hat. Says it's always summer where he is."

I thanked Steve for the information and on the way out to my car I probed a bit further. "Assuming there had been a find, would you possibly know where it would be hidden?"

"Assuming such a find, then the answer is yes."

"Care to share?"

"Negative." Then he gratuitously added, "But it's not all that hard to figure that part out."

A quick update of my notes and I was off to see Malone. The look on her face when I came through her door was not at all pleasant. In fact, it was downright nasty. "That scowl directed at me?" I asked, ready to make a hasty exit at the slightest provocation. This situation highlighted a major difference between Jimmy and I. Whereas Jimmy would typically charge directly into the discomfort zone, I tend to skirt the edges.

"No. Sorry. In fact you're just the person I need to talk with. Pull the door closed will you."

Malone, not the friendliest person on the island, came around her desk, motioned for me to sit at a small table in the far corner. She uncharacteristically pulled another chair around beside me. We ended up with our knees almost touching.

"First thing, how's your partner doing?"

"Holding his own, I suppose."

"I don't detect a high confidence level. I'm sorry. Thrown from a horse is the official story. Accident or foul play?"

"Officially, an accident."

"You believe otherwise?"

"Polo ponies of the caliber of Lip Sync don't throw riders. This one did."

"I take it you two were in Jamaica because of that polo pony here on the island, actually the foal, that went missing? I think the foal's name is Sync Opate."

"Of sorts." One thing I did learn from Jimmy. Give out as little information as possible. "It wasn't really Sync Opate, but a substitute. It's a long story, short version the mother wasn't Lip

Sync. Phony foal's name is Strike One. But you already knew that from your investigation of Conc. He was the trainer."

Malone's face set hard. "That's just it! I was... relieved of the investigation."

"You were wh..." I began, but then realized what had happened. "Because of the video! That's exactly why Sal impersonated you. To keep you off the case."

"Exactly, now some dumbass from Brownsville's in charge. Case'll be cold as the fish-bait in my freezer before that guy even learns the names of the players."

"What, if anything, can you relate?"

"Only that the killer is the same person who killed Billy Jaspers several years back. I'm sure you remember him. Known around here as Paco. Same knife pattern, same angle, same height. Lab even believes it's the same knife."

"Shadowy Sal!"

"Floraline Maldos as she's known to Interpol."

"One of her may names."

"Speculation has it she was hired to eliminate Conc. I did confirm he was DHS. She left the drugs, so it wasn't a heist. Someone wanted the kid dead. I'm betting that someone is Santiago because he also learned Conc came over to our team."

"Any idea where she is? Still on Island?"

"For all I know she's hiding right among us,

taken over the life of our desk sergeant—or even you for that matter."

"Sobering thought. Should I be worried about you?"

"As we know, she already has all she needs to do me. For that matter, you as well."

"I suppose I should tweak your nose, or yank an ear, to assure myself you're you."

"I wouldn't advise that," Malone warned. "But you could do what I do. Just watch eyes."

"And—"

"And yours are just fine."

"Speaking of Shadowy Sal, how's Angel Garcia doing? His lunch with Trump was postponed I understand. Did they at least meet?" I had been so engaged in my own life that I had lost track of the larger world.

"I haven't been directly involved, but Chief says Garcia claims he didn't need your partner to tell him his wife Valencia had been impersonated. He said he knew it the moment she walked into the hotel room."

"That's not the way Jimmy tells the story. In fact, had Angel actually known, he wouldn't have come as close to her as he did. That's what allowed Sal to take him hostage."

"That's not the way Garcia tells it. In fact, when Jimmy's report didn't match Garcia's, bells in Spook Haven sounded, the Secret Service got

nervous, and the President's schedule suddenly changed."

"Bet that didn't play well."

"To say the least. President is pissed and Garcia
blames Jimmy for screwing up."

"Make up session?"

"Actually, yes. Not announced yet. But the two
men, Trump and Garcia, will hold a small rally to
show border solidarity very soon."

"Don't tell me it'll be here on the island."

"That's what Trump wants. He refuses to ever
back down. Says, 'they win, when they force me
to back off. Can't be having that, now can we?'"
Malone had captured Trump exactly. "It's either
Brownsville or here," Malone continued. "I'm told
he's leaning toward the island. It's more a media
event than anything, so the island flavor, the Gulf
of Mexico in the background, fishing boat captains
being interviewed about how the new tax law helps
them, how exports are up. You know, the working
man's President, the whole nine yards. The island
plays to his message."

"And it's hard to mount a protest out here. The
way you're talking it's already set. When?"

"Not at liberty to say. But be on your game."

"Listen," I said, by way of thanking her for
reading me into the Presidential plans, "the coordinates for the site where Castro dug up the
fossil are 26.65 north and 97.32 west. If you can
arrange a drone we can go up island together and

fly it across the Mansfield cut, see what we can see. I assume checking on fossil dig sites outside city limits doesn't interfere with the murder investigation."

"It certainly doesn't, not in Kenedy County, but to be on the safe side I'll run it past the Chief. That'll get us an ATV as well as the drone. By the way, I'm impressed with your memory for the numbers."

"Thanks. I rounded those up a bit. I have more accurate coordinates written down. By chance, can you operate the drone yourself, or do we need—"

"I've been trained. Be back in a few," Malone called, quickly leaving the room. I was happy to note the swagger back in her step.

TWENTY-TWO

Malone drove along the beach, the wheels of the ATV skirting the surf. "Smoothest ride is in the wet-packed sand," she said. "Up near the dunes the sand mounds will shake your teeth loose." We had traveled a good five miles since seeing the last human, a turtle patrol woman wearing a white long-sleeved T-shirt, a bandana mask covering her face and nose. "Did you know," Malone asked, "that over five thousand hatched turtles are released on this island every year? And the number is increasing exponentially."

"Tribute to the folks who spend countless hours on their behalf."

"Not that much further," Malone called, her words mostly blown away by the wind.

"I only hope we can fly this thing with all the wind," I replied, practically screaming to be heard.

"This one's designed for forty knots. My guess the wind's under that."

"Hope the batteries are good and charged, if that means anything against the wind."

"It certainly does, but they're full. Okay, I'm heading over toward the dune line. Hold on."

A few minutes later we were stopped and out of the vehicle. The Mansfield cut was just ahead and this was a good place to set up our pad. The sun was now in the west sky so the car provided enough shade to see the display panel.

"I'll set it so the coordinates will be displayed along the bottom of the screen," Malone said. "Been awhile since I played with this puppy, so it may take a few minutes before it all comes back. You ready?"

I reached in my pocket and retrieved Hathcock's written coordinates. "Ready when you are."

The drone, which resembled a miniature table with helicopter-like propellers at the four corners, lifted off the pad and circled overhead. Malone touched a button on the console and the beach around us came into perfect view. A quick movement of the control stick brought the drone overhead, our heads now prominently displayed on the screen.

Malone nodded toward the key pad and I knelt in the warm sand and punched in the numbers Steve had given me. "Okay, she's going north," I said as the first set of numbers went from 26.56050 to 26.5813 to 26.6003. "Take it a bit west, and go in high. We can always come lower if need be," I instructed Malone.

The second set of numbers moved from -97.28599 to -97.3002. The drone was going a bit west. "Now go northwest," I instructed, focusing on the numbers.

"What the hell's that?" Malone asked. "That thing on the screen? On the far left."

"Looks like we have company! Another drone." A bird, more like a duck, was hovering over a spot. Our drone was slightly above the duck drone.

"Go higher," I instructed, "and position directly above that...that duck."

Malone did as instructed and when the duck was directly below our drone the coordinates read: 26.65 and -97.32. "That drone is positioned precisely over our sweet spot," I told her.

"You called out the coordinates back in my office. You think I'm being bugged?"

"That's as good an explanation as any. Can't think of another explanation."

"There's nothing down there. Nothing I can see anyway," Malone said.

"Are we video recording?"

"Yes."

"Okay, let's see if that duck has eyes overhead. Fly northeast, see if it follows."

A moment later, Malone said, "Didn't move. Doesn't seem to see us."

"Good," I replied, "let's go back to our coordinates. But do it high for now."

"Direct me."

"West and north," I said watching the numbers close around 26.6549 north and 97.32565 west. "Stop. Hold. Good. Now zoom in, but keep the bird high. Don't want them to know we're here."

"You see something?"

"Looks like early exploration equipment. Mostly buried in the sand, so I can't be certain. Should we go lower and challenge the duck?"

"Battery's down to a quarter," Malone responded. "Gotta make it fast."

"One pass and then bring her home. See if they bite."

Malone circled the buried debris twice, not more than twenty feet off the sand, then turned the drone south and climbed back to altitude. The Mansfield Cut came into view and suddenly so did the duck. Only the duck was coming upward on a collision course for our much slower drone.

"Is the recording device on the drone, or is it all in the console?"

"Camera in the drone. Recording down here."

"Good. They get nothing if they intercept us."

"Except a valuable piece of equipment, of which I am responsible."

The image on our monitor caught a close-up of the duck's beak slam into the legs of our table-shaped drone. The picture jumped and twisted. Then stabilized. But the duck was again coming directly toward the camera.

"Bring it south," I said. "If it goes down, let it be in the water. Makes it harder for them to recover whatever it is they think has been recorded. We have what we need."

"And that is?"

"That Hathcock's coordinates are correct. The fossil find is at a possible oil drill sight. Castro may want the jaw for its intrinsic value, but some big money wants to keep the fossil off the market because of the billions of dollars in oil that might be in jeopardy."

"So who's flying that duck you think?"

"Whoever has a bug in your office."

"Lotta good that does me."

"Great, the duck turned away! Our drone's heading home. A bit nicked, but still functional."

"Angella, you just described me to a T."

"Know anyone who goes by the name Q?" I asked Malone on the way back to police headquarters. The name Quinton King that Hathcock gave, me I kept to myself.

"Description?"

"Meager. Well-dressed might be a descriptor."

"Anglo?"

"Assume so, but not certain."

"I'll see what I can find out. Oh, by the way, I had them sweep my office."

"Find it?" I asked, hoping they had, but also realizing the bug could just as well have been planted on me.

"Oh, we found it. And...and planted by the phony herself. Got her on tape impersonating me."

"They certain of that?"

"Most certain. I was off-island at the time the video captured me entering my office. Got to say even I wouldn't know the difference. Didn't stay but a moment."

"Better give your staff magic decoder rings."

"Very funny. Now get out," she said bringing the four-wheeler to a halt beside City Hall. "Have work to do."

I drove over to our condo and Castro wasn't anywhere to be found. I didn't see any evidence that he had ever even been there.

"Merry," I said a few minutes later when Attorney Ayers' voicemail intercepted my call, "I need to speak with your client Castro. Have him call me, ASAP." I left my number and hung up with little expectation that my phone would ever ring with the kid at the other end. But we were being paid to keep him alive and I had to do my best.

TWENTY-THREE

My phone made a sound I had never heard before. Looking down I saw nothing, so I ignored it. I parked in the Riviera parking lot and was about to step out of the car when the buzz sounded again. This time there was a small red area flashing in the corner of the Great Southern app. I tapped the app causing it to open and spread out across the screen.

An image formed, and at first I thought it was Silver, but was surprised when I realized it was Jimmy. He had his right forefinger across his lips and his left hand up by his ear. I knew he didn't want me to speak, but it took a moment before it came to me he wanted the cell off the speaker. When I complied, he said, "Say nothing at all. Drugs are out of my system and I'm doing fine. Tiny's briefed me on your up-island fly-over with Malone. Silver says our new digs are ready, so do me a favor and go to the condo and get clothes for a few days for both of us. We'll need my suit and something dressy for you. Trump's hosting a lunch, or perhaps a dinner, for a few officials. We'll be invited. Don't yet know how formal it will be."

I started to ask a question, but before the words came out, Jimmy cautioned, "No questions. Save it until we're in person. Also, be careful, ole Sal may be masquerading as a hotel employee. Gotta go. Love you."

The screen went blank. Jimmy looked and sounded fine, good even. Assuming, of course, it had been Jimmy. I felt foolish doubting what I had just seen, but then again, Shadowy Sal had a proven history of making people look foolish—and dead. I didn't think the person I had seen was anyone other than Jimmy, but he hadn't used our code and there had been no way for me to demand it. But then again, the code protocol required response from me and that also hadn't been possible, so I was left in limbo as to the genuineness of the call. No harm would be done by my compliance, but Jimmy was right, I had to remain alert.

I didn't see any Gable mustaches as I walked through the lobby. In fact, I saw no mustaches at all. Not in the lobby and not by the pool, unless the dark shadow under the nose of a rather large woman in the gift shop counted.

I had been instructed to go to our condo and pack, so I proceeded back to my car, drove north to our soon to be given up home, parked and went upstairs. Jimmy's clothes were easy to put together, but mine caused concern. Real concern. I had an outfit we had bought for just this type of situation, but it wasn't hanging where I had left it. After searching the entire condo, which didn't have all that many hiding places, I concluded someone had taken it.

"Well, my backup outfit will have to do," I told myself, as I struggled to shake off the feeling of extreme violation. Anger would be another way to express my feeling.

An hour and a full suitcase later, I walked out the front door to the car. Seeing nothing suspicious, I heaved the suitcase into the trunk, checked the backseat for unwanted passengers and slipped into the driver's seat. Only then did I see a small slip of paper lying on the passenger seat. A scrawled note instructed me to drive north.

So drive north I did. Past Paragraphs On Padre, past Teds, Parrot Eyes and the Island Fitness Center. Past the Turtle Rescue, the Birding Center, Clayton's and the Convention Center. I didn't know how far north I was going or how I'd know to stop. But I did know that about four miles ahead the road would end with nothing but sand and more sand for the next ten miles.

I drove past the old horse stable where we had first met the imposter Lighting Strike and where Castro had discharged a shotgun in my direction. Then past The Shores, and a mile after that, past Andy Bowie County Park, I slowed where sand had drifted into the roadway closing the right lane.

No vehicle was coming south, so I moved to the left into the southbound lane in order to continue my trek north, still not knowing why I was even going in this direction.

I was about to pull back to the right lane when a rock, or something, bounced off my side window. Castro was standing halfway up a massive wind-created sand dune. He pointed to an opening in the dune just in front of my car and I spun the wheel hard left fully expecting my tires to sink into the soft sand as I had seen several cars do over the course of my time on the island.

But at this location the sand was hard packed and in fact led to a narrow opening in the dunes that the kid motioned me to go through. Once on the other side, the terrain flattened out, again revealing a wide expanse of what looked to be a parking lot.

I stopped and waited for Castro to approach. But he had disappeared in the dunes and wasn't visible. I waited. This was his show and he could direct it however he wanted.

Five minutes of not knowing what was expected or what was coming next is a long time. Castro made me sit almost fifteen minutes before he cautiously approached. He motioned for me to join him outside the car and I did as instructed. The kid was almost as jumpy as he had been when we first met him, but the good news was he didn't have the shotgun—or any other weapon I could detect.

"Follow me," he said moving quickly away from

the dunes toward Laguna Madre Bay. The sand was hard-packed and I had no trouble keeping up with him. "Your car is most likely bugged," he began when we were close to the water. "Some of the new devices can record even outside the vehicle." His hands were now steady and his eyes focused.

"So it's all an act. You're good at it."

"I'll take that as a compliment coming from you."

"Tell me what you can about Conc and about... Shadowy Sal."

His eyes went soft for a moment and then regained their composure. "Conc was a friend. A good friend. I wish I could have...saved him. I had no idea he'd be killed."

"Why didn't you intervene? That's what's been bothering me. You saw the figure approach him. You could have—"

"I've been asking myself that very question. Beside the fact that I'm undercover, I thought...I thought the figure was Lt. Malone." Castro looked away for a moment, then continued. "I figured she was part of the drug shipment. Implicating a local police lieutenant in a drug operation couldn't hurt my career so I laid back thinking even if she had gone bad she would never murder anyone. Man was I ever wrong."

"When did you learn you'd been duped—like the rest of us?"

"The next day. I got back and found you with

the foal in the yard. I needed you out of there because I had to tattoo the foal. That's why I had gone up the beach to begin with. Conc was waiting for the text with the picture of the real foal so I could make the foal we delivered passable as Sync Opate."

"You actually tattooed the baby!"

"I painted him. I don't know what this deal's about, but typically in a money laundering operation having the genuine article is not as important as having goods that are plausibly genuine. Kidnapping the foal came as a surprise."

"How did you expect the horse to get into Mexico? Assuming Mexico is the destination."

"Walk him across the Rio Grande down by Boca Chica."

"That's SpaceX country."

"Not yet it isn't. If the cartels have their way, launch pad'll never be built. Too much security comes with it. Eyes everywhere. Bad for business."

"So what happened?" I was thinking of the time frame and unless I was mistaken, Ole Sal was in McAllen, impersonating me and Valencia roughly at that time."

"That's all I really know. When I caught them stealing the foal I was supposed to follow them, but...but that's when I got caught, and tied up."

Conc was dead, so blowing his cover to another agent was no longer a breach of secrecy—or so I told myself. "Did you know your friend Conc was a DHS agent?"

Castro's eyes froze and his lips pressed together. He looked away.

"Look, he's gone now and nothing will bring him back. I'm sorry for that, but maybe, just maybe if I knew all the facts I could...well, who knows what will happen."

"He's the one got me into the agency. His family, as well as mine, know Santiago all too well and it was a hard decision to work against the old man, even though he's in jail. But the drugs are killing people—on both sides of the river. Conc had enough. I knew my father was against the drug traffic. Conc played along with Santiago, helping him and at the same time tipping DHS to the drops. As I told you, this was to be the last one for him."

"You think Santiago had him killed?"

"Can't be certain, but that's my take. His way of telling his mules not to turn on him."

"How'd Santiago find out?"

"He's tight with someone. Maybe the mole, I don't know."

"Okay, go to our condo and lock the doors. I have arranged for off-duty cops to watch the place."

"Better yet. I'm no longer required for this operation so I'm being moved out. Being picked up in an hour."

"Picked up. Where?"

"Right over there." Castro pointed to the flats not far from where we stood. "Thanks for your help and...and sorry to have...well worked you and Redstone."

"Goes with the territory, I'm afraid. Good luck to you." I shook his hand, which was now steady as a rock. I was happy DHS was cleaning up loose ends. In parting, I asked, "In your opinion, is Lip Sync and her foal safe now?"

"I assume you're asking on behalf of Great Southern about the real horses, the ones on my father's ranch. Not the SPI imposters."

"I am. The ones that are insured."

"I have reason to believe they're on their way to Jamaica. You can tell your employer the risk is back to its normal level. Not zero, but it's never zero. Not with horses, not with humans either for that matter."

A true statement if ever I heard one.

TWENTY-FOUR

I left Castro sitting in the sand, his back against a sand dune waiting for his ride. He was a good kid and would make a superb agent, given half a chance. For my part, I wanted to be as far from criminal activity as I could get. Unfortunately, that wasn't going to happen anytime soon.

On the way back to town I thought about the discussion I had had with Castro concerning his find. He had confirmed that the guy Q was tall, slender and sported a mustache, but he couldn't confirm whether or not it was a Gable mustache because the name Gable meant nothing to him. He also confirmed the location of the fossil find. He had hesitated when I asked if the mammoth had been found on his off time or as part of a DHS assignment. When I pressed him, he said, "In my mind, on my own time. I was up there on surveillance and decided to camp out a few days and poke around."

I doubted if his poke around had been entirely random, but I let it drop. Not my concern. "So, how much did Q offer?" I enquired.

Again, the delayed hesitation before he had answered. "Depends upon if its genuine or not. If it's the real thing then they can't drill and that'll cost them billions. If it's not the real thing then who cares?"

"Well, is it real?" I had asked.

"Don't rightly know. Carbon dating will give the age. Historian Hathcock says it's real alright. He thinks it actually might be older than ever before found. He suggests the bones might have been pushed up by natural gas pressure, leading him to conclude there's a large natural gas field down there."

"You send the find to experts for evaluation?"

"Not sure I want to know."

"Why not?"

"Q offered a million up front and ten percent of the mineral rights. If it's a useless bone then... nothing. And if it's genuine then the field will be shut down. What would you do?"

"Not a fair question. So, where did you hide it?"

"Not a fair question," he had chuckled. The first time I had seen his face come alive.

I walked through the doors of our spanking new digs ten minutes after I left the kid and set my suitcase on the entryway floor. Gorgeous, is how I would describe the place. But my heart was empty. Without Jimmy I didn't know how I'd manage to stay here. I turned, locked the door and drove back to our condo to spend the night.

I fished out my key and was about to step from the car when a shadow appeared in my peripheral vision. I looked up to see young officer Ortez standing next to the car window as though he had just pulled me over. I rolled down the window as one would who had just been busted for using excessive speed, or for running a red light.

"Sorry to startle you, Ms. Martinez. Saw you pull up and well, I was surprised is all."

"Surprised? Why so?"

"Well, I've been driving by, keeping a lookout for that guy Castro you asked us to look after."

Having forgotten to call them off, I felt bad. "Oh, I for—"

"Well, here's the thing. I haven't seen Castro all day and, well, I was waiting for you to come back out to ask you if he was okay, and...well, you never did come out, but...well, here's the thing, you're here now and—"

"Hold it Ortez. When did you see me enter my condo? How long ago?"

"Ten, maybe fifteen minutes ago."

"Wasn't me. Call it in. We're going in."

"Need to wait for backup. Won't be but a minute, two at most."

"Okay. There's another entrance around the side. You watch that door. I won't move from here until backup comes, so if I come out that door take me down. No hesitation. Better yet, give me your hat. There's no way that imposter would know to wear a police issue hat."

"You got it." Ortez hurried around the building, unsnapping his holster as he ran.

Backup did indeed arrive, not in two minutes as Ortez had promised, but within four, and in the form of Lt. Malone. "I was on my way home," she said when she approached where I was crouching. "What the hell's going on? Why the hat?" She had abandoned her private car in the middle of the street, a strobe positioned on the dashboard causing blue and red pulsating reflections from house windows up and down the block. "Who exactly is in your place?"

Before I could answer, two additional police cars skidded to a stop beside Malone's car. In the distance I could hear additional sirens.

"Officer Ortez," I reported, "is around the side. He saw a person who he thought was me enter my condo about ten, fifteen minutes ago. That person never came out, at least not through this door. Wasn't me."

Before Malone could respond, Captain Remington Franco, Malone's boss, called out as he ran toward us, "What's going on, Lieutenant?"

Malone quickly briefed him and then said to two of the uniformed officers, go around the side, don't allow anyone out. The person we are looking for may appear to be Angella here, don't be fooled. Nobody leaves. Send Ortez around here."

The two ran off toward the side of the building and a moment later Ortez appeared. "See anything?" Malone demanded.

"No, Lieutenant. No one even came near the door."

"Then we go in," Captain Franco announced. Kelson, Brown, you go in with Malone. Ortez take the front door. Martinez, I understand your unit is on the third floor."

"Unit 3C," I answered. "When you come out of the stairwell, turn right. Door on the right." I didn't know how he knew where I lived, but now was not a good time to sit down and discuss it.

"How many floors?"

"Eight. Four units on each floor. Two to the right of the stairwell and two to the left."

"Elevators?"

"Two."

"Anything else we need to know?"

"Can't think of anything." I handed my keys to Malone. "Here, no need to destroy my door."

Captain Franco turned to his team. "Bring both elevators down and lock them off. If the person in there is the imposter then she's dangerous. I don't want you shooting the place up, but don't hesitate if you believe your life's in danger. Okay,

Malone, you're up." While the captain was issuing his orders, we were joined by two Cameron County police vehicles, an ICE police enforcement unit, a fire department truck, complete with hoses, ladders, several firefighters, and two ambulances. One thing for certain, if the scumbag was in the building they were determined that she not escape. Dead or alive seemed not to matter. And that suited me just fine.

The captain issued several commands into his radio that I didn't hear. He then went over to where the non-SPI law enforcement had gathered and briefed them on the situation. A Texas Ranger car had now joined us as well.

I walked over to the captain so I could follow the progress of the invasion team. As I approached, the radio announced that both elevators were secured. A moment later Malone's voice said, "Approaching three C. Door locked. Going in." She then issued instructions to her team pertaining to where they were to stand and how they were to enter the apartment.

Then the radio announced, "We're in. Nothing unusual. Living room's clear. Kitchen's clear."

Silence followed. Then, "Guest Bedroom's clear. Guest bath clear." Silence. "Master bedroom clear. Master bath...clear. All seems in order."

"We now need to clear the entire building," the captain said, "I want every unit searched. We might have a hostage situation on our hands. Hold up a moment." The captain then consulted with a State

Police Lieutenant and in his next communication with Malone he instructed her to secure the third floor while a separate team went to the roof. "Also, be advised," he told Malone, a resigned tone to his voice, "the State Police will conduct the apartment search. They plan to begin on floor one and secure each unit other than floor three. Stay alert."

It took almost three hours before Captain Franco issued the all clear. Whoever had gone into our condo disguised as me managed to get out before the search began—or was still there in another unit disguised as someone else.

* * *

"Listen, Angella," Malone said as the two of us were having dinner at the new upscale restaurant called F&B, "I'm not surprised we didn't find the scumbag. For all we know, she's one of the permanent residents in your building. Wouldn't put it past her. Perfect place to hide. Rangers will do backgrounds on all the tenants, but she'll be long gone before results are back. Besides, she's most likely taken the identity of a real person, so tracking her down will prove impossible."

This was a decompression dinner as Malone had called it, so this tidbit was just that, a tidbit, passed along for information only. Malone wasn't going to discuss business any further than that. When she had proposed dinner after the search ended in frustration I had agreed, but with the stipulation that I pick up the tab.

The decor was excellent, the food was excellent and other than the high noise level around our table, the atmosphere was also excellent. Malone and I discussed our lives before becoming police officers and as we did so it became clear that we had more in common than I had initially thought. Both divorced, neither having children, both in serious relationships that could possibly lead to marriage, yet neither of us were prepared to force the issue.

"You know," Malone said over dessert, "you and Jimmy work together as well as any partnership I've seen. Better than most. And I've seen a lot in my time."

"Thanks for saying so. At times I feel...well, like I can't keep up with him. He's always thinking, planning, doing. Yea, does he get it wrong? Sure he does. But...but not very often. The man is focused like no one I've ever been around."

"So, Angella, what's that cloud in your eyes. It's hanging over you like you're about to drown."

"It's only...only that this accident, so called accident, resulted in a head injury and...and frankly, a personality shift. They have some name for it, but the result is they don't know if he'll shift back, or...or even if he does will he be the same." I wasn't yet prepared to discuss the picture Jimmy had on his person. The thought of the ring being for some other woman, well...even the thought was too raw to contemplate.

"You look so down, Angella. Didn't you say

you spoke with him earlier and he sounded better? Now you look like you're expecting bad news."

"That's just it. He spoke, but wouldn't allow me to. That's not—"

"If we assume...and based on today it's a good assumption...that the scumbag has you monitored, then he's right in not having you speak."

"Perhaps. Perhaps not." I didn't tell Malone about our secret code protocol, but I added, "Something in his voice was...well, off."

"What?"

"That's just it. Can't place it."

"Hopefully, a good night's sleep will do the trick."

I didn't think sleep would cure anything, but I didn't go there. "Perhaps," I compromised, "perhaps. And speaking of sleep, I think its time I get home."

"You staying at your old place or down at the hotel?"

"I can't bring myself to move into the Riviera without Jimmy so I think I'll hang at the condo 'till he's well enough to join me."

"I'll arrange for a patrol."

"Appreciate that. But the Berretta will be under my pillow."

"Just remember you do have a roommate. I don't want to be investigating a homicide if Jimmy comes home in the middle of the night."

I assured her that wouldn't happen, but my assurances fell short when Malone pointed out that Shadowy Sal could impersonate Jimmy as well as she could me.

TWENTY-FIVE

Sleeping with one eye open is never a good thing. Knowing the SPI police were keeping their eyes on me helped, but not all that much. Sal proved over the years that she could avoid the very best surveillance. And if she actually was a resident of the building then she could be my next-door neighbor for all I knew. Somehow I managed to get a few hours sleep, just enough to take the edge off. A quick coffee and a bagel smeared with cream cheese at Bada Bing Bagels and off I went to the Riviera to unpack our suitcase and move us in as much as possible.

I took a leisurely tour of our new digs and the excitement mounted with each room I went in. I saved the kitchen for last and to say it was magnificent is an understatement. I couldn't imagine an appliance this kitchen didn't have. To top it all off, the bar fridge was stocked with our favorite beverages.

I carried the suitcase into the luxurious walk-in storage space that Silver's architect had designed in conjunction with the master bedroom. I began by hanging up my dresses and several blouses. I turned to retrieve Jimmy's suit and nearly came out of my skin when an old man, wearing a Texas Rangers baseball cap, shuffled in. "Yes," I managed, "can I help you?" My mind raced as I uttered those words. This was private space and the front door to the suite had been closed and locked. Sally in disguise? An accomplice of hers? How do I call security?

"This the Redstone, Martinez suite?" the old guy mumbled, still moving in my direction, his head down, the beak of the hat covering his eyes.

My gun was out of reach, but a wooden clothes hanger was lying on a shelf perfectly positioned as a viable weapon. Old guys aren't always old guys. Trust nothing! If he takes one more step forward, drop him. You have only one chance, so make the swing count.

I planted my feet.

"Don't take another step closer," I ordered, backing away as far as I could, but remaining within range of the hanger.

His head started upward followed by his right hand.

My arm flew out, my fingers quickly closing on the hanger.

The stranger, sensing what I was about to do,

took a quick step backward just as the hanger passed through the space where his head had been a second earlier. His hat flew off and his head rose a good six inches.

"Jimmy!" Oh my God! I almost killed you. What are you—"

"I forgot how fast you are," my lover said. "Come hold me."

Recalling Lt. Malone's words and not yet certain Jimmy was really Jimmy, I stalled. "Your old man routine was perfect. You fooled me." I studied the man in front of me a moment and my resolve faded when I saw that both of his hands were devoid of weapons. I reached out. "Come hug me," I said, abandoning my concern that this man could very well be a phony. Stupid, I know. But some things just can't be helped.

Jimmy started toward me and something in his movement was off. I took a step back, still struggling to determine for a certainty if this was really the Jimmy I knew. If this was Badman Tex I'd still be in a world of hurt, "Aren't you forgetting something?" I hoped he would answer with our secret passcode routine. That wouldn't solve the personality shift, but it would definitely eliminate the scumbag possibility.

"If you insist." Jimmy answered. He then uttered the right phrase. I answered with my part of the protocol and he responded properly with his part. The sequence was spot on, which prompted him to say, "See, no permanent brain damage."

"No, Jimmy. All you just proved is that you're not the scumbag. Now talk to me about the trauma."

"Mostly drug induced. I may have bumped my head, but I was injected."

"You're not...not that guy Tex anymore?"

"Badman Tex. That was all drug induced. Drug's gone and so's he."

"A simple concussion then?"

"There's no such thing as a simple concussion. But if the question is how am I doing? Then the answer is, as well as can be expected. Not allowed to do a few things."

"Such as?"

"Jump from planes for starters."

"Not that you were planning to." But truth is I never know what Jimmy will do next. "What really?"

"Ride horses. Play football. Can't go out for the boxing team. They don't want another concussion."

We hugged for a long while and all the questions I had for him vanished. I didn't want the hug to end, and I certainly didn't want business, any business, getting between us.

Jimmy pulled me toward the bed and that's where we spent the next two hours lost in each other. "So," I finally asked, "what was the old man routine about? And don't tell me you were interviewing for the scumbag's job."

"Didn't want anyone knowing I'm here. Something's wrong in the hierarchy of our government. I don't know where the problem is, but I know there's a problem. Whoever's orchestrating this wants me...dead or at least out of the way. I prefer alive. So...so the fewer people who know I'm out of the hospital the better." He paused for a moment, then added, "Me showing up when unexpected could just possibly screw something up. And for operations at this level, timing is critical."

"You then must think it was staged? Being tossed."

"The lighting causing Lip Sync to buck may have been gratuitous. But I even doubt that. But for certain, me being injected had been planned."

"You certain you were drugged?"

"That's what the docs say. Traces of propofal and midazalam were found in my blood. Along with other stuff."

"Why?"

"So I wouldn't remember what happened."

"Propofal? I know that—"

"Michael Jackson died from an overdose. In his case it was used as a sleep aide. Listen, to be clear it is Tiny who thinks the drugs were injected before I came off the horse."

"For what reason?"

"That's what I can't figure. But it's clear someone wanted me out of the picture. I keep asking myself what threat am I? And to whom?"

"Your conclusion?"

"I saved Angel Garcia's life a few years ago and may have saved it again last week."

"You think Garcia is still in danger?"

"Maybe not the senator. But what about the president? Could it be they're planning to assassinate Trump and don't want me interfering."

"Why not just shoot you?" I asked, mostly joking but shuddering at the thought.

"Killing me would have set off a major investigation by at least two governments which possibly could have uncovered the plot, if there had been one. Being thrown from a horse, death or not, would fall under the radar for Secret Service concern."

"Your imagination is well...let's just say active. You have an assassin in mind?"

"If I did, I'd inform the Secret Service. But that's why I need to be at that dinner or whatever they're holding with Trump. Get a firsthand feel for who's there. Maybe something will jump out at me."

"That's a leap too far, even for you, Jimmy. You're not making sense." In truth, I was worried about my partner. What he said could be true, but it could also be a result of his hallucinations. "How do you plan to get on the invite list?"

"Silver took care of that an hour ago. I'm sitting at a table with Silver and some other big donors.

You'll be escorting Valencia Garcia."

"Know any names of those donors?"

"None at the table I'm at. But I was told the guy named Q will be in the audience."

"Full name's Quinton King. He's a lawyer, represents the families who own the mineral rights on NPI federal lands."

"That's some pretty rustic land up there. Hope they never drill."

"They can't if this mammoth jaw bone of Castro's proves to be genuine." I briefed Jimmy on my conversations with Hathcock and Castro, but I had the distinct feeling he had lost interest.

"Truth be told, Angella," Jimmy said when I stopped talking, the real reason we're invited to the reception is because Shadowy Sal is on everyone's mind. She's been impersonating you, Valencia, Malone and God knows who else. The best way for the Secret Service to take away those disguises is to have the real people right there where they can be accounted for."

"How does that work? She just uses some other disguise."

"Yes, but she needs to know ahead of time who's on the guest list and then make that person go AWOL. Each of the possible candidates for impersonation will be given a code word an hour before time. You won't get in without the code."

"Not foolproof, but a start," I agreed. "When's the reception?"

"Tomorrow. Don't know lunch or dinner. They're taking a tour of the Rio Grande in the morning, followed by a border rally in Brownsville. I think they're leaning toward a lunch reception here at the Riviera."

"I thought you told me to bring dinner clothes. Now I have all the wrong stuff."

"Moving target. Part of it is to keep everyone off guard, part of it is Trump won't commit until the last moment. For all I know it'll end up a breakfast meet with a few donors."

"If they're Trump donors why are they such a danger to him?"

"The target may not be our President. Might be Senator Garcia."

I thought for a moment of the possibilities. "The folks who drugged you in Jamaica are most likely highly connected to our government and in a position to move many tons of drugs, weapons, people, and who knows what else across our borders almost at will."

"And to the Mexican government—as well as the Jamaican government. My car runs on gas. Politicians run on money. Take away the gas and you know what happens to the car. Withhold the money, same result. Simple as that. I have no doubt Shadowy Sal—if she's involved—will know the time and the dress code far enough in advance to plan a proper disguise. But she'll have to arrive at the check point in enough time to monitor who arrives so as not to double up."

"As nimble as she is, that's a walk in the park."

"Let's just be certain we interrupt that walk," Jimmy responded. "If we're right in our assessment, Sal will be one of the last folks to enter the room. That should make it easier to spot her."

"Good luck with that. Who do you make for the target? Trump or Garcia?"

"Unless the senator has changed his position on the movement of contraband, I'd say he's more troubling to them than Trump."

"Granted," I reasoned, "but given Trump's border stance he's gotta be high on their hit list as well."

TWENTY-SIX

An hour later I was back in our condo, again loading clothes into a suitcase. This time I had no problem with my wardrobe, but Jimmy's another case. He hates clothes shopping and his motto, as he's explained dozens of times, is travel light and don't get fancy. That translates into only a few casual dress shirts and five dress whites. And the only reason he has so many white shirts is because of our new job where suits, or at least sports jackets, are considered proper attire. That meant a shopping spree in McAllen a few weeks back where we had picked up a tux, at Silver's insistence, as well as all the trappings. Jimmy had me pick out the ties for his jackets and I bought him eight, seven were stripped variations and the eighth was a gorgeous paisley that, among other colors, had purple splashed among the swirls. Jimmy had made a face, but it was my favorite and the one I now planned to take for him to wear for the Trump lunch.

On second thought I pulled out a more formal blue tie with a faint white line running diagonally across the face. More presidential, I told myself. All packed, I turned to leave. On a whim, I changed my mind and decided to take both the paisley and the blue tie and make Jimmy select. With the tie rod fully extended, I searched for the tie I wanted. Two times through the ties and I couldn't find the paisley. "You didn't!" I said aloud. "Tell me you didn't throw that tie out!"

I looked again, this time counting the ties. Discounting the one old tie he had hung at the back of the rack despite the fact I had told him to throw it out, I counted seven. With one in the bag, that meant one was missing. I started to call him but remembered he was napping. Instead, I counted his suits and shirts. In each case I came up with one missing. Now I knew who had been in our condo—and why.

Back at the hotel I told Jimmy what I had found. He was as baffled as I was. We kicked it around between us. Scumbag? Someone else? If so, who? Jimmy stands six feet tall. No one really knows Sal's actual height, but best guess is five-six at most, but among her many talents she's obviously also a good seamstress. But adjusting a suit made for a six-foot man to fit a woman six inches smaller was not an easy task. But what if she used stilts, or very high heels? No, heels were unlikely. But five—or six—inch stilts might be a possibility. Speculation was all we could muster, and a promise to each other to keep our guard up. A quick kiss and we each headed to separate entrances of the hotel, Jimmy again dressed as an old man.

There he was directly in front of me. Actually, I should say, there it was. The Gable mustache. But the guy was closer to five-ten than he was to six-two. That argued against this being the right guy. But how many Gable mustaches could there be? I walked toward him with every intention of engaging him in conversation. I had the advantage since I knew his business and I knew what I wanted to get from him and he had no idea who I was. But what really is his business? On the surface it was lawyer representing mineral interests in coastal Texas? On second thought, any advantage I thought I had was illusionary at best.

I was a yard away from Q when two men who I hadn't previously noticed stopped in front of him. They shouted greetings as though they had just been united after a long absence. Hands were shaken all around, backs were slapped, large smiles exchanged and an invitation was extended for Q to meet them out by the pool for a drink. I had never seen either of the men before this moment and was pretty certain they didn't live or work on the island.

"You here for the pep talk by the President?" One of them asked.

"Yea. Duty calls. Hey, that drink sounds good. You buying? Lead the way."

Jimmy would have put himself in the middle of the scrum and by now would have memorized a few new names and faces—and perhaps had a few new contacts. I satisfied myself with memorizing the faces.

When the man I had taken for Q was out of sight I studied the lobby for faces I knew, but saw only Secret Service faces. It wasn't that I actually knew any of the agents, but their eyes—eyes that never stopped moving—gave them away. Every person coming out of an elevator or going into one; every person coming or going to the snack bar, to the bookstore, to the jewelry shop, to the pool area, was scanned from head to toe.

At first I thought the bulge under their jackets was a weapon, but I was wrong. It was a camera. Everything that moved was being recorded. After a bad act they would know exactly what happened. But that was after the bad act. I wasn't certain how the camera helped prevent that bad act, but that wasn't my job. Thankfully.

* * *

We had dinner brought up to our suite and while we ate Jimmy confessed that the missing tie was in his car. Why hadn't he told me that immediately? My hair stood up. Who was this sitting opposite me?

I began the protocol routine. Jimmy looked at me funny, scowled, then simply grunted.

What action do I take if he's an imposter? I repeated my part of the protocol, hoping Jimmy would go along.

Again, he scowled.

I adjusted my legs in preparation of quick movement. Surprise, I knew was the key, but I just couldn't make myself act.

Then, as if a switch had turned, he answered with the proper response. My heart rate slowed. "Sorry, Jimmy. Isn't this the reason we set up the routine? Better safe, than dead. Isn't that what you taught me?"

"It is, most certainly. I was angry with myself for forgetting, that's all."

"So," I said, easing the tension, the tie's out in your car waiting for a chance to throw it out?"

"Not at all. You loved it, so I was going to try and see if I could buy a couple more like it. I just forgot about it. Gotta broaden my horizons. Isn't that what you keep telling me?"

"Glad to see even you can learn." But Jimmy forgetting things was most unusual—and troubling.

"Got a text from Secret Service earlier," he said, as if just remembering to tell me. "Tomorrow, no weapons. You'll be sitting on the dais next to Valencia. I'm now going to be with Angel. This is per his direct request."

"I thought he's pissed at you."

"Not after he saw the video of 'ole Sal cutting Conc's throat. He's again my best friend. Besides, even if he's pissed at me he'd want me next to him. Who better to stop a bullet with his name on it?"

"Not a comforting thought. Hey," I said, redirecting the subject, "what do you make of the fossil?"

"Funny you should bring that up. As far as I'm concerned, the mammoth, or whatever the hell that find is, is behind us. Deal with the painted pony is done, so no one cares about the kid Castro. So why should Silver care about whether or not they drill on North Padre Island?"

"Think Castro will have the find tested, carbon dated?"

"If he was a scientist, yes. But he'll do the smart thing—take their money."

"You're certain?"

"Sure thing."

"You willing to put money on it?"

"Can't take your money. Fossil's over at the SPI Historical Museum. Mounted on the wall."

"On the wall? In full public view?"

"Mislabeled as an early ox jawbone. Found here on the island."

"Museum know of the deception?"

"They only know that Q donated it to them and...and made a nice contribution. They believe Q is a collector. Who are we to dispel that notion? Of course, Silver won't insure it."

"Seems wrong is all."

"People have for many, many years parked all

manner of artifacts in museums around the world. Many a scientist has made his or her best find searching through dusty museum basements. One day that might happen here as well."

"Yea," I agreed, "but not until it's too late to stop the drilling. I suppose the ancient mammoth will have to wait a bit longer to be discovered."

"What's it been? A million years? What's another five or so?"

TWENTY-SEVEN

First thing in the morning I walked over to the History Museum to see the 'Early Ox Jaw' as it was now labeled. It might have been that I knew better, but the jaw did seem, even to my untrained eye, much too large to be an ox. But who am I to judge? Bet the first paleontologist to visit the museum raises hell though.

I turned and came face to face with the last person I had expected, Quinton King, known to Castro as Q. Actually, he was Jimmy's height, so that did put him at around six feet. The folks around him in the hotel lobby last night must have been very tall because Q had appeared so much smaller. That's exactly why witness descriptions are typically unreliable, especially in emotionally charged situations. As was the situation when I last saw him, his left hand was in his pocket.

His face was indeed slender, but not as slender as Castro had led me to believe. But the mustache was right. Clark Gable if ever I had seen one, slim and well trimmed. "Pardon me," I said as he moved past on his way to where the jaw was hanging, "but I'm a friend of Hermes Castro."

"Who?"

"Skinny kid. Name's Hermes Castro."

"I'm afraid I don't know any such person." Q stepped around me. I'd been dismissed.

To his back I called, "You are Q, are you not?" I wasn't sure where this was going, but I wasn't willing to drop it.

He took another step, then stopped and slowly turned to face me. "You have me at a disadvantage, I'm afraid. And just who are you?"

"Angella Martinez. As I said, I'm a friend of Hermes Castro."

"And I said, I don't—"

"You represent folks who own mineral rights on NPI. That ox jaw you're heading for was found—"

Q's eyes darted around, clearly relieved when he determined we were alone. "Come, let's go outside. Never know who's about." In the parking area, he said, "You say you're a friend of Castro. You a lawyer?"

"Do I look like one?"

"More like a cop."

"I was at one time employed in that capacity by this very city, SPI. Now...well, now I work for Great Southern Insurance."

"Investigator?"

"Yes."

"So you're the one moving into the penthouse. You and your partner Redstone."

"Didn't know it was the talk of the town. You know Jimmy?"

"In passing. He had business with my father back when my old man represented a good ol' boy who tended to overbill the great state of Texas. Didn't end well for my father's client. I was too young to be involved, but I recall my father re-marking, 'Ranger Redstone's a pit bull. Sinks his teeth in and nothing opens his jaw'. He said that on more than one occasion about your partner."

I couldn't dispute that pit bull is an accurate description of Jimmy. "Many occasions for one client. Or multiple clients?"

"Both."

"Your father must have been a real..." I was going to say operator. But instead, "I said, popular lawyer in south Texas."

"Indeed, that he was," Q said, pride showing in his otherwise hardened eyes. "That is until... until the Texas Rangers, led primarily by your partner, made overcharging the state, in the words of Redstone, 'a not-for-profit enterprise'."

"So now they've moved on to bigger and better things."

"I don't follow."

"Your father's clients, or perhaps their offspring, went from bilking the state to...to collecting royalties from mineral rights under government land."

"That characterization is most unfair." A nerve had been touched and Q struggled to hold his tongue. "Collecting on mineral rights is, as I'm certain you're aware, part of the deal that allowed the taking of those lands for a national park."

The ultimate bilk, a government sanctioned bilk at that, is what I wanted to say. But instead I offered an olive branch. "Is that the jaw bone in question?" I pointed toward the museum. "The one you discussed with the kid Castro?"

"I've had no discussions with anyone named Castro."

"What about a guy goes by Conc. Conquesta."

"I did have a discussion with someone named Conc."

"The subject of that discussion is what I've come here to see. Sign says it's a jaw from an ox. Castro, Conc. believes it's an ancient mammoth."

"Doubts make the world go round, Miss Martinez. You know that as well as anyone."

"If that jaw were the real thing, I mean over a million years old, then I can't imagine it remaining in this exhibit very long."

"My, my. What a low opinion of humankind you hold. We're not all evil."

"Comes with the territory," I responded, playing along with him.

"Like a doctor who only sees sick people, I suppose."

"Something like that."

"I can't verify that it's an ox, that's for experts to say. But I can tell you it's not what...what Conc thought either."

"You saying it's worthless?"

"Not saying that at all. Might be valuable as hell for all I know. But I do know it's not from an archeological site below the property I represent."

"That a fact?"

"That's a fact. No dispute over it either."

"Does that mean you'll be drilling up there soon?"

"I'm not privy to the time frame. But if you're asking can my clients drill if and when they desire, then the answer is certainly positive."

"Can I assume you're no longer concerned with Castro, or with the ox—or mammoth—jaw?"

"That's indeed a valid assumption. Good day Miss Martinez, I have a lunch to attend." Q turned toward the only other car in the lot.

Suddenly a thundering noise came out of nowhere and my hands flew to my ears just as a small Air Force jet roared across the island seemingly just high enough to not take the roof off the Riviera Hotel. Higher overhead the white contrails of three other jets vividly contrasted with the deep blue sky. A helicopter displaying the Coast Guard insignia was hovering a hundred yards off the beach, its side door open with a person sitting, feet dangling toward the water with an assault weapon across his lap. I was certain there were several patrol vessels in the bay as well. The President was either on site or about to be on-site and what I was seeing was only the tip of the iceberg.

Not knowing if we had heard the last of the jets or not, I allowed my hands to linger up by my ears for a long moment. Q did the same. That's when I realized the hand he kept in his pocket was a prosthetic hand. Born with it? Farm injury? Service related? Always more questions than answers. Jimmy would have asked, but I chose to remain silent. His infirmity was not important to anything I was working on.

Checking my watch, I said in answer to his lunch comment, "So do I as a matter of fact. I also have lunch plans." We were going to the same place, but he didn't have a need to know.

TWENTY-EIGHT

Jimmy had met on more than one occasion with the former President. But Trump, as everyone knew, was a different person altogether and I had no idea what to expect. Jimmy kept telling me to relax, but the more he said it the less relaxed I became. He received his code word while I was in the shower and left for his assignment, calling 'goodbye' to me as he left.

I quickly stepped out of the shower, dried off and went to my phone only to find a message instructing me to remain in the room until I received my code. Cells were banned from the meeting room so going down early would be a problem. I checked the time and was shocked to realize the banquet doors would close in six minutes.

I hurriedly pulled my clothes on and if I hadn't been nervous before, I certainly was now. I had a job to do protecting the Senator's wife and until I received the code I had no way to do it. My only hope at this point was that Valencia would be ushered in after everyone else was seated and I could go in later with her.

All dressed and no place to go. I felt like a high school senior whose prom date hadn't shown up. I kept glancing at the silent phone and again thought of calling Tiny but knew that doing so would prove futile. He had been uncharacteristically quiet and I wasn't even certain he was involved in this operation. But the one thing I did know was that he knew how to reach me. Could they be cutting me out? If so, why? And what could I—should I—do about it?

Two minutes until the doors closed.

One minute.

I jumped when the cell finally vibrated, almost dropping it on the ceramic floor. "Could you wait any longer?" I barked into the air. The screen, said, Three Green. Go down now. V running late."

I stepped into the hall and just as the door was about to close, my phone rang. I would have ignored it, but it was Tiny's special sound.

I raced across the room and caught it before it went to voice mail. Without preamble, Tiny said, "Chatter's being picked up. Secret Service's pressing to cancel lunch, but POTUS refuses to run his life around chatter because chatter's all he ever hears."

"Man's got a point," I said into a dead connection.

Waiting for an elevator when you have less than a minute is horrible. If I didn't know better, I'd say it took that elevator a good fifteen minutes to arrive and when it did the doors opened in ultra slow-motion.

A checkpoint, complete with airport-type scanners and uniformed Secret Service agents, armed and alert, had been established in the hall leading to the banquet room. "Doors have just closed," the nearest agent said. "I'm afraid you're a few moments too late." The man stretched his arm out to block my passage.

"I'm to be escorted in with Senator Garcia's wife." My command voice had eluded me, being replaced with something resembling a sheepish begging tone. "I need to—"

"Credentials please," the man then demanded, his eyes taking in every detail of my body.

"I fished for my Homeland Security cred pack only to find my Texas driver license and a Great Southern badge. I went with the license. At least that had my picture on it. Our official company badges had yet to be delivered.

"Miss Martinez you are indeed on the escort list. Code please."

In the panic to get down here in time, the code I had received less than two minutes earlier escaped me. Early Alzheimer's? I struggled a moment, then said, "Three." I knew there was a color, but I couldn't remember which one.

The man checked his electronic screen and looked up. "Picture matches, but the code—"

"Green," I blurted. "Three green." A plainclothes agent just beyond the checkpoint had pulled his jacket open and moved his hand so it rested on his weapon.

"You're good to go," the uniformed agent in front of me said. "Put your purse on the belt and walk through the scanner, arms overhead."

I did as instructed. The man with his hand on his weapon kept it there while a second uniformed agent ran a hand-held scanner up and down and across my body.

"I hope I don't look suspicious," I joked.

He wasn't having it. "Those are the most dangerous ones," he said, his expression never changing. "Okay, you can go in."

I assumed he was talking about the not suspicious folks being the most dangerous, but I wasn't going there.

I started down the mostly empty hallway, the only person in sight being another uniformed Secret Service agent. I turned a corner and found two suited men wearing earpieces and one woman whose ears were covered by a scarf, but whose eyes locked on me.

"Wait over there by the door," the woman commanded, "they'll be arriving in a moment."

"Thank you," I replied, hurrying to where she was pointing. I wasn't in position more than five seconds when I became aware of a commotion further down the hall in a direction away from the scanner. The two male agents, after glancing in that direction, both resumed their intent focus back toward the scanner.

The President's entourage suddenly appeared in the far corridor and passed into the banquet room through a door that was quickly closed after the entourage passed through. I caught only a brief glimpse of Mogul's head as he went by.

A woman, looking very similar to the woman standing not ten feet from me, approached from the direction of the scanner. Next to her walked the person I had found in the McAllen dressing room. Was this Valencia Garcia or Shadowy Sal? I had to devise a method of determining which it was.

When the woman who presented herself as Valencia approached, I held out my hand and said, "Good to see you again, Valencia. How did those shoes, the blue ones, work out?" I was referring to the conversation we had had on the drive from McAllen to SPI. This was my way of separating Valencia from Sal.

"Actually wore them yesterday to a dinner in Matamoras. Love them."

My guard went up because the shoes we were discussing were green, not blue. I now needed to confirm my concern before acting. What else had she bought? Nothing that I could recall. We approached the main table and Valencia's seat was directly beside the President on his left side.

Shadowy Sal, being left handed, only had to swing around to her right as if she were about to whisper something to the President, bring a knife up and his throat would be cut before even the fastest Secret Service agent could react.

There was no time for indecision. The nearest agent was directly behind the President. Valencia was between him and me. I held my arm high and pointed to Valencia. "She's an impos—"

"Green," Valencia said, her voice barely audible above the ambient level of the now full room. "You mean green shoes, don't you? I didn't buy blue—"

"—never mind!" I called to the agent, but not before he had alerted the full security team. "All clear," I said, hoping to quickly de-escalate what could prove to be an embarrassing situation, not only for me, but for the President himself.

The agent I had alerted stopped just behind Valencia seemingly ready to pounce at the first sign of any movement toward the President. Several other agents had their eyes on the President.

"Code!" he demanded. "Give me your code!"

"Three green," I responded, thankful I could recall it promptly.

"Clear," he said, obviously into a microphone I couldn't see.

Several men and three women, all of whom I had identified as Secret Service, immediately lowered their chins and said something into invisible microphones. If Mogul knew what had just taken place he made no indication. The whole incident had taken less than fifteen seconds, but I could imagine what had transpired around the world in that brief instant. Alerts to embassies, military command centers, attack war assets, you name it. My body shook as I took my seat beside Valencia. Like the President, she didn't appear to be aware of what had just occurred. Or perhaps she did and was skilled enough not to let on. People constantly in the public scrutiny become skilled thespians out of self-defense.

It's amazing how time slows, even seemingly stops, during a tragic and unexpected episode. I once interviewed a car accident victim where the car overturned pinning the passenger inside. The car had run off the road and turned upside down. She described how the trees slowly rotated counter clockwise until they seemed to be planted green end down, hanging from the earth. She told me about watching individual leaves and branches as they slowly moved through her field of vision, the slow motion of it all indelibly etched in her brain.

So I suppose it's not surprising that images of what had just transpired ran through my head as if I were watching a video in slow motion. I clearly saw the agent drop his head, his lips moving, perhaps uttering code words. I then witnessed him moving toward me, his hand reaching behind him. I saw his lips move again and I assumed he was now talking to me while his eyes alternated from their focus on Valencia to darting around the room. Then his body slowly straightening.

I saw the room as he must have seen it. People sitting at tables, making the expected moves, nothing unusual, no one preparing for hostile activity. A trained professional can see it all in an instant; a hand out of place, eyes focused on something other than what they are doing, facial expression at odds with their eyes or hands, any one of a thousand things out of whack.

Replaying the scene in my mind, some things didn't happen that should have. Vividly remembering my DHS training, this very situation had been scripted. A guest on the dais sitting next to POTUS suddenly is thought to be a potential assassin. Once the alert code is issued the actions taken by every agent in the room are prescribed and rehearsed until they are second nature. I know the drill, it was trained into me. And that drill, the drill designed to save the Mogul's life, did not just occur.

TWENTY-NINE

About halfway through lunch, my agitation still running high, my eyes continued to scan the room. I now focused on Q, sitting at a table with one of the men I had seen him meet in the lobby yesterday afternoon. Q was doing nothing out of the ordinary. He was spreading butter on a piece of bread with his right hand, his left was in his lap as I would have expected it to be. His head was down apparently concentrating on his bread plate. All seemed right.

A few minutes later waiters filled the room serving lunch and nothing seemed to be out of line. Soon the mayor walked to the speaker's podium positioned at the side of the main table. After welcoming the President to the city of South Padre Island, he introduced the SPI and Port Isabel council members who were present. Port Isabel being the community at the mainland side of the causeway bridge. Then the mayor introduced several county officers and judges, a few other local mayors, and then he said, "I'm told the President will not be speaking today, his schedule doesn't permit the time. But he has agreed to spend what time he has listening privately to what you have to say about anything—including U. S. Mexico relations, the wall, the economy, anything at all. This is your opportunity to tell him directly what you think. We'll be doing this table by table. Secret Service has requested—hear that as requires—that only one table be up at a time. So we'll go in order beginning with table two over there in the far corner and following the numbers on each table. Unless it's your table's turn, please remain seated. Okay. Now table two."

The six men at table two then proceeded to walk over to where we were seated and lined up directly in front of Valencia waiting for their brief moment with the President.

The line actually moved much faster than I had thought, with the President shaking hands across the slim table, listening, saying a word or two and then turning his head to the next in line.

Table three stood and followed behind table two. This group was mostly women who Trump seemed to spend more time with. But even then, the line kept moving and soon table six moved past, followed by table seven.

The mayor then pointed to table eight where Q was seated. That table was evenly split among men and women. Lawyer Ayers was now in line, together with Griff and Joni from the Paragraphs On Padre bookstore. They were followed by, of all people, Joy Malcom, who couldn't possibly be a Senator Angel Garcia supporter, nor a Trump fan given that she was in league with a Mexican drug lord. Malcom was followed by Q's friend, the man I didn't know, then by Q himself.

Q's eyes were focused on the floor, his mustache standing out clearly against his smooth face.

But the picture was wrong.

What made it wrong?

Was I paranoid?

I was edgy from my near disaster an hour earlier with Valencia and perhaps still experiencing the aftermath of a massive adrenalin rush.

Is it the mustache that's causing my edginess?

No, not the mustache. What then? His cheeks might be a bit rosier than they had been earlier in the day when I saw him at the Historical Museum, but that could be the result of sun—or, more likely a few pool-side drinks.

He was now directly in front of me. I leaned across the table. "Hello, again," I said.

Q glanced up. "Angella," he mumbled and quickly resumed his study of the floor, his right hand stuffed in his pants pocket.

"Angella," he had said! Adrenalin again kicked in good and strong. I stood, focusing on the scene outside the museum just a few hours earlier. He had referred to me then as, "Miss Martinez". Why now call me Angella? Far more important, the out of place fact now screamed at me.

During lunch the prostatic hand had been his left. That was consistent with the man now in front of me buttering his bread with his right hand as I had seen him do. His left hand had been hidden under the table. Now it was his right hand that was out of view!

But if Sally was impersonating Q she would never get such an easy fact wrong. With her skill, she nails all the marks, lines, imperfections, nuances. That's what makes her impossible to stop, her perfection. So why would she...

"Crap!" I said to myself, that's how she got the knife into the hall. It's most likely ceramic so the scanner wouldn't see it. Inside a fake hand that consists of nothing but a thin cover, maybe even lead lined, to block any image of the knife.

Agents, even trained folks, would perhaps know about the prosthesis, but wouldn't focus on which hand it had replaced. She was proficient with her left and the risk of screwing it up if she used her right to cut the President's throat was greater than the risk of being uncovered because she wore the prosthesis on the wrong hand.

Q was almost directly in front of the President. I glanced back at the Secret Service agent I had communicated with earlier. I wasn't certain he'd respond again, but that wasn't the issue at this moment because his full attention was on the person directly in front of, and speaking to, the President.

There was no way I could divert him. But even if I could capture his attention, it was already too late for agent intervention. Q was moving into position, not three steps from the President. Her right hand was now hanging limp at her side, clearly showing the prosthesis. That would then make it natural for her to shake with her left hand, which, as it moved in the President's direction would not trigger concern because the motion was within the ambit of expected movements. The knife would be concealed until the very last moment when it would flash out from her sleeve and cut the President's jugular, all in one smooth motion.

As before, the motion slowed as Q's left hand passed directly in front of me, his—or should I say Sal's—sleeve covering what I knew to be a knife. I thought about throwing my body between Valencia and the President, but the space was too narrow and the angle was wrong. Even more critical, the timing wouldn't work.

It was now or never. If I waited to see the actual knife I'd be too late. I knew all too well how fast Shadowy Sal's hands were. I'd witnessed video of several of her killings, never once, except in slow-motion replay, did I see the full movement from pocket to neck to dead. She was just too fast.

Wait or go? "You can't overthink these situations," Jimmy had scolded me on several occasions. "Use your training—and your instinct. You can't apologize to a corpse for acting too late. You can only be wrong if you fail to act when you should have. The reverse is never true."

This one's for you, Jimmy. I planted my feet, flexed my knees, threw my arms straight out over my head and dove across the table. Not aimed for Q, but for POTUS himself.

THIRTY

I was out of my chair the instant I saw Angella stand. I can't say I knew what she was about to do because I didn't. But I had been watching Q approach the main table and thinking about ancient times, another life long ago when I visited his father up on the family ranch. Q was a boy then and had fallen off a tractor which then proceeded to mangle his arm. He hadn't yet been fitted with a mechanical hand and he showed me what had happened. The stump was still raw-looking and swollen and hard to look at, even though I had seen more than my fair share of amputees as an Army Ranger. The boy wanted to know if not having a hand would prevent him from becoming a Texas Ranger when he grew up.

What do you tell a ten-year old boy who now only has the use of one hand? "Not at all, son," I remember saying, "just so long as you can draw with your right, you'll be just fine. Matter of fact,

I've seen major league baseball pitchers with one hand. Pitch with their glove under their arm and after they let the ball fly they put the glove on ready to field. A bit difficult, but anything's doable if you put your mind to it."

Draw with your right, I kept repeating to myself, draw with your right. But that couldn't be how it was because this guy's right hand was lost, not his left. Memory's going, I told myself.

Memory might be going, but my visual memory remains clear. I see the little boy with no left hand. That was an image burned into my brain and I knew it to be accurate. If there is one thing that triggers me it is inconsistency, inconsistency in any aspect sends a jolt down my spine and focuses my mind as nothing else can.

I was clearly on edge, so when Angella made her move it triggered my pent-up energy and I went for Q, not because I knew what was about to happen, but because the scene was wrong and I couldn't idly stand by.

I hit Q shoulder to shoulder and drove him to the floor on the other side of the table. I had thrown myself with such abandon that I flew over the table, landing on Q. No sooner had we hit the ground than the barrels of several service weapons were pointed directly down at us.

One of the agents stomped her foot firmly onto Q's wrist just above where my fingers were locked. The other had his knee on Q's side. If Q had moved an inch I suspect more than one bullet would have ended his life. A third agent stood three feet away, his Glock pointed at my chest.

"On your feet Redstone," the female agent demanded. "We got this from here. Move slowly."

"This is an imposter," I said, making certain the Service knew who we were dealing with. "I believe it will turn out her name's Shadowy Sal. Interpol has her as a code red. She's dangerous."

"They know exactly who she is," a voice from the past called over my shoulder.

I turned to see Interpol Agent Lillie Holland standing not two feet away. Lillie was the world's foremost expert on Floratine Maldos, the woman lying on the floor beneath me. "What are you—"

"Not here. Over there in private." She motioned to a far corner. What was coming next, I couldn't imagine. But my choices were limited. Actually, non-existent.

"The President?" I asked when I turned to face Holland. "Was he—"

"Your Trump's perfectly fine."

"What actually—"

"Something caused Maldos to stand down. She may have a blade, but she never actually had it in her hand. But it's clear that had Ole Sal deployed a blade and without Martinez's intervention, Trump's carotid would have been severed and Pence would now be President."

"How's Angella?"

"About to be loaded onto Marine One. Two doctors are with her."

"I thought you said there was no blade. I don't—"

"Charade at this point. This was sanctioned very high up and that person, or persons, would have received the initial code red. The plan is to confuse the leader and just possibly a screw up, a hasty action taken, something that will allow his or her capture will occur. A long shot, but worth the chance. We need a major mistake to catch the big one."

"But the all-clear would have gone out immediately. The world is thrown into chaos if news of an assassination goes out."

"Very true. But the news isn't getting out to the public, just to those in command."

"How they going to pull that off. What with everybody packed full of electronics."

"Signals are being blocked from this room. Nothing's going out except what those in charge want out."

"How do you know all this? You're Interpol, not—"

"I'm here for Maldos. You're right, this is Secret Service all the way, but I've been read in. That's why I'm wearing the ear piece. Keeping up with the moving parts."

"I need to be with Angella."

"That'll indeed be a good trick, Redstone, even for you. The USNS Mercy is standing by off-shore. Heard a moment ago that's where they're taking her."

"The Mercy?" A medical ship stationed a few miles from the President while he's on the U. S. Mexico border is not a bad idea. Knowing how well the President is protected I wondered how much of this had been anticipated. I was getting jittery from the adrenalin and started walking toward the door. It took a moment before I realized the doors were still closed and no one was being allowed out. Truth was, I had nowhere to go anyway, except perhaps upstairs to our apartment where I knew I'd pace for hours waiting to learn the fate of my lover.

Suddenly, despite the chaos in my head—or perhaps because of it—the pieces fell into position. I looked around to find Holland who was now in deep conversation with the agent who had removed me from Sal. I charged in their direction. The agent, seeing me coming, quickly walked away.

When I was inches from Holland, I said, "You being here means Secret Service knew there would be—"

"Please, Jimmy Redstone, consider your surroundings and lower your voice. You are, indeed, correct. An assassination attempt from Maldos was anticipated. As you know, Interpol has a vested interest in apprehending her and putting an end to her murderous activities around the world."

"But," I added, the adrenalin still pumping, "there's something even bigger going down. Secret Service would never knowingly allow Mogul to be injured, so if everyone knew there could be an attempt on his life it follows that Angella didn't really save him. Am I correct so far?"

"Indeed you are. He was wearing body armor," Holland confessed. "There's no reason for you to have noticed, but his shirt collar was bespoke to run high up his neck. We know Sal's knife attack pattern all too well. And we know her reach ability. From the way the tables were positioned she could not have possibly positioned the knife above the collar. You're spot on. Angella couldn't have saved him because there was nothing to save him from. But she did provide a cover for why he's not dead. And that is a major factor. That's what I was saying before. The top gun, Alpha, may now be confused and this could lead to an error, a mistake. The intelligence community must capitalize on that mistake."

That caught me by surprise, but it did mesh with my thoughts about being drugged and thrown from a horse. But focusing on the present, I asked, "So how'd Sal even get in? Everyone had a code. How'd she get past the checkpoint?" Before Holland could answer, the full scope of the operation hit me. "Oh, shit! Someone high up wanted her in! Someone did something that allowed it to happen."

A sudden rush of movement behind me indicated that the doors were now open. Indeed, Holland said, "Now that we can leave, follow and stay close. We don't have time to waste."

"Where are we going?"

"To watch some telly my good man. Have a look see what clues the electronic birdies can provide."

THIRTY-ONE

The control trailer was parked behind the hotel and despite the fact that it appeared generic with its dull gray paint, the inside was impressive with plush swivel chairs and banks of monitors, control panels, and glass work surfaces. It was partitioned into several sections connected by a narrow passageway down one side of the trailer. I didn't immediately see any live video feeds so I assumed that area was private, or there was a separate trailer for current activity. The later was probably more accurate.

Holland and I were motioned to sit in swivel chairs that were positioned in front of a wall of monitors. As soon as we were seated a woman in navy-issue jeans and a starched white shirt, one of several darting about, handed me what looked to be a typical TV remote. "The monitors in front of you are numbered," she instructed us, "but for your purposes you'll only need the top two rows numbered one through six. Press the number of the monitor you want to control, then press enter." She paused to check that we were following, then continued, "You can fast forward, or go back, slow, zoom, the typical stuff. But you can also mark portions that will then be available on a separate feed on monitor seven. Just use the button labeled 'mark'. The time stamps and original camera info will be preserved for each marked portion. Any questions?"

We both shook our heads.

"Okay then, you're good to go." The young woman was friendly, but her manner radiated business. "Oh, I forgot. Press the 'position' button and the metadata for each feed will display. I don't usually advise showing the metadata as it tends to mask things that could be of importance to you."

"Thanks," I said.

"Just click the call button at the bottom if you need me," she said before disappearing down the narrow hallway. A few moments later, the six monitors she had pointed to flickered alive with video running on each in what seemed to be endless loops.

One of the monitors showed the front door to the hotel. Another was the security checkpoint. The other four were various angles within the meeting room itself.

"Mind if we begin with the security checkpoint?" I asked Holland. "See what we can see there?"

"Go for it," the Interpol agent responded, seemingly content that I had taken control.

I touched the two button followed by enter as instructed. I then found a beginning button and pressed it. Sure enough, the image on the second screen went blurry for an instant and then showed a time stamp reading 11:38 in its upper right corner.

Nothing unusual jumped out as person after person passed under the monitor and was waved through the checkpoint. I paid close attention as Q approached and walked through the scanner without providing a security code. Obviously, he was not a person they thought the scumbag would impersonate. I noted that the prosthesis was on his left hand as I had remembered it. He was then patted down and instructed to proceed. Since we didn't have audio, everything we were seeing was in pantomime.

I watched myself pass through at 12:03. We had been told to be in the holding room no later than 12:10. The President was set to enter the main room at 12:23.

Up to this point nothing had caught my attention, but then again, I had no idea what I was looking for. I paused the video. "What, exactly, do you think we'll see?" I asked Holland.

"That's the cornerstone question is it not? Maldos is slick. We would have had her in custody long before now if she but left a crumb. Best I've ever seen, by far. Always a new MO. And always a few steps ahead of our best agents. She's single-handedly sent more than one career down the loo."

Back to the video. At 12:12 Captain Remington Franco, wearing his crisply ironed white uniform shirt approached the scanner. Words were exchanged and while our video was without sound I was certain that had we wanted the audio it was available. I pressed the 'mark' button just as Captain Franco reluctantly withdrew his weapon, checked the safety, and handed it to the same uniformed Secret Service agent who processed me through the checkpoint. He was then waved around the scanner. I started to say something to Holland but was interrupted as Angella appeared on the screen. For an instant it appeared that she would be forcefully prevented from entering, with one of the agents actually putting his hand on his own weapon. Because Shadowy Sal had impersonated Angella so well on several occasions I was alert and hit the mark button. I actually didn't know if I was watching Angella or the imposter.

Then Angella—or Shadowy Sal—was allowed through. I hit the mark button a second time to end the portion I was interested in.

No one came behind Angella. The video began from the beginning. "See anything," I asked Holland, "I certainly can't be certain I did."

Actually I had seen something of interest, but wasn't yet ready to share.

"Redstone, we both know Maldos came through that check point. But neither of us know how. She's that good. What did you mark?"

"Captain Franco and Angella. I think the problem with Angella was she might have been slow with her security code."

"That's my take as well. Monitor six is focused on Q's table. Let's observe six next."

Captain Franco sat to Q's right, but the two had no interaction. Q was talking to the man on his left, a man I didn't know, but one that I recognized from the video of him passing through the scanner. A few minutes later I hit the 'mark' button a second time. Clearly, Q had his left hand in his lap and was holding his water glass with his right, as I would have expected.

While Q's head was turned to his left Captain Franco leaned close, as if to catch Q's attention. Instead, his hand passed over Q's water glass and just as quickly moved away. I pressed the 'mark' button to end this marked portion.

A few moments later Q took a sip of water and I again hit the 'mark' button almost certain of what I'd see next.

"What'd you notice?" Holland asked. "Something seems to have captured your attention."

"Unless I miss my guess, Captain Franco spiked Q's drink. Q should get wobbly about—"

"Captain Franco! Never! I know the man and he's—"

Q's head fell forward and would have hit the table had Franco not caught him.

"Chief's helping him up," Holland said,

"What's this about?"

"Now we know how Sal got in. Walked right around the scanner. That's not the Police Chief in this video, it's your Maldos in all her glory." I marked the video to end the section as Franco led Q away from the table. "Unless I'm way off mark, within a few minutes Q will return to his seat and Captain Franco will remain out of the room.

In exactly six minutes what I had anticipated took place.

"By the grace of God!" Holland exclaimed, "You're a corker all right! So the real Q is cold cocked in a loo?"

"Or worse."

"So where's the real Captain Franco in all this?"

"Bet we find an island emergency somewhere that required his attention. Sal and her handlers wouldn't want two Captain Franco's turning up at the check point."

"Of course you're right. But why the ruse? The phony Chief could have just strolled up to your President and done the nasty deed."

"Now that's the question of the day. I'm thinking they were afraid that if the phony police chief was the assassin then too many questions would have been raised, such as, how was the real chief actually diverted, who set it up, how'd they get the timing right? Someone didn't want those questions asked and the best way to avoid focusing on Franco is to not make him appear to be the villain. Investigating how Franco was diverted could possibly lead back to the mole, if there is such a person. With the double switch the road back to the source is vague at best."

"And how did Maldos obtain the Franco's code?"

"Whoever was passing out codes gave it to her, I suppose. Or perhaps because he's the Police Chief he didn't require a code."

"Mind spilling how you knew Q was drugged?"

"As I said, Q's left hand was severed as a young boy. The reason I dove on him—her—when she was in line is because the scene was wrong. You can see on the video his left hand is useless as he's being escorted, mostly carried, out by the Chief. In line, the prosthesis was on the right hand, so I studied the video to learn when the switch occurred. I knew what to look for. When Q returns to the table the damaged hand is his right. Maldos needed her left for accuracy."

"At least now the mystery is solved. I hope they lock her up where she can't escape. She's done that a few times already. Before I leave, let's get an update on Angella. She slammed into Mogul pretty hard." Holland hit the call button and almost immediately the Navy techie appeared beside us.

The young woman listened to Holland's request for an update on Angella, her eyes saying nothing. When Holland finished, the techie said, "I'll do what I can," then disappeared down the corridor.

Holland's phone buzzed, she studied the screen a moment, then looked up. "Your theory's been confirmed. Captain Franco was never at the hotel. Around eleven-thirty a call came in identifying a person wanted for murder as being on the island. Turned out to be a false alarm. That knock about your head did nothing to disturb your mental facilities, I note."

The main monitor came alive and instead of images of people sitting at tables having lunch, or waiting in line to shake the President's hand, the screen revealed a ship with several landing pads spaced across its massive front deck. A copter, which I assumed to be Marine One, was hovering over one of the pads while two Marine guards stood at attention. I also assumed the copter was landing, but it could just as easily have been taking off.

A moment later the copter was down on the pad and the rear cargo door flew open. Two men dressed in white ran up the ramp and disappeared into the belly of the craft. They quickly emerged, a transport gurney between them. On the gurney lay a person covered from the shoulders down by a blue sheet. The camera zoomed in to reveal the person to be Angella.

The gurney stopped, a man who I immediately recognized, appeared from the shadows and leaned down as if whispering something to Angella. My partner then immediately looked directly into the camera, a lopsided smile spreading across her face. She wiggled her left hand free of the cover and gave a thumbs up. Her lips puckered into what I choose to believe was a kiss. This all looked very real and it was hard to accept Angella had not been hurt.

"Okay," I said to Holland, "learning how Sal got in the meeting room is doing nothing to push the ball up the hill. Tell me what's really going on."

"Actually, that's way above my pay grade, Red-stone. I got what I came for so I must say it's been peachy working with you again." She touched my shoulder. "Until the next time I have the pleasure my dear sir."

"You can't be serious!" I snapped, refusing to believe Holland was about to walk away. "You can read me in, you know."

"Sorry, mate, lips are sealed. I'm sure you recognized your pal Levi Ben-Yuval out there on the medical ship. He's coordinating efforts, perhaps he'll include you in his plans."

"Means Israel's involved. How bad is it?"

"Means Tiny's been removed. Your government is drawing the perimeter tight. They have no idea who to trust, so the fewer the better."

"What's that mean?" Her comment set my mind spinning. Was Tiny the mole? Was he working with the mole? The questions were coming faster than I could digest them.

"I'm not the person authorized to brief you," Holland said as she turned toward the exit door, "but I can assure you, Angella is just hunky-dory."

"So, who do I get briefed by?" I demanded.

"Who's going to..."

"Slow your engines my dear man. One of your mates will be along." Holland blew a kiss. "Cheers," she called, and was gone.

I paced the tiny space trying to figure out what Israel had to do with the attempted assassination of our President. Ben-Yuval's interaction with Angella clearly signaled that Israel and the U. S. were working this together. Didn't sound or feel right. But when spooks are involved nothing ever feels right.

THIRTY-TWO

A small man entered the space from the corridor where I had last seen the techie. He wore glasses that belonged on the face of a man twice his size. "Let's get down to it, Redstone. I'm Secret Service Deputy Director Gladstone and as you very well know there has been an assassination attempt on Mogul. He escaped unharmed, but—"

"As per plan," I interrupted, showing this guy I wasn't one to be pushed around.

"What's that mean?"

"Means it was a pantomime. She didn't have a knife."

"Oh, she had a knife alright! Your information is...shall we say, stale."

I studied Gladstone a moment, trying to recall what I had learned about him over the years. Straight-shooter, dedicated, efficient, no-nonsense, no-BS, tough, short-fuse, were adjectives that popped up. I decided to play it straight. "Secret Service knew an attempt was going to be made. And they knew it wouldn't succeed."

"Don't know where you got that intel, but it's highly classified! You still have your clearance, so keep it that way."

That sounded very much like a threat. "But—"

"But, as a matter of fact, the perp did have a knife, but...but she never took it out of her pocket. We speculate she received a stand-down order, but not confirmed. Enough. I don't have time to waste on BS and niceties! You understand me?"

I was on his territory and he had just told me who was boss. This was one of those times it was wise to go with the flow. "Yes, Sir!" I snapped. I threw him one of my mock salutes to save my dignity, at least in my own mind.

"What I'm about to depart is also highly classified. As I said, you still have Top Secret Clearance, so if you repeat any of this to anyone I promise you will disappear. You understand me?"

"I understand." That threat wasn't just lip service, this man meant what he said. That was another adjective I now recalled; ruthless. I had no doubt he had the assets to make it happen. To the public it would appear as though I fell down a flight of steps, or stepped in front of a bus, or perhaps got mugged in the park, my wallet gone to show it was a robbery gone bad. Or perhaps lost at sea—or out of an airplane. Or tossed from a horse. Or, as the Russians do, a little poison added to my morning coffee. The possibilities were endless.

Gladstone glared at me a moment before saying, "As you know, the assassination attempt was thwarted, not necessarily by your partner, but because it was apparently called off."

"But yet you wanted those in the chain of command to think it had occurred. Isn't that—"

"Okay, wise ass, you brief me then! Go for it!"

Never one to duck a direct challenge, I responded, "Someone, or some group, high up is running a counter operation and you don't have a clue who it is."

The little man didn't blink or miss a beat. "You know who they are?"

"Certainly not."

"Then shut up and listen! You're right about us not knowing who's running it. But you're wrong about not having a clue. It's taken a lot longer than we'd like, but...and this goes no further than between you and me...it's someone very near the top...or at the top. We have it down to three possibilities."

"Political appointment or permanent?"

"Good question. People at the top are almost always political appointments. But...but for the Secret Service it's become customary to select its very top people from career folks. Because there is reason to believe this person infiltrated long ago, we're leaning toward career."

"Secret Service?"

"It's becoming more and more certain that Service operations are being compromised by someone very knowledgeable about operational plans, someone with unfettered and untraceable access to the computer systems. Suspicions do lead us to the Service. But... but there are anomalies."

"For example?"

"I'm not at liberty to brief you on all of this, but like this attempt today. Chatter had it on, but it was actually off. How it was called off we yet don't know." Gladstone paused for several seconds debating how much more information to depart. "We are pressed for time here, Redstone, but the thing is, it was on until...until the very last minute. Your informant was spot on, Maldos had a knife, but it was tucked away when...when your partner intervened. I'll tell you this, had Maldos had the knife in her hand your partner...well she'd be lucky to have any of her fingers at this point."

"I suppose the false murder suspect call to the local police department came from Alpha. But truth be told, anyone could have called that in."

"Wasn't just a simple call, Redstone. A BOLO was delivered for a murder suspect along with an alert from the causeway license plate detector. Professionally done I must confess." Gladstone fell silent, walked to the wall, turned and came back, his brow wrinkled as if he was contemplating his next move—or his next statement.

"The timing of the Police Chief diversion had to be spot on and for a valid enough reason to have prevented Franco from appearing at the Trump meeting."

"This may have been a dry run, but I assume you believe the ultimate plan is to assassinate Mogul."

Gladstone didn't immediately answer. For a man in a hurry he was taking his time, sizing me up I suspected. "This wasn't the first attempt on Mogul's life," he finally confessed. "With a group, or even an individual, as determined as Alpha is to destroy him, I'm afraid it's only a matter of time until they succeed. Alpha has access to our communication channels, so a false order or misdirection at a critical moment is all it will take. I've instituted several failsafe mechanisms but... but we're only as good as the scenarios we can envision. As you know, Maldos is the best ever at what she does. I believe Alpha is even better. The fact we've remained a step ahead of him is a blessing—a blessing we have every reason to believe is about to turn negative."

"I'm here for a reason. Why?"

"Two reasons. Primary, you are now outside the government and your movements are, shall we say, less prescribed than they would be if you were still with DHS."

"And the second?"

"At this very moment," the Deputy Director began, obviously uncomfortable discussing this with me, "there are twenty-one commercial aircraft over international waters heading for the United States. One of them could have an ISIL terrorist aboard." He studied my face a moment, before continuing, "Problem is, we don't know which one."

I had no idea why I was being given this info, nor what they thought I could do with it. I certainly wasn't an expert on anything ISIL.

Gladstone continued, "Thanks to our Israeli friends we have eliminated twelve."

"That leaves nine," I replied, showing off my math ability and very little else.

Gladstone rolled his eyes.

"We also believe with a high degree of reliability that the terrorist is carrying a chemical weapon of mass destruction."

"There's more to this. Give it to me."

His eyes hardened. "Redstone, you need to appreciate that destructive weapons are at this very moment locked onto each of those nine aircraft. ISIL was planning on Mogul being dead at this point and our response efforts being confused enough to put rationality aside. They expect us to shoot down all twenty-one flights. Their loss: One hapless terrorist who will spend the rest of eternity dancing with virgins, or some such rot."

"A major propaganda win for them," I acknowledged, "not to mention the loss, at our own hands, of perhaps, four thousand innocent civilians."

"We are murderers if we act, and if we don't

one of our cities could be devastated by the release of poison gas."

The implication of what Gladstone just said took a moment to settle in. If the ISIL attack was timed to coincide with the death of the President then the timing of this assassination attempt had been planned long in advance and supports the theory that someone high-up on the inside coordinated the attempt. "Is it really an option to shoot down commercial flights?" I asked, not wanting to believe what I expected as the answer.

"I'm not prepared to discuss our military options, other than to say I hope we don't get to that point."

"How accurate is the nine number? How do you know there are not say fifty terrorists on their way here?"

"Intelligence is always a best guess. Israel's current best guess is nine. Well, actually that's not exactly accurate. Of the twenty-one we identified, Israel has confirmed twelve are free of terrorists. I'm not at liberty to explain how that number was generated, but it's the number we're officially prepared to go with. But, privately, I agree with you, there could be others. But—"

"In for a dime, in for a dollar. What's the but?"

"But it strikes me that if Alpha, or someone, called off the assassination then the ISIL attack would also have been cancelled."

"Sounds right," I agreed. "But you need to double check?"

"Spot on."

"And that's why I'm here now," I said, anticipating what was coming next, but clueless how
they planned to use me. "So how can I help?"

"Actually, simple. As I said, we're confident—
again only as confident as intelligence ever is—that
the person now on that plane carrying the poison
gas was in the car when title to that painted pony
was exchanged."

"But...but I was drugged. I didn't—"

"Long shot. But we must try everything. I understand the drugs are out of your system. Doctors
tell me they believe you have full memory. I'm
about to show you pictures of men we've identified as possibilities. They're all known terrorists."

This didn't make sense. "Listen, Director, I
respect you and what you're doing, but from the
looks of what you told me, the U. S.—or perhaps
Israel—had surveillance on the transfer. That's
where I'd look."

"You're a fool if you think we haven't gone
down that rabbit trail, Redstone! The person of
interest was inside the car and the windows were
covered with a polarizing film. Or—"

"Or, what?"

"That storm rolled in all too fast. My guess is
the reason the assassination was called off was
because the terrorist—or terrorists—never made
it to the ranch."

"Before we do this I must tell you my memory

is still foggy at best. I don't recall—"

Gladstone glanced up at the digital wall clock. "Time's of the essence now. Need to get on with the identification before it's too late. Truth is, you're all we have." He pressed a button below a monitor and it immediately came alive, this time with a Semitic face filling the screen.

"No," I said, "if the question is, have I ever seen this guy before, the answer is not that I recall."

"No time for the disclaimers, Redstone. Yes or no will do."

Another face. "No."

Another face. Another no.

This went on for seventeen more faces. All close ups. Perhaps too close. All answered no.

"Last one, Redstone," Gladstone announced, as if I was about to flunk some mythical test.

The last face came up and without hesitation I pointed my thumb down.

"Hell," the director exclaimed, "not a single one!"

"We take that as a no," came a voice from the ether.

"Joint Chief's," Gladstone explained, referring to the new voice. "First plane enters U. S. airspace in eight minutes. They need to decide on a course of action."

"Redstone," a different voice said, "This is General Richards. I don't suppose it would help if we replayed those faces for you."

Richards was the Chairman of the Joint Chiefs and perhaps the most powerful military person in the world. "No, sir," I said. "But if I may —"

"Go ahead, Redstone, floor's yours."

"If you have video of my time up at Conquesta's spread we can match faces against those on the flights."

"Negative! Tried that. Next?"

"Display for me video of each plane's passengers and I'll try to recall if any of them was up there with me. Or perhaps I saw them while I was in Jamaica. Start with the plane closest in."

"Worth a try," Richards responded. "We have nothing else better to go on at this point."

Within thirty seconds faces began coming across the screen. I ignored the kids and women because I saw neither up in the mountains. "We can speed this up if you can adjust the software, skip the children," I said, implementing my version of profiling. "And take out anyone over sixty."

Almost immediately the old and young disappeared. As the faces came by I couldn't help but realize that every one of the people I was seeing could soon be dead. My job was to keep them alive. Disasters are never easy, but when the victims become real people, with real faces, the heart — at least my heart — takes over and the task becomes infinitely more difficult.

Concentrating on the faces on the screen forced

me to focus even harder on my time up in the Jamaican mountains. The drugs had wiped my memory clean of everything after a certain point and no matter how hard I tried I could recall nothing. But events before that point were beginning to come back, but in reverse order beginning with the drive up to the Conquesta ranch.

Then an image of...of a head...a head behind a car window. But...but the face was missing. Not so much missing, but rather...in shadows.

What about shape?

Nothing focused.

The images on the screen ended.

"So, Redstone, where are we?" the voice in the ether asked.

"Sorry, sir, but not one face looked familiar. You can run them again, but—"

"No time. Let DD Gladstone know immediately if anything comes to you."

The screen went dead.

I turned in time to see the Deputy Director disappear through the door leaving me alone with memories that had rushed back into my head of the drive from the coast up into the Jamaican mountains.

THIRTY-THREE

I recall that within twenty minutes of climbing into the van at the Montego Bay resort I was ill at ease. Not because of anything that had been said, but because of the deteriorating weather conditions. Compounding my agitation was the driver's enthusiasm for showing us the island tourist attractions. His guided-tour of the beaches and resorts continued as the car followed what was marked as Highway A1.

When we approached Ocho Rios he offered to stop. We declined that offer, as well as his offer to drive us up to see one of Jamaica's famous waterfalls. We were assured the view was spectacular and had long been a popular tourist attraction. We also declined his suggestion that we stop for drinks at the Sandals resort. "Beyond Sandals," the driver-guide had said, "the road turns inward and weaves up the mountain with no place for you to stop and...and refresh yourselves."

Angella's glance in my direction indicated she was good to continue. So I instructed the driver yet again to just get us to our destination, so turn we did and up we went into what can only be described as jungle that grew denser as we drove. The highway was still labeled A1, but the narrowest lane on South Padre Island was a major highway compared to what we were now traveling on. Almost two hours into the trip we turned onto what was now called B2. Why it even had a name made no sense. The sky was totally masked by trees that were barely tall enough for our vehicle to pass under. The treetops were rhythmically swaying as the wind continued to increase.

Two things were perfectly clear. One, it was impossible to monitor the road from above. Two, we were now a caravan, with a car in front and, I assumed, a car behind, although I couldn't see or hear the rear car. From the lead car's lack of bounce I guessed it to be heavily armored.

This was the perfect terrain for drug growing and transport and we were at ground zero for much of the Central American drug traffic. It was reasonable to assume that around the next bend, which was never far in front of us, we'd come face to face with weapon carrying guards blocking the path. My back and neck muscles tensed waiting for the sound of gunfire.

"Almost there. Just a few more cut-backs and we turn off." The driver announced, sounding disappointed, as if he enjoyed driving in these conditions.

"Depends how you grow up," Angela commented, her voice low, sensing what I had sensed about the driver getting his kicks on this goat trail of a road.

A moment later, without touching the brake pedal, the driver jerked the wheel to the right, apparently to circumvent a deep rut in the path. Angella was thrown into me and it was all I could do to keep from collapsing against the doorframe.

What kept the chassis from breaking was beyond me. My head hit the ceiling several times and finally I said, "You always drive this fast up here? Mind slowing a bit."

"Sorry," he said, not sounding a bit sorry. "Need to keep close to our escort. Thought you were in a hurry to get here."

"Should we be?" Angella asked.

"Storm brewing. A big one. Horse buyer due any moment."

I glanced at Angella who was just as puzzled as I was as to how—and why—this driver knew about our business. "How the hell do you know that?" seemed an appropriate question. But instead, I asked the driver, "Are you speaking of the polo pony?"

"Valuable foal I understand."

"Rumors on the valuation?"

"Word is, upwards of fifteen million."

"Know the buyer?"

"By way of rumor only?"

"Have a name?"

"Middle East. Heard several names. All sound the same to me." His laugh had a nervous edge to it. The car served to the left, this time throwing me against Angella.

"We're even now," she said, pushing me upright.

"Try one of the names," I said to the driver.

"About missed that cutoff. Concentration, mon, need to concentrate."

The car slowed and around the next bend we came to a full stop behind our escort. A makeshift guard station stood between two trees at the side of the road. Three guards were visible, two inside and one outside. The outside guard had an assault rifle clutched close to his body and I assumed the guys on the inside had the same. Our driver leaned his head out of the driver's window and motioned the tall wiry outside guard with the full black beard to come over to the car. They exchanged words and a moment later we, and the car in front, were moving again. The bearded guard seemed to be glaring at us — or at the driver — as we accelerated. The third car, if there ever had been one, was not in sight.

A second checkpoint loomed shortly thereafter. Both cars passed this point with the simple exchange of a thumbs-up, neither car fully stopping.

"How many control points are there?" I asked. "Seems over-kill for a ranch this far up in the mountains."

"Several you don't see as well. The horses are very valuable. Up here, the law is what you make it to be."

"How would a horse thief ever get them out?"

"There are ways to move anything. People from all over the world, people with big money, with air assets even, are always in these hills. A million here, a million there, don't care what the commodity is. Movement of goods, any goods, are details best left to underlings. The scent of money draws them like flies to dog shit. Don't care who gets hurt either. Best to take precautions." He patted the empty passenger seat as if to say he had a weapon tucked away.

Suddenly we turned into what at first appeared to be a cave cut into the rock face, but was, in fact, a stone arch. Once through the arch, the overhead foliage was gone and spread before us was a vast plateau. Off to the left stood a magnificent structure as would befit a Saudi king.

It was the faces of the people standing in greeting that I now mentally concentrated on. Indeed, several of the faces were Middle Eastern.

Living in the past is typically not a good idea. I have found that not much good comes from it. But while I'm trying to reconstruct my life, the past is the only way to do it. I confirmed to myself that none of the facial images that had been displayed on the monitor a few moments ago matched any of the faces that I now visualized standing in our arrival reception line up in the mountains of Jamaica. Nor did they match those of the driver or any of the guards I had seen. That left only the faces of the two people in the car that had been parked next to where I was thrown from Lip Sync. I systematically tried to recall each person's face, but nothing more emerged.

"Redstone, you with the program? Or what? Snap to it, man. Time's not on our side." The voice had come from the overhead speaker and unless I missed my guess it belonged to Levi Ben-Yuval. "So far, none of the faces on the airplanes were faces you remember from Jamaica. Right?"

I turned back to the screen and there he was. The shot was too close, or the background had been blocked, for me to determine if he was on the hospital ship. But with the image changing software our government was now using I really had no real way of knowing if he ever had been with Angella on the medical ship or simply superimposed. Angella could have been photo-shopped as well. Reality, it seems, is becoming ever more difficult to keep track of. And the older I get the more true that becomes.

"How's Angella," I asked.

"I'm in the air, can't answer you."

"Where you off to?" I asked, disappointed Angella was being left alone. "Same place you are, my friend."

That made no sense, but I played along. "Where's that?"

"Need to know basis only."

Spooks are impossible. Always have been, always will be. Going to the water cooler is on a need to know basis in their world. "Have it your way. But if you want me with you you'll have to tell me how to get there."

"No need. Be at the Coast Guard station in five."

"It'll take five minutes for me to get to my car and deal with the traffic. I won't—" But the line was already dead. Tiny must have trained Ben-Yuval—or perhaps the other way around. Is there a universal global-type spook school?

"You heard the man," Gladstone snapped, reappearing like a magician's rabbit. "There's a car waiting at the door. The copter lands in...in four minutes and...thirty-five seconds. You'll be on it."

I knew better than to ask where I was going or what my assignment was. Some things just never change. I snapped a salute, was tempted to add a middle finger greeting, but considering the number of cameras in the vicinity, dropped that idea. Instead, I turned on my heel and went through the door.

THIRTY-FOUR

Precisely five minutes after I had hung up, a Navy Sea Dragon helicopter appeared out of the late afternoon sun over the blue-green water of Laguna Madre.

"Get out there," the military driver barked. "Stand on the X—"

I didn't need to hear the rest. My Air Force Ranger training kicked in and I was out of the jeep and running to the pickup point. This was going to be a swoop and grab operation with the copter never stopping and never touching ground. There were many reasons for such a dangerous operation, one of them being deniability.

Under oath, the testimony of the pilot—or the Secretary of the Navy—or whatever unlucky person drew the short straw—would go something like this:

Questioner: Did you have occasion to pick up Mr. Redstone?"

Unlucky witness: "I'm never told who the pas-sengers are." Or, if the unlucky witness is the Navy Secretary, "I am unaware of passenger names. I will check the records and get back to you, Senator."

Questioner: "Isn't it a fact a Navy Sea Dragon MH 53E set down at Coast Guard Station South Padre Island for the purpose of receiving one Mr. Jimmy Redstone?"

Unlucky Witness: "I see no record of a Navy Sea Dragon MH 53H setting down on South Padre Island on the date in question."

Truth is, whether or not the copter actually touched the ground is irrelevant. What is relevant is that I was taken aboard and no one will ever be able to prove it one way or another, lending sub-stance to then Secretary of State, Hilary Clinton's famous testimony answer, "What difference, at this point, does it make?"

"I see your training didn't go to waste," Ben-Yu-val said when I clambered aboard.

"But my body has, alas," I confessed. "Only made it on with the crew's help. Back in the day, if I couldn't pull myself up they would've left me on the ground. It's hell getting old."

"There are lots of hell's out there, my friend. Be thankful living beyond fifty is all you're com-plaining about."

"Put that way, I suppose being able to complain is a good thing. Last time I saw you was in Mexico. You were going down a river I believe it was."

"No lasting issues with memory, I note. Oh, by the way, thanks for delivering Moshe Abrams. Even by Israeli standards he was...how do you say it...one bad dude! Scored lots of points with my government. Sometimes the spoils of war are... worth it."

I didn't know if he meant I scored the points or he did. Again, what difference, at this point, does it make? "Glad to have been of assistance," I replied, duly noting the not so subtle manner in which he let me know he—and his employers—were of the opinion the proceeds of the Great Bank Heist, as some were now calling the SPI bank robbery, were in my possession. Or more accurately, that I knew where the forty or so million was hidden. "So where are we going?" I glanced out of the window and realized we were about to land at a far corner of the Brownsville airport directly alongside a Navy jet fighter. "I mean, after we board the jet."

"My, aren't we curious today," Levi said, a semblance of a smile forming at the corners of his lips as he prepared to jump down from the copter. "Hurry, my friend. Tight schedule to keep. Can't keep these folks waiting."

My seat belt had barely clicked closed when the jet's engines screamed and my head was thrown back against the headrest. I had never witnessed, from inside or out, a plane move so fast so quickly. It seemed as if we were off the ground in less than ten seconds, possibly closer to five. And we shot almost straight upward.

Ben-Yuval reached for the oxygen mask hanging on the partition in front of him. I was already experiencing light-headedness as I followed his lead.

A few minutes later the plane leveled off in an indeterminate direction. "So," I asked again, "when am I to learn the destination? The real mission if you will." Based on the speed at which we left the ground, if Ben-Yuval had told me our next stop was a space station I would not have been surprised.

"Now would be a good time. But first, slide that partition over to the left. The co-pilot needs to hear this as well."

I did as I was told and the right half of the cockpit essentially became part of our meeting space. Levi tapped the co-pilot on the shoulder and motioned to switch the headphones to conference with us. The co-pilot then dutifully reached forward, twisted a dial and said, "Gentlemen, what can I do for you?"

"Oh, my God!" I exclaimed. "How did —" I turned to face Ben-Yuval. "You rat! You could have told me!"

The smile on his face told me all I needed to know. I turned forward. I knew not to unbuckle my belt, but it was all I could do to restrain myself. Angella was less than two feet away, yet I couldn't touch her, or even see her face.

"Angella!"

"Hi, Jimmy. Surprise."

"Best ever. How are you? No injuries? What —"

"He'll buy you a diamond bracelet," Ben-Yuval volunteered, "for just being alive and for not having a Secret Service agent put a hole through your head when you dove for Mogul."

"Oh, Jimmy. I'd love it!"

"The son of a diamond merchant knows what a woman wants. When this is over, Redstone, my father will fix you up. Ok, down to business. Sorry to keep you both in the dark, my friends, but this operation is high level."

"Was that picture book routine with the passengers Kabuki theatre or real?"

"What are you talking about, Jimmy?" Angella asked.

Ben-Yuval cut her off. "Fill you in later. Mostly theater, Jimmy. But there has been information, perhaps, misinformation, about terrorist infiltration threats. Here's what we know and don't know. Israeli intelligence is one hundred percent certain there will be a second attack on your President. At the—"

"Sorry to interrupt," I said, "but let's start from the beginning. You seem to be saying the attacker, or rather the organization behind the attacker, knew—"

"ISIL. ISIL is the organization believed to be carrying out the planned chemical attack on an American city. Speculation, with an eighty percent confidence level, is that ISIL is acting in concert with a person, or persons, well-placed within the American government."

"You know this how?"

"Intelligence sources. Highly placed assets."

Angella turned as far in her seat as her oxygen mask would allow. "Fill me in, please," she demanded. "I can't help you if I'm in the dark about what's going down."

Ben-Yuval nodded in my direction and I gave Angella the short version, ending by saying, "In some circles you're a hero, my dear, because if you hadn't intervened there's a chance 'ole Sal would have made a widow out of Muse. There had been a last-minute stand-down order from the top but with Sal who the hell knows what she would have done. But by your intervention they were able to pantomime an assassination for a few minutes and that, they believe, is all they needed to trigger a mistake from Alpha."

"Who's Alpha?"

"Code for the top person. The mole, or moles."

"Here's where we are," Ben-Yuval said, his eyes dead cold, "Intelligence assets from several countries have been working to expose Alpha and every time they get close he pulls back into his shell. It's as if he's part of the offense as well as the defense."

"Sounds like that's exactly what he's doing."

"And wreaking havoc with your government, and some with ours as well."

Angella said, "You know the definition of insanity is doing the same thing over and over and expecting different results. Is there a new plan?"

"Indeed there is. You notice Tiny's been removed from handling you. Alpha knows we've mounted an attack, knows time is short for him, but he doesn't know the critical thing."

"And that is?" I asked.

"Who's coming—and when."

Angella added, "And how. He doesn't know how we're coming."

"And how are we coming for him?" I asked. "What's the plan?"

"First, let's go over what we do know. Frankly, not a lot for certain. There are many moving parts, including the ISIL terrorist attack. But we now believe that was a diversion to get the focus wrong. So I've gone through all the material in depth and here's what I distill. Alpha has a deep need to own the foal Sync Opate. Intelligence picked that up over a year ago and that's when they began the substitution operation, by arranging for a second foal to be introduced into the mix, all without Alpha knowing. By my calculations, it's all worked, except...except we don't know exactly who Alpha is."

I had worked most of this out myself and was getting impatient.

"Here's what I believe happened," Ben-Yuval said, sensing my agitation, "Tabina Matawani, who, by the way, is well-connected in terrorist circles, brokers horses. She let it be known that the foal was up for sale and this opened an opportunity for Alpha to funnel cash to Hamas, one of her best clients, in the guise of a horse purchase. Alpha couldn't resist the opportunity to wreck havoc, whether that be with Israel or the United States or both is unclear, and at the same time score a prize polo pony in the bargain. His plan was to pay between seventeen and twenty million pounds for what might otherwise be a five million pound foal."

"Wouldn't that set off alarm bells? Angella asked. "Certainly, those kinds of transactions are monitored."

"Perhaps. But auctions are hard to predict and the money ran through several entities. Hard to follow under any circumstance. That's where Ma-tawani came in. She bought the pony for about five-six million pounds from Bar-C Ranch working through Malik Conquesta in Jamaica prior to the auction. The auction was set up as a camouflage to further blur the money laundering operation. Alpha's passion for owning the foal was so strong that he just had to be there to see and touch the young horse and if the weather would have coop-erated, he would have been able to spend quality time with the foal privately. But, as we know, he had to land early and ended up in the car with Matawani. Not what he had planned"

"So what's caused the confusion?" I asked, knowing the answer but wanting to see how much Ben-Yuval trusted us.

"Actually, a combination of things. Primarily,

as we know, the weather caused Alpha to come ashore early and that meant the terrorist buyer, who also had planned on visiting the foal, would be on island at the same time. A major no-no as taught in spy-school 101. So the storm pissed off the buyer, but...but even worse, you showed up just as Alpha slipped into the car with Matawani. Second lesson in spy training, never be seen with a principal to a terrorist transaction. From Alpha's perspective, he had to assume you saw and could identify him."

"So just why are we going back?" I asked, not having yet having worked that part out.

"Matawani took possession of Strike One, not Sync Opate. But the money transferred before anyone figured out there had been a switch. When the phony foal was discovered, actually by Alpha himself, all hell broke loose. He cancelled the deal which pissed off ISIL, and, of course you see what happened on SPI with Mogul."

"Confusion," Angella said. "Total confusion."

"That's been the plan all along. Confusion and timing mishaps. It's hard to pull off major operations when you can't control all the elements. We took timing control out of Alpha's hands. And, we got a bonus with the storm and Jimmy being on scene."

"So why the secrecy with Angella? Moving her off the medical ship disguised as a copilot is...well, most unusual."

"As I said, the both of you are required if we

have any real hope to stop the next attack. Alpha, of course, knows you were both in Jamaica for the horse trade. Angella, so long as he believes you're still on that ship then he possibly will take chances that otherwise he wouldn't take. Not a big advantage for our side, but large enough. The intelligence game is played with microscopic pieces and a sliver of an advantage could prove huge."

"Won't Alpha be told I'm off the ship?"

"You're not off the ship." Ben-Yuval reached over to a console on his left side, pushed a few buttons, moved a curser to an orange circle, pushed another button and voila, a hospital-looking room appeared on a screen in front of me and on the cockpit hood in front of Angella.

"Hey!" Angella exclaimed, "that's where they had me on the ship. I recognize the yellow flowers."

"Look closer," Ben-Yuval said. "Here, I'll zoom in a bit."

There was now no question that Angella was lying in the bed, a bandage on her wrist. "What about—" I was about to ask about myself. Wouldn't Alpha be concerned about my whereabouts as well? But I had no need to ask the question. There I was, big as life, sitting beside Angella.

"Two can play their dress-up game," Ben-Yuval confessed, the first smile of this trip fleeting across his face. "While Alpha believes you two are both on that ship he just might be bold enough to do something stupid. Otherwise, back into his shell he'd go and it could be years before we get another chance. If ever. As I said, a sliver is what we play for and a sliver is all that we need."

"So who's playing Angella?"

"A young Marine gunnery officer who happened to graduate from Carnegie Mellon's School of Drama."

"I can't imagine who's playing me."

"Better not knowing."

"How in hell do you spooks ever keep all the lies straight?" Angella asked.

"Darwin at work, my friend. Get yourself mixed up, get yourself dead. Simple formula. Weeds folks out mighty fast."

THIRTY-FIVE

"What's the expectation from us," I asked, resigned to our fate at the hands of our government masters. Or whoever was now pulling our strings.

"You're both going back to the Conquesta Ranch to do two things. First to give the money back, and second, well second's a long shot. Jimmy we're hoping just being up on the ranch will...jog your memory. I'm told that visual memories are often triggered by spatial objects associated with the physical space where the memory was created."

"In other words, me being in the same place where I was thrown from the horse might cause my visual memory of who was in the car to improve. Is that what you just said?"

"Something to that effect. Yes."

"That's okay for Jimmy, but what's my role?"

"Ease the whole thing. Make it less obvious

what we're doing. They're naturally very...sensitive. Matawani is essentially under house arrest. ISIL has a bounty on her for reversing the money flow. In fact, Matawani is seeking new employment, her terrorist broker days are now behind her. That is, assuming she can keep her head attached to her body. And...in all honesty, Malik is going along with this because he took a liking to you Angella."

I didn't like this last bit of information, but there was no point in shooting the messenger. "I assume the money's on the government. The money we're paying back to...and just who are we paying the money back to?"

Ben-Yuval looked across at me. His eyes focused directly on mine. "Madam Matawani. This is her deal, let her sort it out."

"You expect Alpha to show up?" Angella asked, her voice sounding muffled, almost unintelligible.

"That would be a major bonus. But I seriously doubt he'll chance it. By now he knows we're close on his heals."

"If the purchase of Sync Opate would have been real wouldn't that have led directly to him? I mean, follow the horse."

"Not exactly. The horse would pass through several owners and a few years from now Alpha would take full ownership. For him, this is his passion and it's enough to know that he can control the horse's future. That's why he was up there in person. Just had to see and touch his dream."

What Ben-Yuval was saying made sense from my experience. For people with hobbies, people who collect, it's all about the owning, the possession, the memory, not so much about the every day seeing and touching. That's why it's so hard to track down art thieves. The stolen piece is acquired, viewed a few times, then hidden away for years, sometimes forever. "You didn't answer my question about where the money's coming from."

"Out of your share of the last deal. Where else? That's how you're going to pay back what went missing."

"I've about had enough of that crap! You know damn well I put that money in the bank! Government refused to claim it. Bank heist cleaned it out. Go talk to the frigg'n robbers! And stop already harassing me about it!"

"You're a sensitive lot, you are. Shooting the messenger, my friend. Cash will be supplied."

"By whom?"

"Now you're asking too many questions."

"We're putting our lives in jeopardy and—"

"Everyone involved with this operation has his or her life on the line!" Ben-Yuval snapped, the first time I had ever seen him display anger. I didn't like what I saw. "You've been there, you know that all too well. I'm giving you what you need to know to increase your odds of remaining above ground."

Ben-Yuval was right of course. And I did know

better. But in my defense, I was no longer working for the government. I was trying to be a private citizen. And that wasn't going all that well.

The plane was now low, just off the coast of Jamaica and we were minutes from landing. Ben-Yuval turned to me, "Jimmy, the reason we believe you were drugged is because you actually saw Alpha. We need to know who that person is and stop him before...well, before he wrecks more havoc on your country."

"And that's what this mission is about. Memory jogging."

"And protecting Angella from Conquesta." Ben-Yuval winked.

"And to protect Angella," I weakly added, knowing full well the Israeli way was one fire, one ranger, so why the both of us? I still didn't know my mission and doubted I ever really would.

"We land in a few minutes. Time to relax."

"I reached through the open hatch and touched Angella on the shoulder, my way of telling her I had her back. Turning to Ben-Yuval I said, "This may be the most convoluted operation I've ever worked."

"You're not alone my friend. It's most devilish to catch someone at the top. Alpha has spent years as a mole and moves around almost with immunity. That's why Mogul called on our government to help, but the truth is we need to get very lucky."

Before I could respond, he added, "And we can't lock Trump in a lead vault miles underground while we figure it out. The show must go on."

"And you trust Deputy Director Gladstone?"

"He's a bit...well, unconventional at times, but straight as an arrow. Known him it seems forever. And I can vouch for him. Can't say the same for the Director."

"Why Israel? Why reach out to Israel?"

"We may have a larger stake in this than your country. Alpha is in league with Libi. Full name is Abu Sholeh al-Libi. He's Abu Bakr al-Baghdadi's top deputy. In fact, some would say Libi is actually the top guy. We showed Libi's picture to you and you didn't recognize him. So he must not have been among the ones you saw, or your memory is blocked. But he was on one of those planes we were watching. He flew out of Grand Cayman, so he was in position to be in Jamaica if the weather had cooperated."

"Since I haven't been told of a plane being shot down, I assume this guy al-Libi was arrested when the plane landed," Angella said, more by way of comment than question.

"Bad assumption, Angella. Actually, we have nothing concrete on him."

"But you know he's the top—or near top—terrorist! What am I missing here?"

"Your government insists he be tried before being imprisoned."

"I support that. So?"

"Angella, he can't be tried without Israel's co-operation and Israel won't expose its operatives. They're deeply imbedded. Taken us years to get there and its not duplicable. So no public trial."

To my mind that meant the Israeli agent—or agents—are Muslim by birth. To expose one could wipe out a family as well as eliminate a valuable source of information. "So," I said, "our government must allow this man freedom to come and go as he pleases because Israel refuses—"

"No lectures, please. The information we provide keeps your country safe. Be grateful."

"The lecture part goes both ways. Okay, what exactly are we doing when we land?"

"Going back up to the ranch, buying back the pony and viewing everyone who is up there. We'll have surveillance cameras posted, but those folks are experts in blocking themselves. We use filters on our cameras and they have counter filters. Ain't technology great?"

"In my experience," I said, "people, especially trained terrorists, who don't want to be seen, aren't. As you say, that's just Darwin at work."

"Hopefully just this once there'll be an exception to the Darwin theory."

There's never an exception to Darwin, so I was now certain it was my presence on a ranch high up in the remote mountains of Jamaica that would create whatever variance they needed. In essence I was the bait and that didn't bode well for me in the least. Especially when there was a better than even chance that when the trap springs I'll end up inside the belly of the target.

THIRTY-SIX

"**I** won't be joining you," Ben-Yuval said as the plane skimmed just above the angry dark water of the Caribbean, seconds before touchdown. In truth, I couldn't see the runway and could only hope this wasn't one of his, Oh, I didn't tell you that you two would be jumping out and swimming to shore, moments.

I don't know if Angella had heard something in my voice or had her own thoughts about what was about to happen, but she strained around and glanced at me through the side of her mask. I couldn't exactly interpret the message she was sending, but it was not a happy one.

I reached out and put my hand on her shoulder just before Ben-Yuval reached slammed the partition closed.

Suddenly the engine pitch changed, going from a deep hum to a high-pitched scream. Angella's head swiveled around and both us were thrown forward, restrained only by our seatbelts. An instant later all sense of forward motion was gone.

"What the hell's wrong with you, Redstone?" Ben-Yuval snapped, getting to his feet. "Get your ass off this plane. There's a driver waiting. This plane has a schedule to keep and we have to get off this island before the window closes again."

I believe the window Levi was referring to was the window before the authorities reacted to a plane landing on their soil and not a weather window.

The door was indeed already open and I looked down, expecting to see water lapping below us, but instead there was rock-strewn earth barely wide enough to accommodate the jet. The runway lights, if indeed there had been lights, were already switched off and it was pitch black out. The base of a mountain that reached skyward not fifty yards beyond where the plane was now positioned was visible only in shadow. On the other side of the plane I could hear water lapping at what I envisioned as a beach. From what I could see, the entire runway was no longer than half a football field. I had no idea that jets could land—or take off—in such tight quarters.

The lights of a car parked on a narrow roadway that ran along the base of the mountain flicked on. One thing was certain, I had no idea of where we were—or that we even were on the Island of Jamaica. I shrugged my shoulders in answer to Angella's non-verbalized question.

"It smells like Jamaica," she said as we walked toward our waiting ride. "But don't all tropical islands smell of sunscreen and coconut oil?"

"Is that a hint that we should travel—or vacation—more?"

"Just a statement. But I wouldn't quibble about the vacation part if you were so inclined." Angella stopped and turned to face me. "What was that about on the plane? You had a strange—"

"Not important now. Just a bit of paranoia. We didn't land at the Montego Bay or Kingston airports, so obviously we're not in country—or at least the State Department can deny we were here with a somewhat straight face. That plane came in so low I doubt if the Jamaican government even knows it landed."

The runway lights came on and the sound of the jet screeching into the air interrupted my thought. The lights went off almost immediately.

"Certainly," Angella said, "with all that noise this is not a stealth operation."

"The Jamaican ministry might have been given a heads up, but they'll never admit it. They're accustomed to planes coming and going at all hours. Drugs and whatever else. That landing area didn't build itself."

The rear car door opened and Malik Conquesta stepped out. The last person in the world I had expected to see.

"Show time," Angella said, "Game faces on."

"So we meet again, Mr. Redstone, Miss Martinez. My pleasure. Am I to believe your head injury
was minor, Mr. Redstone."

Conquesta was in rare form. He kissed the
back of Angella's right hand, motioned for me
to sit in front while he slid in the back seat next
to her. Seems he was resuming where he had left
off. At least I now knew for certain what Island
we were on.

"We will be spending the night at the Half
Moon. It is far too late to drive up to the ranch,"
Conquesta informed us. "I suppose you two are
hungry. The main kitchen is closed, but I've asked
them to have kippers and eggs brought to your
room, along with some beverages. We have much
to discuss, but it can wait 'till morning."

The drive to the Half Moon took less than fifteen minutes and instead of stopping at the main
building the driver took us directly to a remote
bungalow. After again kissing Angella's hand,
Conquesta said, "Have a good night you two. I've
ordered breakfast be brought here to your quarters
at nine. I'll be joining you. Goodnight."

The late-night snack Conquesta ordered was
perfect and the champagne was even better. Angella and I were alone, the only sound was water
rolling over the white sand—a bit more rambunc-
tious than the last time we were here—but sooth-
ing nonetheless.

* * *

"I understand there's a package waiting for pickup," Conquesta announced when he arrived at precisely nine in the morning. "Breakfast will be along in a few minutes. Or, if you wish, we can all go up to the main dining room."

I assumed the package was the money we were to return to the terrorists, but in truth I didn't exactly know what to expect. I wasn't hungry, but didn't know how Angella felt about having breakfast at our cottage.

"Breakfast out here would be lovely," she replied, not answering my question the way I had hoped she would. "Do we have time before we...I don't even know what time we are due at the ranch."

"Time is what we always have, my dear. Time, a beautiful island, and of course, a beautiful woman. What else is there?"

Neither I nor Angella responded.

Conquesta, filling the awkward silence, remarked, "Storm's down to a low grade tropical depression finally. Ranch suffered some tree damage, but not much at all considering. This weather is most unusual, must be that climate change everything's being blamed on. How they got you out, Jimmy, I'll never know."

"I'm glad they did," Angella said. "Saved his life."

"That's what I've been told. I note breakfast is not here yet and I apologize for that. The food here is excellent, but alas, often the service is not," Conquesta said by way of apology. "They take relaxation to an extreme at times." In response to Angella's puzzled expression, Conquesta added, "I mean, the guests are supposed to relax, not the wait staff. Often they are in no hurry to perform their chores."

While we were waiting for the food to arrive, I felt a tap on my shoulder. Turning, I found a stiff-backed uniformed bellman waiting to say something.

"Yes," I asked, "is there a problem?"

"You will please follow me, Mr. Jimmy Redstone. There is a package waiting for pickup."

"Please bring it to me."

"That will be impossible, sir. You must sign for the package."

"I can sign here at the table. Now please."

"I please request you to follow me. I'm instructed to summon you."

"Better to go with him," Conquesta advised. "I have found that once instructions have been given it is not possible for the workers to vary. He must carry out his orders."

"Don't make a scene, Jimmy," Angella said. "It can't take all that long to get what we came for and besides, you're never hungry in the morning anyway."

I had been dismissed and wasn't happy about

it. I stood, turned on my heel and commanded, my tone none too polite, "Lead the way. Let's get this over with."

The bellboy, a wiry youth with a pointed goatee and angry eyes, debated for a long moment the wisdom of taking me on. Had he followed his instincts, the poverty rate on the island being what it was, the opportunity to earn a steady wage would have been forfeited. When he spun on his heel, much as I had done a moment earlier, I knew that eating regular meals over a long period had outweighed his immediate satisfaction of decking me. All to his credit.

I was two steps behind him and the faster I walked the faster he moved. We passed in and out of several buildings, all elegantly furnished and open to the beautiful horseshoe shaped white sand beach. Across the beach I could see the individual huts, one of which was where Angella and Conquesta were sitting. I strained to see which one that was, but the spray blurred the view.

We had been walking a good five minutes and I doubted if I could find my way back to where I had left Angella. Our destination seemed to be a building at the far end of a crushed stone path sitting farther back from the beach than the others.

Mr. Angry Eyes held the door for me, something he hadn't done with any of the other buildings. I read that as a sign our journey together was about to come to an end. A moment later that assessment was proven correct when he closed the door behind me with him on the outside.

The room had no water views and did not seem to belong to the resort facility other than the name Half Moon Bay in gold letters on the wall above a counter. All very corporate looking and official. A woman sat behind the counter, her head hidden until I was almost upon her. "You're Mr. Jimmy Redstone, I take it?" she said even before I could manage a hello.

"I am. I have a—"

"Identification please."

I pulled out my driver license and handed it across the counter.

She studied the document. "American?"

"Yes."

"Passport, please."

This was not going to end well. I was not allowed in the country without a passport, but once I showed mine to her she would immediately check for the entry stamp. Not to hand it over, I concluded, was the worst of the two evils.

She flipped the passport open to my picture, compared it to my face, then said, "Good likeness," and reached for her phone. "He's here." She didn't bother checking for the entry stamp, obviously instructed to overlook the passport irregularity.

Almost immediately two uniformed and armed men appeared from a hallway. The smaller of them, by way of height, but not girth, said, "Follow me please."

I followed them back into the hallway and into an office on the right. The door closed behind us. "This yours?" the burly guy barked, pointing to three very large boxes sitting on a table next to a fourth somewhat smaller box.

"How would I know who those—"

"That your name on the address labels?"

Sure enough, Mr. Jimmy Redstone was prominently displayed along with the words, Half Moon Bay. Private, open only in presence of addressee.

"They're addressed to me if that's what you mean?"

"Open them please."

I did as requested. To do otherwise would have only provoked these guys. And who knew if Jamaica had the U. S. equivalent of Habeas Corpus. I didn't want to find out the hard way.

Each box was loaded with euro banknotes in the denomination of five hundred, a denomination I had read would soon disappear primarily because of its use for so called illicit activities. Witness this transaction.

From calculations I had made in the past I knew that fifteen million Euro banknotes in the 500 denomination would equal 30,000 physical bills. The banknotes were banded into bundles and again from past experience each bundle typically would be a hundred notes. Each box would then contain a hundred bundles. So if three boxes contained fifteen million, then why the fourth?

There are times when one's mind just doesn't click fast enough. This was one of those times. Then it came to me in an ah ha moment. "Jimmy, don't be so stupid. Can you say bribe?" Three boxes to buyback the phony pony. One box to buy off the authorities! The fourth box is half as large as the other boxes, i.e. the going rate must be more or less fifteen percent. With emphasis on the more part of the equation.

So how's this going to work? One doesn't just walk up to the BRIBES ACCEPTED HERE counter and plop down two and a quarter million euros. I wondered if there was a posted menu of rates; say fifteen percent for allowing cash into the country; twenty, possibly thirty percent for allowing drugs to be exported. I can't imagine what the rate would be if I really needed the government to do anything.

Is it appropriate to ask for a receipt?

THIRTY-SEVEN

A glance through the dusty window told me I wouldn't have long to wait. A truck came to a bouncing stop and three heavily armed men jumped from the covered rear end before the vehicle had settled. A moment later two other men, a short wiry guy and a taller well-proportioned man who had the classic command presence of a leader, slid from the passenger side of the front seat. Escorted by the guards, the two men proceeded to enter the building. I had no doubt where they were heading. Nor did I have any doubt what they planned to do when they got here.

The uniformed men in the room with me came to attention when the truck squad came through the door. A quick nod in the direction of the boxes was all that was exchanged. The leader picked up the smaller of the boxes and each of the armed guards took a box. The truck was their destination and without being instructed to do so I followed them out. The large boxes disappeared into the bed of the truck followed by two of the armed men. The third armed man stood by the corner of the truck his eyes following my every move.

The original two uniformed men remained inside the building. The driver walked to his side of the truck and climbed in behind the wheel. The leader proceeded to the passenger side, opened the door, placed the box he was carrying on the floor, and hefted himself up onto the front seat.

Not one to allow fifteen or so million to simply disappear from sight without protest, I ran to catch up, my focus being the passenger side rear door. The armed guard shifted his weight, but the business end of his weapon remained pointed upward. A good sign if ever there was one.

The truck lurched forward just as my fingers touched the door handle. The momentum threw me off balance enough so that my left foot dragged across the sandy ground. Luckily, my hand tightened around the metal handle.

"Hurry, Redstone," the leader barked, his voice U. S. trained, "we have a flight to catch. Finance Minister's waiting. Not a patient man."

Using the handle as a support, and praying it didn't break away from the rusty frame, I pulled myself up onto the small running board as the truck gained speed.

I managed to wrestle the door open and fell inside an instant before the truck turned onto the main road and the driver accelerated to merge with the traffic.

"Well done, Redstone. I was—"

The engine noise made it impossible to hear what was being said from the front seat and that was good as it gave me an opportunity to think. Problem was I didn't know what to think about. But I did know where we were heading, Kingston. Belafonte's lyrics passed through my mind and I was reminded that he had sailed away and was sad to say he wouldn't be back for many a day. He had left a girl in Kingston town just as I was about to leave my love here in Montego Bay. I hoped my time away would go faster than Belafonte's.

The lyrics were wiped away when we passed under the Sangster International Airport sign and the truck made a sharp turn onto a dirt road. The jarring of my spine increased in proportion to the banging and rattling noises filling my ears. The men in the front seat didn't seem to be bothered by either the noise or the pounding. This seemed to be just another day on the job for them.

The truck came to a skidding, screeching stop at a gate in an otherwise impenetrable fence. Excited words were exchanged between the driver and an armed guard while another armed guard kept his rifle pointing directly at the cab. There might have been more firepower in the covered truck bed behind me than there was in the shack, but little good that would do if one of the gate guards got trigger-happy.

We were at a standoff. The leader yanked the door open and jumped to the ground. The good news, at least for me, was that both guards had their weapons pointed directly at him. I didn't hear what he said, probably because I wasn't meant to hear it, but suddenly it was over.

The leader climbed back into the truck, the gate swung open and onto the airport property we rumbled. The truck gained speed and the noise increased as we crossed several runways. Our destination appeared to be a small plane parked as far from where we entered as physically possible.

The driver apparently had only three driving speeds. Actually, only two could be called speeds. Full-off, over-rocks fast, and full-on. Our throttle was set at full-on until we came to within ten yards of the plane's tail and then it went to full-off with a brake pedal-to-the-floor override.

The screech, I was certain, could be heard in downtown Montego Bay. The dust cloud could be seen even further. How we missed slamming into the plane I don't know. The important fact is that we did stop a few yards before we hit anything. Piece of cake I could hear the Jamaican driver saying to himself. Maybe I should not have applied the brakes quite so soon.

This must be where New York taxi drivers train.

"Out, Mon," the leader scolded. "We're behind schedule. Hurry, hurry."

Money box in hand, he bounded up the portable stairs to the plane and disappeared inside.

I delayed long enough to make certain the other three boxes were being transferred, helpless to do anything about it if they had other plans.

Lucky for me they didn't. All three boxes went into the small freight area of the plane and I ducked though the door as it was being closed. The plane immediately began to taxi.

That's when it hit me. Again, a beat too late. They removed the money from the boxes in the back of the truck! All that remained in those boxes was white sand, if that. Next thought, again too late to do anything about it: They're about to dump me in the Caribbean. The land sharks will be fifteen or so million dollars richer and the water sharks will have had dinner.

I've often mentally debated whether I would be better off clueless or knowing what was about to happen and helpless to do anything about it. A stupid thing to waste brain cells on, totally un-productive, but yet all consuming. My conclusion: put up a good fight. But if I had any chance at all of surviving the fight I had to start before they began executing their plan.

The odds were not in my favor, but, by doing nothing, the odds were worse. I focused on the weapon on the leader's hip. It was on the far side from where I was sitting across the aisle. The other guy was behind me and hopefully not paying much attention to my movements. But sudden movements on my part would quickly rouse him to action.

I tensed, trying to gauge the right moment, believing I had time before the plane was far enough off shore for them to feel confident in dumping me.

Thinking of the plane made me realize we were in trouble. The wind was tossing us around like a cork in an ocean, right to left, up and down. When the plane was thrown to the right I caught a glimpse of a mountain directly ahead. Then it was gone as the nose of the plane rotated left. Then the ground loomed as the nose fell, replaced a few seconds later by sky, then the mountain, then water. One instant it seemed as if we would slam into the mountain and a moment later I was certain we'd turn upside down and land in the bay.

Slowly, ever so slowly, the small plane gained altitude, but not enough, it appeared, to clear the mountain. Then the nose turned to the right, north, and as it did the winds seemed to soften a bit as we passed the shore line and flew out over the Caribbean.

Kingston, where I had presumed we were heading, is on the far side of the mountains and south of Montego Bay.

"Just where are we heading?" I asked, adding, "clearly this is not the direction to the minister."

"Life is good. No sweat, Mon. You must learn to enjoy," came the leader's reply.

"I'd enjoy it a lot more if I knew what was going on. Who are you, anyway?"

"For your purposes, call me General."

I searched my memory for what I knew of Jamaica and their politics. And the only general who came to mind was General Christofer. This man was at least twenty years older than the picture that came to mind, but he did have a scar across the back of his right hand, supposedly obtained in a sword duel the one time he had been imprisoned. Christofer was known for his brutality; particularly his penchant for chopping off heads at the time Jamaica was gaining its independence from Great Britain. The duel had ended, or so the rumors went, when his opponent's head landed in the dirt of the exercise yard. If this was the man the locals simply called X, it was no wonder the guard at the airport capitulated to his request. The guard understandably had wanted to keep the view he saw during his morning shave.

Unattached heads aside, I wanted to know what the plan was. "Okay. General, you said we had an appointment with the Finance Minister. That would be Kingston if I'm not mistaken."

"You are not mistaken. Unfortunately the flight plan called for this plane to go to Havana. Wouldn't want to explain on the record why we needed to go to the Capital. Paperwork all too often interferes with the proper functioning of the government. Don't you agree, Mr. Redstone?"

"At times," I responded, not adding that I didn't consider bribery, or in this case, official extortion, as being the proper functioning of government either. "I assume we still plan to meet with your honorable minister."

"In due course. Would a hefty glass of rum help in calming you? You seem very much distracted. We may be over water a while."

How far did they plan to go before dumping me? I can't say the rum was a bad idea, especially if my two guards partook. Actually, it was exactly what was needed.

Beside everything else, I was worried about Angella. But truth was, Conquesta had known all along what the drill was going to be and by now he would have explained it to her. Without warning my stomach tightened into a rock-hard mass. Perhaps jealousy, perhaps fear, but whatever, it was real and powerful. The thought of my lover alone with a world-class ladies' man at one of the world's most romantic hideaways with private white-sand beaches and villas was almost disabling. Logic told me Angella would be above it all. But try to explain logic to a panic attack. Different leagues altogether.

I had had enough. My fists clenched as I turned to the general. But before I could get the words out. The left wing dipped and the plane began to turn to the left. When we again leveled off the sun had moved from port to starboard. We were finally heading south.

A half-hour later, ten-thirty, eleven at the latest, judging by the sun, a truck, maybe even the same truck as before, came to a stop beside our parked plane. Unless the driver had gone to driving school in the interim, this was a different driver.

As before, three armed men jumped from the rear and this time focused their attention on the plane.

"Time to move out," the General said, motioning me to follow.

Down the steps we went, the cardboard box firmly in his control. Once on the ground, he turned and barked, "Hurry it up!" The kindly uncle voice he had employed on the plane was now gone. And his strut was again firmly in place. He spun on his heel. "You two," he commanded, "stay here and see that no one enters or leaves that plane. And I mean no one!"

To the man he had not addressed, he said, "You! Get in the back of the truck and see no one disturbs us." He then put the box in the cab of the truck as before, motioned me into the back seat and then climbed in next to the box.

The truck started to pull away. General X shouted, "Stop!" He rolled down his window, stuck his head out and yelled, "Turn around you fools! Face away from the plane. The enemy is out here!" To the driver, he said, "Go! Minister of Finance. No siren, but make it fast! Ten minutes!"

"But General—"

"Just do it!"

There was no further complaint, just a screech of tires and a hint of white knuckles on the steering wheel.

I reached for a seat belt and found nothing. "Enjoying the ride, General?" I asked several blocks later as it became clear we were mostly driving on the wrong side of the street, with cars and trucks frantic to get out of the way. We actually nipped the rear fenders of two cars, but our truck never slowed down.

"As a matter of fact, I am. This, dear sir, is far better than being late, I assure you."

Exactly ten minutes later we jolted to a stop in front of what appeared to be a five-hundred-year-old building with the words Ministry of Finance sandblasted into the grey stone.

"Wait for us," the general commanded the driver and the guard as he lifted the box from the floor of the cab. Once out of the truck he shoved the box into my chest. "Here, this is yours. You carry it."

I don't know if my imagination was playing tricks, but the box seemed to have gained weight along the way. I suppose, considering the merchandise, gaining is better than losing, but it could all be sand. The five-story building was constructed long before elevators came to the island and, of course, the minister's office was on the top floor.

Approaching the third landing the two plus million euros in banknotes felt as if they had become five million. I was afraid if I lowered the box to the floor I wouldn't be able to hoist it back up. My back and neck hurt and the muscles in my arms were quickly approaching the failure point. I struggled the last few steps to the fourth floor landing and just managed to balance the box on the railing before I lost complete control.

"Careful there Redstone," General X cautioned, "it would be a shame if all that money fell overboard at this point. Its already due and owing. I trust you'll be able to cover any losses."

"Not a chance," I responded. "Not even close."

"Then hang on tight. And get moving. Clock is ticking."

THIRTY-EIGHT

"I'll wait out here," the General said when the Minister's dreadlocked male associate pointed to a door, saying, "Minister Rasmutin is available now. Go right in. And take that filthy box with you."

I had only been kept waiting ten minutes, a very low number of minutes in the world of government officials, perhaps because the Finance Minister was anxious to get his hands on the money—or on me. The part about the box being filthy had to be the associate's acknowledgment of the bribe because the waiting room had soiled coffee cups acting as paperweights on every horizontal surface. "And close the door behind you, I don't want to hear a word of your conversation."

Rasmutin was overpoweringly tall. Taller even than Tiny. He was standing behind his massive, Texas-sized, desk when I entered his office. I imagined I was feeling roughly what David had been feeling when he first met Goliath, only in spades. I stand six feet. The man on the other side of the desk stood well over seven feet. He had not an ounce of fat on him. Giraffe came to mind. Skinny giraffe.

"This is the world famous Jimmy Redstone," his voice was loud and deep enough to vibrate the walls, "came to Jamaica Island thinking those black Jamaicans are rubes. Don't know a real polo pony from a painted fake. You take fifteen million for a dollar ninety-eight horse. You get caught and now you're here begging to stay out of jail."

Jail! This has gone off the rails! I've been set up! Better get it righted sooner rather than later. I looked up at the Minister. "The buyer was—"

"Was what, Redstone? A woman? Muslim? In your world you think it's okay to cheat Muslims? Or is it because the buyer is a woman?"

"I didn't—"

"She's a visitor in my country. In your home do you treat guests poorly?"

"I—"

"Yes or no, Mr. Redstone? Do you cheat guests in your own home or do you not?"

There was no answer to this question. Yes, and I've confessed to being a criminal. No, and I'm guilty of ill intent with respect to the Jamaican people. Shit, I'm being taped! "Mr. Minister, if I may. I have—and had when I was here a few days ago—no intention of cheating anyone anywhere at any time. Too many words. Say as little as possible. "Not in my home and certainly not in your home," I finally managed.

His eyes lit up as if on fire. The desk shook from his fist slamming into it. "You dare come in here and say I am lying!"

I hope this is more of their Kubuki theater. If not, well there better not be an 'if not'. Better play along. "Most certainly not, Mr. Minister. The buyer received a horse that was painted, I grant you that. But please allow me to assure you I didn't paint that horse and I don't know who did. I thought I was delivering a valuable pony worth fifteen million. I didn't know someone substituted a painted horse for the real horse. When I learned a mistake had been made I quickly returned to buy the horse back. I'm here now to fix the problem, set it right."

"You expect me to believe this is all a big mistake? It's a fraud of the first order! You want me to laugh it off as if nothing has happened. As if you didn't cheat a guest of our country? The Justice Minister must be informed! Our jails are full of people such as you who make these kinds of mistakes."

"It is what happened, your Excellency. I had no hand in it."

"Why are you here now?" the Minister bellowed, the walls resonating to his powerfully deep voice, a voice that did not match his stick-like physique, but certainly matched his physical height. "Why are you in my office, taking up my time?"

"I was brought to you by General X along with this—"

"Oh, General X! I should have known he had a hand in this! What you did is criminal! You should be across the road with the Justice Minister arguing your way out of prison, not here with me groveling for whatever it is you are groveling for! But lucky for you I have no proof you are lying, so get out of my office before I...before I change my mind and inform the Justice Minister."

Do I take the box with the two and a quarter million or not? I glanced down to where it sat.

My dilemma was immediately answered when the minister again bellowed, "Move! Get your ass out of my office and out of my city! And do it now! There is no further reason to hang around my office. There are bad men all around. Good day Mr. Redstone and keep your nose out of trouble."

I had now been given clear instructions. I was not to mention the money—or even the box. No receipt would be forthcoming. And best of all, he didn't care one bit about the Justice Minister. "Good day, your Excellency. I appreciate your time."

"Appreciate nothing! You were never in these offices!"

*   *   *

The plane gained altitude, but the mountains seemed to be rising just as fast. I had no idea so many people resided in these hills, huts everywhere

I looked. Judging from the housing density, I'd say most of the population of Jamaica lived well above sea level, surrounded mostly by trees and dense ground cover. Large swatches of that ground cover had been removed, replaced by what appeared to be farms and some ranches. My suspicion was that the crops of choice were cannabis and sugar cane. The population density dramatically changed higher up where the mountains flattened into wide expanses of winding dirt roads doubling back on themselves with smoke billowing upward from time to time. Rum distilleries. Most likely bootleg. This would not be a good time or place to have engine trouble.

We flew another fifteen minutes and then the plane nosed downward, not because we were landing, but because the ground was receding and we were following the terrain. We were over the mountain and while I couldn't see any evidence of the Caribbean I assumed we were heading down toward Montego Bay.

Then the plane banked to the right, rose again to avoid dense trees and up the side of a different mountain we went. The trees on this mountain gave way to a wide expanse of beautifully cultivated golf course quality grass spread over slowly rolling hills with patches separated by white picket fences. This must be the high rent neighborhood.

A moment later I realized we were flying over Conquesta's ranch, which seemed to cover the entire mountain. Then we were down. I hadn't seen a runway, but the landing was one of the smoothest in recent memory. The surroundings were, as before, magnificent. But the best sight of all was Angella standing off to the side of a small gathering of folks, a welcome smile spreading across her face as she realized who it was stepping out of the small plane.

She ran toward me, relief clearly spreading across her face. I took a step toward her, my arms wide to embrace perhaps the only person I have ever loved.

"What happened?" she exclaimed when my hands closed on her back. "I've been so worried about you! You just disappeared. Malik said you had business to attend to. What business?"

"Tell you later." In fact, I wanted to tell her now and even more pressing I wanted to hear what her morning had been like. I didn't trust Conquesta and truth be known I was jealous. I pulled her even closer and in a voice I intended as a whisper, but came out with much higher volume, I said, "I love you, Angella."

"I love you as well."

"That hat!"

I was professing my love for Angella, but my brain was processing an image, an image that by all rights it should not have been processing at this time. The hat was perfectly positioned on the head of an attractive tall slender woman.

The hat was large, and floppy, and hid her eyes, casting deep shadows over her nose and mouth.

Conquesta had his arm around the woman's waist as if to draw her closer to him. However, her focus was on Angella—or on me.

The hat. White, silk, large brim and perfectly matched to her white outfit. I knew the hat from somewhere. But where? Nothing came to mind. Time frame? Nothing.

"Something wrong?" Angella asked, her eyes going from happy to puzzled. "You look...well confused. And what about a hat?"

"That woman over—"

"Your timing sucks. You know that."

"The hat—"

"Which is it, Jimmy? The hat or Tabina?"

"You know her?"

"Joined us at the Half Moon this morning. Conquesta and her have a...a business relationship."

"He seems to have relationships with a variety of women. Was she here the last time?"

"Didn't see her. Doesn't mean she wasn't. And don't be nasty."

Angella's 'nasty' comment caught my attention. She seemed overly sensitive when it came to Conquesta. But this wasn't the time to press the subject. Even if I had wanted to say something, the remaining three boxes of money had just been placed at my feet.

As if on cue, Conquesta approached with the woman Angella had called Tabina in tow. Her hat continued to block the top section of her face allowing only brief glimpses of her mouth and chin as the brim fluttered up and down in concert with her footsteps across the meadow.

Angella's hand tightened around mine and when I glanced sideways her narrowed eyes communicated displeasure. A lot of displeasure. I was concentrating on Tabina a bit too much for her liking. A good sign actually. But the hat had captured my imagination.

Was this a remembered image?

"I understand you have a little something for me," the woman said, a slight middle-eastern accent hanging over her very polished words.

Her host stepped forward. "Jimmy Redstone let me please present Tabina Matawani, the owner of a horse named Strike One masquerading as Sync Opate. It appears that a grievous mistake... so to speak...has been made. Madame Matawani has graciously declined to press charges in return for a full cash refund."

"How do I know—"

Conquesta reached in his leather bag and produced an envelope that he handed me before I finished my lame protest. I slipped a title certificate from the envelope and studied the document as if I knew what I was actually doing. On its face it purported that one Tabina Matawani, a citizen of Jamaica, owned a Thoroughbred/Criollo Equidae named Sync Opate, foal of Lip Sync, and that said Equidae, by this document, was being sold, transferred and quit-claimed to Bar-C Ranch, as represented by one Jimmy Redstone, a citizen of the United States of America.

Truth was, I had no idea what document or documents were required to transfer horse ownership. Furthermore, I had no reason to believe said Tabina Matawani was a Jamaica citizen. Actually, about the only fact on that document I knew to be accurate was my name and citizenship. But I had been instructed to hand over fifteen million in Euro banknotes to reclaim the horse thought to be Sync Opate, but who actually was named Strike One, so I saw no reason to hold up proceedings. "Everything appears to be in order," I announced, breaking the awkward silence. "The full amount is in these boxes. Count it if you wish."

"I have every intention of counting the money, Mr. Redstone. You can be certain of that. Fooled once by you is more than enough." She nodded to a man standing in the shadow of a palm tree, a man whose face had spent so much time in the sun it appeared to have been crafted from cracked leather. The man walked toward me, his eyes never leaving my face. He bent down and effortlessly lifted the first box.

He didn't have long to wait before a black limousine pulled up and the trunk popped open. The driver scrambled out, ran around the front of the car and opened the passenger side rear door. Madam Matawani climbed in without so much as a goodbye Mr. Redstone, nice to have met you Mr. Redstone, see you around, Mr. Redstone.

Leather Face proceeded to place the box in the trunk, then produced a long-bladed knife from under the mat and proceeded to cut the top off with one deft swing of the blade. From the speed and ease with which that knife appeared and the box was laid open, this wasn't the first time he had put that blade into play.

I studied the banknote count, knowing that since I had not pre-counted the money we might have a bit of a situation on our hands. I felt Angella tense as he approached the end of the first box. I assumed she had seen what I had seen. The box contained four and three quarters million, not the anticipated five. At this rate, we would come up three quarters of a million short. This was setting up to be a major problem.

I took a step backward, being certain to be as far from the circumference of the knife blade as possible. Angella did the same.

Leather Face picked up the second box and placed it beside the first. With a flick of the wrist the cardboard top flew away revealing the neatly stacked money bundles. I couldn't help receive the message that if the count didn't add up my neck would suffer the same fate. I didn't doubt for a moment his capability—and more importantly—his willingness to take such action.

Some good news. There were more notes in the second box than in the first. But unless the third box was packed even denser we were still going to come up short.

Two additional men appeared out of nowhere and positioned five large suitcases at the rear of the car. The men then proceeded to remove the notes from the open boxes and pack them away in the suitcases, recounting them as they proceeded. Nine and a half million filled three of the suitcases by the time the second cardboard box had been emptied. The three suitcases were closed, locked and heavy blue/red/green zip lock security bands were pulled around each and locked tightly. These folks were not neophytes at this rodeo.

The top flew off the third box and landed at my feet as the counting and repacking process continued. A few moments later, fourteen million eight hundred and fifty thousand Euro banknotes were locked and secured within the suitcases. A hundred and fifty thousand Euros were missing.

THIRTY-NINE

I focused my attention on the knife while at the same time mentally reviewing my Ranger training for just this situation. I knew to visualize each step and to plan exactly where my feet would be planted, what my hands and arms would be doing, how my torso and head would move. I was as ready as I ever would be. Unlike when I went to take down Castro back at the horse stable, I even made allowances for my diminished dexterity. The main advantage I had was the all-important element of surprise. I knew what Leather Face was planning and unless he had been briefed on my background he wouldn't anticipate what evasive action I was about to take.

He started in my direction, his weapon of choice down at his side. But instead of coming directly toward me he detoured to the rear window of the car where Matawani was sitting.

The hat! That's where I had seen the hat!

Not a white one as Matawani was now wearing, but a black one, also with a brim that mostly covered her face. The silhouette I now saw was the exact shape and size I had seen as a bolt of lightning had streaked across the sky illuminating the terrain for an instant. It was as if a photograph had been embossed on my brain. The photograph contained the nose, mouth and chin of a woman. The nose, mouth, and chin of the woman now sitting in the car matched the photo perfectly.

As I studied the visual image I began to realize that there had been another face behind, actually beside, this face. A male face, a distorted male face, distorted perhaps by the lightning, perhaps by the glass. The forehead was out of proportion wide as compared to the narrowness of his chin. The image I now saw was more akin to a caricature portrait one commissions at a sidewalk festival than to an actual photograph. Very narrow chin, wide brow.

Lip Sync must have been spooked because the next thing I recall was hitting the ground. I may have blacked out, but if so only for an instant, because when my eyes had opened, the car door was just coming open and the man, not the woman, was stepping, out. Indeed, his forehead was broad, but I don't recall his chin as he bent over me. I do recall that he moved with a cat-like smoothness. His hand had come toward me and for an instant I thought he was about to plunge a knife into my chest. Only it wasn't a knife, it had been a syringe with a needle at the end and before

I could roll away, Mr. Wide Head had injected me with something.

Now a man was again coming for me. This time it was Leather Face and his hands appeared empty. But I knew the knife, or the needle, was only inches away from his fingers. This time I was ready.

And so was Angella. She had moved away from me in the direction of the car. That meant that he had to pass her before he got to me. Problem was, if he was a trained agent he would take Angella out as he passed. One quick swipe of that lethal knife would be enough. The wound wouldn't necessarily need to be fatal, just temporarily debilitating.

I tried to warn her with my eyes, but she was concentrating on the approaching subject, not on me. I changed my strategy. I'd go for his legs the instant I sensed even the slightest motion in Angella's direction. The spacing between him and myself was further than I would have liked, but still within striking range.

As I continued to study him, he passed the danger point to Angella without incident. Either he had discounted Angella or he had been instructed not to harm her. In any event, she was now behind him. My own countdown began.

One.

He continued walking toward me, his eyes told me nothing.

Two.

His pace slowed, his right hand moved slightly forward toward his hip—and the knife.

Three.

Leather Face is left handed! Every time he had used the knife for slashing open the money cartons it had been with his left hand.

He stopped. His right hand continued toward me. It was empty as far as I could see. His left hand was hanging straight down.

"Mr. Redstone," he began, still several feet in front of me, "I have been instructed to thank you for honoring the transaction. We know it was not your fault someone substituted a doctored horse for the real one. An honest mistake on your part, I am told. No hard feelings."

He was talking, but I was concentrating on his left hand, which hadn't moved. I needed to be certain it continued not to move.

"Madam Matawani," he continued, "hopes to do business with you in the future. Goodbye for now."

An attack would come the instant he began to turn away. The knife—or the needle as before—would smoothly pierce my skin and I'd be down. In an attempt to change the distance between us, I took a small step backward. My heel caught on a rock and I stumbled, falling to my side.

Angella, seeing me fall, launched herself forward, hitting Leather Face behind the knees. The two of them landed in the grass with Angella on his back. Her arm, as she had been trained to do, quickly encircled his neck.

I stumbled to my feet and ran to where they lay and as I did so the car carrying Matawani shot forward heading toward the entrance gate. But she wasn't my immediate concern. Angella was.

I expected to find a struggle going on, but neither Angella nor Leather Face were moving. "You okay?" I called to my partner.

She nodded.

"Roll off to your right," I instructed as I prepared to stomp on the back of the guy on the ground below her.

"I don't know about him," she replied. "He hasn't moved since I hit him."

"Slowly roll off him." I kneeled on his back, my knee replacing Angella's body. Angella was right, of course, the guy wasn't moving. She stood beside me as I slowly released my weight.

Still no movement.

"What happened?" Angella asked, concerned for me as well as for the man on the ground.

"I stumbled over a rock or something. He didn't provoke it."

"He didn't come after you?"

"Just precautionary on my part." Leather Face still hadn't moved and I leaned down to feel his neck for a pulse. "No pulse," I needlessly announced.

The only other person around was Conquesta who remained back, apparently not wanting to become mixed up in our fight. The other two men must have caught a ride with Matawani or disappeared into the vegetation.

"Let's roll him over, maybe he hit his head."

Once on his back it was more than obvious what had happened. His knife was firmly in his left hand and when he hit the ground the blade had run through his stomach and up into his chest. He must have been making an upper cut with that blade at the instant Angella had hit him. I hadn't seen it coming. The man had been good. Angella had been better.

"He knifed himself," I said, stating the obvious.

Conquesta called in our direction, "Come, let's go up to the house. My folks will handle the accident."

"You have a name for that guy?"

"I know him only as Zehedi."

From the chart Ben-Yuval had shown me, Zehedi was not far from the top. "And Matawani?"

"I prefer not to discuss Madam Matawani. But I can tell you, she and Zehedi are cousins." Conquesta said something into a cell phone and motioned for us to join him.

Angella and I had now made another powerful enemy — and quite possibly even more.

A truck raced up, slid to a stop a few feet from Angella, two men jumped off, lifted Zehedi's lifeless body from the ground and placed it face down in the open bed. They both managed to jump on as the truck sped off, stones flying in all directions, leaving Angella standing alone, blood dripping from her fingers where her hand had come into contact with Zehedi's fatal wound.

Conquesta turned to Angella. "Come, my dear, let's get you cleaned up." Before I could protest, he led her toward the big house, his hand firmly on the small of her back.

I started after them and had a thought. I checked my phone, noted a surprisingly strong signal. I dialed Tiny. The call rolled over to an automated voice response system informing me that the party I called was no longer at that number. The line then went dead.

That's when I realized I had no way to get in touch with Ben-Yuval. My lack of ability to contact anyone was no accident. Bait is always expendable, like shrimp on a fishhook, not expected to survive the encounter. That was supposed to be me in the back of the truck, not Zehedi.

If that was true, then Conquesta was not to be trusted. He was up to his eyeballs into whatever was going on and Angella's safety was now my primary focus. They were out of sight, but I trotted toward where I had last seen them as fast as I could move over the rocky and hilly terrain. The mansion was directly in front of me, but the front door was closed and I saw no sign of Angella or Conquesta.

My cell buzzed, displaying the name Ben-Yuval.

"I understand," he began, "you placed a call to our mutual friend."

I told Ben-Yuval what had happened, adding that I now had a mental image of the people in the car when I had been drugged.

"Seems Zehedi has departed this earth," Ben-Yuval said when I fell silent. "Can't say as he'll be mourned from anyone on our side. What you have one the folks in the car is sketchy, my friend, but we'll run with it."

"Sorry, Best I can do."

"At least that's more than we had. One other item to factor in. Hamas chatter on our border ceased at almost the exact same time as Alpha reversed the pony deal."

"Connected?"

"Can't be certain. I say the money to the terrorists was pulled back, but truth is, we all want neat answers, sweep it all up together. The fact remains that at any given time anywhere around the world countless mischief is in progress. It's difficult to tie one to another. It's never a neat package. Never."

"Wouldn't need you guys if it was easy."

FORTY

Angella had now been out of my sight far too long. I took the stairs up to the massive front door two at a time and was about to pull it open when it swung outward on its own. Well, not exactly on its own. A tall, slender, gorgeous woman with perhaps the blackest hair I had ever seen was holding the door handle.

"Slow down, Mr. Redstone," she said, her emerald eyes immediately capturing my attention. "There's really no need to rush. Your friend is being tended to by Doctor Fernald. Just a slight scratch I am told. Come, follow me to the back garden. Tea will be served."

I didn't want tea. I wanted Angella.

"How is —"

"I'm told she is doing fine," the tall woman repeated, her intonation very clearly communicating that she was not accustomed to having her instructions disobeyed. Her fingers locked around my elbow and unless I was prepared to forcefully yank my arm away, I was going where she was going. I matched her long strides one for one. Her skin coloring was smooth caramel, making her age impossible to guess any closer than to say she was over fifty and less than seventy. A hint of a broad nose was centered between high prominent cheekbones, calling to mind sketches I had seen of the Tainos peoples who had been the early inhabitants of the Caribbean, from Cuba to Jamaica. The Spanish had all but eliminated their presence on this island.

The back of the house proved even more magnificent than the front. Garden paths spread out in countless directions, weaving and snaking in and around plantings, each more magnificent than the last. Trees and shrubs and plants were blended to perfection with the colors bleeding one to the next.

We turned a corner and my escort motioned toward a path bearing off to the right, the one that appeared to lead to a gazebo, although I only had a glimpse of a rounded top seemingly woven from hemp. A moment later we turned another bend and the bamboo gazebo came into full view, its sides covered with purple bell-shaped flowers. Indeed its top was woven to allow airflow.

Centered within the exquisite structure was a small table with two chairs. A crystal pitcher of iced tea sat in the middle, a glass of ice positioned on the table in front of each chair. Obviously, the place settings had just been positioned, but I had neither seen nor sensed anyone moving about.

"Sit, Mr. Redstone," she said, patting the seat next to her. "Sit and relax, you're...how do you say it...wound very tight."

"I don't recall being introduced," I said as I followed the sitting part of her instructions.

"My name is Tara. I'm Malik's wife."

That caught me by surprise. There was a spark in her eye that I would not have expected from a mother who had just lost a son. Maybe a second marriage and Conc wasn't her son? But still there would be a degree of sadness. Yet all I saw was an upbeat woman. "Gorgeous spread you have up here, I must say." I was filling the silence, trying to gain my balance.

"Try the tea, I think you will find it quite satisfying. A delightful blend of leaves from our own gardens combined with peppermint harvested just this morning from those plants you passed over there. Tell me what you think."

I sipped my drink and had to admit it was better than I had expected. Excellent, in fact. And I told Tara so.

"I thought you might enjoy it. Lunch will be served in a few minutes. I imagine you have worked up an appetite."

I was more interested in Angella than in eating, but truth was, even though I had managed a pastry on the flight over from Kingston, I was famished.

"Pardon me, I need to find my...partner."

"I know you are concerned, as I would be. She'll be along when Doc is finished." Tara Conquesta took several sips of tea, sat back and said, "In answer to your comment on the land, it's been in my family since...actually since the first people to come ashore. The original settlers, some call them the Tainos peoples, were mostly fishermen and vegetable growers and tended to settle on the low lands down by the water. My ancestors, for some reason or another, went for the high lands. Herded goats at first, then planted tobacco, which expanded several years back into cannabis I'm sad to say. Now it's mostly back to tobacco, tea, sugar and, of course, polo ponies."

"No more weed?"

"Some, but not much. All for local consumption, mostly for the help. If we don't grow it officially, they plant it themselves anyway. Our system keeps the peace."

I waved my arm in an expansive circle. "All of this land up here—I mean there are several mountain ranges I can see and I can't imagine how much farm land I can't see—belongs to...to your people?"

"It's a long, complicated story, Mr. Redstone, better saved—"

"Call me, Jimmy."

"Okay, Jimmy. And you call me Tara. Deal?"

"Deal," I said finishing off my tea.

"As I started to say, it's a complicated story.

Short version, Malik and I are distant cousins," Now it was Tara's turn to wave her arm. "The mountains over there, the ones growing the crops, they were my family's land from the time people were first on this island. Eventually, we received a grant from the King of Spain, but truth is, it was family land long before the Spaniards ever landed."

"And the rest, the—"

"The horse ranches and animals, those lands have been in the Conquesta family, I believe for just as long. The families intermarried many generations ago, and over the years split off, reunited, split off, that sort of thing. Malik and I consolidated our holdings when we were married."

"So how long ago was that?"

"Forty-eight wonderful years. Well, almost forty-eight." Tara's emerald eyes were glowing. "Anniversary coming up a week from today, it is."

"Then Conc, William, was your son? I'm so sorry for—"

Tara looked away, but not before her eyes went soft and her lips quivered. With her head turned away, and her voice barely audible, she said, "Conc was a good boy, he really was." She wiped away a tear, then continued, "I think it was inevitable. With so much drugs moving north we had to get him away from it all. But to where? We failed. My husband wanted him to remain on the ranch, raise horses, grow cotton. But...but youth being what it is he wanted to help stop the traffic. We knew when he joined your government it would be a matter of time."

"I'm so sorry. I know it doesn't make it any easier that he was trying to save lives, but he was."

"I know. I know." Tara shook her head, kept her back to me a moment longer, took a deep breath, then turned to face me. It was as if a switch had turned. The spark in her eyes was back, the brief glimpse into her soul now gone, leaving me not knowing which person was the real Tara Conquesta. The fact that her son worked for our government caught me by surprise.

The bushes rustled as if someone, or something, was approaching. I quickly jumped up from my seat, half expecting a knife wielding hombre to pop out of the vines.

"Oh, that's just Jamison preparing lunch. There's a work pavilion just over there." She waved in the general direction of the trees. "Small kitchen, that sort of thing. I would expect your lovely partner any moment."

"That's good to hear," I said, sitting back down. "Have you met Angella," I asked, playing off Tara's comment.

"Had a most enjoyable breakfast with her this morning down at the Half Moon. Too bad you were...were called away."

Before I could react, Angella appeared in the pathway looking radiant in a long white cottony outfit. Tara was slightly taller than Angella, but not by so much as to rule out that the dress was borrowed from her wardrobe. Either that or Conquesta just happened to keep outfits handy for occasions when women lost their own clothes. I wondered how often that happened.

I ran to Angella and pulled her close, wrapping my arms around her. I stood there rocking her against me never wanting to let her loose.

When I finally released her, she spun around like a schoolgirl. "Is it the bare shoulders or—"

"Legs. Definitely the bare legs," Tara called. "He's a leg man if ever there was one."

Now it was Angella's turn to slow burn. "And how in the world would—"

"Just a guess, my dear. Just a guess. Here, come up here and get comfortable. Lunch is about to be served."

"And my legs are not exactly bare."

"When you move, the slits down the sides give away your lovely secrets. Much better on you than on me I can assure you."

Angella's face turned red. Not one to blush easily, I suppose it was because of my over-extended hug and not the exchange with Tara. I may have over-stepped my bounds. But truth was, I was relieved to see her—and to know Tara had chaperoned them down at the resort.

"You two have confirmed what I had gathered this morning. You are more than partners in...in business. You're partners in life as well."

I took a step away from Angella thinking about how to respond to Tara, but she beat me to the punch.

"On second thought, why don't you two take a walk through the gardens. Say, about fifteen minutes while Jamison sets the table. Then we can all join for a nice lunch."

Angella nodded her consent.

"Be back in fifteen," I called to Tara as we disappeared around a massive raspberry plant laden with baby berries just turning from green to pinkish-red.

When we were out of sight, I again pulled Angella against me. This time kissing her hard.

"Not now," she managed a moment later. "Save it."

"It's just that...well, I thought...anyway, you look so...so lovely. I hadn't expected you'd do your fashion shopping up here in the Jamaican mountains."

"It was Tara's idea." Before I could react, she added, "The dress belongs to her. It's one of her favorites."

"All this over breakfast? You two really bonded. How'd that happen so...so fast?"

"Who knows what these folks are thinking. There's a dead guy out on the lawn and...and their son just died...and they're worried over getting lunch right. Not my cup of tea, as Lillie Holland is wont to say."

FORTY-ONE

"How did you know to go after that goon?" I asked Angella as we walked the gardens. "He had me completely fooled, what with that large smile, the handshake, lack of tenseness. Man was good."

"The smile didn't match the fact the money was light. That crowd may be a lot of things, Jimmy, but when it comes to money, forgiving they're not."

"Never saw the knife."

"In his line of work, he wouldn't have been alive as long as he was if his victims saw the knife coming. Isn't that your Darwin theory?"

"Not my theory. Fact"

"Actually, Darwin's been debunked, but that's a topic for another day. Why can't they just trace the money and roll up Alpha? Can't be all that hard."

"Back when I was a Texas Ranger we tracked money in and out of corporations and through partnerships, on and off shore, country to country until we didn't know which way we were going. These people are really sophisticated. Some countries make their entire income on fees generated by monetary flow. Every now and again we'd get lucky, someone would slip up and leave a crumb for us to nibble on, but not that often. More likely those nibbles led to dead ends—or to competitors."

"From what I've heard, Jimmy, you were the best the Rangers had at tracing the money."

"You heard that from my PR folks. Don't believe all that you hear. It's always a team effort. And I wasn't the best, far from it."

"Your take on this deal?"

"Usually, I say, 'follow the money'. But in this case that leads us right back here to the beginning."

Angella fell silent for several minutes, then said, "Just had a thought. And not a good one! What if an attack on Israel coincides with the death of Mogul. Actually, that's backward. Follow me here. Israel is attacked. The U. S. is distracted. Mogul is killed, Homeland Security is in a turmoil, especially if it's compromised at the top. That would make it much easier to detonate a nuclear device—or take out the power grid. Could bring us to our knees."

"All possible, but nothing's ever a neat package," I said, repeating what Ben-Yuval had said about international espionage.

While I was talking my mind again began replaying the events of earlier today. I again visualized the face under the hat, as well as the second face in the car. Just who was that guy?

The image just wouldn't clear any further than it had already. I couldn't place the face.

Tara called us for lunch. The gazebo had been converted into a magnificent dining area rivaling any place I had ever eaten. The dishes and serving pieces appeared handmade, each with its own unique floral impression and coloring, all blending perfectly with the hand-dyed table coverings. Off to the side a serving table held what I determined was salt cod boiled together with ackee fruit, onions, tomatoes and peppers. Another serving plate held fried plantains and still another several loaves of cocoa bread.

"I understand, Jimmy," Tara said when we were seated, "that these are your favorite Jamaican foods. I hope you enjoy."

"You have outdone yourself," I said, putting my hand on Tara's arm as I spoke.

A slight narrowing of Angella's eyes—fleeting, but real—put me on alert. I didn't know if the signal was one of external danger, or of jealousy over our beautiful hostess. I hoped for jealousy, but mentally prepared for the former.

"Angella told me all about your stay at the Half Moon, last week, so if you're wondering how I knew what you liked that's how."

"I take it that Malik isn't going to join us?"

I noted the obvious since only three places had been set.

"He's been called away on some...some business. He sends his regrets."

I was certain the business had to do with finding a final resting place for the dead guy. But what I wasn't so certain of was how much of Tara's naive innocence was a carefully crafted facade. But what was clear; she pulled it off with poise and dignity. Lunch went well and by the time the plantains were served Angella's eyes were no longer sending me signals.

My phone buzzed. I glanced down. "Seems our ride's almost here. I'm sorry, Tara, but we'll have to cut our lunch short. This has all been... over the top."

"Happens," Tara answered, throwing her arms around Angella. "Please come back and visit. You two are welcome here anytime. You do understand that, don't you?"

"We do," I said, answering for Angella as Tara now hugged me. "Sorry to cut this short, and I do plan to take you up on your wonderful offer. Thank you for your gracious hospitality." I kissed Tara lightly on the cheek then turned to join Angella who was already moving down the lane toward the house. I caught up to her just as a Sea Hawk helicopter briefly appeared over the roofline of the structure, its distinctive rotor noise unmistakable in the otherwise quiet afternoon sky.

We both broke into a trot, timing ourselves to

arrive at the landing spot simultaneously with the helo. The door flew open, in we went, the door pulled closed and the bird was back in the air and above the tree line before we were seated. This Sea Hawk was equipped with only six passenger seats along with four crew seats, only two of which were occupied. The other four passenger seats were empty.

It didn't take long before it was clear where we were heading. Actually, that's not exactly accurate. We knew where we were not heading. We were not on our way inland. Nor were we going to an airport, commercial or otherwise.

The shoreline was soon behind us with only emerald water in all directions. We were going north, that much I knew, perhaps a bit toward the east. I searched my memory for possible destinations and the first place that came to mind was Guantanamo Bay.

FORTY-TWO

"Guantanamo?" Angella exclaimed as we flew north. "Why Guantanamo? Could be any number of places, starting with Grand Cayman. Even Miami. I'll settle for Key West."

"I'm afraid this isn't a tourist excursion. Not with a Navy Seal at the controls. Can't imagine setting down on anything but government property."

"We're not enemy agents, Jimmy. Last I checked we're both American citizens. So why Guantanamo? You thinking the prison? That's only for foreign terrorists."

"When did you last see your passport?"

"Not funny," Angella responded. She studied the water below, then exclaimed, "You're right! That's Guantanamo just off over there!"

A moment later we touched down.

"Both of you! Out! Now!" The command from the cockpit was clear. Also exceedingly clear was the fact that the pilot wasn't going to issue the command a second time. Also exceedingly clear was the fact that the rotor blades hadn't turned off. This puppy was itching to leave.

"Aye, aye, sir," I said, snapping what passed for my rendition of a salute. And out the door we went. And leave the Sea Hawk did. The chopper was fifty feet in the air before the door snapped closed, its nose then rotated south as it accelerated out over the Caribbean, heading, I presume, back to its mother ship.

"I suppose the chopper wasn't supposed to be here," Angella commented. "Wonder what its log book will show?"

"Sitting at an airfield down Jamaica way. Never left the ground all day."

"You sound like a Bellefonte song. Keep that up and you can entertain our troops." Angella, in her white flowing outfit, was ill equipped to do anything very active. Realizing what she was wearing, she said, "I can't do much of anything dressed like this, that's for certain."

"Now we wait. First Tiny went silent. Now it seems Levi's done the same. I suppose Alpha's onto us as well. What happens to us depends upon what team we're on."

"What's that mean?"

"Tiny has—had—our backs, but he's off the team. Levi took his place and who now knows about him. We're civilians and I'm not certain they want us back. Alpha certainly doesn't."

"Hope somebody does. This is not the place to be stranded. Talk about a shooting first situation."

My cell came alive. GO SOUTH HICACAL. There was no indication of the message's source. I brought up the compass, confirmed which way was south, and motioned Angella to follow.

We trudged along the flat sandy terrain in silence, following a well-used, but for the moment empty, pathway. I couldn't help but continue to glance behind me as Angella, being as careful as she could be not to soil the dress, carefully maneuvered around the occasional scrub plant. We were exposed and vulnerable—very vulnerable.

"Unfortunately, Jimmy, this island has a bad reputation for torture," Angella called to me at one point. "If I had an active imagination I'd say I hear their screams."

"That would be an active imagination. From what I've read, that's not happened in years now."

"You think...you think that's why we're here. Get information out of us? If so, that sounds like torture to me."

"I can dream up a long list of folks who would line up. And so can you. But, truth is, I have no idea what we know that's important. Ben-Yuval and his merry gang of spooks have cornered the market on theories and inter-tangled plots."

We continued walking in silence for ten more minutes, all the while feeling we were being watched, but seeing nothing to confirm either way.

The fact that I didn't see a drone meant nothing. The occasional bird flying overhead could be sporting a camera. Or the camera could be miles high. Or even buried in the sand. No use fretting over it, if we were on camera that could be a good thing. With security leaks as prevalent as they had become, if we were beheaded it would be shown on live TV, surrounded with all the necessary commercials and host chatter.

"Hey," Angella said a few minutes later, "that sign up ahead says Hicacal Beach closed."

The name rang a bell. "I think Hicacal is where the old coastal battery was located at one time. That's the battery that protected the island from invasion back in a much less complicated time in history. I've always wanted to see it."

"This how you envisioned getting the chance?" Angella asked, not at all happy with where we were heading. She had pulled the dress up around her waist so that it wouldn't snag on the rocks as the terrain was now raising from sea level.

When we were well past the BEACH CLOSED-NO TRESPASSING sign, Angella said, "Well, Jimmy, I have to caution you to be careful what you wish for. Seems you're about to get your wish to see the old battery."

"It's not so much what I wish for, but who I wish to be with when I get my wish," I replied.

"And that is?"

"Tiny!"

"Tiny?" Angella responded, disappointment creeping into her tone. "Why—" Angella stopped in mid-sentence and turned in the direction I was looking. "Tiny!" she exclaimed. "What the hell you doing up here. And what the hell's this about anyway?"

"In due course," Tiny called, "Come over here out of the sun. I have water if you need it. Sit. Take a load off. What's this? Prom night?"

"Good thing I don't have a weapon, or you'd be minus a head."

"If either of you had a weapon I wouldn't take the chance."

Tiny was out of the sun, sitting with his back against what had been at one time a brick support for a large cannon. When we were all seated, like scouts around a campfire, I said, "I half-expected Levi. But not you. What the hell's going down?"

"Actually, I'm sorry you two got into this. At the early stages, the horse deal seemed harmless enough. A money laundering arrangement for certain, but...but so what else is new. Thought you might like some quiet time in Jamaica."

"It didn't work out that way, now did it?" Angella said. "How about if you let us plan our own vacations? That too much to ask?"

"Testy, testy." Tiny said, a glimmer of a smile appearing at the corner of his lips and disappearing as fast as it had come. "Message received. But we're working a problem and I need full attention."

"Okay," Angella said. "And... apology accepted."

"Shoot," I replied, perhaps a bit inappropriate for the expression now on Tiny's face. I suppose I should acknowledge Tiny's rare confession, but nothing about where we were and what we were doing felt comfortable. Maybe to Tiny this was all in a day's work. But this was not for me. Not anymore anyway.

"Here it is. Unvarnished and perhaps a bit incoherent. You know about the horse deal. Part money laundering, part payment for action taken and about to be taken." Tiny studied our faces for a moment making certain we were with him. "The services part was in payment for Shadowy Sal to impersonate the lawyer Q and assassinate Mogul. There has been so much chatter in the channels pertaining to assassination that it's hard to keep up with what's real, what's possible, what's a hoax. Someone is keenly aware of that fact and that someone intends to use the assassination chatter to achieve several goals at once. All the intelligence agencies around the world are unsettled, they don't know real from fake. The sum of this confusion is that we're possibly very close to having our government brought down."

"Grand planning," I said, "has always overcome this type of confusion. What's changed?"

"Trust, for one. The planning for operations and counter-operations takes place with the knowledge of those at the top of governments. But when the top folks are...are bent...the trust is lost. Chaos follows."

"Israel," I injected. "Israel can be trusted. That's why Levi's involved."

"Israel," Tiny said, pausing as if to consider his next statement. "North Korea."

"North Korea?" Both Angella and I exclaimed, neither of us expecting what we had heard.

"Mogul has asked for their help in this as well."

"To be that widespread, the military must be involved. Nuclear?"

"Actually, I think not nuclear. Because...because only Mogul, and perhaps Hoosier, using encrypted codes can set the nuclear options in motion. But... stand-down orders are much easier to achieve. North Korea attacks and we do nothing. That's why Mogul has discussed this with Chairman Un. Mogul believes he has full cooperation. But, we digress. What's going on now has nothing to do with DPRK."

"Just how   " Angella began, then stopped as the full import of what Tiny had just said took hold.

"Let's back up for a moment," Tiny said, steering the conversation back to practical terms. "Here's my theory. I don't profess to have it all worked out, but I have enough to know we don't have much time." He studied each of us for a moment, then continued, "We have been searching data files, communications around the world, you name it, but have come up empty. One takeaway from that would be there is no plot. Another takeaway, shared by only a few of us, is that one person, possibly two at the most, have infiltrated our government."

So far, Tiny was in agreement with Ben-Yuval, but it seemed as though the two of them were not communicating. We had been told Tiny was on the outside. How did he get back inside? Is this really Tiny? "That person would have to be at the top, then," I said going along with the theory.

"Precisely. And to have gotten to the top that person, Alpha as he's being called, has been in government and around military and national security matters a life time."

"And gone through extensive background checks every few years. I know what that's like. They did one on me a few years back and even spoke to my first-grade teacher," Angella said. "Not much chance of getting and keeping a top-secret clearance if you're rogue."

"It's not just the clearance," Tiny corrected, "but access to different files and systems. It's also the trust that's built up over the years all around the world that allows someone at the top to obtain the most sensitive information."

"Then how—"

"Someone is being impersonated." Tiny paused to let that sink in. "Someone at the very top, Chairman of the Joint Chiefs, Director of Secret Service, Homeland Security Director, Directory of National Security, there are several possibilities, including...

including, the president's own Chief of Staff."

Angella said, "I'm not buying that with all the biometrics, the eye scans, fingerprints, anyone at that level can be impersonated."

"Look Angella, the way the Chinese or Russians hack into our systems it's possible the biometrics have been altered. But the way I have this calculated some mole is impersonating someone at the top. The biometrics were changed years ago, maybe twenty or so years ago."

"Okay," I said, "let me understand this. Some mole, a high placed mole, with—"

"Possibly a her," Tiny injected.

"—possibly a her, with access to our military commanders, is orchestrating the destruction of the United States." Tiny nodded and I continued, "Under Alpha's plan, the president will be assassinated and at the same time our military will be ordered to attack Israel and stand down against a North Korean attack."

"Maybe not attack Israel, but certainly stand down there as well, while they come under attack from Iran. And don't forget there's some thought of a nuclear weapon being set off in one or more U. S. cities."

Angella spoke up. "I'd say that last is impossible."

"Not if Homeland Security is compromised and stands down at a critical time," Tiny responded, his eyes closed against the intense sun. He took a long drink of water, then said, "Look, there are more theories running around than answers. I, for one, don't believe most of what could happen will happen. But I do know we must expose Alpha so we can get back some semblance of normalcy."

"So why are we here," Angella asked, beating me to the punch.

"Do you buy because it's private?"

Angella studied Tiny a moment, perhaps thinking what I had been thinking, he's an imposter. The problem with that scenario is who has the size and girth to play Tiny? Then she said, "Lots of places are private. We were up in the Jamaican mountains, you want privacy, that's privacy. Didn't have to come to this...this troubled island for privacy."

"So why Guantanamo, you ask," Tiny said, ignoring Angella's Jamaica comment. "First, wanted to show you where your friend Shadowy Sal was brought after the assassination attempt. She'll be known as Floratine Maldos or Person 2745. Arrived early this morning."

"How did they swing that?" I asked. "She was in the United States, doesn't she—"

"There is no Floratine Maldos in the United States. She never came into the country. There certainly isn't any Shadowy Sal either. So officially, she has no identity. She's always someone else. Let the Center For Constitutional Rights work through that for a while."

Fitting, I had to admit. "And second?"

"We're getting to second. Levi reports you saw Alpha."

At least now I knew Tiny was in contact with Ben-Yuval—or at least a common database. So unless they are both rogue, Tiny is genuine—or as genuine as a spook can be. "Truth is, I saw a man in the car with Madam Matawani. It's pure speculation that the person I saw was Alpha."

"Speculation is what my world lives on, Jimmy. Speculation based on a ton of factual information."

"Such as?"

"Such as we have a high degree of confidence that Alpha was in that car. And we have an even higher degree of confidence that no one who matches the description you gave Levi was in that car."

"As I told Levi, there could have been, and probably was, a distortion from the rain. How good was the surveillance up there?"

"Best there is in the world. Israeli's are even better than we are. No one fitting the description you gave entered or left that car. Period."

FORTY-THREE

"So why did Alpha, if that was Alpha, drug me and not kill me?" I asked after thinking about the events surrounding my being thrown from the horse and injected.

"If you had died, all eyes would have focused on your death. The result being that the killer would have been detained. Not good for Alpha's plan—or for his identity. You were knocked out, and as such all efforts focused on getting you to the hospital. His plan, once you saw him, was to eliminate your memory so you wouldn't remember him."

Eliminating me would come later.

"To do that," Angella said, "he would have had to preplan the drug. Is that likely?"

"We think Alpha's done that several times in the recent past. He's become more hands-on active resulting in having to eliminate people who could identify him."

Angella took that in, thought for a moment, then said, "That's consistent with someone running a complicated operation without much help."

"The intelligence community very much agrees with you on that, Angella. And that's why a massive push is on to uncover Alpha now. It's thought he's near his end game."

"You think the attack was just postponed?" I asked. "Not cancelled,"

"That's the consensus, I'm afraid."

"So," I asked, "what progress has been made to identify Alpha from what I gave Ben-Yuval?"

"There are five top government officials who have the capability to pull off what I outlined and whose precise whereabouts at the times in question are suspicious. Everyone else is accounted for." While Tiny was answering my question, he was busy with his phone. He found what he was searching for and turned the screen so I could see.

The glare was too bright. I turned the phone out of the sun and cupped my hands around the screen. Slowly I cycled through the five faces, not recognizing any of them, except from TV coverage. Then a thought came to me, a thought that had been continually reinforced for the past several minutes, yet not acted upon. "The five pictures you have here are of men. Yet you continue to remind us that Alpha could be female. Where are the females?"

"That would explain the small chin," Angella said.

"I don't know why these are all men. Let's find out."

I have never seen Tiny move so fast. It was as though the big fellow had been shot out of his seat. In an instant he was towering over me, his phone now back in his massive hand, his fingers moving wildly over the keyboard.

I guessed he wasn't using audio because of security concerns. Or perhaps, as would be his normal operational mode, to keep us in the dark. While we waited, I took a small self-guided tour of the battery thinking about the soldiers who stood guard with the artillery that had once been mounted on this hillside guarding the entrance to the inner harbor. Those men were long gone, as were their weapons of war, only the circular stone bases now remained.

"Jimmy," Tiny called, "look at this!"

Was that excitement in Tiny's voice? There never was excitement in Tiny's voice. Angella must have heard it as well because she hurried over to where he was standing, his back again against the brick wall.

Spooks, I decided, always keep their backs against walls. They remain alive longer that way, I suppose. "What'd you find?" I asked.

Tiny held his phone out and there, smiling out of the small screen, was the exact slender chin I had seen sitting in the car up on the ranch with rain pellets hitting the window. It also was the same chin who bent over me with a syringe. Only in this picture the forehead matched the chin in size and shape.

"That's it! You got it! Who is she?"

"Homeland Security Assistant Director Murphy," Angella answered. "Megan Humphrey Murphy."

I looked at my partner and started to ask how she knew.

"My exit interview. Remember my interview was in Brownsville. She said she was just passing through, happened to be down our way and thought she'd like to meet me. Didn't think much of it at the time."

"Coincidence?" My question was directed to Tiny?

"Perhaps. Perhaps not," he responded. "No time to sort that out now." He again turned his attention to his phone, his large fingers moving nonstop across the keypad.

It took a full ten minutes before Tiny looked up, an expression of deep concern consuming him. "Coincidence, maybe. But I think not. But timing will be...almost nonexistent." He thought for a long moment, I assume fighting his natural instinct to say as little as he could. "Look, I'll level with you. I think we're in deep trouble. But...but there's a slim possibility. Murphy is the lead security official in the President's hosting of, get this irony, Kim Jong-Un at Mara-a-Lago. The event begins in," Tiny checked his watch, "twelve minutes. If she's going to take Mogul out that would be the time to do it. She has unfettered access to him and more importantly they already are on event muster, so all communications to the Secret Service detail go through her until muster is over."

"You can't just do nothing!" I exclaimed. "There must be—"

"I've communicated to everyone I trust. But truth is we don't know what orders have been posted. Because of Kim's visit, our military around the world are on advanced readiness, so any order coming from Alpha will not be questioned. Particularly, stand-down orders."

I had not at first appreciated the fact that a military order to do nothing was far easier to execute than a go forward order. But human nature being what it is, even for generals, launching nuclear weapons takes grit. In contrast, standing down is easier, if not procedurally, then mentally.

"Do you anticipate Alpha will kill the president in the guise of Assistant Director Murphy, or under another disguise?" Angella asked. "I mean, if she does it as herself, then how would she be able to issue orders afterward? Wouldn't her authority be cut off at that point?"

"That's what we're thinking, Angella. But with someone as clever as Murphy it's hard to anticipate exactly what she'll do. Or, in fact, when she'll do it."

"Has to be soon," I said, "because the whole operation was predicated on absolute secrecy.

That's now gone, so the clock's ticking."

Angella had been studying her phone for the past several minutes. "It seems that Murphy is single and has been so for the past twenty-two years. She joined the CIA fresh out of Purdue, had several minor assignments, went to Penn, I'm assuming on the Government's dime, then posted to Germany for several years, France for a few years then off to Saudi Arabia."

"Get all this on the Internet?"

"Jimmy, you'd be surprised what's on here. Anyway, she's high enough up now in the government that Wikipedia has a page on her. Her husband, who also was with the CIA, but assigned to Turkey, went to Saudi Arabia for a visit and they were in a car accident. Husband died, Megan survived."

"What year was that?" I asked, remembering something Lillie Holland had said about Shadowy Sal's teacher.

"Ninety-six. Why?"

"That's when Sal's teacher's other disciple disappeared."

Tiny looked up from his cell. "That's how they changed the DNA and biometrics. The accident was staged. Bet she had no parents, siblings. Let's see." He returned his attention to his cell and after a few minutes of key pushing, said, "Thought so. Parents died when she was twelve, no siblings, left a large farm in southern Indiana to her. Oh,

and she has a horse stable now. Into Thorough-
bred racing. Doesn't say anything about Polo, but
I suppose a horse is a horse."

"So, if you couldn't get through to Mogul's
detail who did you speak with?" I directed my
question to Tiny, fully anticipating he would ignore or deflect as he was prone to do.

True to his nature, Tiny leaned back against
the crumbling stone structure and closed his eyes.
But to my surprise, in a moment of what for Tiny
passed as candor, he said, "Muse. She has instant
access at all times."

Angella was busy clicking sites on her phone.
She looked up and announced, "I have the news
feed from Mara-A-Lago live. Meeting is delayed a
few minutes is what they're saying." She returned
her gaze to the screen and then excitedly exclaimed,
"Hey, they're panning the folks in the room and
guess who's front and center? Homeland Security
Assistant Director Megan Humphrey Murphy."

"Delay's good news," Tiny said, "means Muse
took it seriously."

"Why wouldn't she?"

"The threats have been constant. And from all
sources. It's easy to let your guard down."

"But from you?"

Tiny looked away before responding. "I've been
read out. I'm tight with Gladstone, so he broke the
rules with that communication just now."

That explains the secret nature of the communication. Can't be logged, even by the snoops.

Tiny added. "Threats are coming from inside as well as out. My God, a Congressman even called for the military to take over! Mogul's enemies will stop at nothing. This must be carefully orchestrated or—"

"How do you orchestrate around treason, when the treason is by the highest ranking official?"

"That, my friend, is the question of the day. As you know, an assassination is only a part of it. They may have destruction planned around the world, all triggered by Mogul's death. What we don't know—or at least what I don't know—is whether the further damage will be automatic based on the assassination, or whether Murphy must personally initiate that action. It's critical to know because how her attack on the President is countered depends upon the answers. But...but until we have proof beyond a reasonable doubt, Mogul refuses to cancel the meeting."

"I just thought of something that's been nagging at me," Angella exclaimed. "You know, the Scumbag backed off the assassination attempt and we've been wondering how that was communicated to her. How did she know to stand down?"

"Go ahead," Tiny said, "that's been troubling a lot of us."

"Simple, now that I think of it. That is, if I'm right. My thought is that Murphy had physical duty on SPI and would have been there just as she is now physically present in Mara-A-Lago.

The storm kept her in Jamaica and without her presence, Sal stood down."

"Easy enough to check." Tiny busied himself with his cell, his fingers moving like a piano maestro over the keypad. In less than three minutes, he had the answer. "You were spot on, Angella. Murphy had indeed been scheduled to be the Chief Duty Officer for the South Padre Island luncheon. But, according to the duty log, she was detained in Grand Cayman due to weather. Deputy Director Gladstone had taken over command."

FORTY-FOUR

"If it were up to me, I'd lock Murphy up. But, knowing our government as I do they won't be so quick to act," Tiny said, standing, his back still against the smooth cut stone. "The good news, if there's any good news in this at all, is that we're about to get answers."

No sooner did he say that than two uniformed Marines appeared on the ledge beside us. One held his firearm across his chest while the other carried a canvas bag cradled against his body. He carefully lowered the bag onto the top of the nearest gun turret and stepped back.

"That will be all, Corporal," Tiny said. "Stand down."

The man saluted Tiny, turned and walked back down the hill. The guard with him followed suit, but without saluting. Since it is not customary for military to salute civilians and Tiny's khaki pants and fishing shirt certainly bore little resemblance to a military uniform, I concluded Tiny still held rank in the Marine Corp.

When the men were out of sight, Tiny unzipped the bag, revealing what appeared to be an old Philco TV with a round screen. "Latest technology," Tiny commented when I leaned closer to examine the apparatus.

At first I thought he was pulling my leg, but as he began turning knobs and entering information, I realized that the machine was reading his eyes, because a note floated across the screen to that effect. Tiny's finger was now positioned over a yellow square that had appeared on the screen and soon the screen indicated that his blood oxygen, or some such parameter, was within range. A moment later the screen displayed PARTICI-PANT CLEARED.

"Your turn, now, Redstone. Look directly at those two yellow areas."

Indeed, it appeared that two yellow eyes had formed on the screen. I did as I was told and the screen then asked me to place my right finger on a square. Several more requests and I was instructed to repeat a sentence. At the conclusion of my statement I also was cleared. The procedure was repeated with Angella.

"How the hell did they get all that information on me?" Angella asked when she was cleared.

"You'd be surprised what all they have on half the population of the world," Tiny responded. "Now I'd advise you say nothing more as this is about to go live. Both of you put on these earphones. Jimmy, plug into speaker position two, Angella, you use three. I'll use one."

"Who's on the other end?" I naively asked.

"If they want you to know it'll come up on the screen. Know this, the link cannot be hacked, and no one can be on either end who's not authorized. It doesn't just set up the link, the equipment continuously monitors the entire communication session and the instant a biometric becomes unverifiable or goes out of range the link ends."

"Mr. Redstone," a voice in my ear suddenly said, "we've received your input pertaining to Alpha. Before we proceed further, please confirm that the only persons on your end participating in this link beside yourself are Angella Martinez and the man you know as," he paused, "Tiny. Is that accurate?"

I recognized the voice as belonging to Secret Service Deputy Director Gladstone. Indeed, his name was now displayed at the top right corner of the screen, and a live shot of him sitting behind a desk came into focus on the screen. "That is accurate."

My speaker went silent, then a moment later Angella said, "Confirmed."

"Confirmed by me as well," Tiny said a moment later.

The names NCB Head Lillie Holland and FBI Deputy Director Chris Kagan then appeared below that of Gladstone.

"National Central Bureau," I whispered to Angella when she puckered her nose at the new names. "Interpol. Holland seems to now be Head of the U. S. office."

"I believe you both know Director Kagan and NCB Head Holland," Gladstone said, "so let's move this forward. We have reason to believe you are accurate in your assessment that the person you saw when you took that unfortunate spill from the horse is, in fact, Assistant Director Murphy. Further, if that proves to be accurate we have reason to believe Murphy is a mole. But, and this is in consultation with the National Security Council as well as Mogul, we are not yet prepared to take action based on your observation alone."

"Even given the fact that Murphy was relieved of her mission assignment at SPI causing the assassination to be aborted?"

"Could be coincidence," came the immediate reply. "And...and frankly, we are not positive it had been aborted."

"Check her DNA, bio—"

"Let me assure you, Mr. Redstone, that we have employed everything at our disposal to cross-check her and also let me assure you every parameter matches. If indeed someone has been impersonating Murphy they have been doing so for so many years that all traces of her early DNA and other biometrics have been replaced."

"Then check—"

"Let me add," Director Kagan added, "Murphy has been under the FBI's watchful eye for many, many years. Never once has there been any question of her judgment or loyalty. So while it's certainly possible she's been compromised, there's very little to suggest, other than what you've just provided, that she's Alpha."

"Holland," I asked, "do you agree with this assessment?"

Silence followed for a long moment. Then Interpol Agent Holland, a woman Angella and I had worked with on several occasions, and a woman I very much trusted, said, "The time frame seems to fit with a protégée of Shadowy Sal's teacher going missing. So, it's possible CIA agent Murphy died in Saudi Arabia and her place was taken by the mole. But, in mitigation of that fact, we have recently located the grave of the protégée. Thus, nothing is conclusive and Murphy could be who she says she is. I would have to agree with your president and toss the benefit of the doubt her way."

"But you're not certain?" I pressed.

"In the imposter world, no one can ever be certain. These imposters are good. Better than good. I suppose we can dig up the protégé's body and see what we can find. We plan to exhume her parents, but that'll take a while."

"Bet you find the real Murphy at the bottom of that grave," I said.

"Enough of that speculation, Redstone!" Gladstone snapped. "We cannot arrest AD Murphy on suspicion of... of...having a small chin! That seems to be her only...crime if I am to understand your analysis. That and a coincidence."

Gladstone was quickly getting under my skin. "So tell me why you went to so much trouble to set this link up just to tell us you're doing nothing."

"Truth is, we do have doubts and the clock is ticking. Mogul is right now under Murphy's exclusive control and even an instant's delay in making the right call could spell the difference between life and death. Yet...yet we're helpless to take action unless we're positive. Speculation, chin size if you will, simply won't cut it. Unless you can positively identify Megan Murphy as the person you saw in the car with Matawani, Mogul insists we stand down."

Now it was on me. I knew the answer was yes. Yet, I couldn't honestly say I was absolutely positive. "No," I admitted. "As much as I want to say yes, I can't be positive."

Director Kagan said, "Listen Redstone, we've had Murphy under surveillance for years and truthfully have found nothing. If she's a mole then she's done nothing we can lay at her feet. My hope," Kagan acknowledged, "is that you would have more for us. You or Angella."

I had a thought. "If Murphy's been under surveillance as you just said then where was she when I saw her, or thought I saw her, in Jamaica?"

Now it was Kagan's turn to consult notes. "Give

me a moment," he said. "Oh, yes, we did have her at that time. Let's see, she flew commercial from National to Miami. Caught Lift over to the Coast Guard Air Station at Opa-locka."

"To Opa-locka? Isn't that unusual to fly out of a Coast Guard Station," I said, thinking of all the clandestine times Angella and I had been airlifted off SPI.

"I suppose, with the foul weather in the Caribbean, commercial flights were being disrupted and nobody thought anything about the U. S. Homeland Security Assistant Director catching a military ride into the heart of the problem."

"So you actually have her going into the Caribbean at the right time?" I was puzzled as to why this wasn't enough for them. "Isn't the fact she's on her way down here at the right time enough?"

"It would seem so," Kagan acknowledged, "but...but I'm going to share surveillance video with you and you'll see why we are skeptical. Tiny, bring up the Guantanamo footage from your end. Begin with 12:54."

A keypad popped up on the screen and Tiny typed in a passcode along with other information and a moment later a video began playing. I recognized the location. It was exactly where Angella and I had landed an hour or so ago, the airfield at Guantanamo. Megan Murphy stepped from a red and white Jayhawk, threw a quick salute in the direction of the cockpit and then walked toward the massive hangers.

Tiny touched the screen again, typed in some more numbers and then we saw Murphy enter a house, which I assumed was officer's quarters. The time stamp on the screen was 13:04. The time sequence went into fast forward, but nothing changed on the screen. Then at 13:57 the sequence went back to normal and at 13:58 a man emerged dressed in khaki pants similar to what Tiny was now wearing, and a white shirt. The man walked off screen to the left.

The screen went blank.

Tiny said, "The surveillance team did not follow the man leaving the premises and for two days nobody was seen leaving the building. Unfortunately, the hurricane came through and under orders of the base commander they left their post. Frankly, we don't know who left the house or when.

"Where did that man go?" Angella asked.

Tiny brought up a set of notes showing a Sikorski leaving the base at 14:32, destination Grand Cayman Island. "No record of any craft landing after 14:00 that day on Grand Cayman or on any island," he said.

"Before you read too much into that," Kagan said, "let me assure you that due to the weather, many aircraft came and went in the Caymans and on many of the islands, including Jamaica, and none of them were properly logged."

"The best we can show," Gladstone said, his voice tired and resigned, "is that our target remained at Guantanamo."

"I was told," I pressed, "she was unaccounted for during the time in question. By unaccounted for you mean nothing positive."

"Exactly," Kagan acknowledged.

"That man's a disguise. You must know that. Right?"

"That's where you come in. You say you saw Murphy in Jamaica at the start of the storm. But you couldn't be positive. Is there anything you just saw that makes you more or less positive as to who it was you saw in the car up on the ranch?"

There it was. My speculations against video evidence placing Murphy 200 or so miles away. Memories are strange things at the best of times. I had fallen from a horse and been drugged to boot. I saw a face. Same chin. But wide forehead. Not as wide as the person I just saw. But...but the face in the car could have been distorted somewhat. Was his shirt white? The person coming out of the house on the base had been wearing a white shirt.

Yes, it was white!

I started to respond, but paused a moment to force the image back into my mind. On second thought, the white shirt could very well have been the lightning strike on the window. And that's what I said.

"Still far too much speculation to have her arrested I'm afraid," Gladstone concluded. "Does anyone disagree?"

"It's possible it was her," Holland conceded,

"but we have no assurance of accuracy. And that video is...well, will be damming in court."

"I concur," Kagan said. "We must allow this to play out. Good day Mr. Redstone. Ms. Martinez."

"Wait!" I yelled, hoping it wasn't too late "I believe I saw something! Let me think a moment. Yes, yes, now I remember!" It was too late, and perhaps too lame. A sudden memory at the last instant.

The screen went blank. I turned to Tiny to see if he could do anything. "Link is controlled from their end. I could call them." He started tapping numbers into his cell just as the TV screen flashed back on.

"Did you say something?" Gladstone asked. "The others are off, but my line didn't go down."

"The man who bent over me," I said, struggling to talk slowly, yet knowing the words were coming out faster than I intended, "the person who injected me, had a smudge of red on his left collar. I recall thinking just before I went out that it was strange a man had lipstick on his collar."

"Tiny," Gladstone commanded, "play the surveillance footage of the man leaving the house. Enhance it and slow it way down."

Tiny did as he was asked, and it seemed an eternity before the camera caught the collar, but when it did, there was no lipstick.

"Freeze it right there," I shouted. "Hold that view. Now blow it up."

Slowly the image grew larger—and blurrier.

"There!" I exclaimed. "See there!" Indeed there was a smudge. Only it wasn't lipstick. It was make-up.

"Good show, Redstone. I'll take it from here," Gladstone said as the image faded to off.

Tiny, for the first time ever, grabbed my hand. "You've done well, my lad. Really well. Capisce?"

"What do we do now?" I asked, knowing there was nothing we could do. Trump, being Trump, will handle this how he handles everything else, in some unpredictable way. But at this point it wasn't up to Trump alone. His handlers, the Secret Service would intervene. If I read Gladstone right he was now convinced that Murphy was the mole. Or was he?

"Do we just leave this equipment here or what?" I asked Tiny.

I followed Tiny's eyes as they moved slowly to his right. Sure enough, the heads of the Marine contingent appeared off to the side as they made their way back up the hill to the battery where the three of us stood.

They said nothing as they went about their assigned task of retrieving the sophisticated field communication equipment and then proceeded back down the hill from whence they had come, all without exchanging a word.

I felt in my pants pocket for the picture of the engagement ring. Locating the now crumpled paper, it struck me that right here, high above the

Caribbean, would be as good a location as any to propose. At least it would be memorable. My fingers tightened around the picture.

"Angella," I began, walking over to where she was standing and putting my arm around her hip, "before we head back to the base and hitch a ride home, I have something—"

"Hopefully home is somewhere other than one of those brigs over there," Angella replied, her eyes not leaving the sprawling detention camp across the inlet. "That must be one miserable place."

Wrong place, wrong time, I quickly realized.

"So what is it you want to—"

"Only that it's time to head home." I turned back to see if Tiny was planning on joining us on the trek back to the airfield. But the big guy had vanished, leaving us to our own thoughts—and a clear view of the massive prison not all that far from where we now stood.

Angella was right, there was nothing good about this view. Nothing at all.

EPILOGUE

What Jimmy and Angella didn't know, had no way of knowing, was that Tiny immediately informed Levi Ben-Yuval, who in turn briefed Prime Minister Benjamin Netanyahu. Netanyahu took two crucial actions. First, he ordered the Sayeret Matkal, Israel's elite special operations force, to interrupt any and all communications between United States Department of Homeland Security Assistant Director Megan Murphy and any entity located in the Middle East regardless of security level and regardless of designated importance.

This action, it was later determined, caused Iran to postpone a coordinated missile attack on Tel Aviv and on the new U. S. Embassy in Jerusalem.

The second action the Prime Minister took was to place an emergency phone call to his friend, Donald Trump, who was just about to step out of his private quarters at the Mar-A-Lago to appear at a televised news conference with First Chairman Kim Jung-un.

Taken from the official White House call log:

(Israel PM / Mogul) (date and time redacted)

"Mr. President, I have just been informed by a trusted source that your Department of Homeland Security official Murphy is...let me be blunt...a—"

"My friend, Bibi, I thank you for your candor. Please allow me a moment here and I'll read for you a prepared statement that is at this very moment being loaded onto the teleprompter."

Pause in the call log:

Resume call log:

(Israel PM / Mogul) (date and time redacted)

"Ah, here it is. I will read it just as I will deliver this message to the American public. Here it is. I wish to announce that Department of Homeland Security Assistant Director Megan Murphy came to me several weeks ago and tendered her resignation. Today I have granted that request and Assistant Director Murphy's resignation is now official and effective immediately. I thank her for her service to our country and wish her well in her future endeavors."

Call log ended: (date and time redacted)

Private Conversation with the Prime Minister of Israel:

(date and time redacted)

"As you know, Bibi, there have been several attempts on my life. I can't say for a certainty that Murphy was behind them all, but she's a traitor to our country and we can't have traitors."

"Will she be tried...I'm thinking for treason?"

"Attorney General thinks not. Too much will be exposed."

"I support you in that, Mr. President. Murphy was uncovered, as you well know, by a top-secret joint operation between our two countries. I wouldn't want any of our operatives exposed. It would wreak havoc—"

"With us as well. Too much will become...exposed as you say. Let's just move on from here. Do I have your continued support?"

"You most certainly do, Mr. President."

"Be well, my friend. Be well."

"Shalom, Mr. President. Shalom."

Other Books by David Harry

Jimmy Redstone / Angella Martinez Series
the Padre Puzzle

the Padre Predator

the Padre Paranoia

the Padre Pandemic

the Padre Poison

the Padre Phantom

General Fiction
(Under the name of David Harry Tannenbaum)

Standard Deviation

Out Of The Depths

General Fun
(Under the name of David Harry Tannenbaum)

Adventures In The Law

Weird And Funny Tales Told

By The Lawyer Who Lived Them

Thank You

As always, I want to thank my editor, Marvilyn Miller, who does a fantastic job correcting my many errors of spelling, grammar, and plot.

And a big thank you to Steve Hathcock, the man who knows everything worth knowing concerning the history of Padre Island and the environs. Even the history of mastodons and mammoths didn't throw him.

About the Author

David Harry and his wife, Mary, have a home on South Padre Island, Texas. When he isn't writing, David enjoys biking, traveling, and model train building. If David is off the island, he, Mary, and their dog, Franco, can usually be found enjoying their old stomping ground of Pittsburgh, Pennsylvania, and more recently, Miromar Lakes, Florida.

Communications

David Harry can be reached at: authordavidtannenbaum@gmail.com

You can follow David Harry on Facebook: davidharry (or patentguy) and on twitter: david1harry.